PENGUIN BOOKS

THE CASE OF SERGEANT GRISCHA

Arnold Zweig, a German novelist, playwright, and essayist, was born in Grosz-Glogau in 1887. He was a volun-
teer during World War I and served in France, Hungary,
and Serbia. In 1933 he was expelled from Germany and
his manuscripts were confiscated. He lived in exile in
Haifa until his death.

THE CASE
OF
SERGEANT GRISCHA
BY
ARNOLD ZWEIG

PENGUIN BOOKS

PENGUIN BOOKS
Viking Penguin Inc., 40 West 23rd Street,
New York, New York 10010, U.S.A.
Penguin Books Ltd, Harmondsworth,
Middlesex, England
Penguin Books Australia Ltd, Ringwood,
Victoria, Australia
Penguin Books Canada Limited, 2801 John Street,
Markham, Ontario, Canada L3R 1B4
Penguin Books (N.Z.) Ltd, 182–190 Wairau Road,
Auckland 10, New Zealand

First published in Germany under the title
Der Streit um den Sergeanten Grischa
by Gustav Kiepenheuer Verlag, Potsdam, 1927
First published in the United States of America by
The Viking Press, Inc., 1928
Published in Penguin Books 1986

LIBRARY OF CONGRESS CATALOGING IN PUBLICATION DATA
Zweig, Arnold, 1887–1968.
The case of Sergeant Grischa.
Translation of: Streit um den Sergeanten Grischa.
Reprint. Originally published: New York:
Viking Press, 1928.
1. World War, 1914–1918—Fiction.   I. Title.
PT2653.W4S713   1986   833′.912   86-742
ISBN 0 14 00.7057 5

Printed in the United States of America by
R. R. Donnelley & Sons Company, Harrisonburg, Virginia
Set in Old Style

CONTENTS

✡   ✡   ✡   ✡   ✡   ✡

Book One

BABKA

✡

Chapter 1

THE PLIERS

THIS earth of ours, the little planet Tellus, went whirling busily through pitch-black, airless, icy space, forever swept by the waves of the uncharted ether. In darkness made electric by her passing contact, she moved among mysterious influences, baleful or benignant. Swathed in her thick, woolly veils of air, she had now outrun that stage in her elliptical race which keeps her north-westerly parts furthest from their life-spring in the Sun; and she was turning them again towards him in the ceaseless revolutions of her course. Now the rays of the great fiery ball beat more exultantly upon the face of Europe. The atmosphere began to seethe and everywhere fierce winds rushed from the Arctic wastes to the warmer regions, where, lured by the magic of reviving light, all things awoke and blossomed. In the Northern lands life's tide was slowly rising and to her peoples came bewildering changes with the changing year.

A man stood in the thick snow, at the foot of a bare and blackened tree, that rose up slantwise in the charred forest, black against the trampled white expanse. Encased in many coverings, the man plunged his hands into the pockets of the outermost of these, and stared before him, thinking. "Butter," thinks he, "a pound and a half, two and a half pounds of meal from a farm, a loaf that I can put by, and some peas. Yes, that'll do. She can carry on for a bit with that. I'll give it to Fritzke to take with him to-morrow when he goes on leave. Perhaps I can swap my tobacco for a bit of dripping: if I throw in a mark from my pay, cookie will hand it out. Butter," thinks he, "a pound and a half." And so once more in his heavy, deliberate mind he spread out the contents of a parcel which he was planning to send to his wife, wondering whether he could not find room for yet something more.

3

Somewhere down in the vague depths of his inner consciousness he felt he would have liked to rub his feet together, for they were rather cold; but they were enveloped in thick boots, and wrapped round with rags and the lower part of his trousers, so he let them be. His legs were embedded in the deep snow, side by side like the hind feet of an elephant. He was wearing an iron-grey cloak, with absurd red squares on the collar under his chin, and a strip of blue cloth with a number on each shoulder. And tucked closely under his arm, while he stood thinking of peas and dripping, was a long, heavy, cudgel-like object of wood, affixed to an odd-looking iron contrivance, the whole being called a rifle: with this he was able to produce cunningly directed explosions, and by their means to kill or maim other men far away from him. This man, whose ears were hidden under soft black flaps, and in whose mouth was a small pipe adapted for smoking dried leaves—a German working man—was not standing under this tree in the burnt forest for his pleasure. His thoughts were continuously driving westward, where in two or three cubical rooms in a walled house his wife and child awaited him. Here he stood, while they lay huddled in a far-off room. He yearned for them, but something had come between them, unseen but very strong: an Order: the order to watch other men. The time was winter 1917, and, more exactly, the middle of March. The inhabitants of Europe were engaged in a war which had for some time been pursued with no small determination. In the midst of a forest in these eastern marches, wrested for the time being from the so-called White Russians, stood this German soldier musing, Lance-Corporal Birkholz from Eberswalde, guarding prisoners, soldiers of these same Russians who must now labour for the Germans.

A good seventy yards away from him, on a railway line, the huge red-brown and grey-green freight-cars were being loaded up with timber. Two men were handling each car. Others dragged up on their shoulders heavy, carefully graded beams and planks, which others again, a few days before, had hewn from the dead pines whose once green and reddish brown expanses had been eaten away in many directions by the hatchets and saws of the prisoners.

Much farther than the eye could reach between the tree-trunks, a day's ride in each direction, the black pillars of this corpse of a forest stood out stark against the snow and the sky—fifty thousand acres of it. Incendiary bombs from airplanes, shells from field-guns, had each in their own time during the past summer done their work upon it faithfully. Pines and firs, birches and beeches, all alike: burnt and singed, or withered and choked from afar by the fumes of battle—all perished, and now their corpses were made to serve their turn. There was still a reek of burning from the scaling bark.

In the last car two Russians were speaking in their own language about a pair of pliers.

"Impossible," said the slighter of the two. "How can I get you such a thing? I'll have no hand in such foolery, Grischa."

The other, turning upon his friend two strangely powerful grey-blue eyes, laughed shortly.

"I've as good as got them in my pocket already, Aljoscha."

And they went on piling up the yellowish-white props, that were to serve as supports for those human caves called dug-outs and communication trenches, in a certain order in the car, the side of which hung down from its hinges. Grischa worked above and superintended the stacking of the planks; from below Aljoscha kept passing up to him the fragrant bolts of wood. They were a little shorter than a man, fully one and a half inches thick, and so grooved that they could be neatly fitted into each other.

"All I want now is a pair of pliers," persisted Grischa.

Five prisoners in a row, each with four of these props on his shoulder: they flung them down in front of the car, with the hollow clatter of dead wood, then all seven of them stood up for a moment in a group. They said nothing. Those who had carried the planks let their arms fall by their sides, and looked at the huge heap of timber.

"That'll do," said Grischa. "Go and warm yourselves, boys: time's up."

"Right you are, Grischa," answered one of them. "We'll take your word for it," and they nodded to him and went off. Further up, between the rails of the two lines that met at this point, a small field railway track and the main line, a large, fragrant fire was burning. Beside it, standing or sitting on ties, planks or stumps, were the guards and the Russian labourers with their German foremen, men of the Landsturm Army Service Corps. Iron cauldrons of coffee were hanging over the flames, and here and there a man was toasting bread on a green twig. The mighty element devoured the resinous wood with spurts and hisses and crackling leaps of flame. In front of the railway the forest fell back to left and right. Like rusted ghosts of the living, the great trunks towered above the snow, the thick, powdery, frozen March snow of western Russia on which the sun flings blue and golden light and shadows, seamed by the tracks of heavily nailed boots. From the loaded white branches moisture dripped at the contact with the sun, and froze in the circles of shadow. A remote, deep blue sky drew the men's glances upwards. "Spring's coming," said Grischa, meaningly.

"Don't you do it," Aljoscha answered in a coaxing voice. "Yes, spring is coming, and then things will be better: we shall have moss to lie on and there'll be more food. Don't be a fool, Grischa, stay here. It's madness, what you mean to do. You won't get forty miles away. The whole country is overrun with Germans—outposts, police, and all the rest of them. If you get away and they catch you again—you'll be working like a nigger for them for years after the peace."

Grischa alone had charge of the stacking of the props, and now he went about this task silently and in most unwonted fashion. No authority could possibly have ordered this waste of space: between the back of the car and its load of timber he kept a passage free, above the floor, where the shorter, heavier beams were put to steady the load, and this passage was cunningly roofed in with timber.

"Quick, Aljoscha! Before they come back!"

And Aljoscha obeyed. He knew why his friend was calling him. In this hiding-place Grischa meant to escape that night, for the car would appear fully loaded. Aljoscha did not for a moment approve of the attempt. He had set his whole heart on dissuading his friend from an undertaking that seemed to him hopeless and foolish. But he obeyed. In the whole company of prisoners, two hundred and fifty men, who for the last nine months had been employed in sawing timber at the prison camp at Navarischky, there were not two who would refuse any request or disobey any order of Sergeant Grischa Iljitsch Paprotkin, now Prisoner No. 173.

He had a jest for every man, and above all he had won the St.

George's cross as far back as the siege of Przemysl: and also, every one of them knew that for his part Grischa Iljitsch would, and often did, help them in any way he could. Aljoscha, working with a passionate keenness born of his affection for his mate, began to sweat: he was passing up one after the other of the squared pine planks to his comrade, who almost snatched them from him and handled the heavy soaking planks like matchwood. One, two: one, two: with the muffled ring of wood against wood, the roof-timbers that were to conceal the tube-like hollow fell into place. Grischa, standing on the fully laden part of the car, tested the hollow with his toe: it held. It was a neat piece of work. He had hauled up some of the planks and set them on end against the sides of the car; thus at the same time keeping out the cold and giving support to the covering timbers. To-night he would creep into this hollow and lie there like a badger in his earth: towards morning about four o'clock an engine would draw the whole train eastward out of the forest. And eastward went his heart. A good many of these timber cars went up to the Front with the countless supply trains, and that was his goal. It was still early in the year 1917: the Russian armies, weary from countless defeats and shattering losses, had, first on their own initiative and then with the approval of the new regime, brought the War to a standstill. Strange things were happening in Petersburg: the almighty Tsar, the Little Father, Nicholas II, had abdicated to save the ancient imperial crown for his son: the Grand Duke Michael, chosen as Regent, transferred the power into the hands of that evanescent parliament, the Duma: soldiers firing on the imperial police: the red flag waving in hungry Petersburg, in Moscow, Ekaterinburg, Kronstadt, and Kazan . . . the Schlüsselburg blown up, criminals let loose, generals imprisoned, ministers hounded into exile, admirals drowned, shot, driven from the country. And in their stead, what strange new people! At that moment Russia's destinies were guided by a handful of civilians, a substantial merchant, Rodzianko, a landed proprietor, Prince Lvof, Miljukoff, a Professor, and the astute and dexterous poor man's lawyer, Kerensky.

Russia was reshaping, Russia was awaiting peace with her rifle at her feet. Firing had ceased between the German and Russian trenches: all was brotherhood. As the War must needs end soon, deserters were thronging back to their native villages and towns where, if they were lucky, their relations would still be waiting for them. But Grischa Iljitsch Paprotkin, sergeant, lived in Vologda, far away to the north-east of the vast land of Russia, and if he wanted to see his wife and children he must look for them behind the Russian front.

That was his plan. He would escape from the Germans: he could stand it. no longer. With the beginning of the new year and the confirmation of all sorts of rumours, his heart had become strangely restless: slow heavy-footed thoughts had day after day fixed themselves more firmly in his head: he must get home. He had waited far too long. What with the barbed wire, the kaleidoscopic orders of the crazy Germans, so scared that they would scarcely let you breathe, and would almost have you breathe by numbers: "breathe in, breathe out, wipe your nose, now go to the latrine"—what with the cramped sleeping-quarters in the barracks, and the staring eyes of the officers—all this stifled him. He had been their prisoner for sixteen months, and he would not stand it for another day. That very night he would start on his way to Marfa Ivanovna, and his little tiny Jelisavjeta, whom he had never yet seen. As a stone falls, so his mind was set. And because he needed the pliers for his purpose, and Aljoscha was orderly to the sergeant in charge of tools, Aljoscha could easily steal them so that he could cut the wire. The latter part of the journey would be easy enough.

"Now for it, hurry up, Aljoscha," he replied inexorably to his friend's mute refusals. The thought of leaving Aljoscha made his heart a little heavy. But when the War was over they would meet again. He had thrashed it out with him a thousand times. He could not have waited if he would. In his heart was no more room for waiting. His arm thrilled with a measureless, ever fiercer impulse to beat down all before him, and hew a way out for himself; the random words of insolent corporals danced in his brain like sparks. He must go, or worse would come of it: and this Aljoscha knew. Their hands moved swiftly backwards and forwards and the pile of timber grew.

At last not a plank was left upon the snow. The two workmen swung their arms across their chests, cabman-fashion. Grischa jumped stiffly from the car, and pulling on the huge grey mittens, that they could not use while working, they stamped over to the fire. In the meantime, the five men who carried the wood had trotted back to their distant comrades who brought down the freshly cut timber in the small tip-wagons and trolleys of the field railway. The saw-mills (and the prison camp close by), a small hutment village right in the middle of the vast desolate forest of Navarischky, stood on a little hill about three kilometres away. To protect it against aircraft, the junction of main and branch lines had been fixed at the lowest and most thickly wooded point in the forest. As far as this junction, a skilful man who knew how to slow down his lorry by thrusting a stick between the wheels, could send it thundering down the light rails without an engine. Just then, Lance-Corporal Printz, a fair-haired young rascal who, after recovering from a wound, had been drafted to the Landsturm battalion, appeared on one of these lorries . . . crashing and roaring like the Fiend.

"And you are going to bolt from the camp to-night on a thing that makes a row like that?" whispered Aljoscha maliciously to Grischa, who was stuffing his pipe with the dubious prison tobacco and held out his pouch to his friend with a meaningful gesture. Grischa dug him good-naturedly in the ribs with his elbow:

"You're a fathead, you forget the wind: as soon as the sun is down, the old trees make as much row as if I'd paid them to, as if the Devil and his grandmother were in it. I don't want you to slip me those pliers till eight o'clock. At half-past, after evening rounds, I'm off. Why don't you come, brother? Aljoscha—the two of us! We'd get through."

Aljoscha smiled. If they had not been sitting quite so near the fire, the smile would have looked more rueful still.

"I don't think so, Grischa: I don't like the looks of it."

"What doesn't your friend like the looks of?" asked Sergeant Leszinsky from the fire; he understood Russian well, knew the two as friends and favourites among the prisoners.

"The weather," answered Grischa, cheerfully. "He thinks it will rain."

Lance-Corporal Birkholz, who had sauntered up from his pine tree towards the fire—in five minutes it would be the midday interval, the field kitchen would be brought up at any moment, and he had nearly finished making up his mental parcel—Birkholz, the joiner from the Berlinerstrasse in Eberswalde, propped his rifle against a tree and held out his hands to the glow, while he sat down on a pile of planks, and the Russians moved up to make room for him. "Rain? Oh, it won't rain in a hurry, you can bet on that. Why, the way it's been blowing, evening after evening, you'd think the huts would fly away—such a row you can hardly sleep. But in the morning the sky looks as clear as mother's table-cloth on a Sunday, Russsky, my boy."

Grischa put a small ember with his bare hands on the tobacco in his pipe, and puffed. Aljoscha stood beside him and smiled nervously. When he had finished speaking, nothing could be heard but the crackling and sputtering of the flames, for the words had touched the sensitive point in all of them: their longing for home. All these men, no longer young, for years now cut off from their habits and their friends, were home-sick. And while this feeling had become part of the structure of their souls, in some sense the centre of their hearts' gravity, the measure of all that was within them, they noticed it themselves only from time to time. Even if the difficulties in their way had not been so insurmountable, not one of them would have contemplated making a dash for home like Odysseus, the Homecomer of the Trojan War, and let himself, like him, be whirled backward and forward in his perilous course, drawn as by a magnet, and sure in his inmost heart of his return. The most passionate soul of them all was at work in Grischa, and thus it was that what many millions of men, dressed in all manner of different clothes, and all, caught in the machinery of War at that moment, only longed to do, he did. But this measureless urge, which had been present to them all for one instant, passed over their heads like the smoke of a fire. Suddenly they all looked up: harsh trumpet-calls, like the rasping of rusty hinges were heard in the blue air. "Geese," one of them called out, and pointed to the white gleaming wedge of the great birds in flight, like a half-open pair of compasses hurtling through the air, now overhead, far above them, white and dazzling under the clouds; then speeding away over the woods—the squadrons of the spring.

"Yes, they are flying home," murmured Corporal Leszinsky.

"Eastward," said Grischa, softly, amid the significant silence of the Germans and the Russians, and in the Russian tongue. The geese were disappearing like a glittering speck against the radiant sky, and the silence round the fire was ended by a shout which came echoing from afar: the "stew-gun" (field kitchen) appeared in the shape of two large cauldrons, and was skilfully pulled up on the narrow-gauge railway.

"Fifteen!" shouted Corporal Leszinsky, the midday call of the timber workers, the welcome rallying cry to rest. All hands were stretched out towards the pots; all of them, workmen in uniform, rallying each other in the slang that reminded them of their freedom, of the time when they were not soldiers and struggled hard for their daily bread. They all ate standing. Amid the metallic clatter of the tin or aluminum pans, Aljoscha said to Grischa: "At eight, then." Grischa clapped him on the back smiling. Both knew what was meant; they did not even need to look at each other.

"What's for dinner: where's the menu?" shouted Lance-Corporal Printz, dimpling and radiant.

"Beans and bacon," answered the kitchen-corporal. "They feed you up so here, that there won't be room for you in mummy's bed when you get home."

Chapter 2

ESCAPE!

TEMPEST and tumult. From the chimneys, zinc tubes with their little cowls, plumes of swirling sparks went hissing over the flat, huddled roofs of the hutment camp, black against the snow that glittered dully in the moonless night. In the corners, gangways, and recesses—darkness, compact and impenetrable, especially about those places where, from some ill-curtained window, a beam or shaft of light went questing through the storm-rent air. Over the straggling hap-hazard camp, sang the wind, the storm of spring, with maniac fury, in the chords of the barbed-wire fence, three or four yards high, that encircled the barracks, officers' quarters, sheds, and storehouses.

Slipping and stumbling among them on the iron surface of yesterday's thaw, which had frozen once again, came a sentry now soon to be relieved. Wrapped in a monstrous white sheepskin, his gun slung over his shoulders, muzzle downwards, with the nails of his greased boots he crushed the sharp little edges and ridges of yesterday's frozen footprints. Thus staggering, and thinking of his woes, he listened to the wind that cut his cheek as it whistled by. He left his shelter, where a man might sleep in comfort, to meet his relief who should arrive at any minute. Of course, there was no sense in patrolling this place : no one was likely to bring anything into the camp. And on such a night as this no one was likely to take so much as an army loaf out of it much less his own valuable carcass. A mug's game escaping, now the War's over. This was not only the conviction of Heppke of the Landsturm, but also of nearly the whole garrison, always excepting the camp sergeant-major, who, like all his kind, would have thought he had taken leave of his senses, if he did not treat the most trivial matters of routine as solemnly as a private treats his pay-sheet.

Heppke was seething with impatience, wondering when that devil Kazmierzak, his relief, could be coming. But ever and anon he was overwhelmed by the cataract of sound which filled the air. Like a tireless torrent howled the forest gale, heaving and thrusting, piling up the snowdrifts, smiting bough on bough; till at its onslaught many a tree, made brittle by the frost, paid forfeit of its heaviest branches, booming like a cannon. No step could be heard in all this tumult; and so out of the darkness loomed Kazmierzak of the Landsturm in his black cloak, and stumbled against the sentry. "Oho," said Heppke, glad of his relief. "So you've found your legs, have you? I thought you'd got them stuck under the table playing nap."

Kazmierzak of the Landsturm, pipe in mouth against all orders, took his comrade's rifle. Heppke immediately divested himself of the heavy sentry's sheepskin, and while Kazmierzak was putting it on, he pointed out reproachfully to Heppke what he had meant to say on the way from the guard-house. "Look at those windows. You can see an inch of light everywhere; if the sergeant-major sees that, *you're* for the high jump."

Karl—he called Heppke by his Christian name—had better see they were properly darkened. Nonsense, of course: nonsense like the whole War. As if there could be airplanes in the middle of Poland, where the deadliest bombs would be droppings of wild geese. But orders are orders, duty's duty, rum's rum, and it's all sh—— together.

"Get those blighted windows darkened at once," he warned him again. "You must have been dreaming there on sentry-go, as if you didn't know Klappka and the order-book!" Klappka—that was the sergeant-major—was a choleric gentleman with an exceptional gift for exploding with fury over trivial transgressions.

"Friend," said Heppke, in an odd tone of voice. "That's not what I'm thinking. Sticking here makes me feel funny: and this blasted wind always roaring in my ears. I'm sick for home: I shall go dotty if I can't get back."

Kazmierzak said nothing. If Karl thought *that* was news to him or any other man in the army, he might put his brains in a glass case and show them in a museum. But Heppke, who had got a glimpse of his own soul, became yet more confidential. "And the songs! Listen to them singing now, those Russians; like eighteen-seventy! There's a revolution over there, Emil, mark my words there'll be peace: it'll be home, old son, me to my bench again, and the old woman in bed beside me, and the kid crawling round the table leg. Emil, we shall be hanging the old guns on every branch and trekking off home on our flat feet. Spring's here at last: just smell it coming from the forest."

Kazmierzak settled himself in his cloak, slung his rifle, an old-fashioned musket fitted with a modern lock, and opined that there was something in it; the Revolution was coming over there and that was why the Russians in the camp were singing. That was something for a sentry to think of between eight and ten, or two and four. Kazmierzak did not venture to pursue his thoughts further. He was partly Polish, as his name implied, and since the War began, experience had taught the Prussian soldiers to mistrust a Polish name—you never know, they said. The Poles were rather more closely watched than others, Alsatians excepted. And although Heppke had been his comrade and his friend, Kazmierzak was not too free with his confidences. But for the sake of company he went back with him to the guard-house, for he had two hours' sentry-go before him, and snatched at the chance of a few minutes' gossip. And Heppke was bursting with information. "All I want is to get home, and be Heppke the joiner again at Eberswalde, go to the park of a Sunday and have a beer, with the kid on a see-saw, mother knitting and having a crack with Roberta; me playing nap with Rob and Vicky—Oh God, and Rob croaked in hospital last week with spotted typhus. No, my boy, a man gets balmy walking up and down staring into the darkness, thinking—and nothing to keep up your spirits."

In the meantime Kazmierzak was preparing to deliver himself of an observation. He considered it safe to point out to his friend that peace did not seem likely for the present. America was a dark horse, Wilson had all his trumps to play, the U-boat war would tangle them up a bit, and things wouldn't be so easy.

But Heppke was too wrapped up in his own speculation.

"Emil," said he, when they had nearly reached the guard-house door, "I'll go in and have my bit of sleep; then I shan't care if it hails. And I'll dream, old boy: fancy me at forty and living on dreams. If it lasts much longer, I shall go balmy, Emil."

But Kazmierzak would have none of this escape into dreams. " 'Dream, ah, dream of Paradise,' on paper sheets and sawdust, with no extra charge for bugs," he snapped out. "Perhaps we'll have peace after all. At least on our Front. But if it's only on our Front, it's no catch. They must all do like the Russkies, chuck down their rifles, and b—— off home."

This roused Heppke, who had long been of the same mind. "Us first!" he whispered, looking round him cautiously. "But we shan't risk it." And with that he opened the guard-house door, whence a waft of warm humanity rolled out into the night air; and Kazmierzak was left to his solitary task of patrolling the camp.

"Shout it out," thought he, "let 'em all hear: it's true enough, of course it should be us first, but of course we funk it. The brass hats have got us by the short hairs."

His footsteps crunched upon the frozen snow as he walked, staring at the toes of his boots, and ever in his ears echoed the song of the Russians from Hutment No. 3, near which their conversation had begun.

Where Nos. 3 and 4 met at an obtuse angle, out of the shadowy gloom now moved a figure towards the wire fence—a figure trembling at the knees with fear and excitement, fervently thankful for that song of mingled menace and despair, which drowned the hammering of his heart. The Russians were singing the song that rang through the prisons during the revolution of 1905 when the condemned were led out to death, a melody so simple and with so magical a rhythm as could only be devised by a deeply musical and enslaved people over whose heart the ploughshare of sorrow has passed. Although Grischa crawled with the utmost circumspection by the dim light of the snow, over the five or six yards in front of the first line of fence, and while he cut the wires—two, three, four, with powerful strokes of the pliers—still in his inward ear echoed the words his comrades were singing, the words of a vow never to forget the dead and always to stand by the living. When the wires were cut their loose ends sprang apart twanging and thrumming. The

hole, which in a few seconds was large enough to admit, first his
pack, then his bundle of blankets, and finally the man himself, lay
neatly hidden in the shadow of the huts. Now there was no going
back, the escape could no longer be concealed. Soaking with sweat,
and panting with apprehension, Grischa hurried breathlessly towards
the next line of wire, in front of which he paused by the toolsheds
and breathed deeply. Now he cursed the song,—which luckily ceased
at that moment,—for it would prevent him hearing the sentry's footsteps. He knew who was on duty then. Like all men of his kind
who are fond of a glass, Kazmierzak was strict in his dealings with
the prisoners, especially as with many of them he was able to speak
Polish. Still, Grischa felt a momentary regret that this man—for
who could say when his escape would be discovered?—would perhaps
be called to account for it. But Grischa was working his way through
the east side of the camp, and whenever an escape had been attempted,
—there had been four in the last nine months,—the fugitives had
made their way westward towards the town, five-and-twenty miles
away, where they looked for shelter among a population bitterly
hostile to the Germans. The pliers rasped and clicked against the
wires; the wind saw to it that no sound should be heard, for here the
wind blew freely; and its biting blast almost numbed Grischa's
labouring fingers.

Now for the wide and wellnigh empty space between the two
storehouses and the outermost wire fence. Showers of sparks whirled
noiselessly from the narrow chimneys of the overheated crackling
wood furnaces, and near by ticked the dynamo which supplied the
electric light. There had once been talk of setting up arc-lamps to
flood the camp with light, when the last escape cost Sergeant-Major
Busch his comfortable job. But at that time the fear of aircraft
made such a course impossible, and since in the meantime orders
had been given to economize coal, this infallible safeguard could not
be adopted. "When I'm out of it," thought Grischa, "they'll light
the place up. And these nippers will get poor old Aljoscha into
clink. But," he went on, mentally groping in all directions through
the darkness—as his thoughts moved under their own momentum,
heedless of his innermost self, which was ever straining forward, like

the hammer of a rifle at full cock—"but perhaps he'll wangle himself out of it, or won't even be suspected."

With that he drew a deep breath, clenched his teeth, and said to himself: "Now for it!" He tiptoed in his heavy boots across the broad and shadowy enclosure: he was aiming for the point nearest the edge of the forest, where the lorries stood on the field-railway. Here a quantity of hewn timber had been piled against the wire, to put on the trucks the following day: to save time, just before they stopped for the day, the men on this work had passed the planks to one another through the wire. Thus the barrier of wire could not be seen through from either side: this would only be so, of course, until next morning, when the pile would have to be moved to make way for fresh timber. But no man of sense would look so far ahead as that. Early next morning when work was allotted and Prisoner No. 173 found missing, and all the camp in a ferment, these planks might be utterly forgotten and stay where they were till peace was made—or, for the matter of that, if the work were pressing, they might be picked up at once—God knows. From the moment when Grischa, scratching himself slightly on the wire, plunged into the dark shadows beyond, he could be sure his escape would be unnoticed till about half-past seven next morning.

The storm was writhing in the wires; Kazmierzak of the Landsturm was marching up and down. "All serene. There'll be hell with the Americans," he thought. He knew what they were after. He'd been over there, worked there, saved up his dollars, and brought them back like an idiot in 1912. He had lived on the East Side, right among the Jews, and earned good money. The Americans take hold and hang on when they once bite, like bulldogs. *They* had built the big railways, they invented skyscrapers, they made Niagara grind their turbines—they were folk worth seeing. So thinking, with the wind howling in one's ears, it was easy to pass within a couple of yards of a cut wire fence and not notice it in the dark, nor observe that it has been broken through at about the height of a man kneeling, on the innermost line of wire, near the hutments.

A man ran on tiptoe in the teeth of the wind towards the forest, from stump to stump across the clearing. What a din was in the branches! Almost as great as the turmoil in his heart. Sometimes it happened that a badly secured lorry got loose, and rolled slowly at first, then quicker and quicker, down the gentle slope between the high ground of the camp and the loading station. Wheels clattered on the rails. The frozen iron rasped and squealed. But even if there were ears to hear, who could hear this sound amid the general babel? So did the wind rage and boom and bluster in the tree-tops.

Army regulations require that loaded cars left in the forest should be guarded. But what matters when there is none to see? A warm and lighted railway shed, iron-roofed and snugly boarded, if you have two companions and plenty of tobacco, is a rare spot for playing nap in, especially as you can make tea, and your three rum rations in expert hands will yield a good supply of grog. And if you keep friends with the cook there will be no stint of sugar.

Meanwhile a man was climbing into a freight-car, easily enough, as it was open at the top. In a tube-shaped hollow encased in the resinous wood, he stretched himself full length, having first carefully pulled back over him some of the short pine planks grooved at either end; stretched himself out, and laughed aloud, and shook with that great laughter, his shirt drenched in sweat, and shivering all over, in the narrow sharp-edged coffin-like recess. It was hard lying: he could move but little. But he could laugh: and his eyes must have shone in the darkness like those of a panther which had burst its bars at last.

About half past eleven Grischa was awakened by a jolt, a noise of grinding and crashing; he started up in terror from the pack on which he had slept, wrapt in his blankets and his cloak—he had slept more serenely than for many years—and banged his head on the wood above. But he shook off his terror quicker than his pain: it was an engine backing down on to the interminable line of cars, with shrieks and whistles slowly merging into a steady clank and rumble. Once more Grischa sank down contentedly upon his wooden pillow; the train moved on, jolting and spewing forth sparks—while the firemen cursed softly at the wretched coal bricks; and the engine breasted the wind that blustered round it, as if to check its eastward course, towards Russia!

Chapter 3

THE FREIGHT-CAR

HE who would travel in a freight-car, should first remember that it is not sprung like a first-class passenger car, but will beat a devil's tattoo on his hindquarters. Railway rails are about six yards long, loosely clamped together in a simple and ingenious fashion which allows the heat to expand the metal without breaking it. Every six yards, therefore, where one rail meets another, the car passes over the joint with a bump. Thus, if a car travels for several days, at about twenty miles an hour, those who make a hobby of arithmetic may take paper and pencil and calculate the approximate number of bumps imparted.

"D'you want the War to last for ever? D'you want the War to last for ever?" rumbled the train, as it clattered on its way, beating the rhythm into the bones of the traveller in the car who had not so much as a truss of straw to lie on, such as is provided when these cars are used for their proper purpose of carrying forty men or eight horses. But the conveyance of as many officers would require at least eight second-class compartments—that is to say in war-time.

A man lying in a coffin cannot move very freely, even if the coffin is three times as long and high as usual. Breadth is what matters, and broad it cannot be. Moreover the body ensconced in such a coffin may be lying softly upon sawdust: but if it lies there long enough, the saw-dust will be proudly mindful of its wooden origin, and revert to the hardness and consistency of the trunk from which it was so violently extracted. Even a tarpaulin for a shroud cannot make the corpse lie easier. For though a tarpaulin keeps you warm, and indeed has more uses than may be easily rehearsed, still it is no more than a piece of coarse canvas. The man in the coffin—or what may well be likened thereto—turns and tosses from back to side and side to belly. He draws in his elbows, squeezes his shoulders in, aches in all his muscles

19

for a change of position, and must be careful how he sits lest he bang
his head on the timbers of his roof. So he rattles along in the car,
like a wild animal—some panther carried in his cage to the Zoological
Gardens where he must end his life behind iron bars. The comparison
errs only in this important point, that Grischa was free.

The man in the coffin is quite enveloped in the acrid vinagrous atmosphere of hewn timber. This does in fact contain noxious chemical
constituents which, in the long run, will make a man dizzy and even
ill : at least, since he can't get out into the air, it gives him a splitting
headache. And darkness reigns in such a coffin. It is true that the
daylight comes through the boards above his head in thin streaks :
thus he can distinguish day and night by the pleasant warmth which
reaches his wooden cavity when the sun stands right above the train.
So he observes the passage of the flying hours, and also by the less or
greater keenness of the cold, the winter cold of a March day and a
March night. And the change must be well noted for another reason.
For he may not smoke by day ; the brakemen on the train might well
be suspicious of the faint blue cloudlets rising from a timber wagon,
which might have caught fire, so that they would have to reload it.
But at night, with sufficient caution, one may enjoy a cigarette or a
pipe with impunity.

Furthermore, the traveller who carries all his luggage on his back,
and, placed as he is, cannot renew his supplies, must be a trifle
Spartan in the satisfaction of his hunger and even of his thirst. He
sips cold tea from his water-bottle : later on, when his march through
the snow begins, he can do very well with a little salted snow-water.
As for eating, he must be very moderate with the hard bread or the
small biscuits which he has bartered from his guards. And this has
advantages, when a man can only relieve the necessities of the human
body consequent upon the absorption of victuals, at the peril of his
life. It is better for him not to leave his lurking-place, but to subdue
his grosser parts.

Such a man, prostrate at the very foundation of the pyramid of
society, like a small stone thrilling with consciousness, cannot afford
to study over-nicely his personal convenience. The German private
soldier, as belonging to the lowest caste in the army, may get some
hard knocks : but he passes on these knocks to the countless masses

of civilians in occupied territory, for a soldier in field-grey with a bayonet at his side is master of them all. And a Russian prisoner, especially if he is escaping, has everything to fear from these civilians. Every peasant, every Jew, even every woman, whom he meets, is the dispenser of his life and fate and freedom. A man can sink no lower among human-kind than a Russian prisoner of war, escaping, or waiting for the end. For it is but one step lower to the domestic animal, distinguished from the prisoner not by the fact of his working —both must work—but simply by being eatable, a property which has been extended to cats and dogs, not to mention horses.

And yet the man, in such case, cooped up and buried alive in pungent smelling planks, bumped along in the darkness, groping blindly in his pack, tossing and turning, prone or crouching, aching in every limb, his brain, his temples, the back of his head throbbing unendurably:—this man laughed and chuckled to himself in the blackness. Indeed, he could have sung and whistled. Grischa was glad that he had got free and plunged into the wild incalculable adventure of escape, as into icy water. The thought of it, as he recovered consciousness, almost broke his heart. There was nobody now to order him about. Within his wooden abode, he slept and waked when he chose, ate and smoked as it pleased him. He felt the vast delight of being alone at last. Better to feel the hard planks at his elbows, than to have some one at his side every hour of the day and night: better a thousand times the splintering freight of timber above his head than the eye, the presence, the invisible pressure of the officer. That, too, combined perhaps with the narcotic effect of the pine vapours, must have been why he had not slept for years as he had done these last nights and days, numbed as he was, and his head throbbing: yet he slept the sleep of one who returns to health and looks again upon the face of God.

Grischa had not thought out his escape in detail. It is seldom that life approves our exacter calculations: every hour she leaps capriciously across them, led by her own laws, and a wise man follows her caprice. From time to time he had carefully sounded the railwaymen and those in charge of the trains, as to the probable destination of a car so loaded with timber, and enquired the name of the station where the cars were detached from their several trains, like men parted by their destinies after a season of companionship; and he did not forget to ask which way the loads were going. They were all bound for the Front, and the Front stretched between Dünaburg and the Austrians in a bent and bulging line which gashed from north to south the face of holy Russia. It was all one to him at what point he crossed the trenches; but there were certain matters he had to think of. He could—indeed he must—try to reach his goal by the shortest route, to ensure supplies and to avoid discovery: but perhaps these freight-cars, that could not leave the rails, would be making a vast detour from south to north before reaching their most easterly point; besides, they often pulled up for half a day. By the shouts of the men, the jerks and tugs of the engine, by its whistling, and the shunting backwards and forwards, he recognized places where the train was split up or lengthened. He possessed a watch: and though it was not luminous in the darkness, he had matches with which he could light his pipe at the same time. The average run of such a car would be five or six days before it was unloaded on to the field-railways. Grischa had made up his mind to leave his refuge on the fourth night.

But he could not hold out so long: his body revolted. About three o'clock on the morning of the fourth day, when the train had stood for two hours in isolation and silence, he carefully lifted the planks above his head and looked about him. To his eyes, accustomed as they were to sepulchral darkness, the world seemed wrapped in a half-light, and very silent. Strange and exultant seemed the icy air as it poured into his nostrils, smarting with the cold, and into his lungs which had grown quite unfamiliar with real oxygen. On his right rose up the forest edge, like the sheer cliff-face of a plateau through which in the course of ages a river had bored its way. On the left of this river—the line of the railway—and parallel to it, ran a sort of highroad, also bounded by the wall of forest. In front, and far away, he guessed, would be the engine: his view was blocked by the towering loads of the cars. Behind him, lashed securely down with a sheet of waterproof canvas loomed the mammoth bulk of a flatcar loaded with compressed hay.

He had already pushed aside the blankets and tarpaulin, ready for his flight. Then carefully he lowered his unwieldy bundle on a strap of his pack and climbed out, for a moment completely visible, on the load of timber, and lying on his stomach, pushed the roof planks back, leaving a level surface to avert suspicion, and then let himself down into the snow beside his pack. His feet, almost blood-less and unused to walking, would scarcely carry him. The silence seemed at first to vibrate against his temples, then changed abruptly into the noiseless calm of a winter night. Straight in front of him glittered lights, the lamps of a railway building, a shed of some kind: a halt, perhaps a siding, one of the many sidings in the forest. Grischa knew neither where he was nor where he was going. He shouldered his pack and, fully conscious of the danger that he ran, was across the road in three or four strides. His foot struck some curved object like the crook of a walking-stick. He could do with a stick, so he grasped it and pulled out of the snow the ragged skeleton of an ancient gamp which some Bavarians in charge of a troop train had used in carnival festivities, and then thrown away. Grischa clutched the clumsy frame and gathered the spokes into his palm. A second later the forest had closed its drooping snow-laden boughs behind him. In spite of the utter darkness, less black, however, than the darkness of his coffin, for half an hour, panting and soaked in sweat, he stumbled through the tree-trunks.

In front of the hut that housed the three soldiers in charge of the siding, stood the brakemen and the engine driver, drinking hot "coffee."

"Any game here?" asked the fireman.

"Game? I should say so," answered the man at the telephone, which announces the arrival and departure of trains, and receives and transmits orders.

"We've all done a bit of that: there's plenty of it away back in the forest. But don't you risk it; Felix, just tell him how you went after a Christmas dinner, and we had to go shooting and whistling all over the place to get you out of it."

Felix, spreading turnip jam over his bread, shuddered involun-tarily. Though on that occasion he knew that his comrades were near and trusted them to come and look for him, he now shivered with horror at the recollection of having suddenly come upon his own tracks in the pathless forest. Although it was broad daylight, he thought he should never find his way back until he heard the signals fired from the shed.

"No fear," said the first man firmly. "No more Sunday dinners here."

The brakeman, who had just seen something that looked like a half-grown animal, perhaps a roebuck, nibbling at the hay car, was careful not to say a word. The art of goading a man beyond endurance by venomous speeches had been raised to a fine art in the army. Besides that, it was much too comfortable sitting here by the warm stove with a good light and drinking sweet malt coffee, till the telephone should ring to announce "line clear." Time to hunt for tracks later on.

Twenty minutes later, of course, the matter had been forgotten in a discourse on peace and a little game of six and sixty, when the expected signal scattered them and their hopes of winning.

Chapter 4

THE FOREST

It would never have occurred to the fiery old mother lynx, in her thick and tawny winter coat, to eat a man, and a dead man at that. But one day as she trotted between the tree-trunks after the fresh scent of a hare, she came upon August Säpsgen from Tharandt in Saxony, a nineteen-year-old forestry student, near the square caves where she now lodged with her two little whelps, caves which had been hollowed out of the earth by men who shook the forest of a night with the thunder of their huge machines. In those days, like the other animals that need quiet nights for hunting, she had migrated northwards, and, only a few months before, had ventured to return, when the Northern winter looked like being too severe. The men were gone with their great thundering noises, but the caves were left, and in the most remote of them mother lynx made herself a comfortable home.

The savage creature in her hunt for flesh had come upon young Säpsgen in a very sorry guise. He lay stark naked on her track, arms and legs outstretched, dead, but not long dead, when the lynx first got her teeth into him: and a few weeks later the dead man was entered as missing. The gendarmes of the police-post at Cholno had warned the young newly commissioned dragoon, who as an expert forester had been attached to their remote little station to assist them in the suppression of brigandage, not to venture so much as a mile into the forest. But the young man heartily despised them for being so intent on the prospect of peace, and arrogantly informed them that he cared not a damn for deserters—cowardly swine—escaped prisoners, and the whole tribe of civilians; whereat they, Swabians from Bietigheim, made furtive and somewhat venomous comments on the young coxcomb, who said he'd show them what a Jäger was and tempted his guardian angel a little too far. . . . On his handsome piebald Wallach, Victoria, with the sturdy police dog, Lissi, as his sole companion, he was more and more often enticed into solitary rides of a Sunday afternoon along the gleaming forest gorge, which led to the abandoned gun emplacement dating from the year '15. One day, after two glorious hours' trotting, Lissi gave a sudden angry bark, and snarled at the impenetrable wall of forest which fringed the clearing right and left. And instead of immediately turning back, or at least firing his carbine into the moving leaves, the poor young man, suspecting a fox, bent down to unleash the hound, when a shot rang out, a single sharp pistol-shot from very near at hand; it struck the ill-starred youth upon the temple, and two strangers who were hunting so shamelessly near Cholno went home the richer by a dog to roast, a fine live horse, a spotless new cloak and tunic, trousers, boots and underclothing, not to mention a carbine of the '98 pattern with ammunition and some two-and-twenty marks in cash. So they left August Säpsgen lying there in the middle of the track, as a contemptuous warning to his comrades in the ceaseless warfare between outlaw and forester. In the evening when the moon showed her face over the fir trees like a half-gnawed apple, mother lynx made acquaintance with August Säpsgen after her fashion. So on Monday the Württembergers could only trace to the place of their disaster those who went forth so gaily that Sunday afternoon; for it would be unsafe to pursue the tracks of horse and man deeper into the forest, where any bush might shelter a bandit and his rifle. The only signs of Säpsgen and Lissi were great bloodstains on the snow, for in hard winters wild animals are most skilful in burying even their biggest game. This audacious exploit of the bandits was reported to Grodno, and in spite of the awful frost, the forest, impenetrable as it was, was searched so far as might be, from end to end. But what could nine men do in the short hours of daylight, to avenge the unhappy youth, though they searched with all their might in their fury at his murder.

So it came about that the lynx who had eaten one man, was not greatly perturbed by the scent of another. One night she crossed his track for the first time: she laid back her silky, pointed ears and followed. Uneasy, but at the same time hopefully intent upon the prospect of a meal, she licked her lips and, without neglecting her young and her daily pursuit of food, she watched out for him night after night as he crunched and stamped along for reasons which she could not fathom, and in a direction which was not at all to her liking. This man was Grischa Iljitsch Paprotkin, escaped prisoner, and sometime tenant of a cosy, comfortable, lousy freight-car.

He thought he understood forests; in which he was sorely mistaken, as it proved. Through thick undergrowth, which had never known the axe, he forced his way in the noiseless daylight between morning and afternoon, in what he thought was an easterly direction. In the faintness and bitterness of his heart, he had long realized that he had left the camp too soon: now he was in midwinter and mid-forest, saved only by the little compass on his watch-chain from exhausting himself by walking in a circle, and so landing at the station from which he had plunged into the woods. He kept on falling into pits full of snow, picking himself out again, stumbling over rotten stumps of trees which the snow had gradually converted into man-traps, and entangling himself in a network of bramble-bushes. For want of a hatchet, he used the strong sharp dirk of a French sub-lieutenant of Marines, which he had saved and kept in his boot, when he had been employed on the Western Front in bringing in and burying the dead. In his fatigue he had not yet hit upon the road, now partly dilapidated, which wound in spirals from Cholno, concealed as far as might be from detection by aircraft, and led to the disused gun-emplacement. Stubbornly and blindly he hacked his way through the most impassable stretches of that vast forest heath. Among leaf-less beech and ash and elder, which grew freely in the marshy tracts, he went forward rapidly for two days; but as the ground was frozen as hard as a stone, there was no sign of water, and he could not understand why he so often slipped and fell and bruised himself. Then as the level of the wood rose gradually, fir trees appeared, interspersed with giant oaks and pines, and then tall birch trees, whose tapering height rose far above man's stature before the blackness of the bark merged into the silver pallor of the stem.

After the numbing cold of the rocking car, he had now to face the keen sharp cold of the living air, but he was not afraid: fear or regret had never yet subdued his soul. A sullen anger against the difficulties which confronted him, and beneath this the unswerving resolution of a man who has a purpose, were the background of his mind. His boots, which an old soldier's skill had softened and greased to make them watertight, fastened at the tops to keep the snow out, and the brittle and powdery nature of the long-frozen snow, kept his limbs dry. And every evening under the shelter of a pine tree, or a plantation of saplings cleared of undergrowth, he lit a fire to warm himself and cook his supper.

He had long since parted company with civilization and had turned into a hunter like the wild Lithuanian or the White Russian of centuries ago. From the days of his boyhood when he ranged the plains of Vologda and the steppes he had learned the ways of rabbits: so he would not lack for victuals. For a week he had wandered in the snowy wilderness leaving behind him the prints of his feet and the ashes of his fires. And not only mother lynx had marked his presence.

He hunted with bow and arrow: in his hands, the umbrella that he had picked up in the road became, according to a recipe of his boyhood days, an extremely serviceable weapon—five of the steel spokes bound together with the string that every soldier carries in his pack, and a length of tough twine stretched from end to end of the resultant bow, will make a weapon for a handy lad with which he can even shoot down animals. The other spokes, even the short ones, make excellent arrows, if they are notched at the upper end, at the eye where the silk is fastened; a small fork, which can be sharpened with a flint, serves as a barb. When he picked up the umbrella, the curved handle of which he first took for that of a stick, he meant to use it as such; then it occurred to him that it might serve to support the tarpaulin over his head at night. Under the bedraggled skeletons of the trees he soon made out the tracks of animals: besides many unknown to him, which he took for those of dogs (in which he was quite wrong, as we know), hares, rabbits and the smaller fry that prey on birds—the polecat and the weasel, faint and delicate on the surface of the snow; and then he devised his bow.

He still had a long half-full tin of bully-beef, which had cost him dear, one and a half bags of biscuit and a good hunch of stale bread: under the green canopy of a pine, where at noon he had fixed his quarters for the night, he lay in wait like any hunter, his arrow on the string, watching the narrow track in front of him. With his feet wrapped in a blanket, and sitting on his pack, his back against the tree, he could endure for a while.

And when the light of early afternoon shone from the yellow sky he had his triumph: he shot his arrow through the throat of a guileless, confiding little rabbit as it scampered happily along its accustomed path, which had always been safe in the daytime, to nibble at the sapling birches. It was the triumph of the primeval hunter, when Grischa dragged his first victim by its warm ears into the thicket. He was cunning enough to know that a rabbit seldom wanders about the world alone, so he remained on the watch. Quicker than he could say, another with laid-back ears scuttled past, and behind it a white flash—an animal. "Weasel," he thought irritably; for he was impatient to get another shot. Finally he acquired a second smaller rabbit; this made enough, and he would light his fire under the tree by which he was sitting. He cut off a stout branch and swept the ground clear of snow; he made a sort of bed of green foliage and spread it like straw under the tarpaulin. Then he cut an armful of dry wood which, after it has been on the ground for a year, is never soaked quite through, and rummaged with his stick for further firewood beneath the surface of the snow, where lay a welter of creaking trunks and branches; and last of all he found a birch tree, almost uprooted by the frost and snow, and hacked away the few remaining fibres that held it to its stump.

His preparations for kindling a fire now reached a point where the primitive hunter, into which he had transformed himself, reverted to modern civilized man. No primitive hunter or archer could have kindled such a soaked mass of wood into flame with the tinder relic of his time in France, a little round bag of raw silk, about the size of a plate, stuffed full of greyish-black round discs resembling in of old days. But Grischa rummaged in his pack and pulled out a size, thickness, and shape the horn buttons of a sporting-jacket— high-explosive used for howitzers, compressed into this form. Two such discs, lightly touched with the burning end of a cigarette, produced a sputtering flame, which the brushwood of last year could not resist. But before it flared up, he carefully placed a layer of thick branches on the pile, and the tree on top of all, with the fire-craft so familiar to all soldiers in the field. So, in a few minutes, he had everything needful for spending a winter night under a pine tree: a fire to cook by, and to warm him—for the birch tree glowed and crackled gently all night long—and protection against danger, though he knew of none.

Mother lynx gazed mistrustfully upon him from an upper branch, lying flat on her belly, invisible, ghostly: she did not believe he could reach her from a distance—for his stick in no wise suggested those other sticks which she well knew could vomit sound and fire. But she did not like the look of it. That nasty glowing, crackling smoky fire, how she wished it away! Snarling and spitting, she laid back her tufted ears and stared with the round white orbs of her catlike face in its furry ruff down at the fearless thing that lay below her, all wrapped up, whose strong bright eyes had not yet looked in hers.

A day and a half later Grischa came upon a forest glade and started back with an exclamation of surprise. From Cholno he might have used the winding gorge on which the luckless young forester from Tharandt lay stretched four months ago. First he found himself amid ripped and splintered tree-trunks, then in a welter of wrecked timber: further on, by the former gun-positions, the ground was pitted with shell holes, strewn with lopped or uprooted branches; and a narrow path between the tree-stumps brought him to the hillside where once had stood the German howitzer-battery. First he stopped dead, gazing long and listening eagerly in the silent afternoon. "Good," he murmured: "first-rate!" as he realized that all these ravages were nearly two years old. All these stumps of beeches and oaks meant that there would be comfortable dug-outs somewhere in the neighborhood. He would stay in the forest a few days amid this free and pleasant solitude, wash his shirt, rid his body of lice, and stretch his limbs in peace. Only fools lose their way in the forest. North-east, south-east? East at any rate, he said, as he sniffed the breeze. Give him a little breathing space and all uncertainty would vanish: he would soon be on his way, and the Germans would not again have the pleasure of seeing Prisoner No. 173 of Navarischky Camp.

When he found the dug-outs snowed up, systematically de-molished, and stripped of all articles of use, he spat on the snow and cursed the stingy Germans; not a stove, not a rusty dixie, not a solitary shell-case to reward his digging in all this waste of debris! The observer's dug-out, constructed in a mound some distance off, he did not discover in the snow, in spite of tell-tale tracks of animals. Its entrance had been blocked by a lucky shot from the Russian field-guns; and was accessible—though, of course, not to humans—only by the shingled chimney-flue. In this dug-out, licking and playing with each other, kitten-like, on a bed of shavings, sprawled the spotted whelps of mother lynx, now the sole mistress of these forest haunts. Nevertheless, Grischa resolved to spend the night in this place. There were many attractions: wood from the vast wreckage of the trees, and telephone wire to his heart's content, which would be uncommonly useful for making snares, and hanging his stew-pot over a roaring fire. When the moon rose and the lynx left her lair she started back in fury and dismay: the man, that roving, dangerous, appetizing creature, so near her lair, must he not be prowling here with evil purpose? She was as big as a short-legged full-grown bulldog; she had claws of steel, and fangs that would have done credit to a young panther. Sitting erect on the lowest branch of a giant silver fir, the top of which still bore traces of its use as an observation post, she followed with her blazing eyes the sluggish searching movements of the enemy as he went to and fro among the holes and hillocks, stooping and rising, dragging home the wood from which she knew would grow that great red burning flower of fire. Moreover, with his trampling hoofs, clumsier than those of any other animal, even the horse, he scared away all the little burrow-ing beasts that lived beneath the surface of the south side of the hill, of which she could have taken toll to make up for these wasted hours. There, in her fierce bewilderment she cowered, undistinguish-able against the sharp foliage of the fir tree, and pondered over her man-hunting. Nothing so large and active had a right to walk so near her lair.

She knew every hollow of the stripped ravine, every corner, every tussock. Among the heap of empty tins, smelling so pleasantly of pickled herring and rancid fat, she had hunted rats and mice, which in some strange fashion had settled there and multiplied until, still very cautiously, one of the sly rodents ventured to show his tail between the coils of wire and heaps of paper. Under the snow every inch of the ground was strewn with objects which made a noise and moved unexpectedly when the foot struck them; but they did no harm. The man down there was wandering about stooping and picking things up. Soon the fire-bush would be in bloom again. Noiselessly, she slid down the trunk on her powerful kangaroo-like hind-quarters, which distinguish the lynx from the rest of the cat tribe.

The flaming yellow sky flecked the snow with its soft tints and blue shadows. It was evening, and the tops of the firs were full of the soft, silvery twitter of the little birds, which in the thick foliage of the tree-tops, did not need to fear the great owl whose hollow menacing "hoo-hoo" now echoed from all sides.

Grischa looked curiously in the direction from which the owl's cry seemed to come, the hunting call of the great, grim screech-owl: he would have gladly looked upon that spectre of the night. He was passionately in love with all the animal life about him, to which he had been so close. So long as he did not hear the winter howl of the wolves, tales of which had terrified his boyhood, or see the huge bulk of a growling bear across his path, or meet the ugly glare of the tusked and bow-legged boar, his only feeling towards animals was that deep delight in their gambols and their ways which is often found in a hunter out to kill. But Grischa felt no joy in killing, since the Tsar's coat had changed him as by enchantment first into a hunter of men and then into a caged quarry. In any case, he cared no more for killing than most men with an occupation. Above all now, after his escape—or his resurrection, as he called it—he was so brimful of kindness and goodwill, that apart from his dish of rabbit he would have had no hand in the wanton slaughter of live things. When he lay awake in camp he would have given something to understand those mysterious voices, the cries of the creatures of the forest. A certain fear of sitting alone in the darkness by his fire, he could not but acknowledge—and suppose he had had no fire! . . . But with it he kept off everything that he would so gladly have observed: the slender deer, the small, vicious hunters—martins, polecats, weasels—the silent-swooping owl, the tree-cats he had heard of, wildcats as they were called, with their big round heads and gay fur slashed with black.

Slowly, under a green sky, fell the shadows of blue dusk across the snow, merging the slope of straggling forest behind the pitted clearing into a blue-black wall. Time to go back to his dug-out which he had made habitable for the night; he had piled up logs in front of it, and one corner of it was still roofed over. Grischa had grumbled in his heavy way when he found the gun emplacements and underground passages stripped of almost every plank of serviceable timber. The Germans did not usually want for wood: a battery on the move would be hardly likely to encumber itself with planks. "Oh, well," thought he, "if the Devil's taken them no doubt he had his reasons." And feeling his way with the crook of his umbrella, his bow and arrows buttoned through his haversack, he clambered up the hill behind which had been the fourth gun of the battery. It was easy to detect and avoid the snow-filled shell-holes: vast hollows, where the snow had melted under the midday sun and then frozen once more, they were visible as slightly sunken circles of ice.

With much astonishment he saw before him in the snow, a good twenty yards away, a beast, fallow-grey, which, when he came into view, crouched motionless, and glowered at him. Grischa knew nothing at all about lynxes. He saw at once from its humped shoulders that it was no dog: it must, he thought, be a poor half-starved tree-cat on the look-out for bones, when he had finished his rabbit. He called to it with a "miaou," and tried to attract it by snapping his fingers, which is no easy task with mittens on. "You shall have liver and lights for supper, you great hulking brute."

Cowering thus, stiff with rage and terror, the lynx looked no bigger than a well-fed sheepdog, and not half so dangerous as she was, with her sinews of steel, hooked talons like a panther's claws, her vicious fangs which she bared with a slight snarl. This gave her a grinning look. And Grischa, as he gazed more and more closely at the unknown beast, was struck by its attitude, and it suddenly dawned on him that the creature was like him, Grischa! He was hugely tickled to recognize his own round face, with its frill of beard, his piercing blue eyes set somewhat askew, his snub nose and his powerful set of teeth: and he broke into a hearty guffaw, laughing like a boy, slapping his thighs—as he had not laughed since Aljoscha used to crack his jokes.

"Come, little brother," he cried: "come to the fire," and another "Ha, ha" rang out over the stillness of the twilight.

A lynx could hardly be expected to tolerate this: snarling and spitting she made off in terror. She was no match for this roaring, quacking animal with his gleaming teeth, and a moment later, with the noiseless rushing speed of extreme terror, she disappeared into the bushes. There she recovered from the unutterable confusion into which she had been thrown by her first experience of human laughter. For this night she still had enough milk to fill the little creatures' bellies. She could not hunt far afield so long as this enemy haunted the neighborhood. Luckily for the last few weeks she had left the rats alone and near by her lair two or three fat and toothsome survivors of a once-flourishing tribe ran right across her path. From beyond the snow-covered hill she fearfully descried the glare of the great fire-bush and the smoke-tree growing from it.

Never yet had Grischa made such a bonfire. His snug corner was so warm that for once he could take off his boots and heavy trousers and sit toasting himself in his pants, waiting till his stew was ready: rabbit broth with bread, well salted. Meanwhile he was picking lice off his shirt, especially from the folds at the neck, and from under the arms, where they were clustering like bees. He had rubbed down his chest and shoulders in the snow, and it was glorious to feel the glow upon them. Despite his hungry winter, there were great knots of muscle on his arms. From time to time he chuckled as he remembered the tree-cat; her prominent hindquarters had made him think of a woman or a hunchback as she cowered in the snow, and then galloped off like the Devil. It was grand to be out here all alone in the middle of the forest.

But he was not quite alone. Such at least would have been the verdict of two men, who were standing at the foot of a great pine on the far side of the ravine, spying out his tracks: there they stood where in summer a forest torrent formed a little lake. One of them, leaning on an infantry rifle, had made up his mind about him: the other with a fine carbine of the latest pattern slung across his shoulder looked eagerly at the glare of the fire:

"That's not a German," he said; "why's he spending the night in the open?"

"Must be mad," said his companion.

"A madman could make a better blaze than that," said the man with the carbine, smiling scornfully.

"We could put a bullet into him from here," answered Koljä, thoughtfully: "but I don't think we will. He's one of us—a dog could smell it with his tail."

The shorter man, wearing a peaked German forage cap—an officer's cap—pulled down over the back of his head, looked again up the valley with his deep-set, piercing eyes.

"Let's be careful," he said. "It might be a spy sent out as a decoy from Cholno." He thought they had better investigate.

Koljä looked with astonishment into the eyes of his short slim companion; they were steady bright grey eyes and over the flat spreading nose the brown skin of his forehead was cleft by a deep furrow.

"Do you think they're after us? Oh, Babka!"

The man called Babka wagged his head. He did not think there was any such danger, and said so in a deep, husky feminine alto. If he had, he would not have knocked Koljä's gun aside when the fellow yonder basking over his fire made such an excellent target. But he wanted to know more. They were already late, and they would find their way "home" more easily at midnight when the moon was up. It would be best to go and have a look at him. They could either take him with them or—inherit his possessions.

Although behind the dazzling screen of crackling flame Grischa could not have seen even a howitzer approaching, the strangers crept round the edge of the forest, crunched their way through the snow of the Cholno road, and kept in the shadow, until the fire was seen only as an intermittent glare behind the tree-trunks.

Grischa was relishing his meal: he smacked his lips and licked the very spoon. Then he carefully pulled out from the glowing embers an old meat-tin in which he melted down snow to make hot water, and with a handful of pine needles so far brushed the fat from the saucepan that he might reckon on a cleanish brew of tea. With a great sweep of his hand he flung out the dirty water into the impenetrable darkness beyond the fire.

"Damn it all," cried a voice in Russian. "That's a nice way to treat a friend"—and Koljä strode forward into the firelight with a smile. A great fair-haired man in a Russian military cloak with a very shabby guardsman's cap.

For a moment Grischa stood aghast and his heart throbbed wildly. Caught! The new-comers were armed and he was naked from the belt upwards, and his dagger lay under his cloak in a corner at his back.

"Room for us, comrade?" asked Koljä, jauntily, pleased with the dramatic effect of his first appearance. "On the tramp the same as us, all alone in the stormy night? Come along, let's have a drop of tea and a warm at that nice little bit of fire of yours!"

Grischa struck his forehead with his hand. What an ass he had been! A fire like that would attract whatever had two eyes. He shrugged his shoulders helplessly, let his arms fall, and admitted them. The second of the two seemed an odd-looking creature, an ill-favoured loutish youth, wearing a fine green cavalry cloak and an officer's cap in which he looked as silly as a cat in a starched ruff.

So now he had some guests. They were no Germans. He had made up his mind about that at once. He felt comfortable and warm. For a few minutes they sat in awkward silence and watched the balls of snow floating, melting, sizzling in the pot.

"Boys," said Grischa, heartily: "the truth is always best. You're not German spies, of course? You won't send me back to be chased about those damned wire cages, will you? You've got guns, I see, and I've only my bare fists, but before you drink my tea, and sit down as my guests, just tell me how things stand, because I've run away from them, and that's God's truth, and I'm off home to Marfa Ivanovna, my little wife. I'm fed up with the last year or two, and if they make peace over there I'm going to be in it."

The two armed strangers stared at each other in amazement. Here in the depths of the forest was a man telling the truth, a man in his right mind, with a boy's eyes and an honest face, and a good Russian soul.

"You'll get a long way, Brother, if you throw the truth about like that," said Koljä, drily, holding out his hand. "If you've been on the tramp for long, it's a marvel they haven't caught you."

Grischa laughed as he shook the outstretched hand; Koljä laughed as he pressed it, and as he did so they watched the third man stand his carbine in a corner of the dug-out, revealing the green tunic of the dead dragoon Säpsgen: he sat down by the fire, keeping his cap on his head like a soldier, and warmed his legs carefully so as not to scorch his boots.

"Give me your hand too, my lad," said Grischa good-naturedly, and he who was called Babka stretched it out to him: it was smaller then a man's hand, hard and horny, seamed with countless wrinkles, like that of a scullery-maid.

"Tea will soon be ready," said Grischa. "How do you come to be here? And now you know who I am, perhaps you'll tell me who you are. The woods are full of free men, so I heard at Navarischky camp," he went on cautiously, "but I didn't think . . ."

"The forest is a good place for those that know their way about," said the boy in his husky voice.

"Boy or not," thought Grischa as he gazed at him, "you're not much of a man—ugly little devil too, with your flat nose and eyes too far apart!" And while he looked cool and straight at Grischa, he jerked his cap down on to the back of his head, revealing a wisp of grey-white hair, the long and tightly plaited hair of an old woman.

"My name is Babka (Babka is the children's name for grand-mother in Russia): this is Koljä; what's your name?"

Grischa pronounced his full name and title. Grischa Iljitsch Paprotkin, sometime foreman in the soap works at Vologda. Then they drank their tea, and chatted about the business that had brought them to these parts. They had been after a stag, and taken the opportunity of seeing whether the woodwork of the last of the line of dug-outs, the one in which they were sitting at the moment, would be worth another trip to fetch it away. It was they who had so thoroughly stripped these former dwelling-places of the Germans; and at last Grischa found out where he was; his train had made a great circuit to the south, and he too had been moving southward through the forest—the Front lay hundreds of versts to the east, though at this point it stretched in a deep salient to the west. If he had gone on to the south of the railway he would have fallen helpless into the clutches of the field-police. "But now," said Koljä in conclusion, "you'll join us, and you'll be all right, my lad."

Grischa politely concealed his doubts. He looked critically at the old woman with her young voice and young eyes, her stout ankles in boots and breeches which she had certainly not had made to measure. She had "inherited" them, as she put it to herself: for there was war in the forest, too. Grischa got very sleepy. The cooking-pot, now nearly empty, lay sideways in the snow.

"Tired, comrade?" said Babka. "Have a nap; you've got another little trip to do before we get home."

"What a young voice," thought Grischa, "and young eyes." "Woman or no, she's right: why not rest for a few days with these outlaws?" He pulled on his tunic, wrapped himself in his cloak, and lay down with his head on his pack as if he had been alone. Koljä laughed, borrowed one of the blankets and settled himself at Grischa's side. Babka crouched down on the smooth tree-stump which stood in the middle of the dug-out and served as a stool or a table, thrust the crackling embers into the glowing heart of the fire, so that it blazed up once more.

From time to time she glanced at the faces of the sleeping men, Koljä's familiar moustache and the luxuriant whiskers of their new strange friend, who thought he could get across the Front by telling the truth. "He'll get to his grave first, if someone doesn't help him," she thought to herself. "A fellow who takes on a job like that, is properly up against it. He'd better stay with us: it will be the best thing for him, and we shall have another gun." She lit a pipe, and spitting from time to time into the embers, pondered the devious ways of men, and how in these times they wandered through the woods and banded themselves together. She was not much more than twenty years old. She had done and suffered much. It had not been all sugar and roses of late.

But when the half disc of the moon rose above the dark indentations of the trees, she awoke from her doze and sat up. The pipe had fallen from her teeth and lay on the ground between her heels. She woke the men: on the frozen surface of the stream the way lay clear before them in the half-light.

Chapter 5

GOOD COUNSEL

"GOD will protect me," said Grischa, gravely, as he lay stretched luxuriously on the tumbled blankets of Babka's wooden bed, looking not in the least like one whom God would protect.

And Babka laughed. She had washed the soot and grime from her cheeks and deeply lined forehead, and turned her tanned face and bright eyes to gaze at this man for whose sake she had resumed the guise of a young and sturdy girl. She wore a shirt and petticoat, her feet were bare and dirty, and her firm sinewy breasts stood out under the linen fabric; and the white hair that made her look so old hung in long thin plaits against her cheeks. With a cigarette between her lips and her hands clasped behind her head, she sat on the edge of the bed and laughed at Grischa.

"Will God help you?" she repeated. "You silly soldier man. But who's going to help God?"

The dug-out, hollowed out of a sand-hill, and surrounded by birches and beech trees which had stood erect and unassailed by man for nigh two centuries, and braved the storms of spring and autumn, seemed to shiver under the hissing gusts of rain. In the left-hand corner water trickled in a yellowish stream through the leaky boards of the roof into a bucket set to catch it. From time to time the sweeping showers darkened the narrow slit of a window, which had been lifted from a country-house lavatory, to let daylight into Babka's abode.

"Why should we help God, old girl?" asked Grischa, pursuing his train of thought with imperturbable gravity. He looked a good five years younger; the loss of his long beard, which had fallen to Fedjuschka's knife, had carried him back to the days before his imprisonment. The skin beneath his eyes was no longer seamed

40

and drawn with craving and despair, and his cheek-bones were no
longer gaunt and haggard like a convict's.

"Because God's been out of this long ago, silly soldier man," she
said, proceeding with her theological dissertation, as she stared into
the left corner of the dug-out where the water dripped rhythmically
into the bucket. "Because the Devil has shut Him up in the goat-
shed with the Son, and the Holy Ghost is cooing in the dove-cote,
and the Devil is sprawling with his dirty soldier's boots on the red-
plush chairs of Heaven's drawing-rooms. He was never so well off
in his life! He does all the talking now, as any fool can see."

Grischa frowned. "Do you believe in the Devil instead of God?
Why, you were properly christened and called after Holy Mother
Anna, weren't you, Anna Kyrillovna?"

"That's just it. He doesn't want you to believe in him. All he
wants is to do his business and leave you to yours, and he doesn't
care a rap whether you believe in him or not. Do you think the
Germans believe in the Devil? They crack their whips as if they
did. Why, the Germans pay a visit of apology to God in church
every Sunday, because they believe nothing, and then they go their
own way and do exactly as they please. As for the rest of us—
the Russians believe, and the Jews believe, and so do the Poles and
the Lithuanians, all believe, and believe in God, and look at them
now! For three years they've been groaning under the Germans'
boots. The Germans take away your money and seed corn and your
last cow, and won't let you travel about in your own country, and set
the police on your track everywhere, and if you get caught you're
beaten with whips or rifle-butts; then they give you a bit of stamped
paper to say it was all correctly done, and you can put that in your
prayer book, silly soldier man: or you can do what else you like
with it. But the German believes and takes this paper for his law
and conscience. No, my lad," she concluded grimly, "when I was
pestered with papers and police and such-like, I had as bad a time
as any in the country and a bit worse, I can tell you: look at my
hair, white and grey like a cat in the twilight—you don't get a head
like that at twenty-four for nothing. And when I understood the
game and, instead of being frightened of the police, made them
frightened of me so that they wouldn't cross my path when it was

getting dark, and in daylight only in twos and threes, then I was as happy as you please, though God's shut up in the goat-shed, and the Germans rule the world."

Grischa listened meditatively to the April storm roaring in the tree-tops, from which to-morrow's firewood came crashing down, and to the drumming, pattering showers with which spring washed the snow from the scarred face of good old Earth. He felt almost ill at ease in the small, cleanish, carefully boarded room, half dug-out and half hut, built entirely from the remnants of the former gun emplacement—"Tree-Cat Valley" he called it in his thoughts— which stood sheltered from wind and weather like a field-gun from the attacks of aircraft. Rather than sit and argue like this, he would have liked to go to the big sleeping-room where he had lived at first with the others, until he became the Captain's favourite. Of course he would not have sacrificed Anna Kyrillovna, his Babka, even in thought! For the first time for years he had held a woman in his arms—and such a woman!—and all the thoughts in her head, so far as they concerned himself, were good thoughts, a mother's thoughts; and years, a dreary procession of many months, had passed since he had felt such sweet reviving air about him. Like a waft from the glowing furnace of the heart, it made him happy, strong, and young once more. But what wicked talk was this—it was strange to hear such talk from a woman.

Babka broke into his thoughts. "You think it's strange to hear such talk from a woman, you silly soldier man? Do you know what the forest is? Up above, the trees stand in rows, quiet and polite, and if the Germans have had the forest for long, they stand at attention and 'Eyes Right!' when an officer passes. But under-neath swarm the tangled roots; like deadly curling strands of wool, they prey upon each other every hour, and strangle each other every minute, venomous as snakes. If you scraped away a little of the earth on which we and the animals crawl, you would find yourself standing on a seething mass of roots, miles upon miles upon miles of them, and if they had voices they would howl day and night, groaning like a gang of platelayers hauling rails, and like the tree-tops now when the wind has his will with them, like a man with a maid. No, my lad, that world is not God's work, as the priest says, and the Jews read in their book. In the beginning God created heaven and earth;—that may well be so, for sometimes the earth looks pretty, and you know there is some good in it, when the sun shines on you and you lie in the forest, and the smell of the young sap makes you dizzy, and the squirrels up in the trees and the rooks sailing through the air prove that some of the job is well done: but Heaven and Earth are only half finished. You can take it from me that Somebody's meddled with it, and spat a spark into Man's brain, so that it has caught fire, and that fire has spread to every living thing. I can't think," she said after a moment, as she crushed her cigarette end against the edge of the table and threw it into the corner; and stretching out her bare arms with the unconscious grace of an animal, she added, "I can only see."

As he lay there, Grischa gazed meditatively at the cracked ceiling where the long-legged spiders slept their winter sleep. Awakened by the rain, one of these master-weavers stalked cautiously along, a little knot of living substance, as he gathered the swaying framework of his eight legs beneath him.

"Yes," he said. "You've only got to look at the pictures of Emperors and Kings and Generals—how the papers scatter them around! They're not beauties, and they don't look like saints neither. Have you seen old Schieffenzahn's face? He looks like a toad with a bird's beak"—and Grischa laughed. "But he's won three big battles. And his will is law in this country, so the German soldiers say."

Babka looked drearily across at the ikon of the Virgin in the corner where it hung decked with pine branches above a red oil lamp.

"I'll tell you a tale," she went on, pursuing her swift soliloquy aloud. "There was mother and the four of us:—father, who was old but could still plough a good furrow, the two boys, and me. And over in America two more brothers collecting the dollars and sending us a good few, when times got hard: good workmen they were. One of them would sit on his steam-plough and in one day plough up half Lithuania, and the other was slitting pigs' throats in Chicago: several thousand pigs a day, one slit for each pig; they were both doing well. We had our cottage and field and potato patch and little garden and all we wanted, soldier man. Then came

the War, and our boys went marching up; but the Germans weren't
far off, and our men ran a trench right in front of our house. So
we went away, but not very far, and a week later we came back and
found things as we had left them. They hadn't used the trench, and
our house was not damaged, for those sly devils, the Germans, got
at us from another side. As soon as we had settled down we were
swamped with orders and regulations. 'You can't do this, you
mustn't do that: By Order! Prohibited!' We laughed: we're
Russians although we're Lithuanians, and we thought: 'What's all
this? Forbidden to carry weapons?' Not even a shot-gun, do you
realize that? The hares could run over the cabbage patch and the
deer over the crops, just as they pleased. 'Farmer, we want your
gun,' they said. And father wrapped his gun in a cloth and kept it
up in the rafters. Orders is orders, let the Devil find it if he can.
Then they came along with a printed paper in our language, our
Lithuanian language, which the Tsar didn't like, and also in Russian,
which the Pole didn't like, saying that anyone who had a gun was
to give it up, and anyone who didn't give it up and it was found,
would be shot.'

"'Have you ever heard such stuff?' we said. 'Give up a gun
when you've got one? Why, it's madness; who's going to give you
another? And to be shot for having a gun, that's just as mad, when
you've not done anything.' There was a Polish landowner near by,"
she went on, screwing up her eyes with a grim smile, and baring her
lower teeth. "Poles are obliging fellows. Bless you, they can't say
No. They'll promise you anything and say nothing till they meet
another man—then they'll oblige him by giving you away. That's
what Poles are for! Well then, this neighbour, whose land was
next to ours, always had field police billeted on him which did
him no harm, and perhaps not much good either. You can't tell
what's in your neighbour's head. But he knew about our gun up
in the rafters. Then they fixed a time limit for all guns to be given
up. But all my old father said was, 'Fear God and mind your own
business.' 'A still tongue makes a wise head,' with a heap more of
such proverbs that ooze out of the old folk like resin from a tree,
and are just about as useful. And then one day came the head man

of the village with a face on him as grey as dirty snow, and a lieutenant and six men to search the cottage. Of course they found our dollars, but the gun they carried off and the two lads with it— a boy of eighteen and another of sixteen, mere children, I tell you —and in a few weeks they brought them back. 'Anna,' said father, —he didn't kiss me, but just looked at me—'they're going to shoot us, me, Stefan, and Teodor, because we kept the gun. Good-bye! Kneel down and I'll give you my blessing. You'd better go to Peter and Nicholas in America.' I didn't cry out, I was a girl of twenty-two and wouldn't scream before the strangers. So they stood them in the trench just by our house and shot them, and they fell back into it with their faces towards the cottage—they shot them there as a warning to the neighbours. So after that they collared a heap of guns and fines from the poor neighbours—that's how my hair got white like this—and mother . . . every day she got up and cooked the dinner for her men down in the trench; they had gone there, she would say, to please themselves. Father and his sons are masters of the house, and must have their way, said she. An old woman's head is not strong like yours and mine. Every day till the day of her death she cooked a dinner of wood shavings and carried it out to the men who slept in the trench close by. Then I let the farm, when I had buried mother, in the churchyard, of course, and got the priest to consecrate the ground where the old man and the two lads were lying: everything done right and proper, with a fence round the grave and crosses on it, like we do in Lithuania, and a lily for the resurrection carved on top. And then, the day after I went, some one fired through the window of the Pole's house and hit him in the middle of his forehead. Not a bad shot, was it? So I took to the woods."

Darkness came early that afternoon. Torrent upon torrent of the spring showers stormed past the little window, and the draught from a crack in the front of the dug-out caused the light beneath the image of the Virgin to cast flickering shadows.

"Yes," answered Grischa thoughtfully. "War's a big business: once you've started it you can't control it. We've done some dirty work, too. All soldiers are the same: so are all officers. But those

Germans. They've got brains in their heads like a set of pigeon-holes. If they were to catch me . . ." and drawing a deep breath, he held it for a moment in his fear.

Babka said quietly: "Make room," and lay down by him on the broad camp-bed, as a woman beside the man whom she has chosen. "Think of the summer," she said. "There's a good time coming in the forest. Hot days, days in the shade, Grischa, among the bilberries, good work to do and friends to help you."

Here she stopped, gazed at the ceiling, filled with tense expectancy.

"Any fool could stay here," said Grischa. "But it wasn't for that I gave the Germans the slip."

The young woman thrust out her broad lower jaw. "All right, go," said she. She was pale with terror and dismay: something in her was tottering—something that she had herself built up. Grischa thrust his arms firmly round her neck. Into the darkening air he spoke his fixed resolve. "Do you think I wouldn't like to say here, Annja? Wouldn't I like to feel your arms round my neck for a long time yet? Didn't you make a man of me again, and put peace in my heart, as a man sinks a well in the earth, and the water spurts up in a fountain, washing out all the awful memories of prison? Do you think that's nothing? Wouldn't I be a hound if I thought nothing of it? But there's something pulling at me, something that wants to go home. And so I tell you straight I can't stay with you."

There was a boyish ring in his voice, piteous and imploring beneath all the fixity of resolution.

"I shan't go yet if you'll keep me. Why shouldn't I stay here three or four weeks with you and the boys, and help you all, and then go on? . . . Then the gendarmes'll be after me again and I shall have to hide all day. And suppose they catch me!"

His anxious mind began to circle round this thought, which drew him as with the resistless power of a whirlpool.

Babka frowned darkly and said nothing. Still she stared defiantly into the empty air, where a medley of shadows clustered like the phantoms of her ruined hopes. "Will he go?" she wondered. "Will he take me with him?" So her thoughts ran on.

"Perhaps I'll have to work for them for long years after peace is made—carting earth in a wheelbarrow, clearing the soil of barbed wire, or sawing wood in their stone prisons. Wouldn't it be better to run for it, right into the gendarmes and their rifles?—one shot in the back would end it all."

She listened to his laboured breath. By the deep compassion which now filled her, Babka knew the hopeless depths of her affection for this great boy, who had so struck her fancy when she first sat at his fire, this simple Simon, who called a lynx a "tree-cat," and lived alone in the woods with his knife and bow and arrows. Her breast shook with pitying laughter. She threw her arms round his neck, and bit his ear as she whispered (her breath smelling of food) : "All right, go then, and I'll help you, silly soldier boy."

Her words came strangely to Grischa, who lay there propped upon his outstretched arms and gazed into her face. He saw the tears gleam in her eyes as she continued: "There's no need for everybody to know who you are. Just now there are all sorts of deserters coming through the lines, Russian soldiers that have had enough of it, and are off home to their wives and children: though, of course, their villages are on the German side, not over there in little Mother Russia. Here in the hut I've got a coat and trousers belonging to Ilja Pavlovitsch Bjuscheff, who was with me and died here though we tried hard to bring him round. He wore a bit of metal round his neck like all you soldiers, and I've kept it there in the drawer of the table. If they pinch you and your luck's out, you can just say you're Pavlovitsch Bjuscheff from Antokol, No. 5 Company, 67th Rifles, on the way home to mother: you've come through the lines, you're a deserter. They'll swallow that right enough: or at the worst, they'll clap you into a prisoner's camp again, and make enquiries. Meanwhile I'll put the old girl up to it. I know Natascha Pavlova Bjuscheff and where she lives; she'll swear to anything we ask her. What do you say to that, you silly soldier man?"

Over Grischa's round face, dark with anguish, stole an ever-broadening smile: he closed his slanting eyes, and opened them again in pride and admiration: "The Devil's not half as bad as his grandmother," he said, as he laughed aloud, "and his grandmother's an old idiot compared with a good woman that loves you," and like a swooping hawk he threw himself upon the broad, pale lips that had given him such wise counsel.

The rain spattered and poured, and drowned the lingering daylight; the red gleam of the sacred light beneath the Virgin's image shone on her tinselled robes and crown, like sparks of blood.

Chapter 6

DOWN STREAM

THE surface of the earth, covered with forest as with soft green moss, stiffened by the brown framework of the trees, was here gently undulating. The hills lifted their long crests from the shallow dells, slashed with the silver of the brooks. They were swollen with the unceasing rains; translucent over their brown depths, after the muddy days of early spring, they glided downwards towards the rivers of the plains. A practised waterman could navigate them in a flat-bottomed boat, or even take a float of timber down them, though this was not so easy. From the four dug-outs or blockhouses, where the outlaws lived, ugly gashes had been cut in the once-inviolate forest: stumps, many of them still freshly hewn, betrayed the work of the strip-saw, which all day long ate its way with a soft metallic hiss at the foot of the doomed trunks, until, at the will of their pigmy masters, they were brought low by dragging-ropes or felling-axes. The desperate crash of tree on tree or tree on ground only affrighted the jays and crows and the little bird folk of the undergrowth.

From the masthead of a royal fir, Grischa saw about him only a sea of tree-tops, dark green, some stripped by winter, and some, like the age-long birches, lightly clothed in the downy foliage of spring. The vast spreading branches of the oak and beech still kept their tawny garb of yesteryear: but the canopy of heaven hung light and silky blue over the golden haze. Far away yonder in the west, many miles distant, and overgrown by the thickest brushwood of the forest, a small dark spot, like some deposit from the great green river of the trees, marked the site of the abandoned gun position.

They were having their midday rest. After the grey lowering

49

weeks of rain, the men lay about on the moss that dries so quickly in the sun, smoking and blinking at the sky, full of the glad cries of myriad small birds they could not see, the rapturous piping of the tits, the silver call of the finch, the trilling of invisible singers, whose names the men did not know, and indeed there was much discussion whether they were thrushes or blackbirds. On this matter there was no prospect of agreement, however well in other respects the blended speech of the two great armies of the East sufficed for the purposes of agreement or dispute; but it afforded pleasant entertainment.

Some of these companies of outlaws were composed entirely of natives; in this one there were only three of them besides Babka. Koljä and Nikita had, like Grischa, been prisoners of war: three German soldiers completed the band—and each had a story of his own. From his post of vantage Grischa saw them lolling at their case below him. They no longer seemed to him as they did at first, a small closed clique, like a corporal's squad, which takes time to absorb a new-comer. He already began to distinguish qualities in each of them—the peevish Nikita from the friendly Koljä—even if Koljä, as he shrewdly suspected, kept his weightier thoughts to himself; he discovered that Fedjuschka was the son of a well-to-do merchant from Mervinsk whom the Germans wanted to put in a penal-battalion; that Anton Antonovitsch had made up for breaking into a house by breaking out of prison, and that each of the three Germans preferred free quarters in the forest to trundling off smoothly to the Western Front in the cattle-car of a troop train. He had been accepted as a comrade; but there had been a certain coolness at first which melted when he did his full share of work, felling, lopping, dragging home the timber, and bore his part in every jest. It was certain that if on the day of his arrival a vote had been taken, it would have been unanimously in favour of sending him about his business: but he could now confidently rely on a majority in favour of his remaining where he was. Where he spent his nights, whether in a camp-bed among the others, or elsewhere, nobody appeared to mind, although it might be that Koljä and one or two of the others would have liked to deal with this matter with a gun, if it went on too long.

"What's that new fellow doing up there?" asked Koljä, knocking out his pipe on the sole of his boot; "it's a bit too early for crows= nesting."

"After tree-frogs' eggs, I dare say," Fedjuschka answered sleepily.

Grischa, on his tree-top, filled his lungs with the fragrant air which rose from the warm sand and moss. Smells of decay and of new life foretold the spring which already urged and throbbed and sang in all the voices round him. Two squirrels hunted each other up the trunk towards him squeaking and spitting in their amorous game. Their shy vigilance and insatiable curiosity was lost in the wild frolic of the youthful year. He had left off his tunic, and, in perfect ease of mind away up on the tree whose smooth and tapering trunk he clasped, loosely, like a human body, with one arm, he thought of that Bjuscheff who even after death had so kindly rid him of his last anxiety: he had worn a fair moustache like himself, and he, too, had been Babka's man and an honest Russian soldier. He thought of Bjuscheff's birthplace, how he had played as a boy under trees like this, and pelted the squirrels with pine-cones there at Vilna in the Antokol forest; and how he was now to be his patron saint, in a manner of speaking, if things took a nasty turn. How he would have welcomed this spring but for the bullet in his back! He had certainly had a soul, and where it was now wandering—who knew? Perhaps it was fretting at the help which the name its flesh had borne was to give to his successor. Now he, Grischa, was friended by strangers and dead men he had not known. He could not look inside them, but he could try to share their feelings. They were men like himself: he must not be conceited. It was no bad thing to lie rotting in the grave, to be at rest for once, in times like this which hunted men from home. Perhaps the soul was annoyed at its name being continually altered by all manner of people—handed on like a second-hand suit; but probably it did not care, or if there was any sense in baptism, and Jesus Christ had not died for nothing, perhaps it was even feeling glad. The trees were growing their hair again. Everything was coming out of the ground. The dead men below it could send up the strong sap of their desire. Perhaps they would start again—some new kind of life. Why should not souls go by

upon the wind? In the fairy-tales the old women tell there are so
many strange things good and bad—spirits haunting the marshes like
a flickering lantern. And on a high mountain sits the skinny
Babajagaa casting her dreadful spells. Why should not a man be
as good as a fir tree, which grows stouter every year, if it is not
cut down? But then it occurred to him that a fir tree felled or
even rooted up can be used for timber, and only goes on growing
through its seed: and though a tree bears new shoots every year,
so Man, every man, gets new joy in life, like this fir, but like the fir,
only endures in the seed which he has scattered. And with a gentle
sigh he felt his heart turning to Vologda and the little child that he
had never seen.

In a small flat-bottomed boat, like a big orange-box, Babka and
Fjodor Dukaitis were returning from their expedition of two days
ago. Five villages lay along the banks of the stream, like acorns on
a string, at the edge of the forest, where, long since, a tongue of
cleared land had been thrust into the woodland from the north; it
belonged to Count Muravieff, like all the forest round about, a little
province which the Tsar had granted to him from Crown lands
stolen from the people. But now, of course, they paid taxes to the
Germans, just and unjust, dues and levies, and they had no notion
of betraying the good folk in the forest. Indeed, they bought wood
from them, and helped them, for a consideration, in floating down
the timber—those precious trunks which the Germans naturally reserved the right of felling. Why should Reb Eisik Menachem, the
tavern-keeper, or the parish elder, Pavel Gurtkjevitsch, trouble to
enquire too closely into this or that woman wearing plaits of hair
and men's boots, or her fair-haired companion, who had been trading
with them for a year and more? Did not the Germans pry into a
thousand matters that did not concern them—why should one bother
to tell them about the thousand and first? The men jumped up
and ran down, full of curiosity, to help unload the boat. Babka had
brought flour, millet and tea, and five large bottles of brandy carefully packed in hay; tobacco for every man, and for Fedjuschka a
letter from his father, which had certainly not been sent by post.

"In six or seven days the raft ought to be long enough for us to start," she said, glancing for a moment at Grischa and then at the top of the tree, where he had just been sitting. But none of them could hope to stay here long, for as soon as the dry season came, the Germans meant to pay them the compliment of a systematic round-up; and the villagers had been warned that at least two squadrons would be billeted upon them.

"Till they come, our little brothers in the cottages will still be afraid of us and sell us what we want cheap, but with their stables full of German horses, I don't think they'll be quite so matey," laughed Babka to her companions, who were chewing their nails in their alarm, clawing their beards, and puffing furiously at their pipes. Two squadrons? What if they worked their way over here from Cholno, and also set out patrols to the north-west, as they had once tried to do? They couldn't spare any airplanes, but if they went properly to work with dogs and horses they would soon settle their hash. Koljä clapped the German, Peter Ducheroff, on the back, and laughed, provokingly. "As if she hadn't got something brewing in that head of hers, and ready, too; she needn't ladle out that German soup," he laughed. "Just look at the little witch."

Babka threw a fir-cone at his head, saying there were some people who must go telling everyone what they can smell in the oven. Anyhow, she was going to get something warm into her belly, and then the men could show whether they'd got anything in their heads; and with that she went into the kitchen, the door and window of which stood open, and asked if anything had been kept hot for her. Tasty soup of unknown composition, the common ration soup of armies. She ate the broth with her spoon which she drew like a man out of the leg of her boot, peering the while with knitted brows into the sunlit woodland yonder where Grischa was sauntering up from the others, pipe in mouth. He strolled slowly across the forty or fifty yards that parted them, and she caught her breath as she wondered why she could not tear him from her heart, and why, now that the lives of all of them were in jeopardy, she must still feel that he was the nave and centre of her being—a man who pined for his home and another woman. And she confessed to herself that the plan which had flashed through her brain when she first heard the menacing news, would certainly not have occurred to her so readily if it had not given her the chance of following the lad Grischa on his journey.

He sat down beside her rolling a cigarette out of newspaper and pipe tobacco for her to smoke when she had finished her meal. But she pushed it aside and silently held out to him a packet of good Russian "*Papyrosses*" from the shop of Reb Eisik Menachem. He laughed to think that she always had something better than he had. Then, growing serious, he asked her, as she drained her bowl, and a glow of contentment (not from the food alone) coursed through her, what plan she had thought out to meet this danger.

"What's that to you? You won't be in it."

Grischa slapped his knee. It was all one to him. "In five days when the raft is ready they'll get their logs away and then pole them down to the Vilja. They'll take you with them till they get to the water: the water's dangerous in the floods, though that does not matter. The Russian roads are more dangerous still."

Grischa sat, embarrassed by the joy which he did not dare to show, and took her hand. "You're my mother, Babka, and my company sergeant-major," he said. "But if you won't tell me how you're to get away with the boys, I won't go either."

Babka looked at him distrustfully, smiled indulgently, and said that a kind word's as good as a drop of schnapps. She thanked him very much, but anyhow they could not stay together, for on their journey there was as little chance for large parties as for foxes on the squire's drive. They would try to reach Vilna as raftsmen, in three sections, each led by one of the Germans. Their papers had been arranged for, and would cost sixty marks in all. After Vilna they would see what could be done. Of course it would be hard and very expensive, if not impossible, to get further papers for them all so that they could stay in the big town. And there was always the risk of betrayal. But you must eat what you've got and not what you've dreamed about. He, Fedjuschka, and Otto Wild were to start first, and in three weeks their dove-cote would be as empty as last year's fir-cones. "If they go after us with horses, we'll change into fish. If they fish for us with nets, we'll live in houses like the Vilna cats." She wound up in a triumphant voice, wiping her mouth with the back of her hand, and her hand on her petticoat, and let Grischa light her cigarette with a glowing ember. But the admiration which leapt out of his eyes was far more grateful to her than the smoke of the good *Papyross* after her long abstinence.

In the night before their start, there fell from Babka, the rough peasant woman who had fought two fights and killed three men with her own hand, all the steely masculine armour of her soul, and in Grischa's arms lay quivering a young girl, in that entire affection in which mistress and mother are united. She held his head by the ears between her outstretched arms, gazing with passionate questioning into his eyes, then drew him towards her, nestling her cheek beneath his chin. She listened to the beating of his heart; she bit his arm and clung to it, and the red light before the ikon cast little gleams into her pupils or the whites of her eyes as she stared at the roof and watched the sleeper. The fumes of the hut took on the semblance of her wild desires, curling upward towards the image of the Virgin, whom men also hail as Mother. First she would have him stay, then she would have him escape, then she longed to go with him and watch over him—she, not Babka, but Anna Kyrillovna, a woman who had chosen one man after knowing many; and now with the fixed and furious passion of the lynx for her young whelps, she would cleave to her lover's path, to protect him or perhaps possess him for herself. She believed fervently in the goodwill of the Mother of God, and bating a little of the pitiless doctrines with which she had striven to grasp the secret of the times, she said to herself that Satan had of course the power, and the intercession of the Mother of God had just as much weight with him as the prayers of a stepdaughter with her mother's second husband, who had a ready fist and taste for schnapps. But as even the sternest stepfather has unexpected fits of kindness when he will gratify even the most unlikely wishes—such as an appeal for the life of a favourite kitten, though the sack was ready and the stone tied round its neck— so perhaps the Devil, as he stamped in his high boots and jingling spurs through the chambers of Heaven, stroking his imperial moustache, might suddenly let this Grischa through the net with which his Germans kept the land pinned down, and which was drawn closer and closer towards the Front. She stole noiselessly from the bed, stuffed fresh wood into the little iron stove, so that Grischa should sleep snugly in the warmth, and under the bat-like flickering shadows cast by the newly kindled flames she fell on her knees and prayed before the image of the Lady with the silver heart.

In the morning when Grischa stood before her for the last time alone, clad in the patched and threadbare uniform of a Russian infantryman, with her own hands she hung round his neck the copper identification disc of Private Bjuscheff.

"Kneel down," she bade him, as she forced him to his knees before the Mother of God. For a long time Grischa had ceased to care for priests and images, and had quite broken with his Faith, yet now with a thankful tenderness he obeyed the surge of feeling that was wafted to him from the woman's heart. With her eyes fixed upon the picture, and murmuring adjurations from the words of the Litany, she let the copper disc fall beneath his shirt cold against the soft down of his chest, and, without his trying to prevent her, she added an amulet such as Bjuscheff had worn, a Russian amulet of yellow bronze, square and stamped in relief with three holy women guarded by two Angels' heads. She called upon Bjuscheff's soul: as he had obeyed her in life, so he must obey her now, give Grischa good advice, look upon him as a friend and comrade, help and serve him. Meantime Grischa was thinking that this praying business was all very well, but that the time would be better spent in drinking coffee; besides, if he stopped a rifle bullet, these two hard bits of metal might be driven into him. However, the amulet might keep off revolver bullets. There they stood, side by side, once more in front of the hut, motionless. The sky, ethereal green fading into blue, and magically soft, hung above the firs, in whose topmost branches three or four thrushes poured forth a hymn of adoration to the youthful day. Alone in her morning glory stood the star, the visible companion of the sun: and yonder in the east the planet Venus shone steadily, where behind the wall of trees a faint red glow heralded the dawn. Grischa thanked Babka "for everything," as he said clumsily, gazing long and lovingly at that dear face; no tears betrayed it, but transfigured by the exaltation of grief, he saw it upturned to the soft light, framed in its dishevelled plaits of hair, and beautiful with the odd awkward beauty of a homely face. Her great grey eyes were fixed on his.

Men's voices called impatiently from the kitchen where the boiling tea was steaming in the saucepans. Grischa looked once more into Babka's eyes with a radiant smile, then clumsily stroked the oval of her face with his great paw-like hand, and said: "Right, Anninja," and turned sharply like a sergeant on parade. His heels rasped together as they met; then, quivering with the delight of departure, he stamped in his freshly greased boots over the sand and pine-needles to the kitchen.

Babka could not but see his joy; indeed, it was like the smoke of incense rising from the earth. She drew her arm across her eyes, from which a few tears, that she had tried so bitterly to keep back, stole down her cheek. Then with still unclouded gaze she looked up at the morning star shining softly and scornfully upon their leave-taking, shook her fist menacingly at the Lord of that world of War, bared her strong teeth at Him, and swore: "I'll get him out of your clutches"; then with a composed expression, she walked towards the kitchen, to give her last instructions to the two others. After Grischa had left them, Nikita was to meet them at the raft, so that there would be three of them again. In a few minutes the alders and the young beeches would close behind the heavily loaded packs of their departing comrades.

"Thank God," she said, passionately, while she plaited her hair. "It's a good thing the lad's alive. I've got an object in life again. I don't mind struggling for life again with the German and his hordes." And she nodded across the kitchen at three men sitting by the bowls of tea and hunches of bread; two of them, Otto Wild and Fedjuschka, looked deeply dejected—they merely felt how irksome it was to leave their safe familiar home for ever and plunge into the forest. But the third, Grischa, oozed with joy from every pore.

"You've got the true Russian wanderer's heart," she said to him, as all three of them stood up squarely under their loads and made ready to leave the warm steamy room, with their cloaks and blankets rolled up under their packs, and staffs in their hands, like men—and soldiers, for it was the same thing in those days.

"Good luck," she called after them, and of the three only Grischa turned and nodded to her with his round face and little shining eyes. Then she stood for a few seconds alone in the clearing, amid the twittering birds, under the rosy glow of dawn, her eyes fixed upon a point in the surrounding woodland, whence no man came back. No; none came back. And with a toss of her head she returned to the kitchen, to boil a cauldron of hot water, for men must have their tea.

Chapter 7

THE RUMOUR

THE territory under the Commander-in-Chief of the Army of the Eastern Front (called Ober-Ost, or Ob-Ost for short) bulged out into the great notch of the Prussian frontier line from the Baltic coast to Upper Silesia, stretching towards the Duna and the Dnieper. To the south his command marched with the area administered from Warsaw and called Poland, and, further on, with Austrian territory. To the north the Russians still held Riga and the land beyond the river. Ob-Ost therefore chiefly comprised Courland, Lithuania, and Northern Poland—cornland, woodland, steppe, and marsh; potatoes, game and poultry, and cattle; few minerals, small towns, forts and hamlets.

Not many railways enlivened these broad provinces, and none of them served sufficiently the needs of those who lived there. The Russian upper class that ruled over Lithuanians, White Ruthenians, Poles and Jews, officers and officials sprung from a fusion of the warlike races, Balts in the north, Great Russians and Tatars in the east, administered the resources of the realm, as the haughty settlers from the Eastern Marches and beyond the Elbe held sway in Prussia—at the dictates of their instincts; and those instincts were brutality, suspicion, and a craven lust for war. The railway lines, therefore, had been laid with an eye to future wars, and strangled trade and traffic in their narrow net. A host of confederate German tribes clung like leeches to this vast territory. At every centre of activity or wherever the natives had settled in considerable numbers, the Germans fixed their tentacles. They watched, and tightened or relaxed their grip according to the interests or judgment of Headquarters. And they drew from the poor soil its sap and substance to feed the German troops or Germany herself, who, cut off as

59

she was from the sea and all supplies, drained, like a gigantic land-crab, all the countries of what they had to give her. Every town swarmed with offices full of clerks, where officers, and officials im-personating officers, strode continually through slamming doors and down flights of stairs with their noses in the air, shouldering out of their way a population whom they heartily despised as barbarians, and by whom they were secretly hated in return, town-majors, in-spector-generals of communications, staffs, hospitals, depots, civil ad-ministration, censorships, military courts. Every large village harboured a lieutenant as town-major or a captain of mounted police with his staff, or at least a troop of Landjäger or field police, for whom a comfortable lodging had to be provided.

The Higher Powers looked on the whole land as ultimately under requisition. The only disturbing element was the population, and that obstacle must be dealt with as expeditiously as possible. It did not occur to anyone that the land would ever be evacuated. Every temporary usher or sub-prefect thought that after the War the place would still be his by prescriptive right. Some influential officers already had their eyes on large estates which they hoped to receive later as gifts from a grateful Emperor. They thought as little of the population as a patriarchal squire from beyond the Elbe thought of his Polish hinds and scullery-maids. They would have liked to pretend that the danger of espionage made it necessary to lock the door on every inhabitant over ten years of age of this future Prussian province. But they did the next best thing, and for-bade anyone who was not wearing German or nurse's uniform to use the railways; they were however free to use the roads and foot-paths, though only if provided with the necessary papers, in the day-time, and on foot.

Only the rivers moved in their usual course. From the marsh-lands and the little hills they rippled down in the direction of the greater streams—the Vistula, the Bug and the Niemen, on whose estuaries far away in the north lay mighty harbours within the Prussian border. The War was a glutton for wood. Next to human flesh, clothes and corn, there was nothing it so continually devoured as beams, planks, boards, stakes, wood-pulp, shavings, wood-fibre, and sawdust. The timber trade was popular with the authorities and profitable to those engaged in it; and indeed, none deserved better of the Germans than those who gave proper care to the timber in these vast primeval forests, thinned them, cleared them, and replanted them on the Prussian model. Moreover, nobody could tell by the look of a tree-trunk or a piece of planking where, by whom or by what right it had been cut down. Even those who rafted logs down the rivers were regarded with favour: and thousands of rafting-permits were issued to those who showed any aptitude for the work.

In this way Reb Eisik Menachem, on the evening of a certain day, was in a position to produce two such permits: they had been crumpled and smoothed out again, they were very dirty, and a number of plausibly applied grease stains had given them a most respectable and convincing appearance, apart from the innumerable stamps and signatures.

The beasts of the forest and the field live more by night than by day. They make love, go forth to drink, eat, kill each other, and scurry about in the darkness. The people of the occupied territory, when their business carried them further afield than was permitted by the great helmeted Landcrab, had to do as the beasts did. It was impossible, indeed it would be injudicious, to keep a watch at night over the lanes, footpaths, and hedges, by means of which the few great roads, so constantly broken down by troops and transport, and remade, could be avoided. The field-police, even in twos and threes, and well armed, did not at all like going very far from these broad highways. Too many things happened: in spite of the most energetic warnings, searches, and executions, the country was swarming with hidden weapons. And hordes of men, if they could ever be rounded up on the great plains of that enslaved land—vast hordes of men would be found wandering secretly by night over the land that once was theirs.

On an open heath covered with tree-stumps fluttered the black monks' hoods of the juniper, taller than small houses. Grischa shaded his eyes with his hand, looked before him with an uneasy laugh, and said: "They look like nuns in the mist." His two companions were silently baking eggs by a small fire. The swathes of whitish vapour which overhung a forest brook, where its shallow waters had overflowed a meadow to the breadth of a small river as it issued forth from the shade of the trees, changed in the evening twilight into vaporous banks of yellowish-red. And through the peaceful stillness of the falling night rang harshly the late cry of the great raven and the hoarse menacing hunting-call of the awakening owl.

"I feel sad, friends," sighed Grischa, crouching down; he was lit up by the red radiance of the camp-fire, though half hidden by the pine saplings, and the broad spreading juniper trees.

"You had a good time with us, comrade, and you've got soft," said Fedjuschka, mockingly. "You ought to have happened on us in the summer, when the gnats were eating us up and hunger was rumbling in our bellies before the harvest came, or in the autumn when we did our harvesting at night and lit the peasants home with bullets——"

"Ah, well," said Otto Wild, speaking in German slowly and distinctly. "You're going at the right time. It's a good time to go now," he repeated in Russian. And pulling out of his pack a map—the most precious treasure of the little company—and holding it to the glow of the resinous pine splinters, he pointed out to Grischa with his knife about where they then were. "We go up the Niemen, and you go down it," he said, indicating the direction: "we go by water to Grodno, and perhaps on foot to Vilna, or perhaps we'll get on to a freight-car at night. We shall manage, comrade, but it won't be easy," he added in German.

Grischa nodded. An active youth would not find much difficulty in jumping a slow freight-train, and, standing either between the cars on the treadles that work the brakes, or deftly balancing himself on the buffers, travel long distances through the deserted land at night. The thought that he must go on alone gripped and crushed the breath out of him. Stunned and paralysed, he looked at the thin black snaky lines that indicated the Niemen on the map. "That must be a river," he said feebly; "how clever of some one to make it look like that."

"We shall get to it to-morrow at midday," said Fedjuschka,

"the lovely, splendid Niemen. Then you must walk upstream, Grischa, about five miles away from the bank, and go on like that so that you can still see it, and keep your direction, because it comes from the east and you want to get to the east."

Grischa listlessly held up the compass on his watch-chain.

"Yes," said Otto Wild, "but you can't follow your nose and go stumbling across country; you must see where you are and stick to your path. You've put on too much bacon with us, comrade, you've done too much sleeping in a bed I could mention."

They sat in silence. Grischa toasted some bread by the fire, and thought it was a good thing to talk to people when a man is going to be alone for a long time. Otto Wild scowled thoughtfully into the fire, while his boots stood drying placed a careful distance from it so that they should not scorch. The men were lying on tarpaulins, their feet already tucked up in their blankets, and they felt comfortably warm. For him and the two other Germans the position was far more serious than for the "Russians," and he reflected as he pored over the map that they would perhaps run least risk in the Grodno marshes in the summer, where only a few natives of those parts knew the way to those unapproachable hill-fastnesses in that pathless low-lying moorland, dotted with treacherous quagmires. It would certainly be possible, he thought, to hide in Vilna, and finally his face broke into an abrupt ironical smile, as a scheme began to glimmer in his mind: he might, in a word, act as though he were mad, and in broad daylight suddenly stumble against a policeman, pretending to be some sort of shell-shocked straggler, who had lost his nerve and memory, stammering out a mixture of German and Russian—as though he did not know where he had come from or who he was, and present those bloody hospital doctors with a nice little problem of a new kind of amnesia. Perhaps they would turn the Faraday current on to him, but then he could scream the place down. Anyway, he wouldn't fall into the hands of the authorities as a German soldier and a deserter.

Meantime, Fedjuschka watched the newcomer who was now to leave them once more and go his own way. He did not envy him. His eighteen years of life had left Fedjuschka no illusions. "Now you'll be all alone again," he began cruelly, though his expression was not unfriendly. Grischa nodded resignedly. "Yes, I shall be alone, little brother."

"I fancy you'll be a bit cold now and again?" And Grischa smiled.

"I shall certainly be cold, little brother."

"Won't you be a bit hungry too, pretty often, comrade?"

And Grischa, wrinkling his brow, replied: "I shall be hungry when I must be, comrade."

"You'll wear out your boots, and at last you'll fall into the hands of the field police, comrade, that's what I prophesy for you."

Grischa looked long and curiously at the youth's lean and worn face, which seemed quite unnatural with its odd black downy beard. "Why should you be pleased if I have bad luck? Haven't you got enough of your own? You sit around here with all of us, and yet you've got a father and a little mother not far off."

"Mind your own business," said Fedjuschka, haughtily. "When I'm pleased, I'm pleased. But I'm not pleased now. When the chestnut falls from the tree and its shell bursts on the ground, who's pleased at that? We say, of course, it had to fall, it had to burst—that's nothing to wonder at."

Otto Wild, who understood Russian better than he spoke it, looked from one to the other. "Why shouldn't he get through?" he said soothingly at last (though he said "how much," instead of "why"): "he'll get through, with luck." Fedjuschka thought, beginning to throw pine-cones on to the blaze: "Why does he call it luck to get through? It's stupid to live. If I'd been sensible I'd have hanged myself long ago. Everybody hopes for peace, but what's the good of peace? The wearisome old world again. This fellow calls it luck to crawl through the front lines. Then they'll give him three weeks' leave, and as soon as he's got soft and settled with his wife and child, they'll pull him out again; of course they will. It'll be a case of 'Shoulder Arms.' And when he's fairly got the taste of home into his mouth after he has lost the taste of mud and misery—hundreds of miles of it—hunger and thirst and sleepless nights, dodging about and tramping his boots off, he'll be killed in the first skirmish, because his troubles have made him slow and clumsy. And I'm dolt enough to laugh at him. . . ." And gazing at Grischa, as if to imprint his features in his mind, the high cheek-bones topped by the blue-slitted eyes, and pale-red fringe of beard round the chin and up the cheeks, he put his hand into his pocket and handed him a precious gift, a matchbox full of matches.—"Oh well, we're all friends together. There, think of Fedjuschka, who said such nasty things to you, when you light a fire on your journey. And look here: my father sells groceries and brandy, and whatever else he can get, up in Mervinsk. The shop has a green sign with a border of blue, white, and red. His name is Veressejeff, and he lives just opposite the cathedral. If, by God's grace, you ever get there, go to him and tell him you've met me and that he's to write to me, he knows where at Vilna, and tell me how he's getting on: and tell him to let me know how you are too." ("If you are not nabbed by that time," he added in his mind, but did not say so.) "Come on, let's go to sleep, it'll be our last night together. It's a dismal time this: we must make a jolly night of it; we don't know which of us is the luckiest."

They said no more, but wrapped themselves in their blankets and lay, for the sake of warmth, close up together like three great larvæ of some fantastic butterfly, feeling that they still lived and were not alone under the moon whose thin red horn hung in the misty eastern sky. Far off, something was howling, perhaps a wolf, perhaps a dog in some distant byre, and the great hunting owl circled on noiseless pinions round the sleepers and their sinking fire. Above them moved the shining company of stars.

In those days many strange rumours went to and fro among what was called the civil population. Peasants in short sheep-skins, cottagers in long white smocks and trousers bulging at the knee and stuffed into their boots, women in the Lithuanian head-dress, with petticoats hung from their shoulders on gay bands of embroidery, Jews in old-fashioned, mediaeval cloaks—black cloaks, for black is the only wear for the sons of Jacob—with their side-curls hanging over their ears under the black-peaked cap—just as you may see the People of the Book shown in the reliefs on Hittite temples. All these people occasionally exchanged scraps of conversation,

merely to fill up the time—nothing in it, of course—about certain
nocturnal phenomena. Footsteps had been heard at night near this
or that village down by the Niemen. Some said that between the
tree-trunks at the edge of a misty meadow, a ghostly figure had
been seen, and here or there the dogs had barked and howled like
mad. There was something in the wind—the children knew that
best of all. The boys of the village, Jewish and Lithuanian, and
later even the White Russians, whose heads are stuffed with stories
and fairy-tales—the boys, at any rate, had quite made up their
minds there was a ghost about, "The Soldier of the Tsar." He was
taller than a juniper bush, and wore his beard knotted behind his
neck, so that he should not step on it. He carried his musket on
his shoulder; his eye-sockets were of course empty; and thus he
marched along upstream night after night, and that's why the dogs
howled so. He could walk on the surface of the river when he
chose, for he was thinner than air. The spirit of the fallen soldiers,
the Soldier of the Tsar, is marching out of Poland, marching out
of Lithuania, marching through White Russia, through the Jewish
villages, marching, marching eastward.—Woe to the Tsar if the
soldier ever gets at him! Woe to the Tsar if those empty eye-
sockets come upon him, white and bony, and that bayonet red with
Turkish, German, and Austrian blood pierces his quivering entrails!
The avenging soldier goes his way at night, and it is not good to
meet him. April is at hand with its misty nights and blustering
winds, and May will bring the lightning flashing through the falling snow.

The Niemen moved on its sluggish course muttering and gurgling
like a Jew at prayer.

The spirit had no fear of human dwelling-places. When Klara
Filipovna, the wife of Herr Studeitis, opposite whose house at the
entrance of the village the Germans had put up their notice-board—
when this substantial dame saw fit to go out last night to the manure-
heap on her own occasions, she saw the spirit standing in the moonlight. She could not tell how it got there and how it disappeared:
there it stood, grinning palely at the notice-board, plastered with
German notices and proclamations old and new. She threw her
apron over her head with a muttered prayer to St. Philip, the Pre-

server, and to Klara her patron saint, although she was hardly in a
fitting posture for calling upon the names of saints. But what can
one do, if the Devil keeps on raising ghosts in the bright moonlight? And when she scurried into the house and had had to go
back for a slipper which she had dropped on the way, the spectre
was no longer looking at the notice-board, on which were printed
in seven languages the proclamations of the German High Command.

Rumours run much quicker downstream than up, but they do
go upstream, nevertheless. On Friday nights, in their dimly lighted
windows, the Jews sit and talk, when they have sung "Schir
Hamaalaus" and drunk a drop of brandy—they talk of the soldier
that goes by. The older men find nothing very strange about it,
and with their intellects formed and sharpened by the Talmud they
debate whether it is the spirit of a Jewish or a Christian soldier.
The men and women of the younger generation smile knowingly,
and are inclined to think that the Spirit was made of flesh and blood.
Reb Eisik Menachem, when he came home, dropped many a hint
of certain good friends he had in the forest: strange, very strange. . . .
Kindly old Channe Leje knew more. One morning lately in the
half light when the stars were glimmering above the slanting cottage roof, she got up to feed the fat goose, which was snugly lodged
in her dark cellar. A man was standing at her gate, asking for bread.
Can a pious Jewess to whom God sends a beggar, stop to consider who he is? Might it not be the Prophet Elijah, who had taken
upon him the form and features of a soldier, and has come to bless
a Jewish house, and give them an opportunity to do good works?
"*Zedokoh tazil mimowes*," murmured Channe Leje, when she
thought of the good hunch of black bread which she had handed to
the Prophet, and how he had deigned to kiss her hand in gratitude,
"Good works are a deliverance from death." But in the first place
it is not fitting to gossip about the appearances of the Mighty Ones,
and secondly her husband was ill, he had a cough (may the word
not harm him!), and if she took upon herself the burden of silence
touching this appearance of the Prophet, telling none, not even her
husband, the Ruler of the World (whose name be praised) would
regard it and her man be healed.

On the forenoon of next Friday, which was market day, Affanasja Ivanovna, the White Russian peasant woman, was beset by a huge horde of customers: for it was she who had seen the werewolf. She was sauntering out one evening, thinking no harm, to drive home her fat nanny-goat, when a huge bat dropped from the sky through the trees right at her feet, and leapt up: a man as true as the saints have risen, a man with eyes as big as saucers and great fangs like a wolf. She just had time to call on the Holy Mother, draw a circle round her with her stick, and crouch inside it; she was not going to run away, for that was what the werewolf wanted. The magic circle protected her. But the poor goat had to pay for it, for after human blood there's nothing those monsters like so much as fresh milk: for, look you, behind her petticoat which she had thrown over her head, she heard the werewolf grunting and licking his chops, like a dog at his bowl, and the goat bleating. "I tell you he was drinking at her udders for longer than three long prayers: such a snarling and a growling! And as soon as all was quiet and I dared to lift up a corner of my petticoat, I felt something warm against my face—she was butting me gently with her horns, good old Kosinka; her udder was as dry as my apron pocket, but she was safe and sound, and not a sign of the werewolf."

Rumours like this of course provided enlightened minds with matter for ridicule. Moreover, it is the duty of a sergeant of mounted police not to leave the roads unpatrolled at night. As regards the by-roads, the paths along the river or through the meadow, the printed proclamations made it sufficiently clear that their use was absolutely prohibited at night. Of course, the natives could not read. But all the things that they might not do had been well hammered into them—why should a man get his feet wet stumbling into puddles in the dark, or risk his bicycle in the uncertain moonlight, rooting about among the marshy flats, the tangled willow undergrowth, and all manner of trees and bushes? There was so much to talk about, the War, how long they would be there, Red plots, America and Wilson, and the success of the submarine campaign. Every day they read in the paper that England was as good as starved out. To prepare the ground for a new war loan, and collect subscriptions for it from the subject population, was likewise no light matter; and the hens were just laying, and the contribution of eggs which each village had to supply must be carefully assessed, so that provision should be also made for the unofficial requirements of a sergeant of mounted police, his wife, and a few influential friends. Frowning thoughtfully, cigar in mouth, *Litevka* comfortably unbuttoned, for a drill-tunic was too cold at night— Sergeant Schmidt strolled out upon the steps and looked at the market-place below. The weather would hold. How pretty the clouds looked round the moon! "Strange," he thought: "they're exactly like the ice-floes on the Niemen three or four weeks ago: rounded slabs, swollen at the edges, floating on a darker background. Well, well, leave that to the scientists"—and he returned to his grog and his newspaper.

It is a weird feeling for a man who cannot read, to stand in the moonlight staring at a printed paper. A look of longing came into his eyes and he shook his head at the board, with its edicts and decrees in seven languages. If he had been to school this board would have told him where he was. He could not even tell the name of the village, still less how far it was from the Front, or glean any other useful information from those columns of letters. What a sea of strange new knowledge would open out before him, had he but learnt to distinguish those black and white specks from one another! A soldier like Grischa can just recognize the several styles of characters, the crabbed German script, the graceful Polish and Lithuanian letters, the scrolled letters of the Russians, and the square and dotted Jewish alphabet. Musing thus, he stood still in the moonlight: he began to wonder whether he would ever get a warm meal again, or whether he would not fall into the gendarmes' clutches; and yet he must brave every danger, he must go through this village, because the main street was the only dry road between the river and the accursed fences round the farms.

What a fine thing it would have been if a man could read at least one of these seven languages! It might be that one or other of these regulations affected him, although he would not have thought it likely.

Far away at the eastern edge of this country the German Army, embedded in the ground, stands waiting for the peace that must come at last. In this longing, despite the sharp cleavage between caste and caste, officers and men were at one. But the further one looked towards the west, especially within this occupied territory where the pulse of life beat so faintly, in the towns, the military stations, and among the troops, the more sharply officers and men fell into two classes—Whites and Reds. The Reds were the common soldiers, and every fibre of their hearts was straining towards home and peace. The Whites—officers, officials, staffs behind the lines, and Highest Authorities generally, were certainly not against peace, though of course upon conditions. They led quite tolerable existences. They were ready to hold out. They were for victory, which meant keeping their heels on the neck of this vast rich land and its inhabitants, and making the common ruck of soldiery, Reds or not, stoop lower still under the yoke by which in Prussia up to 1914, and still more since then, they forced their wills and judgment on to the toiling millions. All resistance was to be ruthlessly uprooted. The channels through which this vast organization of authority operated, radiated from the room of a certain officer, in a large house in the once Russian and now German town of Bialystok: the office of Lieutenant-General Albert Schieffenzahn.

But the armies think otherwise. The icy-steely, flaming walls of the live lines of trenches have here and there broken, and are crumbling: drops are coming through, human drops. The water is massing at those points where certain strange individuals are gathering, drawn by a new kind of human gravity. Thither some drops have flowed from far away. At such places, of course, the sieve is coarser, and the net of civil authorities, police, patrols, road companies, and the like, was less tightly drawn. Every one of them had the right to force every single man to explain himself and his business—the right, because they had the power.

And somewhere in that house, on a brown chair, sat Corporal Langermann. Since he had been wounded by shrapnel in the shoulder during the great retreat from the Vistula, and had been slowly convalescing, he had acquired very strong convictions: to atone for that wound the Russians must forfeit more land than had been dreamed of in all military history. In his own heart, like many of his kind, he regarded the annexation as already carried out, and he felt it to be his professional duty to do his part in enlightening the German public as to the psychology of their new compatriots. Until Fate had cast him among the transport troops, he had basked in the schools as a student of modern languages; now he was a clerk, and spent his leisure composing with the ready pen of one who knows a little but not much, ponderous articles for the Press News Service, the Government Department which kept the newspapers well posted, flooding every channel of the German public with descriptions full of local colour, droll stories of the natives and even faithful accounts of the newly occupied territory. And as his contributions were rewarded by encouraging letters from Heads of the Department, and also invariably accepted and punctually paid for, Corporal Langermann looked out hopefully over his fair moustache, with his hair well parted and his mind alert, ever in quest of new material. He could always make money as a contributor to the local paper, and several times a month adorn the pages of the *Tenth Army Gazette*, the *Watch on the East,* the *Bialystok, Grodno,* and *Kovno Times.* One day some one in high places might remember this studious, erudite, and orthodox young man when the school was founded and had need of a well-paid headmaster.

The news of the wandering "werewolf" reached his ears and his pen almost at the same moment. He soon filled his afternoon causerie in one of his papers with the "myth-making proclivities of the White Ruthenians." As Langermann suspected in all such popular myths a substratum of reality, which developed through various stages of rumour, from rumour to fairy-tale, from fairy-tale to legend, and thence, it might be, to Saga or to Epic, he sought to disinter this grain of reality even in the case of so recent a ghost-story. He sat by one of those tiny cupboards through which ran a strand of that great net, that tissue of slender telephone wires which, like a spider's web, brought that vast land within the hearing of its masters. As Langermann was no more than a lance-corporal, though the double stripe was a familiar dream which promised to come true, he was obliged to give an official colour to his researches. Thus, information of a stranger wandering by night was received by countless sergeants of mounted police, town-majors—little timid folk, to whom any neglect of duty might mean the loss of a comfortable billet behind the lines. An escaped prisoner? There were plenty of them, but one must catch them first. Of course, once their presence had been officially reported, as that inky-fingered swine, old Langermann, was always doing, anyone who did not get a move on would soon feel a nasty draught. For such vexations a common panacea was "Wrong Department." What was outside the strictly circumscribed area which was the special preserve of Captain A., or the official jurisdiction of Town-Major B., was *ipso facto* outside the solar system. In spite of uncompromising minutes on the file such as: "Not known here," or "Nothing ascertainable at this office," there began by night, incidentally, and amid the pressure of business and beneath the surface of routine, working with a sullen activity, a new current of information passing on words of advice and caution, shrewd hints that it might be well to tighten the night patrols. Friends must look after each other, and if you saved Ulitzki's life to-day, Ulitzki might save yours to-morrow. Moreover, general and special orders laid down that a soldier was never off duty. "And don't you forget it, Private So-and-So: if there's a single gipsy on the road at night, breaking the blasted law, it's up to you to see that he gets it in his bloody neck!"

Book Two

HIS EXCELLENCY von LYCHOW

✭

Chapter 1

MERVINSK

IN A country flat as a pancake, a hill sloping gently up to a ridge two hundred odd feet high has the air of a considerable mountain. A town will usually grow up on its western side with a great broad square for markets and parades, surrounded by eighteenth-century houses built of dull white stone; in the midst of it is the monstrous truculent cathedral which the Russians dumped there thirty years ago, and beyond that, squat, swarming wooden houses, groups and rows and districts of them, with courts, shops, and churches, shrines and grottos—pleasure and pain and faith. And on the high ground north and south are countless country houses; for the townsfolk do not care to live in the streets in summer mornings when the lark is whirring skyward like a rocket of delight, chirping from every feather, and the cuckoo may be heard close by the farms. These wooden villas are called "Datschen." Russians and Jews are equally partial to them, plainly furnished as they are, and there they spend the summer, among their gardens and their birch trees, with the bright and bubbling samovar in a cool and darkened corner of the room. In spring, when the nights are often frosty, most of the people stay in the town, for they stick as fast to the calendar as birds of passage to their seasons. In spring whole streets of "Datschen" stand asleep with doors and shutters closed, behind their low, mildewed, moss-grown garden fences, too rotten to keep out a child of five. But sometimes when an epidemic rages in the town, when water is impure and the food tainted, a careful parent will send his children to the country earlier, in defiance of tradition.

In the glittering light of a glorious May-like day at the end of April, the ungreased wheels of a peasant cart groaned and creaked along the road. Cart-grease meant fat, and in the spring even the

75

peasant had no fat to spare except for baking. Above the traveller on the crest of the hill, a road stopped, half completed, in the midst of the colony of "Datschen." Originally, indeed, the main road below, on which the cart was labouring and creaking, was to have been carried through the clusters of country houses. But at the last moment the local Authority bethought itself that the long detour and steep incline involved in such a construction would be well worth while for the contractor and the landlords of the "Datschen," but would scarcely repay the country and the Government. So from the lower road a branch ran upwards, ending suddenly at the house of the merchant Süsskind, who had already sent his daughter Deborah and her cousin Alexander up to the "Datschen." For Kriegs-gerichtsrat Dr. Posnanski, who was billeted upon him, had pointed out, with the plaintive facetiousness characteristic of him, the dangers of diarrhœa, which just then was turning Mervinsk into anything but a health resort. The schools were still closed for the holidays, and who could tell if they would ever be reopened?

Deborah Süsskind, called in Yiddish "Dwore," sat in a white linen dress trimmed at neck, waist and sleeves with red and black em-broidery, on the bench by the round table, under the light green feathery brush of the tall, slanting, birch tree, and as she finished plaiting her hair, she was arguing with Sascha, who thought her the most beautiful and clever Jewess in the occupied territory, about the rising Socialists yonder in Russia, those men of promise who would stamp their names upon the future. She was for Kerensky, while Sascha, who was twenty-one years old, and had been cut off from his studies for three years, would contend for Lenin, Plechanoff or Tscheidse. He had found ready employment as assistant master in the newly established Jewish "Gymnasium" at Mervinsk, and therefore escaped being drafted into one of the various labour corps that were raised from time to time, as at Gainovka, for example.

Dwore, whom a Russian would call Dawja, stoutly maintained that the liberation of the soil, by which she meant the peasant revo-lution, was the essence and the most notable result of the Russian upheaval. Sascha insisted that the truly progressive and revolutionary will was to be found only among the proletariat in factory and slum. The real issue between the two therefore was whether the impulse towards the transformation of the disorganized bourgeois society was to come from the peasant or from the mechanic.

Sascha was holding a German newspaper between his fingers: he shook it out and kept on reading the Petersburg news which had come via Copenhagen. "Over there," he said, pointing to the east, "the way lies open. If the bourgeois doesn't make up his mind pretty quick whether he's going to stop that war that we've lost or go on waiting for help from England, France, and later on from America, the tortured, flayed, bleeding, starving people of the towns will rise in their might and hunt him down to hell."

"And we shan't be there to see it," said Dwore sadly. "We sit pining here and can't get any news. This is a positive bog," she cried, striking her fist on the table: "We live like rats in a marsh. Nothing ever happens. The world moves on its great new road, and we are flogged into idiocy by our new masters. Oh, Sascha, I could scream." So saying she stood up, smoothed out her clothes, and went indoors to fetch the samovar and bread and bacon for their breakfast. Sascha watched her, the dear tumultuous creature with her two plaits of black hair who would perhaps say "yes" to him at last—not from love, for she was not in love with him, but from a kind of love which was born in her head from a community of minds and thoughts and purposes, and might spread to her body if he ever became a man of deeds and influence and swayed his fellow-men. The expression in her eyes when she looked at him was very different from when the handsome Lieutenant Winfried smiled at her. Here certainly were hard facts, but he was not the man to bow to them: he too, had his weapons, and Sascha would not for a moment accept defeat, simply because Dwore fancied Winfried. "Fancy's one thing, love's another," thought he.

Something made him start suddenly and turn round. Over the fence some human thing was clambering, a man, with a dirty chalk-white face, and terror in his eyes, but with the noiseless movements of a ghost, his Russian uniform and pack covered with straw as if he had slept in a farm cart, a week's beard on his drawn and dirty face; he advanced towards Sascha, who shrank back like a helpless boy confronted with a tramp. But he held his ground; his face grew pale, but no shadow fell on his shrewd and watchful countenance. His dark Jewish eyes met unmoved the piercing bright blue eyes of the stranger.

"Police?" whispered the apparition, jerking its head interrogatively, and Sascha with the like pantomime denied the implication. The creature smiled and said, "Then give me somewhere to sleep, a drink of water, and a bit of bread."

Even in those whispered words could be heard the strained, hoarse tones of uttermost exhaustion. "Only for three days and nights. Don't be afraid. I'm not a murderer."

Sascha answered slowly. "Perhaps I am afraid, but I believe you all the same. I see what you are, too. This 'Datsche' here is inhabited, but the next one is empty; you bundle in there: through the hole in the fence. There's water in the water-butt behind the house. I'll get you some bread. So run in quick!"

Above all Dwore must not be frightened of the stranger. Of course her fear would not last two minutes when she heard the truth; but this was a man's matter all the same.

Grischa nodded; and the apparition vanished, without a trace, except for a few bits of straw left on the sand and the young grass. They made Sascha feel uneasy, so he carefully collected them, crushed them in his hands, and put them in his pocket. Then he walked up and down, still pale, but quite resolved to have a closer look at the fugitive after he had slept. Determined to settle his mind before meeting Dwore, he forced himself back to his newspaper and studied the agricultural supplement, experiments in the use of bulrush roots, nettles, and starwort seeds as adequate substitutes for coffee, flax, and rice, and a lengthy article on the great recent developments of paper textiles.

At this moment a bicycle glided by the fence and stopped. Balancing himself with his hand against a tree, a fair-haired sergeant, wearing the white brassard of the military police, and with a rifle slung round his shoulder, shouted out: "Hullo, you there, my lad, have you seen any mounted police about?" And with no less courtesy and unconcern Sascha shouted back, as he got up and walked towards the fence: "Good morning. No, nobody ever comes this way. The road ends right here at the wood."

In his black Russian blouse and a leather belt round his boyish hips, he stood there, a tall slight figure, he, too, in his way, a soldier.

"O Lord," groaned the sergeant, beads of sweat dripping from beneath his light spiked helmet with its grey linen cover. "Isn't this the main road? I'm a stranger in these parts: I've only been here a week. And this heat's something awful."

"You'll have to go back, Captain. The main road is on the left at the cross-roads. You're bound to go wrong in this country if you go straight ahead."

The sergeant, a cheerful customer, burst into a loud guffaw. "That's true enough. And what a dust you keep here!" And unhooking his water-bottle he offered Sascha a sip of coffee. "Not made of coffee beans, of course; you needn't be afraid of nicotine!"

Sascha thanked him with a civil smile and refused: he thought the Captain would need his coffee later on, and his own tea would soon be ready. And indeed just at that moment Dwore appeared at the top of the steps which led down from the small wooden verandah to the garden.

"Two's company, three's none," said the sergeant with a sly wink, wiping his moustache with the back of his hand, and preparing to let go of the tree. "If those lads at the telephone weren't always hunting us about, I might almost ask myself in," he said; saluted, gave himself a shove off from the tree, and was soon pounding back by the way he had come.

Dwore looked at him uneasily as he disappeared among the trees. Nowadays the police were unwelcome in certain cases, even if one did one's duty faithfully as a schoolmistress. At that moment Sascha realized that he must not conceal from her the visit of the stranger. The weather was much too sultry for the time of year, the sun was hot, and the air close and heavy, and men were not surprised to hear from far away yonder where formerly the faint thudding of the cannon had betokened the Wall where the world ended, the muttering roll of the first thunder, heralding the summer. A whirl of dust and straw swept over the road like a mocking shadow and an echo of the departing cyclist.

"We'll get fresh drinking water," said Dwore, as she looked up at the sky, with a flash of her fine broad teeth; and Sascha decided to tell her, after breakfast, that the house next door had a secret occupant, and ask her whether she did not think it advisable, in case he should be discovered, to go back to the town, which lay panting in the heat under its roofs and towers beyond the pines and birches where the thunder-clouds lowered in the sky.

Chapter 2

THE NEW LAW

THE room with the bow-window, where stood His Excellency's writing-table, was upholstered in a greenish-blue, devised by the sumptuous taste of the manufacturer Tamshinski, and carried out in the riotous rococo of a Warsaw artist upholsterer. The bronze incrustations on the mahogany furniture and the blue velvet of the curtains were an unfailing source of irritation to His Excellency.

"They ought to be cut up for children's dresses; they're no good to me," he would shout jovially when a visitor commented on all the splendour. But as he paid but scant attention to external things (though the beautiful tiled bathroom did give him great pleasure), he left everything as he found it. So it came to pass that the portraits of the lantern-jawed Kosciuszko, the lovely Countess Potocka, and that same Madame Szymanovska whose piano-playing so delighted Minister von Goethe at Weimar, looked down undisturbed from the walls of this once-brilliant salon.

Exzellenz von Lychow, white-haired and tanned of face, his blue eyes looking brightly from their wrinkled setting, youthful, brisk, and almost birdlike in his movements, was gazing attentively at his aide-de-camp who early one morning was detailing to his chief the programme of the day. On the wall, fastened to the damask tapestry with large pins, hung the war map of the Eastern Front from the Baltic to the Black Sea. The section held by Lychow's division was marked with a blue pencil: the large scale-maps showing the position and distribution of regiments were kept in a room above on a trestle-table five yards long, especially constructed by the carpenters at Brigade Headquarters out of carefully planed deal planks, utterly profaning the august bedchamber of Madame Tamshinski—now probably in St. Petersburg.

In his Excellency's opinion the day had begun abominably. He held crumpled in his hand a printed sheet which Lieutenant Winfried had just put before him, a ukase from the Officer Commanding Field Railways, containing among other unwelcome provisions, which threatened to capsize the whole Divisional leave-roster, an express and universal prohibition, addressed to the *Herren Offiziere* in Field Railway Areas IV, V, and VI, to the effect that pianos must henceforward not be carried as personal luggage. The station authorities were instructed to refuse to handle them as from the date of the Order, and, further, to report the officer responsible, etc., etc. What next? Pianos as personal luggage! Von Lychow looked at Winfried with steely eyes. That the officers of his Division could be in any way involved in such an accusation was of course unthinkable. (Lieutenant Winfried had his own ideas on the subject.) The blood rushed to the old gentleman's head at the very notion that somewhere behind the lines there were human beings, German officers, whose behaviour could make such orders possible, orders which were not now issued for the first time, or the second time either.

The fact was—as was only too clear to Winfried from His Excellency's lowering brow and rising colour—the General was prepared at any moment to let loose the floodgates of his wrath. But there was a cunning look in the bright eyes of the slim young officer, who was quite equal to the occasion. He had no desire to have his uncle issuing orders for an investigation (secret, of course) into cases of this kind occurring in the Divisional area. He therefore proceeded at once to the second item. He knew that its contents would annoy His Excellency much more, and would divert his wrath to a wholly unattainable and Olympian object.

"Certainly, Uncle Otto, these musical fellows, you know . . . Nowadays when officers' stars are turned out by the thousand gross, all sorts of things will happen. Now, here, Sir"—and he deftly extracted a second sheet from the Orders of the Day—"is something very choice: His Royal Highness the Grand Duke of Sachsen-Eilenburg will be graciously pleased to visit a quiet part of our line to shoot some Russians."

Von Lychow sat straight up in his chair, erect as in the saddle, and said "I beg pardon?"

Lieutenant Winfried, who knew his uncle thoroughly, and, as the great man's nephew, had nothing to fear, assumed a guileless expression like a boy intent on mischief.

"Shooting Russians seems to be a field sport with the Princes of the Empire, since a certain Grand Duke started the game. Up north in the Tirul marshes, if I'm not mistaken:—drove up to the front line, where it's as safe as a girls' school, and whenever an unsuspecting Russky came along, his Highness bowled him over with a shot in the head. It was a new game for him, and, unfortunately, for the Russian too, and as for that oaf of a General who let him do it . . ."

Von Lychow glared at the young man and froze the words on his lips. For Paul Winfried knew what he was talking about, and the indignation on his uncle's face was no greater than he felt himself.

"The *General* who let him do it . . . please go on !"—

" . . . . Expected a nice little medal, of course, and got it, too. But the people in the trenches, the supply troops, the road companies, and sappers, paid for it with the loss of a hundred and seven men. They sent over heavy stuff the whole afternoon, and did pretty good shooting. Then our guns started in, and there was very nearly a big show on where there had been nothing doing for months. 'Increased artillery activity,' the bulletin said. And now they want to introduce this sport here."

Winfried was waiting till the General should rise with his bronze-studded chair and bring it crashing down on the polished floor, to the great peril of the lieutenant's toes. He had seen so much horror in his fifteen months' service at the Front that he could not take seriously the exploits of these expansive royalties. Von Lychow did not wreak his wrath on the arm-chair, but pushed it carefully back, got up, and pale with wrath, paced nervously up and down the room whose three bow-windows opened on the street, where the golden light of an early May morning glittered in the puddles and the gutters. As he stood in the window he could hear the tapping of typewriters in one of the offices below, and the voice of Corporal Siegelmann reading out to himself the orders of the day, as he copied them off. And with measured tramp, their rifles under their arms, and their grey steel helmets shining above their foreheads, marched the sentries at the gate of the villa in the quiet consciousness of duty faithfully discharged.

"Very well, then," said His Excellency, in the parade voice of a General of Division: "tell His Serene Highness's aide-de-camp that in this Divisional area, owing to the danger of shrapnel and of typhoid, we can undertake no responsibility for the safety of His Serene Highness's person. And I'll have you know that I'll have no more of this d——d medal-hunting. If it is not stopped I shall forbid the officers of my Division, so long as hostilities are suspended, to accept any kind of decoration, except such as may be awarded for past acts of gallantry in the field. Was Schieffenzahn informed of this?"

Lieutenant Winfried smiled at his uncle and said:

"You know as well as I do, Uncle Otto, that Schieffenzahn is careful not to hear about such things."

Von Lychow suggested quietly that he might speak rather more respectfully of his superior officers and said, "I hope not. And as for that d——d Station-Master": he snapped out, reverting to his original grievance: "taking off his trains and stopping all my leave arrangements, trying to rob my fellows of their few wretched weeks —write and say he's a ——, and tell him I said so."

The aide-de-camp laughed. The idea that he, who was barely three-and-twenty and had just been promoted lieutenant, should tell the Director of Railways in a district half as large as Germany, and at least equal to His Excellency in rank, that he was a ——, tickled him hugely.

"As regards the piano luggage," said His Excellency, "he was right. I can't think how they manage to buy pianos here. ('Buy' is a good word, thought Lieutenant Winfried, sighing gently.) But before we are transferred to the west, at least the front line must have a spot of leave. I can't send my men into that filthy hole when they're bursting with rage because their leave has been put off or stopped. If those fellows at Headquarters think you can treat an army like a herd of cattle, someone here thinks differently. Please tell them this. . . . With all proper respect, etc., for economic necessities and the shortage of coal, I must request that the running of the leave trains on our area should in any event be carried out, as heretofore, according to plan. In case of necessity I shall be obliged to appeal to His Imperial Highness in person to ensure that until the existing trains can be replaced by lorries,"—and as he saw his nephew taking shorthand notes, he dropped into official language: —"time-table shall be maintained without alteration."

Winfried looked anxiously at the General, who was known among his men as "Daddy Lychow," because he took a genuine interest in them, and did not merely send them into action, or badger them about in rest billets with reviews and inspection of boots and rifles. "Lorries"—he thought. "If it gets lively here again, we've just enough of them to hurry a few battalions up to threatened points. The Entente is keeping us busy over in the west where I've come from, where I got this thing"—and the Iron Cross (First Class) on his tunic felt like the touch of a dead finger—"in the blood and horror of Pozières cemetery. If they bully that fellow Kerensky at Petersburg into making peace, then God help a great many poor devils—unless that wily old Schieffenzahn has something up his sleeve. Lorries! Yes, Excellency, you ought to see the state of the roads in spring: you ought to see the work our navvies are doing floundering in the mud,—and it's not half done yet."

"Anything more on the menu?" asked His Excellency.

"Wants to shoot Russians," he broke out again, as he struck a match with a slightly shaky hand and began to smoke an enormous brown cigar. "Have you any idea, Paul, how many men they've lost over there up to date?"

The Lieutenant did not know.

"I don't know, either," said Lychow, "but at least eleven hundred thousand. Good God," he added, under his breath; "If we'd had eleven hundred thousand men in '70 we'd have put France in our pocket. And now, on that Front . . ." He nodded significantly. Finally he collected himself and asked if there was anything else.

Paul Winfried drew from the folder a judgment of a divisional court martial which had been sent up for signature yesterday evening, and laid it silently before his Chief. The General of a division, which is an independent fighting unit, is the ultimate legal authority under the Emperor, who in this connection represents God and

Destiny. Von Lychow buried himself in the document, which was a death-sentence on a spy, a certain Ilja Pavlovitsch Bjuscheff, who, as the evidence clearly proved, had been spying for some time behind the German Front. He knitted his thin white eyebrows, and instead of picking up the pen, which Lieutenant Winfried handed him, pushed away the document and said: "No, thank you, no more dead men so early in the morning. Who presided?" With a glance at the signatures on the paper, Lieutenant Winfried answered "Kriegsgerichtsrat Posnanski."

"Posnanski?" repeated the General. "A reliable man: a Jew, but a useful fellow. I'll have a talk with him. Tell him to come here this afternoon, and put that aside," he said, as he gave back the paper to the Lieutenant. "And what else have you got to-day?"

In Lieutenant Winfried's heart there was a real affection for his uncle which was ever ready to show itself: he would smile at him or, in very unofficial moments, thump him heartily on his padded shoulders. "Thank God," he thought, "at least there's one man with a heart among all those ancient butchers." And he resolved to give His Excellency as pleasant a morning as he could. In point of fact, certain inspections had been arranged at the urgent request of the Director of Medical Services, who had just taken over vast typhus-hospitals, and hoped thereby to complete his collection of war medals. But, ignoring this, Lieutenant Winfried said that there were some new timbered roads to the trenches to be tested: "A pleasant morning's work to-day, Sir." He knew that Exzellenz von Lychow liked poking about in the hutments where the reserves were quartered, or dug-outs, or in the sopping, splashing trenches of the front line. Deep down in his heart, he bitterly resented the state of things which had been brought about by the war of position, to the great satisfaction of commanders and their staffs; for the higher a man's rank and the greater his responsibility, the further from the Front was he to be found. These odd fancies earned von Lychow the reputation among the other Generals of being "queer"; as if the safety of the army commander was not all-important to the divisions, brigades, regiments, and batteries. It was strange that the old gentleman, encumbered as he was with all those inconvenient notions, should have been so successful.

"First-rate, my lad," said His Excellency, now visibly relieved. "I thought you'd get chlorate of lime, or latrines and beef tins up your sleeve again. They're necessary," he continued cheerily; "beef tins and chlorate of lime are more important than half the waste paper that goes out from this office, and so are the clothing depots, hospitals and stores, nurses and all the rest of it—though Sister Bärbe and Sister Sophie are, perhaps, rather lively young ladies, eh?"

"Right," said Lieutenant Winfried, clicking his heels together, and smiling in the corners of his eyes; "then I'll order the carriage."

"Yes, order the carriage, please," said Lychow, referring to the huge grey fifty-horse-power touring car, which was now standing ready in its shed. "And on the way you can tell me how the War's going. Any more news?"

Yes, Winfried had news enough, but it would be better to explain it before lunch, at the map-table. On the whole there was little happening at the moment, but there was a good deal brewing in the west. "Posnanski, then, at five o'clock," repeated His Excellency, and rang for Wodrig, his orderly, to bring in his cloak.

The grey car, with the white divisional pennant with its black and red border on its radiator, thrust its nose into the wind like an athlete on his course, and sped onward into the distance which receded into rippling undulations. From time to time the rhythmic beat of the engine was broken by the harsh roar of the horn. Jets of water from the puddles spurted up to right and left as the wheels passed over them, and behind the car the cleft air met in swirling eddies. His Excellency could easily be recognized, for on the facings of his cloak fluttered the bright red which marked his rank. Paul Winfried beside him in his steel helmet, grim and fateful, looked like the embodiment of a new age. Each of them in his own fashion carried with him into the free air, in a corner of his brain, the echo of that postponed death-sentence.

Von Lychow's Division held a vast sweeping salient of the Eastern Front; on the north was a Bavarian Army Corps, while to the south he joined hands with the Austrians. On the right wing were mixed units in which, "for the promotion of a better understanding,"

German and Austrian battalions had been brigaded together. This meant that the Bosnians and Slovenes were to be controlled and stiffened by Prussian companies. The headquarters of the various staffs lay more than a hundred kilometres behind the line, which until lately would have been called the Front. The staffs of brigades, regiments, artillery, gas and intelligence officers, medical services, sappers, air and wireless, wagon lines, roads,—all these were established in permanent quarters in the small towns and villages of the district, and had to communicate constantly with that remote region where men and officers lay huddled together; hence a network of telephone wires, fleets of cars, roads, motor cyclists, and despatch riders. The car churned its way through the forest, across vast brown plains, dotted with little pools, whose yellow depths transmuted the blue sky of May to gold, and the whole mighty organism lay stretched out fanwise, with wire cables for nerves and roads for sinews—a fighting monster compounded of metal, earth, and men.

From the sides of the road the pulsing, sputtering, racing car scattered gangs of navvies who, in mud-stained cloaks and trousers stuffed into their boots, formed hastily into line between the ditch and the road, stiff and surly, to let the General's car go by, while the N.C.O.'s. saluted. The grey car hooted as it caught and passed the straggling lines of transport. High piles of timber in the open fields lay ready for the construction of new buildings: hutments, or possibly a parade ground, or a hospital for horses with the mange, that curse of the soldier's friend. Once they grazed past a column of motor lorries loaded with uniforms and equipment. On the left of the road, in huge tents like quarter-deck awnings, stamped the horses of a heavy battery. An ammunition park in a thinly planted grove of pines displayed the geometrical blocks of shells and cases of explosives covered with camouflage canvas. On a half-dry expanse of sand was a training camp where platoon drill was being practised: further on a handful of children were learning to throw hand-grenades, and the necks and heads of the seventeen-year-olds stuck out thin and pale from tunics far too large for them. The road, which had been improved as far as possible in spite of its sodden condition and a thick layer of sandy mud on its surface, rose slowly up a hill, the sides of which were pitted with abandoned artillery positions; but barely a quarter of an hour afterwards they were passing the emplacement of two obsolete long-barrelled howitzers, masked by a tangle of wire netting, and mottled brown and green canvas, while on the left side of the road two others could be seen with field-glasses some distance away. A narrow field-railway led up to them, for the use of the artillery. The wind brought no disquieting sounds with it: though from a neighbouring slope came the faint rattle and clatter of machine guns which were practising with blank cartridges. His Excellency's car slowed down as it passed, saluted by the sentries, through a huge engineers' dump, in which were arranged, with the trim neatness of a *Hausfrau*, towers of coiled barbed-wire, stacks of timber, piles of planks and boards, deal props, and sheds full of tools. Further on, the roofs of a six-winged field-hospital lay spread out in the sunshine; above it the Red Cross flag fluttered drearily, and the length and breadth of the roofs were painted with the protecting sign. A specially made path led up to the building. The crows circled in black clouds about the tall dishevelled poplars, often quite unscathed, but in many cases bearing abundant witness to the ravages of war: many were now no more than trunks; others had been lopped or split, and the fragments still lay about. An endless cemetery, legions of crosses, stretched stark and drear before them. Field companies were working among the shell-holes of a former battlefield; they had strict orders not to interrupt their work, and among them rode a threadbare major on a sorry screw. There was movement everywhere—men, horses, vehicles, and material. At this point a handful of sick men, suffering from dysentery, approached the General's car; he stopped them, made enquiries, and passed on. The fighting strength of the division was being continually sapped and diminished by the effects of various kinds of fever. This winter the men had been fed on a too monotonous diet, not enough meat not enough bread, and dried stuff and potato parings instead of fresh vegetables: and they were now paying the penalty. At the moment supplies were more important than ammunition.

As there was a shortage of stone in this area, the car throbbed and thudded its way over a track laid with logs, which after a month's use was half worn out, and in many places submerged in mud, though the worst damage had been repaired already. The tangle-bearded men of the Landsturm, and the labour companies, marched with a kind of goose-step as they dragged on their shoulders the round, planed trunks from a point beyond the road, where they had stacked up the timber which they had brought down in the trucks of the field-railway. The car crossed over trenches by bridges whose wooden supports rose steady and secure out of standing rain water. The road soon entered a forest which was dotted with hutments and provided clean and comfortable shelter for the battalion staff of the section. But at the General's arrival they awoke to breathless activity.

The vast barren waste, dotted with circular clearings, was little more than a morass traversed by a network of broad and narrow paths. In all the mire of spring-time and of war, whole forests lay prostrate to man's use, stacked in piles of trunks and branches, and faggots of brushwood. On higher ground, where the soil was dry, the first green sprouts came forth undismayed, and round the huts bloomed daisies and forget-me-nots. The commanding officers, who had received official notice of His Excellency's arrival, came in their full war paint, and clicked their Wellingtons together over their polished boots: they were an odd company—tanned faces under their helmets, piercing bright eyes—some with decorations, some with scars, and some with pot-bellies.

Lieutenant Winfried watched the General as he went to and fro among the officers, nodding and smiling genially, or even graciously, if such a word may be used of one who was so fundamentally human, and a practised eye could have followed the conversation from his face.

Winfried was surrounded by a group of lieutenants, his own contemporaries, who were now company commanders. For some time past battalions had been led by lieutenants, while in the neigh-bouring brigade a certain Captain von Sulsig commanded a regiment. Hints and rumours of the forthcoming postponement or curtailment of leave had already reached the front-line dug-outs of the company commanders, and they came in their threadbare field grey, to ask, some with cynical humour, some with fury or contempt, what truth there might be in these glad tidings. Winfried felt greatly relieved at being able honestly to give the lie to the whole story. In the great wooden canteen they all joined in a sandwich and a glass of brandy, and then started off for the inspection.

Chapter 3

A BARRISTER-AT-LAW

DR. POSNANSKI, barrister-at-law, sat in a large and comfortable chair in von Lychow's ante-room and waited. In ordinary times the busy Berlin lawyer would have been highly incensed at being kept waiting even by a General, particularly as he would only have to make a few observations and then take his departure. But he was now wearing a very peculiar costume compared with the usual garb of a lawyer; about his middle was a belt with a pistol in a holster, the grey of his tunic was pleasantly relieved by the blue red-bordered tabs upon his collar, on his hat was a metal spike, and his two legs, encased from the foot to the knee in gleaming brown leather, had acquired a strange new individuality of their own. His enforced leisure did not surprise him. Never till now had he had so much time to spare.

The soft sheen of that May afternoon lay over Mervinsk. It was half-past five on a Friday. For half an hour the Kriegsgerichtsrat had been sitting with a book at the window, sometimes reading a page, then, for whole minutes together, gazing with vague benignity upon the sparrows who were splashing and preening themselves in the fresh puddles. From the welter of roofs rose the onion towers of the cathedral, all golden in the pollen-laden air. With his fantastic thick goggles, his round and hooded eyes, his high forehead, his protuberant skull, with strands of still fair hair about the temples, his short-legged pot-bellied figure, he had all the air of a bald Silenus. He went on reading. He had gradually transferred to his present quarters a large part of his library, chiefly thin-paper editions; cut off from his office and amusements he tasted to the full the bachelor's delight in books. His taste was comprehensive, curious and fastidious. On this occasion he was holding close up to his nose a small English edition of *Gulliver's Travels*, bound in dark blue leather; he read slowly, sipping as it were, the poignant flavour of the great Irishman's fierce satire. He was a good reader, able to see beyond the printed page, and his heart was gripped by so terrible a knowledge of the frailty of human things, so much pity, wrath, and laughter. He was reading the passage in the voyage to Laputa describing the Schemers and Projectors. "Half a soldier's life is spent in hanging about," he thought as he went on reading; and other such soldiers' sayings half humorous and half ironical came into his mind: "Never trouble the King till he sends for you." "Ah, but I've been sent for," he reflected. "The old man's usually punctual: if he's late I shall miss the *Lechodaudi* in the *Bes-Medresch* of the *Chassidim*!" By this he meant that he was accustomed to attend the Sabbath Eve festival in one of the many little temples of the Jewish town of Mervinsk; on Friday evening his Sabbath began, when he neither smoked nor wrote, but adjusted his duties to the injunctions of the Jewish tradition. For he set high value on a mode of life that had lasted fifteen hundred years, being, despite his subtle intellect, a convinced though very tolerant orthodox Jew.

Wodrig, the General's orderly, came in and asked whether the Herr Gerichtsrat would smoke. He was sure His Excellency would be pleased if the Herr Gerichtsrat would accept a cigar while he was waiting.

Posnanski laughed: "All right, Mr. Wodrig. Now you see how one forgets the most important thing. Here I am poring over my book, knowing all the time I want something, and now you remind me of it." And with that he drew his leather cigar-case from his tunic.

Wodrig, a grey-haired man, well over forty-five, with a round face and honest blue eyes, said: "His Excellency will be annoyed if the Herr Kriegsgerichtsrat smokes his own cigars in here."

Dr. Posnanski winked at him slyly. "I dare say, Mr. Wodrig: His Excellency is very hospitable; we buy the same cigars, and as he gets much more pay than I do, I don't mind if I take one. Bring me one of those long black Brazilians with the red band on it. It's a pleasant-sounding name: I think it means 'Sleeping Beauty.' She

went to sleep among the thorns, you know, but I hope there are
no hawthorn leaves in the cigars."

The old man brought a tray with a bottle of brandy and the box
of cigars. "I can't treat everybody that's kept waiting like this—
Captain Fallas, for instance, whom His Excellency can't abide—we
have to learn to make distinctions," he added meditatively. "If I
weren't treated so well here, and if His Excellency wasn't always
persuading me to stay, I could have gone home long ago. Of course,
Herr Kriegsgerichtsrat, I'm well over age, and it's not easy for an
old man, who's got enough to live on at home, to be hopping about
here keeping things neat and tidy. Now that summer's coming
and there'll be no more stoves to look after, it's not bad, but"—
and here he gazed broodingly before him,—"I really should like to
know what's the sense in our having to go through all this."

Doctor Posnanski, with his book laid open on his knee, puffed at
his cigar as he lit it, while the orderly held out an old yellow lighter
made of a rifle cartridge, such as Russian prisoners turned out and
sold in hundreds. "Yes, Mr. Wodrig," he said, "the sense of it all
is beyond us, take my word for it. But what seems much more
strange, is that man is so constructed that he can't get on without
trying to make some sense of it. You want to, and so do I, and
so do the fellows in the books. And if man cannot get on without
it, one of these days he'll get sense out of it, or put sense into it,
if need be."

Wodrig reflected, and then said, "How is it I can talk with the
Herr Gerichtsrat about such matters, and with Lieutenant Winfried
and even His Excellency, but not with the Herren Pastoren. If
you bring your difficulties to an army chaplain, and we've plenty
of 'em round here—they look at you like a boiled fish, and brandish
texts and catechisms at you; then they say, 'Doubt is sinful.' But
what can a man do but doubt? There's something wrong in it all,
Sir."

"My dear Mr. Wodrig, our colleagues of the cloth have a tougher
job than we have. They're harnessed to their texts."

Wodrig in his soldier's tunic shook his head emphatically.
"There's something wrong, Sir, take it from me, and they feel it
too, if they're worth anything. For instance, 'Love your enemies,'

and machine-guns and flame-throwers and howitzers, don't go very
well together."

The Herr Gerichtsrat was a tactful Hebrew and made no answer.
It was no concern of his. Moreover, he had far too much respect
for the average soldier's good sense and passionate intellectual honesty
to treat the man's perplexity with condescension, or facetiousness.
He was luckily absolved from further debate by the noise of an
approaching car. "I think somebody's arriving, Mr. Wodrig," he
said, carefully laying his cigar down on the ash-tray. "We'll finish
our talk another time."

"Yes," said Wodrig, still gazing at the other with an absent air.
"I wish you wouldn't call me Mr. Wodrig, Sir: I feel as if I
can talk to you as man to man." He ran out of the room and down
the stairs to help His Excellency out of his cloak.

Von Lychow was all fresh and sparkling. After his dinner he
had slept for a good half-hour on the battalion commander's bed,
and would nevertheless have got home punctually but for the fact
that the way had been blocked at the cross-roads by a benzol engine,
which came off the rails and stood there surrounded by a caravan
of requisitioned peasant carts. Rubbing his hands with satisfaction,
he described the resulting confusion to the Kriegsgerichtsrat, not
forgetting the eloquence of the drivers and the calmness with which
the railway troops had got the little monster back on to its rails, and
put all straight again. "I kept in the background," he said, smiling.
"I consider that people of our rank spread terror and alarm, and
are no help to anyone."

The Kriegsgerichtsrat made the mental comment that perhaps
the appearance of an elderly gentleman ought not to spread terror
and alarm, and that if it did there must be "something rotten in the
State." But he did not say so. He had frequent dealings with His
Excellency and knew the type. The fine old Prussian Junker with
his inflexible precision in every official detail was not to be held
responsible for the terror and alarm which he inspired. But he
would only have laughed heartily, if Posnanski had endeavoured
to explain to him that he considered superior officers as obsolete and
inhuman devices, and that rank, force, and the mere existence of
armies, imposed upon mankind the mentality of the Stone Age.

Such was his private unofficial view, but this was no time for laying it before the General.

His Excellency said that he was glad to hear that old Wodrig had waited so assiduously upon Posnanski while Posnanski had been waiting upon *him*, and was enjoying this little joke when Lieutenant Winfried came in carrying the file of papers, and they all moved from the ante-room to the General's office, and therewith into an atmosphere of business.

"Bjuscheff's is a clear case," said the Kriegsgerichtsrat in official tones, without in the least belying his good nature and human-ity. All three of them sat down, lit their cigars, and though the room was gradually darkening in the twilight, bent over the paper, in whose folds a human fate was quivering. "Bjuscheff's case is clear," repeated Posnanski, pulling a document out of the portfolio. The local police had captured the Russian private Ilja Pavlovitsch Bjuscheff, of the 67th Regiment of Infantry, about a hundred and six kilometres behind the Front in the vicinity of Mervinsk, in the villa suburb, asleep in an empty house. Since he admitted he had been wandering about behind the Front for weeks with the quite credible intention of finding his way to Vilna and thence to Antokol, where his mother lived; and since he persisted with some pride in his statement that he had made his way by night from the Russian wire to beyond Mervinsk (which was no great credit to the field-police, though a Russian Sergeant might well succeed in such a venture), nothing could be done to save him. This was just one of those cases to which the order issued by the C.-in-C., at the end of February last, was intended to apply. By this order every Russian deserter who failed to report, within three days of crossing the lines into the territory occupied by the German Armies, to the nearest town-major, or the commander of the nearest military or police unit, was to be forthwith charged before a court martial, and within twenty-four hours of his sentence to be shot as a spy.

After this lucid exposition, all three men were silent for a moment, and the same name was in the minds of all three: Schieffen-zahn.

"That's Schieffenzahn all over," said von Lychow, thoughtfully; "he's a sensible man. The army over there is breaking up, and he's determined at all costs to stop all this war weariness, insubordination, and sedition. Soldiers' councils, indeed! He wants to root out the germ-carriers."

"That's just it," said Lieutenant Winfried, "but I'm not sure if you can do it that way. And if you could, is it wise?"

Von Lychow toyed with the papers before him. He was clearly bound by the reports of the two judicial examinations and the verdict of the Court. Then he dropped the papers and said: "Good God, what's the sense of talking about spying now? Was the fellow going to wireless home what he had seen on our side? Not likely. Of course, he was going home to Antokol. The man is to be shot because he left his unit without leave, so as to go home, and is setting our men a bad example. They're all sick of the War, there's no getting away from it. But I suppose Schieffenzahn's right as usual. I can't go outside my orders: but I don't like it," he said, half to himself, for he had begun to think of the admirable turnout of the battalion he had inspected, of the grizzled veterans and beardless boys in their steel helmets—like an unshakable wall of grey rifles and bright faces—whom it was his business to feed and keep in health, and whose patience he had tried to strengthen by talking to them about the prospects of a speedy peace.

The Kriegsgerichtsrat said half aloud: "Sensible or not, I can see no possibility of cancelling the conviction. I don't think I look as if I went about thirsting for blood. The Divisional Court Martial works like a machine: when once a man is caught in it, he only comes out as a corpse. If anyone were to ask me, Your Excellency, whether there is any sense in the whole business, this legal flummery, this penal code, all this limitless twaddle of rules and regulations, I am perfectly ready to give Your Excellency my opinion. Only, if Your Excellency agrees, we must start our revolution from above."

"God forbid," said His Excellency, as Lieutenant Winfried laughed: "Revolution—I loathe the word."

"Then," Doctor Posnanski went on unabashed, "let us get down to fundamentals. Laws based on any other than ethical grounds are barbarous. 'It hath been told thee, O man, what is good, and what thy God requireth of thee!' All the ordinances we post up here and all over the occupied territory, are no more than regulations

—the merest eye-wash. Unless we admit that the aim and object of all our legislation is the maintenance of the existing authority, we do deceive our noble selves. But if the facts, with a view to which an order has been issued, are clearly established as in the case before us, we must either carry out the order or scrap the whole system. I put myself unreservedly at Your Excellency's disposal for a guerilla warfare of that kind against Ober-Ost. And thus," he added with an agony wrung from the anguish of his heart, "thus we shall set a splendid example and deal the death-blow to military lawyers all the world over."

"God forbid," said von Lychow again. "I'll have no truck with such 'splendid examples' and such 'death-blows.' I am a Prussian General, and do my duty. Not blindly, for we Junkers have eyes in our heads, and look at things as they really are; but what must be, must be. I am sorry for the poor chap; but we have greater matters to think of: discipline, Prussia, and the Empire. What does a Russky more or less matter?"

And in the stillness of the deepening twilight were heard the strokes of the pen with which the Ultimate Legal Authority of the Division brought the case of Bjuscheff to its natural conclusion.

Doctor Posnanski sat upright in his chair. To the young Winfried, who stood leaning against the stone frame of the window, his face seemed weary and sunken. And once he indulged in a quite unmilitary yawn, though he covered it with his hand. Herr Tamshinsky's clock, with its alabaster Cupid and Psyche, struck the hour of six in rich voluptuous tones. The lawyer felt he could not keep awake, and roused himself from his chair. Winfried decided to come to his assistance by placing the countersigned sentence in the file which would start on its official journey via Sergeant Pont the Registrar, and he said in low tones to his Chief: "Your Excellency promised to look over the tariff of the men's canteen before dinner, especially tobacco, cigars, and tinned stuff."

"Why, of course," said von Lychow. "It's a good thing for an old stager like me to be able to give his memory a rest. . . . The Shah of Persia couldn't be better off." And he shook hands with the Kriegsgerichtsrat. "Odd fellows, Paul, these legal lads," said he, stretching himself out on the divan, so as to get a little rest in the half-light before starting work again. "This fellow Posnanski, for instance; I'll bet you he reads the *Berliner Tageblatt*, and votes as Red as he can. But when he's on the job, he doesn't let go. These Jewish lawyers . . . I could swear they love law for its own sake as we love our lands and fields. Not all of them, of course,— I mean the best. But Posnanski"—and here he yawned—"certainly does. He's an ugly dog, and no mistake. But he's sound enough. He ought to be on the right side. He can't have been serious in all that . . ." and with a quiet chuckle the old gentleman sank peacefully into a doze, settling his white hair and ruddy cheeks into the soft folds of a black silk cushion, across which the white and red eagle of Poland spread protectively its embroidered pinions. Lieutenant Winfried (whose mother had married into the middle classes) laid over his uncle a soft brown coverlet of camel's hair.

Chapter 4

GRISCHA HIMSELF AGAIN

In the four-square courtyard of the temporary prison at the Mervinsk headquarters stood three long grey ranks of soldiers with rifles: a company of the Landwehr, on duty here as military police, drawn up for rifle-inspection. Sergeant-Major Spierauge, short and stocky, was walking once more round the ranks, casting a final and approving look at uniforms and equipment, before the arrival of Captain von Brettschneider. Quite unnecessary, of course. The company was lucky to be in Mervinsk, and knew it. It comprised the survivors of a Landwehr regiment—two hundred and ten men left out of two thousand four hundred who, some months before, had been thrown into the line to stop General Nivelle's sudden sally from the Douaumont sector. Those three days, from the twelfth to the fourteenth of December, will never be forgotten by that regiment, so long as there are two of them alive to meet. Under cover of the mist the Senegalese and Chasseurs Alpins swarmed out of their positions. A good third of all the casualties were dead, another third had gone to swell the prison camps in France; and here, on parade, were the remnant of the rest.

In the broad, empty courtyard, surrounded by a wall topped by barbed wire, chickens were pecking. The former civil prison at Mervinsk, faced with crude red tiles, had been considerably enlarged by timber out-buildings. It housed the prisoners of an entire division, German soldiers guilty of serious thefts, or those who had obstinately outstayed their leave, deserted their units, got into the bad books of a sergeant or lieutenant, made a combined protest against the food ("unlawful conspiracy"), had got drunk and unduly violent, or tried to mutilate themselves—all these were to be tried under the military code which dated from the eighteenth century.

If the accused made a good impression, and stood up smart and soldier-like, looking lively but not too clever, he would get off with something much lighter than the terrific penalties laid down in the Code. For they were obsolete and inappropriate, as every one of his judges would admit. Besides, scarcely anything would be a punishment for front-line troops, who, after all, spent their lives half-imprisoned underground, and in danger of death as well. For soldiers behind the lines the severest penalty was to be sent to the Front, but this was neither recognized as a penalty nor prescribed in any Code.

Accordingly, in many temporary prisons such as that of Mervinsk, the offenders were treated very reasonably. The comradeship between prisoner and jailer was based on a common uniform, a common destiny, and a common yearning after peace. This feeling extended even to the Russian prisoners of war, where they did not make themselves unpopular by dirty habits or a sullen demeanour.

Here we find Sergeant Bjuscheff: a very good sort of fellow. Neat, cheerful, and as light-hearted as a fish heading for a weir. Among the Landwehr-men who were standing in three rows, stiff as lines of wooden soldiers, and chaffing each other in whispers, there were many who had some liking for him, and knew that he had, at the very most, three days to live. They were familiar with the Commander-in-Chief's orders, they knew that the deserter Bjuscheff would be treated as a convicted spy, but they did not tell him so—why should they? He would learn it soon enough, for, in soldiers' language, "Late's too soon for news like that!"

The men were standing at ease, with muscles relaxed, but ready for the command "Attention! Right dress!" at which they would straighten their backs and form a level wall of rusty tunics, of every shade of grey from mouse-grey to the grey-green of the Jägers; above them, bronzed faces, and grey helmets, and below, buff-coloured threadbare corduroys. On their arms were white brassards with the letters M.P. (for Military Police) and the eagle, which was the special sign of the Mervinsk Headquarters to which the company was attached for police and military duties.

The distribution of authority in such a town as Mervinsk was a little complicated. Over the civil population, whose existence constituted a necessary evil, stretched, by the same laws of necessity, the heavy arm of the local military post or Ortskommandantur with the staff and troops attached to it. The Ortskommandant had a free hand in all constabulary matters, and was immediately under the particular inspectorate of lines of communication in whose district Mervinsk was included. In cases like the present, where the staffs of armies in the field were quartered in the town, their commanding officers were of course the final authority in all military affairs, but in them only. Moreover, the legal jurisdiction of a town for all major offences lay in the hands of the brigade or the division whose commanding officer was established there—in the present instance, His Excellency von Lychow. But in ordinary local questions, which did not concern the troops, the Ortskommandant and his subordinates took no orders from the General. He could only express his wishes, which would then be carried out as far as possible. Thus, between the shifting personnel of the front-line troops and the permanent garrison, there was no love lost, and a continual game of pin-pricks and obstruction served to enliven the dull round of duty. For example, a member of von Lychow's staff might be challenged by a night patrol of Military Police, and fail to produce a special pass; he would then be reported to the Ortskommandantur. who could require his superiors to punish him. Again, no staff or even company officer could resist an opportunity of reporting those "garrison swine" for any of those peccadilloes which relieve the soldier's life.

So it happened that Captain von Brettschneider, though undeservedly, was in bad odour with the General. Twice before he had had to report to him in full-dress uniform, in order to listen to certain polite reflections on the conduct of his subordinates. He might, however, get even with him by applying through his superiors straight to the Q.M.G. in the office of the C.-in-C. (one Major-General Schieffenzahn), and the Q.M.G. would, if he felt like it, have no scruple in trying conclusions with a Divisional General who happened to be his senior. For the relations of the field-army and the garrison were oddly involved. And when one considers that the field troops were constantly moved from east to west, from the Italian Front to Gallipoli or Palestine, it is easy to realize that the permanent garrison, insignificant as it might seem, seldom got the worst of an encounter.

Permanence is power, at least in the place where it is permanent. This, indeed, is the virtue of the brassards and the letters M.P. stamped upon them. For Captain von Brettschneider, in spite of the presence of Generals, Surgeon-Generals, Artillery Commanders, and the like, could afford to be exceedingly independent and self-assertive, and deal with the men under him exactly as he pleased. At the moment, indifferent to every other power in the universe, he was about to hold a rifle inspection of his Landwehr troops, and was just then keeping them all waiting for his own personal convenience.

The May morning was a marvellous background to the military ceremonial. The inevitable rain had discreetly fallen in the night. The spacious courtyard of the prison, on three sides of which were lines of hutments for the men, provided a dry drill-ground which had been strewn with cinders. The late chestnut trees which divided it down the centre, pointed their sticky fingers towards the glorious blue heaven like pennants of the spring. As the exits from the prison—that is, from the barrack yard—were guarded by double sentries, and other sentries were continually walking up and down the wall topped with broken glass, all the men then on duty in prison were called up for inspection. Even the greater part of the clerks and office orderlies had the privilege of performing in high boots and rifles. It would do them no harm to bring their pale cheeks out into the air of a May morning.

Consequently the guardroom, round which the cells lay fanwise, was empty except for one solitary man. The soldiers' bunks, set in two rows, one above the other, like cages, were also on parade. The pillows stuffed with wood fibre, and the blankets beside them, showed in the military smartness of their folds, and their much but neatly darned corners, how well they too had been drilled in Prussian order and precision. From the right post of each cage hung the cooking utensils, shining and spotless, of those who must cook their food under the open sky. At the head of the bunks each man's pack swung at the same level, and a box containing each man's private possessions stood neatly at the foot. There was nothing on the tables; nothing on the benches. As there was plenty of wood, and warmth permits good fellowship, a small fire burned in one of the two iron stoves. In this room, which at that time had to provide twenty men with space to live and move and have their being—in this skittle-alley with its open windows, the prisoner, Sergeant Ilja Pavlovitsch Bjuscheff, was pacing up and down.

Grischa looked somewhat pale, as he had now been sleeping for nearly a fortnight in a cell, in which a full-grown man soon felt as if he were living in a portmanteau; its tiny window was far too high up in the wall to see out of, and its only furniture was a wooden camp-bed with a pillow and blanket, which might not be used by day. Most of his possessions he had to give up when the patrol brought him into the office. Anyone who had seen him in the forest would scarcely have recognized him now. His hair and beard had been sacrificed to the prison barber. As his Russian tunic had been not unreasonably condemned as lousy, and as Russian uniform was constantly needed to equip the German spies, the clothes which Babka had transferred to him as a legacy from the genuine Bjuscheff, to establish his new identity, were taken away, thoroughly "deloused," and replaced by a German outfit—of such a nature as no army would dare to issue to its own men, even to a private in the Labour Corps. His tunic with its black artillery badges looked unimpeachable from the front, but at the back, unfortunately, a large dark grey patch in the green cloth indicated the spot where a two-inch shell-splinter had shattered the shoulder and reached the heart of its previous owner, one Gunner Lewin.

Bjuscheff's trousers, now thoroughly cleaned, had belonged to a stocky short-legged lorry driver, who had been unlucky enough to stop nine shrapnel bullets with his thigh and knee—from an American shell which the doctors remarked with scornful emphasis had been turned out hastily and so spread its bullets over much too small an area. Every one of the nine holes, from which the poor driver had bled, was darned religiously: but as the available thread was almost white, undyed, and unbleached—for the most common necessities were lacking—in spite of their excellent material, the trousers were not really presentable. As Bjuscheff was so tall, it mattered little that they came only half-way down his legs, for the ends were stuffed into his high boots. His arms and his great

knuckles hung out of his tunic, but as he was an active fellow perhaps this was an advantage. He looked somewhat paler, though
younger, with his close-cropped hair, as he sat on a bench, cleaning
a rifle. Corporal Hermann Sacht had promised him half a loaf of
bread, if he would do the job thoroughly for him and thus make
good the delinquency which the worthy Sacht had committed in the
excitement of a game of nap, and concealed, at the inspection, by
borrowing the rifle of his comrade, Otto Hintermühl, who was in
hospital with inflammation of the throat. Alas, even military man is
frail, and the corporal of the section, Lane, the door-keeper, lent
his countenance to this deceit.

Grischa worked with a will. He loved rifles. Since his arrest
he had returned to soldiers' ways and was cleaning the lock of a
German weapon as if it had been his own. He released the safety-
catch, opened the magazine, extracted the movable parts of the
lock, marvelling at their ingenious construction and yet comparing
them unfavourably with his own rifle, which had held so many
more cartridges in the magazine. Then he sand-papered and oiled
the metal parts, and cleansed the barrel with a pull-through to remove the remains of powder from the last musketry practice. As
this is properly a two men's job, he tied the rifle to the post of one
of the bunks, and drew the cotton-waste with all his might through
the spiral grooves of the long barrel. Things were going well, he
thought. The Germans had believed all his statements, and written
them down too. He had been imprisoned merely as a deserter, Ilja
Pavlovitsch Bjuscheff, of the 67th Regiment from Antokol, who
was awaiting the result of the court martial which would set him
free again. A man who has held a woman in his arms has a stout
heart in him, and can lie till the walls turn purple, with an innocent
face and a good conscience. What questions they had asked him!
What trouble he had had to convince them that he had wandered
so long behind the Front! They had almost begged him not to say
that he had kept dodging them for three weeks—having crept
through the wire, of course, at a point on the Front which for his
comrades' sake he must keep secret. He chuckled. "A cock's comb
was the same everywhere and so was the conceit of a policeman,"
and suddenly he burst out laughing, to think how soon he would

be free. Of course he'd be in for something; that was the way of the world: once you go before a judge, you'll be sentenced right enough, though you're as innocent as a copper spire on the golden dome of the cathedral. But they would have to take his fortnight in prison off their sentence. He was not afraid of what would happen now. As he marched through the town, almost fainting with despair and rage, after they had surprised him in his sleep in that wooden villa, he had passed the cathedral and seen the sign over the shop of Fredja's father. He had not had strength enough to ask permission to go in and buy cigarettes. And in the last fortnight he had not been allowed to leave the prison. But he would soon see about that. All was going merrily, and this rifle in his hand was a beauty. Now that he had done cleaning it, he laid it on a newspaper with each steel part separate, and washed his hands in the basin provided for the prisoners; then suddenly remembering that he had not washed his face, he plunged it gaily into the great bowl. There was a stubby beard upon his cheeks. If he cleaned the company barber's boots the barber would give him a free shave. You couldn't live here as carelessly as in the forest. . . . He must make himself useful to these Germans. . . . But at least he was among real soldiers. Not shaky old men like his guards in the timber camp, that lay so far behind the line, and seemed almost as unreal as his friend Aljoscha, the wire-cutters, and the truck in which he had travelled for four days. They had been through some queer things, and could spin a yarn or two, and he could make out most of it when they spoke slowly and in plain language. They had had hell from the French, after the English had plastered their trenches with shells from their big naval guns. As he had earned an extra half-loaf he could finish his ration of bread for breakfast, with the turnip-jam which the soldiers gave him. They had been kind to him like good comrades, especially since the day before yesterday, when his trial had come to an end. So returning to his labours, he swept up the room once more. Then he thought it was time to reassemble the rifle.

The magazine slid back with a triumphant snap, and in a moment every screw was in its place. Then, several times in succession, Bjuscheff pressed the trigger and the hammer clicked in the barrel. Click, clack, click-clack, went that trusty implement of war; it looked so enticing that he exchanged it for one of the practice bayonets, which stood against the wall on dummy rifles and were tipped with buttons and corks for safety. And now, shouting like a boy at play, he went through every lunge and parry of the Russian bayonet drill. And from the chinks in the floor which he had been sweeping, the dust rose high as he lunged and brought his great boot thundering down upon the boards.

While he was thus engaged, he heard a noise of tramping feet: the door was flung open, and through it, rifle in hand, rushed the first section of the guard to be released from the dreaded ceremonial. They saw at a glance what he was doing, and Paul Schmiedeke, one of the youngest among them, shouted out "Come on, Russky; bayonet attack!" seized a bayonet from the rack and faced him. Laughing and yelling "Go for him! Give it to him, Russky!" the men climbed up on to their beds or got behind the table, to leave as much free space as possible, and the two combatants went for each other with a will. The two men stamped and shouted exultantly as they thrust and parried, and their blunted weapons clashed together with the whole force of the men behind them. Grischa's onslaught forced the German to give ground, though he was only waiting for the chance to make a sudden offensive. But the Russian sergeant, with flashing eyes, possessed by the spirit of attack that had done to death hundreds of thousands of his brothers in Galicia, the Carpathians, Poland, and as far north as Riga, fought like a maniac. The German, a slighter man, had already touched him twice and got jabbed in the shoulder in return. "Go for him," they shouted, each side egging on its chosen champion. They would soon have been laying odds in the excitement of the contest. Grischa handled the dummy rifle like a huge dagger. Step by step he drove the German back towards the cells, which opened out fanwise beyond the guard-room. "Give him hell!" shouted the soldiers, who had now taken off their packs. "Stick it, Paul! At him, Russky! Bravo! Let him have it!" And the shrill voice of Private Sacht, who was so pleased with his fine clean rifle that he at once took Grischa's part, rang out above the uproar: "Russky wins!" And suddenly the tumultuous laughter was cloven, as with a knife, by a sharp word of command: "Attention!"

With one tremendous clatter, they leapt down from the beds and tables and fixed their eyes upon the door. Grischa and his opponent, with hardly any breath left, carried their rifles to "the order," as the drill book enjoins, before shouldering arms. The office orderly sergeant, all straps and buckles, with his cap on his head, stood in the doorway, and behind him, wearing a helmet and gloves, glittering from his boots to his collar, a lieutenant, A.D.C. to General von Lychow, and the Kriegsgerichtsrat who had met Grischa before, carrying a portfolio under his arm, and accompanied by an interpreter. The N.C.O. on duty reported—whether to his sergeant, or to the A.D.C. and representative of the Divisional Commander, was not clear—"One N.C.O., nineteen men of the guard, one prisoner." The sergeant received the report, and simultaneously Lieutenant Winfried raised his hands to his helmet. "Thanks," he said, "stand at ease!" And with these words the spell was broken. Grischa still held his rifle at the "order," he alone still standing at attention, and his face, ruddy after his fight and victory, grew pale; for he saw on every face that his hour was upon him. Try as he would to control them, his knees shook in his baggy trousers; however, he realized at once, with great relief, that his trousers were too loose to betray his trembling muscles. The lieutenant glanced at him, and said: "Put your rifle away. Hardly room enough for that sort of game. Orderly Sergeant, bring out the deserter Bjuscheff."

Doctor Posnanski looked as white as the official document in his portfolio. Then he nodded to the lieutenant. Winfried understood: "Are you Bjuscheff?"

Grischa, in his excitement, found his breath and panted out "My God!" in Russian and repeated in the same language: "Ilja Pavlovitsch Bjuscheff, Sergeant, 67th Infantry, Fifth Company, present."

Lieutenant Winfried raised his hand to his helmet. "Thanks," he said, although courtesy is not provided for in any Army Regulations in the world. Then he stepped back, so that Kriegsgerichtsrat Dr. Posnanski could face Bjuscheff. Beads of sweat stood out upon his forehead, and Winfried could not help thinking what a decent fellow he looked. The Kriegsgerichtsrat cleared his throat and set himself to read the order which the interpreter was to translate sentence by sentence. First, however, Lieutenant Winfried rapped out: "Company, attention!" in the voice he used when the General was about to address the troops.

The thoughts and sinews of the twenty-three Germans were strained towards that eternity where Posnanski and Grischa Bjuscheff stood face to face, alone.

The Kriegsgerichtsrat spoke in his civilian voice, which he vainly tried to steady and control, and in hoarse rasping tones, he read:

"In the name of His Majesty the Emperor: in pursuance of Order E. V. No. 14/211, the deserter Ilja Pavlovitch Bjuscheff, convicted of espionage on his own confession, was condemned to death on the third of May, 1917. No appeal will lie against this sentence, which hereby becomes effective. It will be carried out by the Ortskommandantur, to whose authority the condemned man is hereby transferred.

Mervinsk, 4th May, 1917.

Von Lychow, Lieutenant-General.
For and on behalf of the Divisional
Court Martial.
Signatures follow."

When he had spewed forth this rigmarole, Dr. Posnanski felt quite empty, at least metaphorically, and on the point of collapse. Indeed, he felt something like an ague in his limbs. But fortunately no one noticed him. The sentences poured from the mouth of the interpreter with the passionless but deadly precision of a field-gun (changed indeed, though their purport was evident to all); for the interpreter, a Lett, formerly a lawyer's clerk in Mitau, Courland, did nothing else all day.

The light of reason faded from Grischa's eyes. "What's that?" he asked quietly, and the words which his ears heard took some time to reach his understanding. This man Bjuscheff, . . . a deserter, . . . a gibberish of numbers and letters, . . . and then condemned to death? What? Were they going to shoot him? It couldn't be true. But the Lieutenant brought the scene to an end. "Stand at ease," he said sharply. "Orderly Sergeant, carry out the last wishes of the condemned man, and report to your office, of course."

The sergeant was perfectly at home. And then a strange thing happened: Lieutenant Winfried, one of the high and mighty ones who make decisions and sign death-warrants, turned impulsively to the prisoner, who had indeed put back his rifle, but still stood rooted to the earth, alone in empty space. Posnanski felt oddly irritated by the man's patched trousers. Then Winfried said—and the interpreter translated in his flat monotonous voice: "Bjuscheff," he said. "You're a soldier, pull yourself together. There's a bullet waiting for all of us. Think you're going over the top, and hold your head up. Sergeant, dismiss." So saying, he again raised his hand to his helmet, and strode towards the door. But he was not quick enough. Bjuscheff, heedless of the sergeant's admonitions, bellowed out in Russian, "What's that, what's that?" sank on his knees, and cried out again, now almost screaming, "What's that, Sir?"

Presidents of Courts Martial, who in most unmilitary fashion put their hands to their ears, are not an edifying sight. Lieutenant Winfried and the sergeant covered the retreat and the door closed behind them.

"They've left us a nice job," said the N.C.O. on duty, full of indignation. "Up you get, my lad," he said to Bjuscheff. "Take hold of him, Paul. Quick, Russky, get a move on!" and they dragged him to his feet. Sergeant Bjuscheff looked ashen grey. Saliva oozed from between his lips, and he was shaken by a dreadful shuddering. The soldiers, who were not at all surprised at the sentence, helped him along. "Christus," he moaned, "Christus." And one murmured to another "It makes your blood run cold." However, Comrade Russky was soon taken to his cell and locked in.

"You devils!" he bellowed, hammering on the door. "You German devils! Can't you hear me?" A dull perplexity brooded over the guardroom—not over the individual men, but the common soul and mass of them, for they felt at once responsible and helpless in the presence of this foolish, futile, and irremediable act. Then Private Sacht, amid the general bewilderment, spoke with unnatural resolution. "I shan't shoot him. I'll go sick. 'What's that, what's that?' I can hear him now." And once more he shook his close-cropped blonde skull and repeated to confirm his resolution: "I'll go sick."

"A nice job they've left us," grumbled the sergeant again. " 'Over the top,' says his Lordship—what bloody tripe! He'll never get back, and he's got a paper to say so. If they served out papers like that before they sent us over, not a man'd go through the barrage." And while an atmosphere of silent agreement pervaded the room, one of those soldiers nudged another with his elbow and said: "Can you hear him laughing, or am I going dotty?"

A faint, uncanny laughter could be heard coming from the direction of Grischa's cell. "Good God, he's laughing!" Private Sacht jumped up from his bench and ran to the door. "Laughing is he? I don't think!"

A monstrous shout of laughter, a little muffled by the wooden walls, burst from the cell of the condemned man.

"He's mad, he's off his head!" they said to one another, as they sat quivering at a thing so strange and gruesome. Then came an-other thundering on the door of the cell—"Kamerad!" shouted the prisoner, "Kamerad!"

"Perhaps he's not quite mad," thought the sergeant, and stole out into the dark passage. "Russky, be quiet! Stop laughing! It's against orders! Do you want anything? Papyrosses?"

Through the wooden door—from the sound, his mouth was close up against the chinks and hinges—Grischa yelled "Call the Lieutenant! Fetch the Lieutenant! As you hope to be saved, bring the Lieutenant back!" The orderly sergeant ran to the door, then recollecting himself, gave an order, and a private trotted off as fast as his legs could carry him.

For in the cell, on the bed, sat Grischa, bathed in sweat and grey of face, his hands resting on his knees, and in his mind one thought: he must get rid of Bjuscheff, Bjuscheff, whose death seemed to have been decreed, and whom they wanted to shoot again. He wasn't Bjuscheff at all! He must get Bjuscheff off his back, and as Grisha Iljitsch Paprotkin, escaped prisoner No. 173, No. 2 Company, of the Navarischky timber camp, recover his own identity. There must not be a second's delay. Something made him loathe the thought of leaving the world in another man's clothes. Something made him long to take his own punishment for his own offence. "Every man to his own," says the proverb. He's not the man they sentenced to death! The judges must know this at once. Shoot *him*? And before his eyes came the vision of the lynx, a black face with furtive eyes, as it had crept to him through the snow, the forest cat, with tufted ears like a devil, white teeth, humped hind-quarters, and clawed feet, the beast that had fled before his laughter. Laughter scares away death. Once again he would scare away the infernal beast. This time it was Bjuscheff whom he'd nearly allowed to devour him, him, Sergeant Grischa Iljitsch! "No! *pascholl!* To hell with you!" And half in relief and half in agony he beat his hands together as before, and laughed. "He's not the man! He's saved. Ha! Ha! Ho! Ho! Now for it!"

And that was why the prisoner Bjuscheff laughed.

Chapter 5

YOUTH'S A STUFF WILL NOT ENDURE

SISTER BÄRBE left her white uniform cloak in the hall of a little wooden house, one of fifty or more exactly similar—most of them without doors or windows—on the east side of the town, which Lieutenant Winfried had selected for himself, and with the assistance of the carpenters from the Kommandantur had transformed, as if by magic, into a charming little home. On the plank floor of the room which she now entered lay a genuine English carpet, of a cheerful green and pink design. A green-flowered wall-paper gave the room a cozy look, as did the table, divan, and bookshelf, and the soft window-seat, covered in yellow plush, which tempted one to look out over the young green of the swaying birches, beyond which fields and meadows stretched away into the distance. A single neglected little road, which encircled the town and from which countless by-paths led into the open country, separated the house from the growing glory of the spring. On an openwork tablecloth, tea was laid for two. The orderly, a gentleman of the name of Posseck, in a *Litevka* buttoned up to the throat, brought the teapot, clicked his heels, and vanished.

An orderly is a man of five-and-twenty, or five-and-thirty, years of age who is well content to fetch and carry for a lieutenant of twenty-two, or often eighteen or nineteen, polish his boots, clean his clothes, and generally to make himself his intimate and indispensable retainer. This was a time when, to a far-sighted man, serfdom was more attractive, and considerably safer, than a hero's life among mud, cursing, thunder, and death.

Sister Bärbe stood gazing out of the window, dressed in a dowdy blue and white striped dress with a hood. "He is a long time coming!" she said to herself, thinking in Swabian, and anyone who looked at her then would have taken her for about thirty. Her pretty little head, with its small mouth and glittering black eyes, sat oddly on her sturdy figure. She sighed gently as she entered the adjoining bedroom, where in a tarnished mirror above the wash-stand she could see a sickly image of her singular costume. She laughed gaily, hailing her reflection as that of a seller of pots and pans in Stuttgart, in the Crockery Fair near the Schlossplatz, and twittered to herself like a Swabian swallow. With her friend, Sister Sophie, she managed with little assistance, and no interference, a typhus hospital, in which lay thirty sick Bosnians, who had been sent there far too late and were slowly dying. They belonged to the "mixed" battalions which had been salted with Prussians, and there they lay, thirty swarthy men, soldiers delivered up to die in a place where nobody understood a syllable of their native Bosnian, or rather Serbian—dumb, patient fellows, helpless in the hands of the two nurses and the doctors, one of whom, a Doctor Lachmann, could at least make himself understood in a smattering of Polish. They were fortunate to be under the care of Sister Sophie and Sister Bärbe. They might have fallen into the hands of the ordinary run of nurses, who did their duty—hard as it undoubtedly was—but nothing more. But these were two young women of the right sort, and after six days' hard work, night and day, Sister Bärbe now had an afternoon off.

She was using it to pay a visit to her friend. She opened the lieutenant's wardrobe, and took out—a proceeding which would have petrified an officer of the old school—in broad daylight, a charm-ing bright red tea-wrap, gay with Japanese embroidery, and lined with pink silk, and changed her dress. There she stood before the mirror in her chemise, knickers, and silk stockings, a handsome Swabian girl of healthy bourgeois stock. Briskly she removed her hood and with it went all that seemed incongruous about that vivid birdlike head, with its pointed chin and heart-shaped, curving lips; it was now seen to be poised gracefully on a dainty neck and fine, dark-skinned shoulders. Sister Bärbe! Bärbe Osann, in the fresh-ness of her womanhood, the daughter of a large Swabian family of teachers and professors of Tübingen University, and for the past two and a half years a Red Cross sister and inured to all the hardships of the service. With the heavy red silk kimono draped about her, even her face looked different in the mirror. Here was indeed the face of Bärbe Osann, out in the joyless desert of Mervinsk not far from the fighting-line, amid all the barbarous masculine system of orders and obedience, a young woman of 1914, whose movements and shrewd eyes were eloquent of all that is most creative in the German race and of fifty years of peaceful cultivation of the spirit; and they bore her above the laws of place and time and the scarred and mangled world about her.

Wearing small shoes of soft Warsaw patent leather, she returned to the sitting-room and listened to the electric kettle in which the water was bubbling. "He'll get wet," she said, as she stood at the window, watching the heavy clouds over the vivid fresh green of the fields. "He hasn't even got his overcoat." At that moment he glided on his bicycle from the road into the neglected garden, full of lilac and climbing roses, and cut off from the road by a ramshackle fence, moss-grown, discoloured, and half rotten, which blended so harmoniously with the silky grey woodwork of the house that it had caught Winfried's eye, and he had marked the place for his own. The window was flung open, and a mop of dark hair parted in the middle was thrust out of it; she had hardly time to snatch a final glance at the radiant young face turned up to hers, when she heard him clattering up the short staircase to the upper story, three steps at a time. The kitchen and the room below were Herr Posseck's domain.

He took her in his arms passionately, yet gently, for the buttons on his tunic had already done a good deal of damage to the embroidery on Bärbe's tea-wrap. Then she sat on his knee on the great green sofa which creaked softly beneath their weight. They were lovers, and because they were neither of them sure they would survive the next three months, for at any moment Lychow's Division might be snatched away and hurled into the swamp of Flanders, or the dusty shell-swept slopes and choking lime dust of Champagne, while, in spite of all precautions, Sister Bärbe might be carried off by typhus or influenza, they gave one another what their youth could give. Both hoped to live through the War, but saw no reason to be stifled by the musty sanctimonious air of military officialdom. Among that overwhelming mass of soldiers, every nurse, even the poorest specimen, was the dream and the desire of thousands; beneath the surface of Protestant morality and Prussian virtue, men and women lived, and wrested what happiness they could from every passing moment.

Before Bärbe followed her friend into the adjoining room, she switched off the current from the electric kettle.

Later on they drank tea in the soft twilight. Bärbe chattered away; Winfried, his cigarette between his fingers, looked at her with half-closed eyes.

"One day," he said abruptly, "I am quite sure we shall look back on this month—our month—as the most beautiful and happy time of our lives."

"How long," she said, "do you think we shall be kept here?"

"Only the brass hats can tell you that. It looks as if they wanted to start all over again. We're so stuffed up in this hole that we must get all we can out of life: it might stop dead any moment, and then we should look silly, shouldn't we?"

And the two young hearts felt how the anguish that rent the age rent them, the pain that was transmuting the passions of old days and turning the longing hearts of men towards something good and worthy of desire—for such must be the purpose of the terror that seethed and roared about the confines of the earth, devouring men, extinguishing the light of youth, wrecking human bodies, breaking the neck of Hope.

Winfried began to talk of his official duties. Strange things were happening! They sentenced a man to death and nearly shot him, and then found he was some one else. And he told the tale of Bjuscheff, the "deserter," who, after the sentence had been read out—a death-sentence of course, for spying—had insisted in the interpreter's presence, with a convincing display of indignation, that he was not Bjuscheff at all, but a prisoner of war escaped from some camp far behind the lines, because he was home-sick and could not wait to be released, and because there was a revolution going on out there, which was bringing the War to an end. "Now all of a sudden he's turned into Grischa Iljitsch Paprotkin, and he's given us the number of his company, and the name of the sergeant-major in charge of his section—not an easy thing to get away with, and anyhow, it seemed to be easy enough to test. If it's true, he's saved."

Bärbe bent forward and stared at her friend with her great eyes: "And is it?"

"Wait and see. To-day Posnanski put forward an official report of the fellow's statements. Then he laid the matter before my uncle. He was in his bath, he had almost forgotten the whole business in his annoyance at the head of the M.E.D." Bärbe understood all such abbreviations as well as any soldier, and knew that M.E.D. meant Militäreisenbahndirektion (Military Railway Control), and that her own leave depended upon whether the Divisional General got his way; and she was, of course, deeply interested in it. "The fellow can count on the execution being put off for a bit. Queer fish you get in these days: Brettschneider's wild about it. He considers that we are 'wantonly interfering with him in the exercise of his official duties.' "

Bärbe shook out her hair, which she had not yet done up again, and which hung in two long plaits above both ears. "Good God!" she said. "All this red tape! And what's going to happen to the poor wretch?"

"Need you ask? 'Further investigations' of course. Posnanski has been given a free hand. You should see that Russky, a stout fellow with Kalmuck eyes and a boyish look on his face. He got the Cross of St. George at Przemysl, and how he got from Navarischky here, is more than I can tell you. Bertin's on the telephone to-night, poor devil. The wires are fairly buzzing over the leave-train battle."

Bärbe flung her arms round Winfried's neck and kissed him hotly on the mouth.

"We'll go together, Paul," she whispered ecstatically. "A fortnight together as man and wife. I shall stay four days with my people, not an hour more, and you can go and see your mother at the same time. I do grudge you to her! If I had my way you should come with me to Tübingen and live at Lustnau or Niedernau, and we'd see each other at least once a day. Oh, Paul, the journey together! And the journey back. And all our life together, Paul, as long as it lasts!"

The young man took her in his arms, for that was what he too most desired.

At half-past six in the falling twilight they left the house together, and Sister Bärbe Osann, habited from her woollen hose to the breast-pin at her throat like a modest Red Cross nurse, graciously accepted the escort of Oberleutnant Winfried, A.D.C. to His Excellency, whom she met while she was out walking; he left her near the hospital, where her friend Sophie was waiting to be relieved in that long room which harboured thirty fevered and typhus-stricken Bosnians, who raised their dumb eyes to the ceiling or tossed their heads upon the pillows.

Chapter 6

A LADY OF GOOD FAMILY

SISTER SOPHIE VON GORSE, with her soft, pale, hesitant mouth, large grey eyes and auburn hair, loved a man of the people, Doctor Posnanski's clerk, a certain Referendar Bertin, who, as a Jew and a non-combatant soldier, was hopelessly debarred from any advancement in the army, and who, moreover, in spite of his youth, had a wife in Dahlem. This young man, already an author of some reputation, had been rescued from the Army Service Corps while the Division was on the Western Front, a few weeks before he completely broke down: he had so loathed the slavish and soul-shattering routine of the orderly-room that, like every genuine worker, he had preferred harder and more dangerous service elsewhere. Now he sat safe and sound in the office of Posnanski, who fathered him, and was at last beginning to forget his terror of all the insignia of rank—badges, stars, and shoulder-straps; and he spent every spare quarter of an hour sleeping. A very youthful novel of his, and a *Treatise on Magic and Decadence*, had made some stir before the War, and since then he had been regarded as among the most important writers of his generation. Two of his dramas, which would hardly pass the censor, were handed about in manuscript.

He was now writing up the proceedings of the Court Martial; he did not guess Sophie's partiality for him.

The hospital ward, with thirty iron beds in two long rows, was lighted on the right by a window, on the left by a glass door, and but for a narrow passage between them the beds almost filled the room. Sister Sophie, with her hooded, soulful face and her white apron, was taking the evening temperatures. The poisonous odours of the typhus-stricken Bosnians filled the air about her, but she did not seem to notice them. With the patience and practice born of

119

her two years' service, she put the thermometer in their mouths, read it, marked the degree of fever on the chart above the bed, disinfected the instrument, and passed on. Mercury was growing scarce, and had already begun to be replaced by alcohol.

No sooner had Sister Bärbe mounted the stairs than she put away the secret joy of her womanhood in a corner of her soul, washed her hands, changed her dress, and stood once more on duty, at the service of her friend.

"Evening," they said to each other. To avoid the risk of infection, they did not shake hands again: the more casual and disordered hospitals become, and the more cheaply human life was held owing to the monstrous ravages of war, the more the two friends forced themselves to carry out their duties with composure and zeal. For the nation had grown brutalized beneath the daily scourge of death. But so long as their patients were alive, the two girls showed them friendly faces and gave them unselfish service.

"Bed 11 and Bed 18 will be free to-night," said Sophie to Bärbe. "Lachmann said there would be two gone, and anyhow, it's better so."

From those beds were heard a snoring, rasping sound, broken mutterings, and the moan of the fever-stricken, the heavy whistling breathing of the men whose hour had come. They had been dosed with morphia and so spared their last agonies and the relief of a few last words: a blessing upon home and kindred, or a curse on their tormentors.

Cotton-wool had given out long ago, and in its stead were giant bales of white wood-pulp, which people tried to think was just as good. Through the open windows protected by thick gauze, to keep out the flies, the rain-washed evening air was wafted into this habitation of despair. The matron put her head in through the half-frosted glass door, nodded to the two sisters—she wanted to make sure whether Sister Bärbe had come back punctually—and shut it behind her.

"Is it your night out to-night?" asked Bärbe.

"I shall stay here."

"Why do that?" asked Bärbe. "Listen, a strange thing's happened." And she related the adventure of the condemned Russian.

"This evening Bertin is to try and get on the 'phone to the prison camp from which this man says he escaped. It's as exciting as a novel. I wish you'd bring me some news about it to-night. I should have something to think about on my night duty."

Sophie understood her friend and smiled at her. Her sweet, solemn face was marvellously transfigured by a flash of mischievous delight. "But suppose he'll have nothing to do with me?" was her only answer. Bärbe glanced at her with those blackberry eyes of hers. "He's frightened of you, you little fool. He thinks you're his superior officer. He daren't raise his eyes so far above him. That's as sure as Amen at the end of 'Our Father.' Posnanski says he called him 'Captain' at their first meeting, on account of the polished shoulder-straps that a Kriegsgerichtsrat has to wear." They laughed; and Sophie's laughter stifled an aching in her heart. Suppose it was so, but perhaps what stood between them was the photograph on his writing-table of the young woman with her head on one side and the glamour of devotion in her eyes and lips?

"Won't you slip on an ordinary frock?" urged Bärbe, as she set about her duties. "Just let him see you as a woman. That'll open his eyes."

Sophie had an evening frock in her trunk. Dark blue with short sleeves and a smart V-shaped opening in front. She might attempt the conquest of this humble Bertin. And yet she, the slim Sophie von Gorse, who had come into the world after two brothers, was afraid of being thought of no account. For this reason, she chiefly sought the company of men of alien races and conditions, men of the middle class and Jews, whose views of women were such as she had only dreamed of in her aristocratic home.

Then she briskly shook her head with its stiff burden of brown locks. "I can't possibly burst in upon him uninvited, and in a dress that we aren't allowed to wear. And how can I get from this God-forsaken place to his quarters and back before eleven?"

Bärbe flashed an arch look at her. "You can if you want to. Change your dress quick, put the damned uniform over it, look half an inch fatter, and come back. At eight-fifteen Basse is bringing Winfried's little car to a certain corner, just by the little creaky gate. I arranged that—out of pure curiosity about the Russian."

The little car, bearing the divisional sign like a guardian angel on its radiator, only took eight minutes to reach Posnanski's wooden lodging. Then, lighting her way through the puddles with her electric torch, Sister Sophie, her heart in her mouth, hurried up the narrow path to the door, and knocked. There was a light in the passage, and the humble Bertin appeared in the doorway with his shaven bullet head and protuberant ears, his high ivory-smooth forehead and his great round goggles, and awkwardly greeted Sister Sophie, who mastered her nervousness and hung her damp black cloak upon a peg. She needed time to collect herself. Then she remembered her social breeding and shook her acquaintance by the hand. He needn't be surprised at her visit, she said, he'd be much more surprised in a minute if he would show her to his room. Then, alone in the corridor, she took off her nun's dress, and appeared in her little blue frock with its salmon-coloured sleeves, and in plain shoes, but gay stockings, smoothing out her silk tie, she followed him into the bare austerity of a military office.

The furniture of the room was made of unseasoned pinewood, and had been turned out by the carpenters of the Kommandantur; the native fleshy tint of the smooth planed surfaces of the tables was concealed by sheets of packing-paper. The darkest corner was filled by Bertin's camp bed, with its chequered coverlet of blue and white. The green bell-shaped lamp-shade pulled down low over the table cast a dim illumination over the room, and breast-high along the walls hung a haze of light grey cigar-smoke. Bertin was not too pleased at this interruption, but when he looked up, he suddenly became aware of a woman he had never seen before. His look of astonishment made Sophie laugh a little, and feel more at ease. She was carrying a shawl on her arm, and threw it over her shoulder.

"Don't look so surprised, Bertin," said she, as she sat down on one of the wooden stools. "We can't always be on our best behaviour. Have you got anything to drink?"

"Why, this girl looks like Lenore," thought Bertin, amazed. "Why didn't I notice it before?" And, indeed, a certain sensitiveness about the mouth and half-veiled eyes was common to them both:—the beautiful silk-clad creature in the photograph which in its frame of gleaming bronze was the only flower in this desert of bleak officialdom, and the living girl who was just lighting a cigarette.

"You've a nice room here," said Sophie. Bertin said in his gentle voice that he hadn't hitherto found it so, but it certainly seemed so to-night. "Why, I've never seen you properly before, Sophie," said he, shading his eyes so as to look more closely at the soft face on the further side of the lamp. "Perhaps because I generally see you with Bärbe, who makes more noise than you do, or in the hospital, where you're my superior officer."

"Do you hate your superior officers?" asked Sophie, and he fired up at once.

"Yes, I hate and despise all authority. It's been the root of all barbarism for these many thousand years. It's the spirit of evil, the spirit of the purblind elders, who are so short of humanity that they need force to assert themselves. The spirit of the crazy greybeards who are wrecking Europe. Have you noticed that not one of those who rule the world to-day is less than fifty years old? You come of an old family, Sister Sophie, if I am not mistaken?"

Sophie grew pale. This might be another barrier between them. "I hope you won't think any the worse of me for that," she said jokingly.

"No," he replied. "The best revolutionaries come from your class, men who've looked through all the masks and known the terror of that sight; Chamfort, Lafayette, and above all Mirabeau. Do you know who Peter Kropotkin is, Prince Kropotkin? Have you ever read the writings of Count Tolstoy?"

Sophie was spellbound by the resolution which flashed from his eyes and quivered on his drawn lips.

"Do you know what Byron said in his first speech in the Upper House; did you ever realize the meaning of Stein's reforms?"

"We're brought up like geese, Herr Bertin."

"Then, in two, three, or four years, when the War comes to an end, you'll have some surprises, and there'll be a few things you won't understand, Fräulein von Gorse," he said, scornfully.

Sophie's hands lay limp and defenceless on the table. Such was the force of the man's hatred and denial that she felt the need of some physical support. But the wild youth opposite her divined her thought. He walked round the table, took her hands, kissed them, and said: "Poor Fräulein Sophie. Have you fallen into a robber's den? As a woman, you ought to be on our side, for of all outcast and enslaved creatures, even including children, women are the most downtrodden."

All Sophie's life welled up within her. "Yes," she said, gazing up at him with her great shining eyes. "That's quite true, Herr Bertin. We women are slaves and geese because men keep us so. My brothers ruled the house at home, and I had to play in the kitchen with potatoes when I should have liked to be learning something. I want to hear what you have got to say, and I'm much more ready to listen than you imagine. We see so many horrors every day. As soon as a man is dead, they rob him, and we have to be always on the watch to stop them."

"To-night I begin to feel as if I was back in my student days, which you know nothing about either," said Bertin, his eyes on a sudden fired with the light of youth. "If I wasn't dressed up in this damned monkey jacket, I'd almost think I was living again in my old room in the Bellevue quarter, at 30, Klopstockstrasse, four stories up, with my charming friend Anni, reading Bergson and Husserl's *Essays in Logic.*"

Never before this adventure had Sophie von Gorse heard anyone produce so many unknown names as if they were household words. The kingdom of the spirit opened out above her like an airy world, into which she longed to take flight. But she was more immediately concerned to set a saucepan on the iron stove, and with deft fingers put some logs and little bits of coal on to the blue flames that flickered over the glowing fire. In the meantime Bertin unhooked the telephone receiver, and for the sixth or seventh time asked to be put through. "Divisional Court Martial office speaking. Can you get me Bialystok now?"

"Yes, of course," came the reply from that Beyond where telephone operators live unseen. "I'll put you through in two minutes. But we can't find that camp of yours in our book, and I tell you, my lad, the Bialystok people won't know any more about it unless you can give them the military area."

"Yes," said Bertin. "I'll let you know that at once."

Sophie from her dark corner by the stove watched affectionately his bright, keen face, and self-possessed expression, as she listened to the easy friendliness of his words which were in such violent contrast with the ruthless arrogance of the world she knew.

"Now," he was saying, "it's up to you, comrade."

And in half a minute he was in touch with *Ob-Ost* telephone exchange at Bialystok. Bertin said who he was.

"Have you got a moment, comrade? It's a ticklish business. We want a prisoners' camp—timber camp—saw-mills."

"Must be somewhere about Augustovo or Navarischky," came the answer in a deep bass voice.

"Thank God," cried Bertin, "I can see you know what's up."

"Yes, comrade," roared the other, "and a bit more than you think. But wait a moment, and I'll give you Section VII B, if anyone's awake there."

After a few seconds, a distant croak proclamed itself the "Forest Department," and Bertin patiently asked to be put through to a timber camp, where there were saw-mills, and a Landsturm Company from Eberswalde was in charge: the Court Martial of General Lychow's Division wanted to speak to the camp on urgent business.

The hoarse sleepy voice at the other end of the world woke up a little. The name of Excellency von Lychow had power even there, thought Bertin. The operator in the Forest Department said that he must ring up the trunk exchange and find out whether there was such a camp and whether it was on the telephone. If there was anyone still at the exchange, he'd be able to find it on his list. And he noted it down: Timber camp, Augustovo or Navarischky district, saw-mills, Eberswalde. "I'll let you know all right, comrade," he said, "if you'll tell me how I can get you again." And Bertin explained.

A faint but cheerful smell of coffee pervaded the tobacco-laden air of the room. The stillness of the night shrouded the house as if the world had disappeared. The only sound was the creaking of the floor as Sophie went to and fro. On a rough wooden shelf she found cups, a thick earthenware mug, and a smaller china cup painted with forget-me-nots.

"Where's your batman gone?" she asked. "Your orderly?"

Bertin smiled. "On leave. We oughtn't to have let him go, as we've no one to replace him, and Posnanski has to do the best he can with me."

Sophie looked up in admiration.

"Nothing wonderful about that, Sophie," said Bertin in reply to her unspoken exclamation. ("There's a man who understands me," she thought with secret joy.) "You must not forget that all three of us are just men together. The days when I took Posnanski for my superior were over long ago." And he laughed and slapped the back of his head. "You and your friends wouldn't believe what a stupid sort of soldier I was, but just think for a moment. Untrained men who are suddenly put under military law are wonderfully easy to manage. They don't even know the few miserable rights that they still have even as full privates. They're always in a mortal funk of committing some fearful blunder. That's why they're not trained. Your caste is marvellously cunning," he said in conclusion, as he pulled up for her the large chair, which he used at his desk, not without first spreading a folded blanket over the back and seat.

They sat at the right-hand corner of the desk of plain deal covered with packing-paper.

"This is very jolly," they said almost simultaneously. Then they crossed fingers and wished. Bertin thought, of course, that Sophie's whispered wish would be the same as his, that thrilling word "Peace." But she, emboldened by her swift success, listened to her heart which throbbed with Bertin's name alone. For she had remained a child amid all the experience of her busy life, which had taught her to master her disgust and made her familiar with men as torn and broken human animals, and now, as the minutes passed, her soul began to unfold in this new and delicious ecstasy.

Then, as they sat drinking "coffee," she made him tell her the strange adventure of the Russian, show her the written death-sentence, and describe the fruitless efforts that Posnanski had at first made, to mitigate the man's own damning evidence. Of course these poor wretches did not know what they were bringing on themselves by their seemingly innocent admissions. "Counter-espionage, what rot! The danger of such measures," said Bertin solemnly, "directed against persons who break laws, of which they haven't the foggiest notion, is most obvious in the case of counter-espionage." He almost whispered in the torment of his passion, "Every fool knows there is no espionage about it." What they were really afraid of now was that the men would be infected by ideas. They wanted to prevent the spirit of revolt, which after years of agony had seized upon the Russians at last, from spreading to the German Army. "We've long since given up thinking about war and victory, Sophie," he added in a fiery outburst, as he took off his spectacles and glanced at her from beneath his reddened eyelids. "Now the real concern is politics. The fight for the Class State and the rule of the few over the many. The militarized nation is, say they, the true expression of the modern nation. Seventy millions at the will and pleasure of three thousand irresponsible masters. To-day they've got hold of the women, and to-morrow they'll do what they like with the schools. At six points, of which three are in Germany, two in the west, and one here, huge masses of humanity are being hurried to and fro, and their despair is either conveniently ignored or looked upon with cynical indifference. And what will be the end of it, no one knows."

Sophie, in a sudden glow of rapture, realized that she was now close to something she had yearned for from childhood—revolt, rebellion, and the freedom of the spirit. Moved by a strange impulse, she laid her hands beside his; they both had sensitive, delicate hands, though they bore the traces of hard manual labour.

"A woman," thought Bertin, "a real woman. I wish the place didn't stink of tobacco. I should like to smell her hair." He stood up so as to bend down over her head. At that moment the telephone bell rang, and Bertin grabbed the receiver, sprawling half across the table.

"Hullo!" said the operator. "I've got through to a timber camp, I don't know where. I think we've connected you all right, but the line's rotten. I don't think you'll get much out of them."

Sophie noticed Bertin's eagerness and excitement.

"Look here, comrade," said Bertin in a hoarse, insistent voice. "A man's life depends on what I'm going to say. A man like you and me. Switch on more current, as if the Emperor was speaking.

Turn on all the lamps you've got. I'm not going to dictate a lot of balderdash, it's a matter of life and death."

The operator promised to do all he could, and presently Bertin heard him talking to another station, probably Bialystok. "How these wires go through the night," he thought. "And on these threads hang human destinies. The miraculous messages pass from mouth to ear, by the magic of electricity. God, how happy man could be made by all these marvels of mechanics!" And suddenly his call came ("You're through to Navarischky camp"). "Timber-camp orderly room. Eberswalde Landsturm Battalion, at the saw-mills." Very clear and far away like things seen in an inverted field-glass. Bertin's hands shook, but not his voice. He shouted into the instrument with the sharp enunciation of an actor, and asked whether some time ago a Russian called Paprotkin had escaped from their camp and what he looked like. With his right hand he scrawled the answers in shorthand on a sheet of order paper. Was it as long ago as that? They'd caught a man here who had given all these particulars. Had they got a certain Private Heppke, Corporals Fritzke and Birkholz in the section of the guard under which the man had worked? Was that correct? All correct? And Sophie saw such a light of joy on her friend's face at the good fortune of a poor stranger who had been condemned to death, that she feverishly pressed to her bosom the arm that held the receiver. And so it was that her hair came near Bertin's face, and he breathed its fragrance as he listened to the faint clear words that came from far out in the night.

"Thank God," he said, with a gasp of relief. "Can a couple of men be spared to identify the prisoner?" He would give them the postal address at once and a telegraphic request would be sent off to-night. And he noted down the official designation of the prison camp in the code jargon of the Field Post Office. "A tall fair-haired fellow," he shouted.

A far-away voice replied. "That should be the man. He got away on a stormy night in winter. It cost the sergeant-major his job. He won't be sorry to see him back."

"Let him down gently, old man: you don't know what he's been through; he was to have been shot to-morrow as a deserter." He

heard the other man mumbling, "How on earth did he get so far?"
"That's his secret," shouted Bertin, "and he means to keep it. A
fine trip your fellows'll have; and the Lord knows how they are
going to get here. When they arrive they must fix up rations and
billets at the Ortskommandantur and report at once to Kriegsgerichtsrat Posnanski at the Divisional Court Martial Office. No, they
needn't start to-morrow," added Bertin, "the War won't be over
for a day or two," and as he thought he heard a laugh in answer to
this sally, Sophie's friend laughed too.

"Have you finished?" asked the exchange: "Have you finished?
Right! I'll cut you off." Then followed a loud buzzing, and Bertin
hung up the receiver. He turned an exultant face on Sophie, crying
"Saved, my dear!" Then he embraced her, and as they leant, half-
sprawling over the wooden table, he kissed her as a beloved and
trusted friend. Her hands were pressing his arms against her
breast, and now she let them fall. She raised them to his cheeks,
and with closed eyes she clasped his face under the bright light of
the lamp.

Thus was the destiny of Bjuscheff, the deserter, bound up with
that of the beautiful and tender Sophie von Gorse, and all because
Sister Bärbe had been so good a friend to her.

Chapter 7

EXERCISE

IN the office of the Kommandantur Staff-Surgeon Schimmel stood poring over the register, checking the names of the men on the sick-list and the result of his last inspection. At the name of the prisoner Bjuscheff, which had been marked with a query, he stopped short, and asked with characteristic amiability: "Why don't you put the swine to work out of doors? Then he won't get these fancies." The sergeant-major shrugged his shoulders: "He's still under sentence, Herr Stabsarzt." The grey-haired Sanitätsrat, whose practice had sensibly diminished during the few years before the War, thanks to the insidious competition of the Jews even in Bremen, dismissed the matter with the profound and truly military remark: "It's a damned silly business, in my opinion!" and went to drink his morning glass of brandy, or maybe glasses, with the potentate of the Kommandantur, Captain von Brettschneider.

Bjuscheff—he was still called by that name—according to the report of the guard and the sanitary corporal, Käuer, had become a different man since he had been informed of his sentence. Until then, he had been willing, alert, good-tempered, and active, but now he preferred, when he was not disturbed, to spend the day on the bed in his cell, through which in the afternoon the sun poured an incessant stream of mellow golden light and warmth, but which for the rest of the day was hardly a healthy resting-place, for it was damp and sunless, and cut off from the triumphant radiance of the spring, which after the last few rainy days had settled on the land like a riotous flock of wild duck upon a lake. In the public gardens, the lilacs and the tulips were in all their glory, the young chestnuts spread their tiny green sails to the wind, and after the gloom of winter the gentle breeze and the brightness of the sky made the cheeks of all men glow with something like a second youth.

Grischa—well, he certainly should have had more exercise. He wasn't simply lying idle on his bed: he was thinking. Two days before he had taken his daily walk, of course in the company of a guard, who wanted to buy something in the town, and there had a short conversation in Russian with the bearded shop-keeper, Veressejeff, whose sign with its Russian legend hung immediately opposite the cathedral, while Corporal Sacht was enjoying a drop of schnapps. Besides this, he took the daily-prescribed exercise in the prison-yard, where he marched monotonously round behind four or five other prisoners awaiting trial, who stared at the ground or gazed vacantly up at the clouds. No more jokes and laughter, no more little jobs, or talks in broken Russian and German. The corporal who had been on duty at the time, and who would in due course come on again, was very ready to answer the many astonished inquiries about the Bjuscheff affair; but, with the fine tact of common men, he never mentioned it in Bjuscheff's company, but confined himself to inquiries, direct or indirect, as to why Comrade Russky looked as if he had the belly-ache. But he had to be content with Grischa's evasive though friendly monosyllables. For the first days, however, they did no more than give the prisoner exercise by making him keep himself and his cell clean, and sending him out in the sun to chop wood, but though he was evidently doing his best, he did not get through a third of what he would have normally accomplished. The "sick corporal" was duly informed, and the matter was put forward officially to the staff-surgeon, so that he was subjected to a hasty medical examination. The result of the examination had been expressed by Staff-Surgeon Schimmel in the words that he had used in the orderly room. The man's body was as healthy as one could wish any German warrior's to be; into his mind they could not look, and it was there the trouble was.

Just as a man who has been hit by a hard leather ball in the pit of his stomach, staggers and falls, and at first knows little of himself or the ground where he once walked, except that a ball has knocked him over, so Grischa lay, at least in mind, still motionless on the floor of that incorporeal space where the soul's life is unfolded. And the need he felt of keeping his body stretched out on the bed and staring at the ceiling of his cell, was only the bodily reflex of his soul's condition. He had to recover from the sentence of death which had been brought upon him by his simple and ingenious trickery. It dawned upon him more and more that the world was shod with iron. The icy tortures of his journey, the shivering, sweaty chase of the last ten days and nights of it, since the telephone wires of the police had been humming after him, and now this bludgeon-blow of a death-sentence—there was little to choose between them. The world seemed so bitter a place that his despair and collapse were natural in a man so utterly abandoned.

In this state he had implored Veressejeff, Fedjuschka's father, to write the letter which they agreed upon, and stretch out a shadowy hand into the wilderness behind him, which, if all went well, might reach a place where love was waiting for him and watching over him. His thoughts moved in crazy circles over the world's abyss. Would he become Grischa Paprotkin once more? Would he succeed in ridding himself of this corpse Bjuscheff, which he had once so light-heartedly buckled round him like a breastplate, exchange it for his own face, and find credence and respect once again? It was a dangerous business to have dealings with the dead. They had ful-filled their destiny and they stuck to it. Just as, if they were born again, they must needs have the same coloured eyes and the same shaped nose, if they were to be themselves, so they must have the same fate sewn into their skin. Bjuscheff had been killed by a bullet, and he must again be killed by a bullet. Babka should have thought of that, and so should he. What can you expect from an apple-pip but an apple tree? Possibly he had disturbed the dead Bjuscheff's rest, and taken Bjuscheff's soul upon him, and having made so free with the dead man as to take cover behind him, he had forfeited the sovereignty of his own soul. And because the dead hungered for life, Bjuscheff not unnaturally had the mastery over him and of course would not return without a struggle, to the background, the underworld, the tomb. He, Grischa, lay with open eyes watching the two souls wrestling within him. Bjuscheff's soul, which was certainly the stronger, lay now uppermost, clutching at the throat of Grischa's soul, and driving a knee into his stomach at a particular point between his belly and his heart which Grischa thought he could feel as he lay upon his bed. As soon as the Germans believed him, Bjuscheff would begin to get the worst of it. He would be flung to the ground upon his back, and Grischa's soul would set both its feet upon him and stand upright in its boots again. But he must not think so much about himself! How could he know what his judges meant to do, now they had heard his new story. He knew he would not be shot yet awhile, but this did not prove which of the two souls would win the battle. And so he preferred to lie upon his back, smoking from time to time a forbidden cigarette, and watching with closed eyes the struggle between Grischa and Bjuscheff. He never doubted for a moment who he was; no one could have made him doubt it. Grischa he was, and Grischa he remained, with a wife and child waiting for him at home in a suburb of Vologda, where the great steppe lay beyond the town; he was sure enough, but could he make his judges sure? Yes, Babka, it would have been better if you hadn't been quite so clever, for the Germans, you see, have always got something up their sleeves for people like us.

By means of that oil of good fellowship which circulates from man to man and lubricates the jarring cogs of the official machinery, the clerk Bertin heard of this change in the Russian who, until further orders—that is till the guards from the timber-camp should confirm his statements—was still registered on their books as Bjuscheff, though Posnanski himself had not a shred of doubt of the man's real name. He had heard the staff-surgeon's opinion with a smile. " 'We'll help that man,' quoth Robber Moor," he said gaily to Bertin as he strutted round the great empty office, smoking his cigar. "Why not? Work's no disgrace to any man, and to us it may be an advantage, for the hands of a German author are quite unfitted for chopping wood and sweeping rooms, whereas it won't hurt the man Bjuscheff, in spite of his remarkable dual identity, to be our orderly. Herr Ruppel can stay on leave a little longer, in circumstances which are more agreeable to him than our own. Human ingratitude, mark my words, Bertin, is as constant as the Polar star, and if you set that penetrating brain of yours to call in question any of the oracles with which I favour you, I shall ask you to bear in mind that I draw approximately twelve times as much pay as you, and consequently I am twelve times as right." Bertin burst into a peal of laughter, unduly loud in the presence of so highly-placed a superior, and said, "May I respectfully ask the Herr Kriegs-gerichtsrat, whether I'm to sit down and type out a request for the services of the prisoner Bjuscheff, alias Paprotkin, for orderly duty in the Herr Kreigsgerichtsrat's office?"

Dr. Posnanski stopped pacing up and down, poised his cigar in mid-air, opened his mouth wide, and said, "Did I hear you say, 'respectfully'? Don't you know that that word has betrayed all that duplicity of yours that cries aloud to heaven? Only an officer may use that word. In a private, respect is taken for granted. If I were Cassandra, I should begin to prophesy: if there were a few more insubordinate gentlemen like you about, this glorious War would not last long. However, you have roughly expressed my intentions, so far as your underpaid intellect can grasp them. Yes, that was the tenor of my thoughts: we'll take the man on as orderly till further notice. For," he said, pursuing his homily in excellent humour, "what do you think will happen if this fellow gets the Bjuscheff label off his collar for good and all? I may point out to you as a layman that this is where the ancient military game of cross-questions begins? If this man, having proved to be no deserter, but an escaped prisoner, ceases to be under our jurisdiction, who'll look after him now, what court will take the trouble to deal further with the case? Ha, Ha! the heathen are astonished, and the scribes do marvel. Of course, we can't touch him, because he hasn't been walking on our flower-beds; his offence comes rather under the cognizance of the Court Martial of the Army Headquarters of this area. But what tribunal God in his good providence appointed for the Navarischky saw-mill or timber-camp, we have not the least idea. Of course," he went on, in a rather more practical tone, "we shall do our best to send the documents to the right shop, or else the lad will have to wait months before he finds a man to judge him. The statements of the two guards from Eberswalde, who are on the way to us, may help us to decide what to do. Then, if the whole story is confirmed, though I've no doubt of it already, we'll send the papers to Section IX, that exalted Department—which on the sixth day of Creation.

that is 5677 years ago, was, in a manner of speaking, ordained to be the highest pinnacle of justice in this occupied territory—and throw in a few judicious observations so as to help the case on its way to the right court. Perhaps we'll send the papers to Bialystok by a man we regard as trustworthy, to wit, our clerk Bertin, thus providing him with a little trip, which he may find not too disagreeable."

Bertin, pipe in mouth, listened to this much-loved chief who had made a man of him again, and been a father and mother to him in the desolation of his soul, when he was sent back shattered from the Western Front, and his heart filled with affectionate gratitude.

"My heart is full of gratitude and affection for the fatherly care which the Kriegsgerichtsrat has been good enough to extend to me," he said with whimsical pomposity, and added, "certainly, Dr. Posnanski, I could do with a trip like that. And while I'm at *Ober-Ost*, I might take the opportunity of looking about for a second clerk for us. We can ask for men fit for service—those fellows at the base are due for another comb-out presently. Thank God, my leave's coming along soon," he went on, gazing long and wistfully at the girl in the photograph, the girl with the sweet mouth and tilted head. "And I don't suppose they'll send a girl to help us."

"And why not, pray? In my present war-shattered condition, I should be quite glad to see a few agreeable females about the place," answered Dr. Posnanski. . . . "As things are at present, I certainly get time to read, and I find working with men very soothing to the nerves, but too much peace of mind is not decent in war-time and why shouldn't I suffer the vagaries of lady-typists for a while? I know a few in my office at 7 Tauentzienstrasse who would be delighted to travel second-class to Mervinsk, to come and reveal their unconscious minds according to the great Freud, by their mistakes and delinquencies. Very well, then, Bertin, we'll apply for Bjuscheff as orderly, hold on to him when Ruppel comes back, and we won't send him on his travels till the Bialystok people have decided who's to deal with him. For I have heard it said that in our prisons behind the lines at Bialystok and other centres of metropolitan life, the air is less wholesome for Russian prisoners than in the idyllic little prison at Mervinsk. Besides, I'd have you know that the man is now under our Department, and the soldier fights for his Department tooth and nail; just as he struggles hand and foot to be rid of anything outside it. I am hereby furnishing you with important data on the life of the civilized white races, and I expect a grateful acknowledgment in your next publication, which, if I mistake not, you are producing, or at least preparing, in defiance of regulations, in your so-called spare time, though a soldier is not supposed to have any spare time at all."

Bertin's cheeks reddened, and he saw with astonishment a sly twinkle in the eyes of his kindly chief. "You must not leave things about, my youthful hero, at least among the official papers: especially a certain document which proves on inspection to be a charming comedy in verse on the Spanish campaign of the year 57 B.C."

Bertin blushed again. What could have come over him to leave in the Bjuscheff file, manuscript pages of his comedy "Felix," in which he had tried to recover his shattered poetical power? It must have been only yesterday afternoon that he had read to his friend Sister Sophie the beginning of the second act, and realized with the ecstasy of the artist that these scenes did indeed contain something like the true poetic sweep and magic which he had had at his command until the recruiting sergeant struck the pen out of his hand.

> "Come, sweeting, let us sit upon the grass,
>   And innocently prattle for awhile,
>   Like little children locking hand in hand
>   (Not very clean hands, yet most truly dear)."

"I think that you are more famous than you know, especially in Mervinsk," Posnanski went on inexorably. "Yesterday at His Excellency's house, two charming lips sang your praises. You've got off with Sister Bärbe, my young Don Juan."

Bertin nodded, delighted that Posnanski was on this false scent, and abruptly slewed the conversation round from this somewhat painful topic to a more pleasant one, namely to business.

"Has His Excellency actually seen Bjuscheff? Shouldn't we get him on to it? That might be a useful thing, not for His Excellency, of course, but for the poor devil himself."

Posnanski gave an assenting sniff and Bertin knew that he had struck the right note. Naturally it would do no harm to bring so powerful a personage into touch with a man in peril of his life. Besides, His Excellency needed some distraction at this time. Great decisions, both by the Russians and the German higher command, were impending, and he, penned helplessly in Mervinsk, chafed under his uncertainty. And so the Kriegsgerichtsrat and his clerk discussed in detail how they should bring about this meeting, and they decided to suggest it in their application for Bjuscheff's services which Bertin had just typed out, and Posnanski affixed to the document the illegible hieroglyphic which denoted his name and rank.

When it reached him, it so happened that His Excellency was in a state of considerable irritation. One of the clerks on his staff, hitherto of unblemished character, had been caught without a night-pass and reported to him. On the face of it this was hardly a matter to disturb the sleep of a general in the Great War; but further developments had made it so. Technically the statement on the man's charge-sheet was correct. But the fact was, an officer of the Kommandantur, on the orders of the Ortskommandant, had walked, watch in hand, up and down the dark street in which the Divisional Staff were billeted, and at exactly four minutes past ten had caught Sergeant Rahn returning from the Soldiers' Club and ruthlessly reported him. Unfortunately, from his point of view, he had not reckoned with the *savoir-faire* of the Staff-Sergeant Pont, or with Lieutenant Winfried's obstinacy in believing his men's statements.

Accordingly His Excellency received the report against Sergeant Rahn, but with it a full and dispassionate account of the circumstances which, in the opinion of the Staff, proclaimed the incident a scandal. Such was the rigidity of this military machine that a vast and un-wieldy organization had grown up behind the lines, and there are plenty of people ready to occupy their leisure in disputes of this sort. But Lychow did not like the sport, and he decided to have a word with Herr Rittmeister von Brettschneider about this ridiculous affair: and if a General wants to speak to a mere Rittmeister or cavalry captain, who is in the eyes of a private a god, but in the eyes of a General a very insignificant clay idol, the interview is occasionally a painful one. Immediately after this, several personal matters were brought before the General including Posnanski's application, that the prisoner Bjuscheff, who was then at the disposal of the Kommandantur, should be transferred to his office, in place of his absent orderly, as the circumstances of his trial made Posnanski anxious to keep him under observation.

Of course, His Excellency had already forgotten this Bjuscheff, or whatever his name was. Nobody need be surprised at that, for at such times a Russian prisoner was of less importance than a louse, if the latter should happen to take up his quarters in the collar of a general officer. However, a few comments of Lieutenant Winfried, who was preening himself in his uncle's office with his usual air of friendly geniality, sufficed to jog his memory: "It's the man who ought to have been dead, isn't it?" said the General. "He's been clever enough to keep himself alive, and if he doesn't lose his head he may get out of the mess altogether." Winfried explained gaily that the Kriegsgerichtsrat (whom His Excellency liked very well) was anxious to keep his eye on the lad—of whose honesty he was convinced—at least, until he had been duly confronted with two of his guards who were already on the way. So far, the man had been well enough off in the prison of the Kommandantur; but as he really belonged to the Division, he ought to help the Divisional orderlies, and not "those slackers at the Kommandantur."

Exzellenz von Lychow heartily approved, and the business seemed disposed of. But in the afternoon, after an excellent lunch—the mess cook had shone in other days as head chef in the Rostock Court Hotel at Rostock, and there had been oxtail soup with dumplings, salt ribs of beef with horse-radish sauce and *Salzkartoffeln*, washed down with a sound red wine, followed by Cheshire cheese, Mocha coffee, and French cognac—Dr. Posnanski suggested once more that the General should see the man. He was accustomed to take his strictly *kosher* meal in a Jewish restaurant, but he went into mess for coffee, and was always welcomed heartily. After politely explaining to the new orderly that he took no cream, not because he objected to tinned cream, but because, in obedience to an official order of the Almighty, he only ate anything with milk in it at a fixed interval after the meat meal of the middle of the day, and the commands of the *Torah* must override even the Prussian Field Service

Orders, he asked His Excellency point-blank whether he would be willing to see the Russky.

The man was suspended, he said, between his two identities like a soul bewitched. He had exchanged Bjuscheff for Paprotkin, but he had not yet settled down to him again. You couldn't see such sights every day at Mervinsk, and it might amuse His Excellency. He was a fine figure of a soldier: it was a pity that he had to go about in such a comical get-up . . . and he gave an amusing account of the whole matter. Von Lychow thought he might as well have a look at the Russian if only to please this humorous friend of his. At half-past four Bjuscheff was in any case to report to the Staff Orderly Room.

"Everything," said Kriegsgerichtsrat Posnanski, "depends on circumstances. In the next few days his two champions from Eberswalde will have found their way to us. It is difficult, I fancy, to get from the timber-camp to Mervinsk, unless one is an escaped prisoner and particularly anxious to avoid us. But they must find us prepared. An atmosphere of unconstraint is essential when the two parties rush into each other's arms. I don't want the victims produced for an elaborate scene of identification in court, but an ordinary friendly meeting which will allow free play for all the psychological detail that should go with a discovery of the truth. And I need hardly say that the meeting must take place under my eyes and in the presence of a certain assistant of mine with a talent for descriptive writing. I should like, therefore, to have the man employed during the day around my office. Your Excellency will appreciate my reasons, and if the two men from Eberswalde identify the fellow, then we will cancel our decision with all due formality, send the papers to the Supreme Department of Justice and keep the man with us until the authorities in Bialystok have decided what section of the military administration should deal with the case. As I don't wish to trouble Your Excellency again over this poor innocent, I should be glad if the matter could be disposed of this very day."

Thus it befell that about five o'clock a Prussian General and a Russian prisoner had an opportunity of taking each other's measure. Corporal Sacht had a nasty shock when there suddenly entered his room, not the sergeant, or the clerk to whom he was to hand over the Russian for duty, but the broad and brilliant epaulettes of a general. This was much worse than going through the barrage. The sight of a general nearly always meant disaster for so humble a creature as a corporal. However, Corporal Sacht, though still a little pale from his first terror, stood up stiff and correct, and rapped out: "Private on guard, and a Russian prisoner reporting for duty."

The General liked Sacht's looks. He knew something of the history of the Landwehr company on duty at the Kommandantur, and asked him about his service in the field, where he had been wounded, and whether his company had had a very hot time of it, and he decided in his own mind that the whole battle of Verdun was sheer madness, and should have been broken off after the first five days. He did not say so, but expressed his surprise that the man was not wearing a black and white ribbon in his button-hole. Had his company not been decorated?

"No," said Corporal Sacht. "My company didn't click that time." He meant they had been overlooked: but an interview with a Divisional General might well be expected to upset a soldier's vocabulary. The General winked slightly at his A.D.C. and nephew, and Winfried made a mental note of the fact that, at the next opportunity, Corporal Sacht should receive an Iron Cross as a memento of his meeting with His Excellency. But Hermann Sacht also understood, and although just then there was a slump in Iron Crosses, a slow blush of pleasure spread over his face as he thought:

"I've earned it, we've all earned it, every man of us, who was stuck there in that bloody hole. Even if it comes late and in the wrong way, it's the Iron Cross anyway. I've earned it right enough, and I shall have something to write home about."

Meanwhile, His Excellency was looking at the man who had very nearly been shot for a harmless piece of trickery. With the natural shrewdness of a peasant, Grischa was sizing up the man who stood before him. He could only be an officer of very high rank, certainly not a doctor, but a full-blown general, and he addressed him in Russian, giving him his proper Russian military title: the words *Voshe Prevasschaditjelstvo* rang sharply through the room, and he saluted in the Russian manner.

"I've learnt something this afternoon," said His Excellency, and the interpreter had no need to explain to him. "Whether you are truly Paprotkin, my son, we shall soon find out," he said benevolently, and while the interpreter translated his words, General and prisoner gazed earnestly at one another. Grischa did not move an eyelash. Dr. Posnanski noticed that the General's eyes and those of the prisoner were almost exactly of the same colour, which was a very subversive prank on the part of Nature, or of God. A silent pact was made between Lychow and the Russian, deeper than either of them knew. "Senfke's eyes and figure!" Lychow's secret soul, but not his mind, remembered. At the moment these earliest recollections did not rise to the surface of his thought, but the ineffaceable memory within him saw in Grischa's living presence a manifest reflection of the dead Grenadier Senfke, who had been the little Otto's faithful mentor from the day when his father, Waldemar von Lychow, Captain in the Second Regiment of Foot Guards, had brought his orderly and factotum home. Who made Otto von Lychow his first catapult? Who made him his first bow of bamboo? On whose shoulders did he ride to battle, broomstick in rest, a paper helmet on his head, and his great round shield—mother's largest saucepan lid— on his left arm? Who was it that had always embodied the ideals of silence, loyalty and self-control, and impressed them on the flaxen-haired boy, who to-day, as Excellency von Lychow, held sway over tens of thousands? Karl Senfke of Hohen-Lychow. Like the man before him, he had a guardsman's figure, narrow eyes deep-set between his forehead and high cheek-bones and fine fair hair, but in the steadfast honesty of his expression he was most of all like Grischa, indeed his very image. If at that moment the General had searched his memory, he would not have found old Senfke, yet Senfke's living counterpart had power over him like some unseen starry influence.

"Splendid fellow," said His Excellency with a sigh: "Once upon a time . . ." he began to remember the boys in their steel helmets and loaded with hand-grenades, whom he had inspected a few days before, those pinched and callow creatures who were learning the soldiers' trade instead of a peaceful business. Here stood the true fighting man, a good six feet of him, broad shoulders and sinewy chest designed and made for war, arms to strike with, legs to carry him to the attack, and a skull to stand many a battering under his steel helmet.

"Just ask him whether he's telling us the truth," he said to the interpreter, as he looked sympathetically into Grischa's face, which was working with violent emotion, while without taking his eyes off the General, he poured out a torrent of protestations in Russian. The interpreter, roused from his usual drowsy indifference by the presence of these distinguished officers, translated every word.

He swore he was telling the truth. He was sorry he had not done it from the start. All he wanted was to go home. The news of peace had turned his head. That was why he had bolted: he was afraid that now he had been caught again he might have to remain a prisoner for years, long after the other men had been exchanged. That is why he had "made his lips crooked with lies," and that was the whole truth, as true as he wore the Cross of St. George on his tunic, and he swore it by the head of his little child that he had not yet seen.

"Strange fellows, these," said His Excellency.

"The sacred privilege of lying has been one of the inalienable rights of men since the days of free education," murmured Posnanski, apologetically; luckily, the General missed the greater part of this somewhat venturesome assertion. He noticed Grischa's curious outfit, and asked Corporal Sacht whether the man couldn't have been turned out a bit better. Sacht hastened to explain that though there were thousands of uniforms hanging up in the Stores, the ordnance officers were as chary with them as God Almighty with his lightning. Von Lychow laughed indulgently.

"They have to be," he said, "that's what they're for. The War won't be over to-day or to-morrow, and we need our good uniforms to keep the soldiers warm. The tunic doesn't look so bad," he added hopefully.

"But you should see his back, Your Excellency," said Sacht, confidentially, and he made Grischa turn around. Grischa knew what was meant: for a moment he showed his strong yellow fangs in a broad grin, then he turned sharply round and showed His Excellency his shoulder-blades where a great patch perpetuated the memory of that frightful shell-splinter. His Excellency examined the place;

and he caught his breath in a sudden gust of sadness. So this infernal War had sent one more tall soldier West, and it was not yet over. Indeed, if the prophets did not err, they would soon be busy on this Front again. Confident as he was, the words, "How long, O Lord," were on his lips, so he silently dismissed Grischa and his escort, and turned to go.

"I like the look of the fellow," he said to Posnanski. "Don't forget to let me know what happens. For to-day he can take an hour's stroll with his guard. A little fresh air will do him good." So saying, he took his departure and went to see his Chief of Staff, Major Grasnick, immersed in his statistics, maps, and paper flags. Perhaps Brest-Litowsk, where the Operations-Section of the Higher Command sat silently working out their plans, might have deigned to wire a little news.

Grischa was still standing with his face turned to the wall: he heard footsteps move away into the distance, but waited for a definite command. Hermann Sacht tapped him on the shoulder.

"Turn round, Russky: it's all right; you've got 'em all stiff; and I've got the Iron Cross. Come into the canteen, and let's wet it."

Grischa heaved his great body slowly round, sat on a bench and said he wanted to rest for a bit. A strange quivering of the knees and heart betrayed the strain of these last ten minutes: but it had been worth it. It would be all right now. A general had looked upon him and there was the gift of life in that look. He would certainly see once more Marfa Ivanovna and his little girl whom he had never known. Then, rubbing his hands, his great round hooded eyes beaming behind their goggles, the Kriegsgerichtsrat came into his room, and said:

"We've done it."

Punctually on the thirteenth of May, the day of the three Ice Saints, Servatius, Pancratius, and Mamertus, Winter set a snowy and frosty signature to his yearly account. Grischa came in with an armful of wood, which he had just sawed up in the courtyard, and standing in the glow of the office fire, piled the logs on the flames, while the Kriegsgerichtsrat dictated to his clerk Bertin a statement to be used in defence of a soldier of the Army Service Corps against a charge of "Concerted insubordination under arms on active service." Suddenly there was a violent knock on the door, and two elderly soldiers in infantry uniform, foreign caps, with haversacks, water-bottles and drinking-cups slung round their middles came into the room. They clicked their heels as they noticed the officer's bright shoulder-straps, and were about to rap out their names and designations:—"Sergeant Fritzke, Lance-Corporal Birkholz, Fifth Company, Eberswalde Landsturm battalion"—when Grischa rose up from his stoking operations, and prepared to leave the room. "Pretty good stage management," thought Posnanski, just as Grischa, raising his arms like a dancing crane flapping its wings, shouted: *"Boshe moi, mein Gott,* Sergeant Fritzke!" And at a signal from Posnanski, his former guard replied:

"Ah, Paprotkin, old bird, we've got you by the leg again."

Then they shook hands, sparkling with joy at this reunion, for men that have once gone through hard times together, love to meet again and learn how each of them has been faring since they parted.

At this point Bertin picked up a document on which several signatures proclaimed, for all eternity, the identity of Bjuscheff and Paprotkin; it bore the official seal, and was attested upon oath. This was the seventh and concluding document in the "Bjuscheff *alias* Paprotkin" dossier, and consisted of only three lines of text, four signatures, and a seal. The rest of it, a generous expanse of white paper, was a positive challenge to "further observations." Bertin lifted his scissors to cut it, for the order to economize paper had gone forth, but Posnanski decreed that this should be graciously spared in honour of the day's events. Then he sent away the two Eberswalder with Grischa, so that they could have a look at Mervinsk, get a meal at the Soldiers' Club, and thence to the canteen for a beer. Officially they were in charge of him (though he was really in charge of them), and they were to bring him back to the office at two o'clock.

"He won't fly away again," said Sergeant Fritzke confidentially to the Kriegsgerichtsrat, whom he at once divined to be a very harmless breed of superior officer, "he's knocked himself dizzy against our window-panes," and then, no doubt in acknowledgment of this apophthegm, Posnanski awarded the two warriors a couple of cigars apiece, which he stuffed between the buttons of their tunics.

Grischa left the warm room with a feeling of vigour and happiness, which blazed in his eyes and thrilled in every movement of his body. Now at last he was himself again. No more Bjuscheff, thank the Lord! No other than Grischa Iljitsch Paprotkin was walking with his two friends through the spring mud. Now all his sufferings would be washed away just as his boots would be cleaned that evening and, after a few weeks' waiting, the whole affair would be put right. It was as though an essential part of himself had passed out of him into his reflection in a mirror; and now the glass had been shattered and the image was restored to him again. Again he walked among his fellows safe and sound, and if his once gay demeanour was now touched with seriousness, that very fact made him feel stronger and more self-reliant. His soul, benumbed by army routine, and awakened by the living experience of his escape and the deadly bludgeon-blow of his conviction as a spy, had begun to grow older and wiser. Though he did not know it, his joy was far other than he once had felt.

Meanwhile Posnanski, with his own hands, tied round the file "Bjuscheff *alias* Paprotkin" a piece of that gaily-coloured ribbon used for parcels sent to the soldiers in the field by thoughtful prof-iteers, and put aside by the careful Prussians for future use; hence the black, white and red ribbon which encircled that bulky package.

"And now away with it to Bialystok," said the Kriegsgerichtsrat, with a twinkle.

✿ ✿

Book Three

MAJOR-GENERAL SCHIEFFENZAHN

✿

Chapter 1

THE POWER OF PAPER

IN those days the War was gripping Central Europe in a hoop of steel. With titanic force, in a welter of savagery, degradation, and cruelty, thirty nations, bent on bringing peace to a distracted Europe, surged against those lands which only the narrow wall of the front line protected from their onslaught. The struggle was at a standstill. Against all the peoples of the earth, the German troops, with the help of the loyal Austrians, Turks, and Bulgars, held their ground, grey, haggard men, without tanks, with only a few airplanes, and a dwindling fleet of submarines. In Palestine, in Macedonia on Lake Doiran, in Roumania and Italy, athwart France and Belgium, and facing England along the Channel and the North Sea; thence through the Baltic to Libau, and on land again through Russia from Windau down to the Bukovina, they fought, sickened, cursed, and died . . . far, far indeed from the clinking spurs of Emperors, Kings, Princes, Field-Marshals, and Generals at the Base.

Meantime in Paris and London the statesmen and politicians trembled at the possibility that the Germans might become aware of their desperate position and make a mighty effort. As the entry of America brought the certainty of their defeat nearer every month, they might nerve themselves to a terrible act of justice—they might evacuate the eastern territories, leaving enough troops to hold the German frontier, and then launch all their forces, nearly eight million bayonets, with guns and shells, gas and flame-throwers, at some given point on the Western Front. If they broke through successfully, there would be no more talk of "concessions in Alsace-Lorraine" and "the restoration of Belgium"—they would virtually have won the War. The Allies, therefore, resolved to set the broken Russian armies on their feet again, but at the same time to make peace overtures through the Pope. Meanwhile the deadly work went on: throughout Champagne and Flanders grenades and machine-guns whizzed and clattered, the limbs of men hurtled bleeding through the air, tunnels filled with dynamite exploded under teeming dug-outs, bombs from airplanes hissed down upon the heads of scurrying men, and rattling machine-guns hemmed the borders of the nation's garments with the chain-stitches of death. The scales of decision, trembling gently, hung level.

In Russia, the corps of officers, especially the Generals under Brussiloff, declared that they could break through the Austrian Front wherever they pleased. The bourgeois Democrats and Socialists, well disposed to the Entente, who sat side by side with old partisans of the Tsar at the head of the new-fledged Constitutional State, thought it very undesirable to darken the birth of their new regime by a defeat and the cession of territory. It was only on the extreme Left that the leaders of little groups of industrial workers, the proletariat strictly so-called, shook their fists and shouted for immediate peace, separate or not. They spoke for the common man; more than two million dead, and some four million wounded, were at their backs. At the moment, the southern part of the Front was a line of lakes and swamps. The spring floods had brought the War to a standstill just at the point where, in the Russians' opinion, their defence would have been weakest. There was time for discussion and decision. Europe lay groaning from loss of blood, hoping against hope for a speedy end to her sufferings, praying with many million silent voices for her deliverance from evil. The simple instinctive wisdom of the people looked beyond the cleverness and cunning of the greybeards and saw that the peace which came earliest would be the best peace of all.

Bertin, the clerk, like many a poet, loved fine paper. An empty page of smooth, richly-grained, dull white paper with the imposing deckle-edges of a patent of nobility, entranced his eyes and thrilled his fingers. He had a collection of books of English handmade paper, of Venetian, yellow-grained paper from the little paper-mills on the Brenta, and great heavy sheets of Dutch manufacture with watermarks and the makers' names upon them. When Posnanski discovered this one day, he sent him to the military store, which was housed in the former Municipal Offices of Mervinsk. There, in the courtyard, he discovered piles of volumes bound in ancient leather, worm-eaten, tied together with string, and sealed. Some of them lay on the ground, torn and tattered; the orderlies had instructions to make use of these old documents to light the fires. Bertin was turning over the leaves of one such tome when he noticed, horrified at this appalling waste, that page after page had been marked in a faint brownish script, "to be left blank." He could read Russian, so he turned back to the text, and his mania for paper laid hold of him when, after reading a few words, he noticed dates varying from 1808 to 1856 upon the pages—registers of a long-forgotten poll-tax on the serfs, payable by their owners, who had been rotting now these hundred years, and recorded by clerks who had long since been crumbling skeletons: it had been paid on "souls" whose grand-children, now free, had died in the armies of the Tsar, or looked forward to a life of widowhood among their orphan children. The Russia of those days was dead, even her fruits were decayed; but here still lay the heap of official paper, ivory-tinted, dove-grey, or dark blue, almost spotless, a century old, and ready to endure for centuries yet, if it were rescued from the hands of the orderlies who had used these treasures to light their fires all the winter through. When Herr Ruppel came back from leave, half-refreshed and half-despairing—he could not say what Germany looked like, but he knew well enough what his wife looked like, and how much she weighed—nobody bothered any more about Grischa's fate, for the simple reason that Captain von Brettschneider in his turn was enjoy-ing four weeks' leave, and Posnanski set Grischa to the task of tearing out blank pages from the heap of documents. He would sit on a stool in the courtyard, or under the roof of a shed, as he preferred, and he, the heir of many serfs, unknowingly destroyed the documents in which his forebears and his kinsmen had been assessed like beasts or chattels. There he squatted with bent back and stiff knees, turning the leaves and tearing them. A dusty vapour rose from the thick bundles of sheets; the chill of winter passed from them into his hands. Incessantly the birds fluttered and chirped in the garden whose low wall adjoined the courtyard. Winter had shot his last shaft and fled. Light and radiant sailed the clouds of June over the magical flax-blue canopy of day.

Grischa was happy. He was safe enough, now that a General had taken up the cudgels for him. When he heard from Bertin, who came every afternoon to feast his eyes upon fresh treasure-trove, that the fighting would probably break out again, and that at any rate there was no sign of peace just yet, he bore his confinement the more patiently and chafed less often at the thought that the spot between the German trenches and the Russian wire, which he had so longed to find, was only a hundred miles or so away. He did not want to fight any more: he wanted to go home. As things now stood, if he got to Russia, he could only hope for a few days' leave. Yet for all his resignation, a frown would often come upon his forehead, because the feeling which sustained his life had been transformed. Grischa felt like a man who has once been wounded, and never risks his life again with the old innocent abandon: objects, sights, and events touched him more deeply now. In the early morning when he had left his cell, where he slept so soundly nowadays, he would sit ruminating over his breakfast, chewing the greenish bread and pouring down his throat the hot brown coffee, made of the juice of burnt turnips, while he stared at his guards' rifles on the opposite wall. (He had got to know the whole company, and every one of them knew him, and his strange chequered history.) Only a few weeks ago he had held the rifle lightly in his hands, a pleasant and familiar thing. The joy of the slayer, slaying from afar, as though he could puff out a human life like the flame of a candle, a full thousand yards away, had filled him with exultant ardour; then he was the man with the bayonet, the fighting man, thrusting and lunging, in the passionate splendid fury of his wild limbs revelling in their strength. But now he was dimly aware of the man on the other side, not only as one who could fire a bullet at him, but also of one who could be hit, whose flesh could be gashed and pierced and could feel the blow and the agony in every fibre of him. When he was splitting logs with his axe, outside Posnanski's door, his soul went out not only to the swinging blade and the steel wedge of the axe behind it, wielded with all the sundering strength of wooden haft and human sinew, but also to the patient wood which split so silkily, and fell apart into smooth-faced fragments. He thought—nay he saw—with his unreflecting, groping vision, the slender, mangled body of the pine or fir, which he was now converting into lifeless logs, and in his disgust he kicked away the block and spat on the haft of his axe as he picked it up again, for that, too, had been hewn out of a tree, and both of them were conspiring traitorously to destroy their brother that had once, like them, been living wood. As he made the fire, he watched the flames leap up, sputtering out blue and yellow sparks, calling forth light and warmth once more, and he stood amazed before the burning logs, the ashes, and the blaze, that seemed to have long slumbered in the pine, and now brought comfort to the races of men, to Posnanski, Bertin, and Grischa Paprotkin.

His mind moved deliberately, dwelling on one object at a time; free from the snares of language he grasped the thing itself and made it his very own. He passed slowly from the active to the contemplative world; without abandoning either, he was equally at home in both. The basting-thread of the great volumes which cracked under his strong fingers, he examined with a knowing eye; they don't spin such thread nowadays, he thought. It lasted longer than the lives of the spinner and the bookbinder. And now it was perishing thus miserably in the fire; it should have been locked up in a cupboard, like Bertin's blank sheets of paper. Here was all this paper, covered with faded ink by men long dead, finding its way into the stove, and no one troubled about the people—the poor serfs whose names and ages were recorded there. He was no scholar; a hundred arts and mysteries were hidden from him. Reading would have saved him from the trap which the Germans had set with their printed notices in seven languages—and he stared at the ground, and sighed heavily when he thought of a certain village far away, and of that night when he had stood silent before a notice-board outside a peasant-woman's hut. The art of writing seemed a thing potent and uncanny. He had seen the "Bjuscheff *alias* Paprotkin" dossier, which lay packed up, ready and waiting for an occasion when it could be sent forward on the first of its official journeys. A duty trip to Bialystok could be pretty easily "wangled," but the Bjuscheff affair alone did not warrant taking a man from his staff duties even for a day; it must wait its time. So day after day Grischa saw his dossier, its blue label and superscription, tied up with the black, white and red ribbon, lying in its appointed place on the broad pine-wood shelf. And he thought to himself that he who walked about here, was much less potent than what was written there between the covers of the file. For what was written there was the truth: a serious matter, certainly. If the paper between those covers lasted as long as the paper in the books he was now destroying, then his story, his lies, his court martial, his sentence, the words of his comrades from the timber-camp, looked like outliving him—him, the man standing there, able to rip the whole package to pieces with his finger and thumb. Such was the magic of reading and writing. It made things live. But Bertin had told him that in these days people did not know how to make such paper. And he shook with sudden laughter; no, the Germans were clever dogs, but nobody on earth could make such paper as the Tsar's mills wove a hundred years ago, except the yellow folk away in China.

But one morning when he appeared at the office, to stave off his hunger with a slice of bread and dripping promised him by Herr Ruppel, for whom he had done many a good turn, he fell back startled and amazed. The papers were no longer on the shelf: *his* papers! Now he knew that his affairs were going forward.

There was nothing now to remind him of Bjuscheff; what a terror he had been! Out of the grave he had leapt upon his neck, or clutched at his throat, and hung there. He was now finally disposed of, sent back to his grave far away in the Cholno forest, in the sandy earth among the tree-roots where was his home, and where the sap and salt of him mingled contentedly with that of the silver firs and pines. Grischa gazed longingly at the tops of the trees, which were straining with all their might to enjoy the short spring of that country. In the intense heats of June one could almost see them growing. In a few days the myriad tiny leaves that formed a feathery canopy above him had turned a dark green. How he would have loved to lie on his back in the forest; strip himself naked on the sunny slope, stuff his clothes into an ant-heap, and so rid himself of lice and of their eggs, for the ants, those silent and assiduous executioners, knew how to root out that

abominable race. He would drink in the intoxicating smell of turpentine and resin, bark and moss and pine needles, and forget the winter which makes a man's bones freeze in his body, the chill of his travelling coffin, the icy fingers of the white forest, the wet boots and clothes he had worn throughout those snowy weeks, and the awful, unappeasable exhaustion of his endless journey up the Niemen. He felt now that his present labours as a prisoner were but a less arduous sequel to what he had then endured, for he had to sleep in a little wooden box, and was always bumping into Germans to the right and left, before him and behind him, with their four-square habits and commands. If only he could once stretch out his arms, and fill his lungs with freedom again! Now his "case" would soon be over, all this cursed foolery that Babka's loving care had brought down on his head. Certainly he would have liked to see her again. "Silly soldier boy," she would growl at him, much too proud of her little stock of cunning—she was too clever by half; and now it was she that was the silly one. Why, she was just like the Devil in the fairy-tale who is always mighty clever and always taken in, cheated by Jews, peasants, soldiers, and everyone else. He would love to tell Babka face to face all these discoveries he had made so slowly and laboriously—to take her by her two plaits of hair and kiss her, and sleep at her side again of nights, the buxom grey-eyed witch. But she was at Vilna, at Antokol or at the Green Bridge: she had forgotten her soldier, and perhaps she had a new one in her arms—why, of course she had. He laughed softly: why shouldn't she? She had a man's head and a man's heart. That sort didn't wait shyly till men married them. And his letter, which the shopkeeper by the church had written, had not been answered. Yes, she had forgotten him, and he, shut up as he was, and always brooding, thought of her more and more. Why shouldn't he?

Yet, in his secret heart he was convinced of Babka's constancy. Indeed, instead of a letter, she herself was coming, walking barefooted through the burning dust of the highroad from Vilna into the heart of Russia—with her grey, piercing eyes, plaits of grey hair, and on her back a basket, for she had to pick berries and mushrooms and sell them, as thousands of women do to earn their daily bread.

God lets the raspberries and strawberries grow for the women and children, so that poor and feeble folk may pick and sell them, and live on them in hungry times. She need fear no policemen: her papers were in perfect order. She was no weakling, and when she chose she could crack a man's head with a cudgel—she need not be afraid. Even if it was forbidden to walk about at nights, there's many an honest traveller that can't get in by dark. So every day, every hour, had brought her a few versts nearer to Mervinsk, ever since she had received the news that her silly soldier man had, of course, been caught by the Germans again, as she foretold. She was really pleased about it. For, once he was over the wire he could have escaped her, but now he could not. She was his, and now she must stand by him. She knew nothing of the details of his story, nothing but the one sentence that Fedjuschka's father had written:

"A prisoner gave me your address. He brought your message. It is awful what low fellows you go about with. God and St. Cyril grant that the English will soon break the Germans' backs. The prisoner's name is Bjuscheff, Ilja Pavlovitsch. I gave him a glass of brandy and two cigarettes. He is imprisoned at the Kommandantur. They want to shoot him."

That he was still alive, Babka did not for one moment doubt, for however she looked at it, she could not see any grounds for shooting him; she knew that the German is methodical and does nothing without a sufficient reason, for in his eyes the reason is as important as the act. And what harm could Grischa have done, unless he had killed some one on the way? She quickened her pace unconsciously, wrinkling her smooth low brow, troubled in heart and tortured by misgivings. If he was still alive, all would be well. If they had shot him, then woe to his murderers! She knew every poisonous herb that grows on the middens and in the woods. There were enough of them anywhere to exterminate a whole company. These thoughts seethed hot and hazy among the normal preoccupations of a harmless, commonplace old raspberry= woman, as they may be seen in any market-square, or of a morning in the streets of any town in Western Russia. Barefooted, her shoes slung by their laces over her shoulders, she hastened on, leaving in

the dust behind her the short broad footmarks of a woman, on the right-hand edge of the road, onwards, ever onwards towards Mervinsk.

Meanwhile, Staff-Sergeant-Major Pont, enthroned behind his table in the orderly room of the head office, raised a well-thatched head and looked at Lieutenant Winfried, who was speaking to him in low and friendly tones. He understood: he was to make out railway passes and papers for Landsturmmann Bertin, the first pass from Mervinsk to Bialystok and back, the second from Bialystok to Berlin and back. His duties might be assumed to occupy him for a week, if the Herr Oberleutnant would sign the order. The A.D.C. smiled and nodded; the official seal and signature of the A.D.C. to a Divisional General counted for something in this world . . . and Laurenz Pont smirked feebly. The army would be unendurable for men from sergeant-major downwards if a mild "wangle" or two did not breathe into it some semblance of humanity. And a quarter of an hour later the sergeant-major, who had once been attached to a regiment of Landwehr artillery, brought back Bertin's papers for signature: four railway-warrants and a type-written document in which all and sundry were requested to facilitate the journey of the bearer, who belonged to the Staff of the Lychow Division, and to give him any assistance he might need; together with a certificate of freedom from lice, forms of obtaining travelling allowances from field-cashiers, and special papers of the Judicial Section at Ost Headquarters. Winfried was glad to observe that nothing was missing from the bulky little packet of papers. By the help of a certain Sister Bärbe, not quite unknown to him under more than one disguise, her friend Sister Sophie had obtained this singular favour for Bertin the clerk. The official part of his journey would take him to Bialystok, where he had to deliver an important bundle of papers to the Intelligence Section (III B), and the documents in the "Bjuscheff *alias* Paprotkin" case to the Judicial Section (IX). Kriegsgerichtsrat Posnanski had arranged the papers in careful order, and added an illuminating summary of the case, in which it was clearly and pointedly set forth what the Higher Judicial authorities were expected to do: which was simply and solely to ascertain which military court in *Ober-Ost*, that vast microcosm of Empire, with its many provinces, was competent to deal with it. If possible, Bertin was to go and call on the Kriegs-gerichtsrat of the military area, a certain Dr. Wilhelmi, in peace-time a district judge somewhere in the Mark of Brandenburg, give him Posnanski's hearty greetings, and so make him directly and personally acquainted with the case—which was more effectual than the strictest adherence to official procedure, and much more so than any pedantic pretension to strict justice. Posnanski had hammered his cynical thesis into Bertin's head with jocose and curious examples. Little effort was needed to take in the learned and sceptical apophthegms with which the lawyer scarified human society for the edification of his clerk. But Bertin's attention was temporarily off duty, and with good reason too. He was afire with his good fortune; his friend Sophie had procured him the happiness of several hours in the company of his wife Lenore in Dahlem. Yes, he said, he would do all he could at Bialystok, see the papers through to the competent authority, and call punctually on the gentlemen of the Press Section, who had telephoned requesting him to do so; but no man who understands the bond between man and woman will be surprised to learn that his strongest impulse was to leave Bialystok as soon as possible, not for the east again, but westwards. . . . It was four and a half months since he had held Lenore in his arms, breathed the fragrance of her hair, seen the soft, veiled look in her grey eyes, or listened to her thrilling, tremulous voice. The harsh arithmetic of army-leave, which treats the common soldier as a man of different clay from the officer and even from his orderly, had ordained that after eleven months' absence Bertin should only be able to stay a day and a half in his own house, and that by favour and against the regulations. The brutal sergeant-major of his A.S.C. battalion had been forced to consent to his last regular leave in July, 1916, though with much ill-will and gnashing of teeth. For four whole days and two days on the journey he had escaped from the almost fetid atmosphere of the 1st Company of the 120th Royal Prussian Army Service Corps Battalion. He would have been due for leave again in March, 1917, at the earliest. . . . At the end of January of this year, however, just previous to his breakdown, he had been summoned by a telegram from Lieutenant Winfried to join the Staff of the Lychow Division, just immediately before it was transferred to the comparative safety of the Eastern Front.

It goes without saying that men who were newly attached to a unit—and a Divisional staff counted as a unit—had no claim to the leave to which they would otherwise have been entitled. In practice, rightly or wrongly, as the latest comers they started at the bottom of the leave-roster, and must wait their ordinary turn. Sergeant-Major Laurenz Pont had pointed this out with unction to the new clerk of the Divisional Court Martial, and added:

"I think the exchange between your A.S.C. company and this office is 'well worth a Mass'."

Then when he heard the answer to his automatic enquiry as to the nature of Bertin's civil occupation, he had opened his eyes incredulously, as he suddenly realized that here was no trumpery little Jewish lawyer, like those that fussed and floundered in every A.S.C. company, but Bertin, the essayist, Bertin, the novelist, Werner Bertin, in fact. . . . So Sergeant-Major Pont had observed:

"Duty is duty, Herr Bertin, and I can't ask you to sit down. I may tell you, however, that when I'm not wearing this coat, I'm an architect and a master-builder, and if my father had not been a foreman-mason up at Kalkar on the Rhine, I should have been Captain of my battery and long since lying with a smashed breast-bone somewhere in Flanders or in Poland. So I'll try to get you a breathing-space in Berlin, if we leave these charming solitudes and go trundling eastward. Of course, you'll count this breath of freedom by hours, not by days—that'll make it sound more" (and he laughed). "As a pretext, I shall entrust you with a small parcel for my wife, on whom you might pay a friendly call at her home in Zehlendorf, only twenty minutes away. You will find her an assiduous reader of your books, Herr Bertin. We must see what can be done about sending you on a duty-trip and so fix you up some leave, which I am sure you deserve. But I must put you on the list in the usual way."

Bertin, who was little enough of a soldier, felt quite overcome by this human and friendly tone, and stammered out some words of thanks; in that hell of an A.S.C. company, that grim, grey desert on the Flabas road, men didn't look and talk like that. And the sergeant-major had positively shaken him by the hand. A sergeant-major!

This time he would manage to cut short his business as before. There must be express trains to Berlin, which took twelve or thirteen hours—a mere trifle! He could be away seven days, and must start back on the afternoon of the sixth day; a day and a half in Bialystok, twenty-six hours in the train there and back, would give him roughly four days in Berlin—four days as a civilian and a Man! Up, then, and forward! His whole soul was quivering with joy. Duty came first, of course, and the documents must be scrupulously conveyed to the proper quarter. . . .

He put nothing in his pack except food for Lenore: a large tin of war dripping, a small smoked ham that he had got from Veressejeff's shop (not to mention seventy-two eggs specially packed in cardboard, which he would carry in his hand), four Russian pounds of lentils, five pounds of peas in small bags, carefully stowed away, and, last and heaviest of all, three loaves of bread, though these were worth their weight in gold. The late spring of 1917, that hungry spring that had left its mark on Germany for many generations to come, should torment his Lenore no longer; indeed, she would not have lasted through the winter without what Bertin had sent her. And then he did something very sensible: he asked Sister Sophie, who with smiling lips and large appealing eyes, was helping him in his preparations, for a sleeping-draught; he was tolerably certain of a seat on the first train, but in any case it would be well to get a little sleep beforehand, for he proposed to brave all the hardships of travel, and go as quickly as he could from Bialystok to Berlin, if he had to stand up all the time or lie down in the luggage-rack.

So he travelled westward, wedged among seven other men of the Division on leave, and huddled into a corner, his luggage between his legs or piled on the rack above his head. The chill evening air of spring was wafted through the half-open window of the overladen, dilapidated carriage, as it pounded on through the approaching darkness. Sleepless and excited, the men about him talked of peace, past battles, and future prospects: whether the Russians would be mad enough to yield once more to the persuasions of the wild men of the Entente, make up the strength of their divisions and launch them in a last attempt against the Austrian Army. God help them if they did! They might have a success or two at first, but then they'd find themselves laid out: grey and set, mad to make an end of it, as once before, the German Landwehr and first-line troops would beat them down, and when the plains were strewn with Russian corpses, perhaps they'd give up the game. This time they'd be home for Christmas, sure enough. Thus, under the dull yellow glare of the lamp, the men sat and smoked, as the train sped through the darkness.

Bertin slept in his corner, his small head in its uniform cap tilted backwards, and jerking forward every time the train stopped and new leave-parties swarmed into the crowded carriage. At last there were ten men crushed against one another, not to mention their packs and equipment, which were piled up on the seats; they were squatting on the ground, huddled together no matter how, after the manner of privates and N.C.O.'s, who, whether they came from the Front, from garrisons, or lines of communication, had no sort of claim to go roaring through the night in comfortable express trains like their betters. And then, as it was night, and they were all friends together, middle-aged men of the Landwehr, Special Reserve or Landsturm, all of them "old hands at the game," who could read between the lines; and as the only youngster among them was crushed up in a corner and snoring loudly, that young —— of a Headquarters clerk with his courier's bags (by which they alluded to Bertin's boyish, sleeping face), they began to speak more and more openly; old soldiers every one of them. . . . Beneath a mask of indifference and scorn they muttered their despair, their infinite and now hopeless exasperation at the monstrous cleavage between the officer caste and the private soldiers, which affected food, clothing, lodging, leave, pay, and even the right of making a complaint. How this gulf was shamelessly and deliberately widened hour by hour; how officers were cold-shouldered for being too friendly with the men; how the "good" officers of each company were ignored, except when it came to fighting. How everything was done to break the self-

respect of the seasoned private soldier, who was only allowed to get
it back by the favour of his officer. They gave instance after instance of the cold brutality of all that was called hospital treatment or medicine; or, indeed, all that was honoured by the name of
science; of the "tripe" their Education Officers, or whatever name
they might be cursed with, crammed into them as "patriotic instruction," grown men and Germans as they were, men between twenty-
five and forty-five, who had long known more of life, politics, political economy, and the duties of a citizen than any rabbit-brained
Colonel or his pack of subalterns. And in the semi-darkness of
the rocking, reeking carriage, some one pronounced the name of a
certain member of the Reichstag, now in prison, one Karl Liebknecht—only casually, of course, for not one of them felt quite
sure of his neighbours, though for seven or eight months they had
suffered and endured together. Beneath all their talk there was an
undercurrent of passionate sympathy for the man.

"You mark my words! We shan't see Liebknecht again. He's
too much our friend."

"Can't we get him out?"

"Not we. You don't know Fritzie. Of course we can't. We're
not Russians. They can do what they like with us."

It was only when the train pulled up with a rasp of the brakes
at Bialystok that the little company aroused Bertin, and chaffingly
helped him out of the train; then he entered upon another world.
Later, he remembered his time in Bialystok as a warm surge of
forty whirling hours. Suddenly he found himself speaking, laughing,
arguing with his fellows. In the yellow house of the Press Section,
faced with tiles, like the greater part of the town, in the ludicrous
style of the 'eighties, he met men like unto himself, intelligent men
of his own generation, passionately concerned for the future of
their country. Among these journalists, authors, painters, teachers, and lawyers, not one of them above the rank of sergeant, all
his constraint fell from him, and the native fire of his spirit leapt
into life that night, as he sat up smoking and talking with them all
in their shirt-sleeves, discussing the horrors of Verdun and Germany's dark destiny. Bertin tried to enliven the conversation by
telling various stories of his own, and among others that of Bjuscheff,

to prove that there was still justice in the army, when a General could hold out a protecting hand over an innocent man, a Russian soldier, and that in spite of all the insanities of war, reason and decency had not perished.

"Glad you think so," said his hearers, and grinned.

Not till next day did he feel once more the gyves of slavery upon him.

About midday, in response to a telephone message from the Press Section, Private Bertin presented himself at the entrance of the Department of Justice, and climbed the majestic staircase. His instructions were, if possible, to see Dr. Wilhelmi personally. But he had no luck. The dossier got no further than the Record Office, and his letter was taken charge of by a spectacled sergeant-major: he could set his mind at ease, the matter would be attended to in due course, but at the moment the Kriegsgerichtsrat was lunching with Major-General Schieffenzahn. If he must see him at all costs, he could communicate with him in the proper way, and in two or three days he would receive an order to report at the Department.

"There's a war on here, my boy," said the sergeant-major, plaintively. "You can stroll about in your pants out there, I suppose. We do things decently here, I can tell you."

For an instant Bertin's heart beat against his ribs. Posnanski had impressed on him the value of a personal interview. But here, behind the lines, where the garrison salved their guilty consciences by adhering to the most rigid etiquette, he would find himself speechless when confronted with the great Wilhelmi, and provoke his highly military strictures on the uniform and appearance of so unsoldierly an envoy. Dreadful prospect! It would be far better if Posnanski himself, or perhaps Lieutenant Winfried, took the opportunity of discussing the matter with the Herr Kriegsgerichtsrat over a bottle of Beaujolais. Thus he reflected, but he deceived himself, for all he wanted was to get straight back to Lenore. And when the sergeant-major peered at him over his glasses, and asked: "Well, my lad, shall I send in your name?" he shook his head in a bewildered and most unsoldierly manner, cleared his throat, and said awkwardly: "No thank you, sergeant-major; if you wouldn't mind just sending the letter forward in the usual way."

"Right!" said Fröhlich, with gruff satisfaction—Wilhelmi hated having anything to do with common soldiers, except insofar as they appeared before him as prisoners—signed a receipt for the "Bjuscheff *alias* Paprotkin" dossier, handed it to Bertin, and let him go.

Late in the afternoon of the same day, a private soldier leapt like a two-year-old, in spite of his heavy pack, on to the footboard of a "D. Train," which bore him away into the happiness of four glorious days at home.

Chapter 2

DOCUMENTS

IN lawyers' offices and judges' chambers bundles of documents are heaped up round the walls. In blue, white or grey cardboard covers, with strips of paper hanging out of them recording the names of the parties and the nature of the case—human fates sprawl over each other like pressed plants in a herbarium, the dried essence of things once alive: momentous actions great and small, strange catastrophies, all the meanness, wickedness, and mistrust of men, pride long trodden under foot and now turning against the tyrant, human dignity for ever worsted in this foul age, naked souls clothed in the arid garment of a legal document, typed, or engrossed in the elegant copper-plate of clerks. Cases concluded, lives that have run their course, lie there tied round with tape and stamped with many seals. It is there that many a conflict ends in victory or defeat, men sicken and pine and die or pass thence free and forgotten. But the documents remain.

Among these documents the order of precedence is dictated by the rank of those concerned. The head clerk regulates the flow of men's destinies from his table in accordance with the eternal laws of the division of labour, viz. much work and little pay, or much pay and little work. Now, in war-time, he puts on a *Litevka* and takes charge of the records; a somewhat smarter tunic adorns the lawyer or the judge, who can afford to be a little testy. Local affairs within the town, or the immediate neighbourhood, he must handle with dispatch, especially as there are other gentlemen interested in them, whose uniforms are as smart as his, and who are quite ready to administer a gentle reminder. Such matters are the test of a good sergeant-major (Records). Against the ground-bass of chronological sequence, he plays skilfully on the key-board of urgency. For thanks to that most tyrannical of all social organizations, the Army, which uses all the inventions of the twentieth century and the exultant cruelty of the human animal to rivet its yoke upon men's souls, the comfort of the High and Mighty Ones, even their daily moods, is the law of life to their poor subjects. Their displeasure falls like thunder, their goodwill brings fortune and the bread of favour. The whole duty of the Subordinate is to make himself agreeable to his Superior.

In the administrative section of the Staff, to which the Judicial Department belonged, a division in the field was not regarded with inordinate respect. As the Commander-in-Chief's chair was the hub of the military universe, values diminished as they receded from the centre to the circumference; the front line meant very little. (In the Operations Section, of course, a somewhat different scale of values was applied.) The Divisional Commander, von Lychow, an infantry general, did not often show his face here at Bialystok or at Brest-Litovsk either. He was a comical old fellow, a father to his men, but with no great social gifts. Once or twice in the mess, of course in Lychow's absence, Major-General Schieffenzahn, the all-powerful, had made him the subject of his bitter wit. On the other hand Lychow stood surprisingly high in the Emperor's favour. Hence, according to Staff mathematics, which restored the old courtly arithmetic under a modern guise, anything from Lychow was to be treated outwardly with supreme respect, but not much real attention need be paid to it.

The cases coming in to the Department of Justice in a single day, still more in a week, made an astonishing total. Crime in the army grew apace. The military prisons at home were long since filled to overflowing, so that thousands of condemned soldiers were confined in the civil prisons, while thousands more were enrolled in penal battalions and many others after conviction were sent back to their units to earn their pardon, an official phrase at which they often laughed. In those days the army was the nation. Penalties dating from the days of the Landsknechts were inflicted on men of thirty or forty who had been blameless citizens in private life. Their superior officers were often little prigs of twenty years old, five or six of which they had spent at their mothers' apron-strings and ten under the schoolmaster's rod; or moth-eaten old dug-outs, whose arteries ossified at the very name of socialist. So the higher authorities of the Military Department of Justice had enough to do in appeasing these fire-eaters and finding extenuating circumstances in the cases sent up to them. For men in the trenches, very few suitable penalties could be found. Field-punishment had aroused a great deal of bad blood in the army, and led to countless disputes; moreover it had given an inconvenient handle for attacks in the Reichstag. There had been an endless succession of speeches, instructions, and orders to hush up awkward cases. There were also the civil courts in the occupied districts, which were administered under Russian law, but not in accordance with the generous Russian temper, which that law presupposes and requires; and thirdly, the multifarious cases in which the civil population had suffered at the hands of the soldiery and vice versa. In a word, the Department of Justice (IX) was far from idle. The dossier with the two Russian names upon it, and its accompanying letter from the Kriegsgerichtsrat of Lychow's Division, and a Jew into the bargain—there could be no great hurry about that. It rested snugly, somewhat on one side of one of the innumerable pigeon-holes, soon to be half-hidden by other papers. That corner of it on which the contents were inscribed gradually began to collect the dust of time. Wood-shavings, tiny particles of coal or ashes, the offscourings of all human things, and myriads of tiny living organisms, gathered over it.

Meanwhile the man, the living man, upon whom the dossier in that far-off city had cast its shadow, pursued his occupations peacefully from day to day. Grischa was watching and waiting confidently for the unravelling of his tangled destiny. The General had seen him, he had stood up to a General—there was no more cause for anxiety, especially as that clerk with the goggles had assured him that his period of arrest here would shorten his subsequent imprisonment considerably. Prisons cannot afford to feed many idle mouths in war-time. He would be sent to work in various places. At the moment he was helping a Jewish carpenter who had been called in specially by the Kommandantur to make more coffins. Every morning a soldier of the guard opened the great shed where the tools had spent a cheerful night together with the nails and wood; then the short, grey-bearded Täwje Frum, his bright eyes looking out from myriad wrinkles, his hair and the side-curls that marked his race already almost white, his reddish, goat-like beard streaked with grey, took up the plane and hammer and, under his guidance, Grischa, almost a head taller than his little master, set up the sawing-trestles and the bench in the open air. Then they began to work: Grischa in his grey patched drill trousers and jacket, much stained, while the master had thrown off his greenish-black caftan, rolled up his sleeves, and tucked his trousers into his boots, in such a way that between his trousers and his waistcoat four long, bright-coloured tassels hung down—for it is written: "Make thee cords and tassels on the four corners of thy garment."

Reb Täwje was a little brisk Jew, with a lively tongue, much given to jesting. Round his eyes a smile was always lurking, and he was as quick to anger as to laughter, though his wrath never lasted very long. His great delight was brandy—not that he drank heavily, but he liked a drop now and again out of a flat bottle, such as can be carried in one's boot, and could only be filled because he was popular with the Kommandantur. For distilling and selling brandy was a German privilege; it put the Jewish innkeepers out of business, or tempted them to start illicit stills, while it sent up the price of their beloved schnapps. "Alas!" thought he. "What other comfort hath man upon this earth? The Torah serves the soul, a page of the Gemara or a verse of the Talmud may refresh his mind, but what remains for the body, poor forsaken creature, if brandy cannot be come by? Herrings are as rubies. And as for eggs—they could not be bought before the War because there was no price for them—three could be had for only two kopecks—but now, in war-time, eggs have vanished. And what about the bread, I ask you! brown like gingerbread, but otherwise not like anything on earth, God forgive me for saying so! War eats up all men, old and young alike."

Mervinsk was a Jewish town. In the mean, timbered houses of its straggling or winding streets dwelt thousands of Jewish families. As at Vilna, their beloved capital, so in all the smaller hamlets, villages, and towns they amounted to nine-tenths of the population. They were the tailors and shoemakers, the glaziers and the tinkers, the carpenters and cab-drivers, bookbinders and wheelwrights. They were the shopkeepers; and they were the citizens. Even in peace-time they had lived in grinding poverty, huddled in dreadful squalor, Jew snatching from the mouth of Jew his livelihood and profit, like the fish in the glass tanks of the great fish-shops, not because they liked to live so, but owing to the policy of the Tsardom which had driven them at the beginning of the nineteenth century, after the partition of Poland, out of all the villages and cooped them in the towns, for they were forbidden to emigrate into Russia proper. Incessantly were children born to them, and, as incessantly, they died.

At Mervinsk and all over the province they were dying of dysentery. At Bialystok, in that month, thirty or thirty-five bodies were buried daily, but Bialystok had many more inhabitants, so that at Mervinsk only four or five would be taken off. Just starvation.

"Men," Täwje would explain to Grischa, "are such stupid crea-tures, that they'd rather eat green apples than nothing at all."

And if you ate too many green apples you would die. Täwje was one of fortune's favourites, for the soldiers of the Kommand-antur, when he came for his pay, gave him bread, good ration-bread, well-baked, which did not weaken the stomach and lie upon the guts like a lump of dough. It was in Russian that he told him all this and more, for language is no barrier to a Jew; and Yiddish, their mother-tongue, is so like German that Jews and German soldiers could understand one another easily enough, though of course with frequent blunders. And so God, whose name be praised, gave work to Reb Täwje Frum. Coffins were so much in request because the body of a Jew or Jewess could not be flung into the earth without one! Such a heinous sin was inconceivable, and as the Kommand-antur now held the keys of worldly power, it had to provide the cof-fins, not only for the soldiers who died in the hospitals, but also for the civil population whose swollen or shrunken bodies were silently carried out from the dysentery huts—for the religious rites of the various sections of the population were scrupulously observed. And so, since Bertin's departure and return, Grischa stood every day in that corner of the carpenter's shed of the Kommandantur helping to plane coffins for dead Germans or dead Jews. At first Täwje only let him hold the planks along the trestles while he sawed them level; later on, Grischa himself was allowed to saw. It takes a long time to learn to handle a plane, which is a sensitive instrument whose laws must be mastered like every other tool that is an extension of men's hands. But the art of driving in nails so that they hold together two planks, straight and true, at the right angle, or glueing them together—he was already learning from Täwje. So they made friends over their work.

The sunshine lay in a radiant haze over the broad lands of Russia. The great chestnuts in a corner of the court-yard gave welcome shade, and the rich colour of the heavens was fading to a pale monotonous blue. In the trenches yonder at Naroczsee, on the Stochod, on the Zlota Lipa, as on the Dvina further to the north, the ground was gradually solidifying; no longer the soldiers floundered in the squelching mud. The dust began to whirl about the streets, and beyond the Front, hung, like the fingers of great yellow gloves, the captive sausage-balloons. The earth was dry enough; now blood might flow once more.

And this is what Grischa and Täwje talked about. Of course the old Jew knew the precise history of his assistant: he took a great interest in it, thought it over, and asked many a shrewd and searching question. He knew a deal of the ways of the world, did this old carpenter. As the Torah and the Talmud contain the whole life of man, he thought out Grischa's story in their terms. The reality of military regulations, and their validity in law, had no great weight with him. He saw it all: here was a man who wanted to go home, like his own name-sake Tobias, from a far country, or, like Absalom, had listened to ill counsel on his road; who had sinned in taking a name not his own, almost like Abraham when he gave out that his wife Sarah was his sister—for a man does not receive his name by chance but from the Spheres of Heaven. So this man had been cast into a den like David or Joseph, and, like Uriah, been condemned to die. But God had opened his mouth like Balaam's ass, and he was returning to the truth like Jonah; and now he found favour as Esther had found favour; the mighty man of valour heard him graciously: his condemnation was forgotten. And as it had been put away, and the sin of his false name purged, some better thing would certainly befall him. Täwje found matter for reflection in all this: men and women came from far and bore testimony to Grischa, and he found righteous judgment, though he was a prisoner from among the company of prisoners. All this was marvellous in his eyes and plainly showed the hand of God. He was elated when he thought of Grischa's story and he would talk of it on Sabbath nights to the old man who studied the Gemara with him. A man must refresh his soul after the day's work, and forget his hunger.

So Reb Täwje would contemplate his assistant, as they sawed planks together in their shirt sleeves. They planed them smooth, nailed them together, and heaped the shavings into a little pillow at one end, that the head of the sleeper might be honoured, and lie a little higher than his body. Burying the dead was a great and solemn duty. At the Last Judgment, when they should all arise, they would testify also for those that had made their coffins. So here in their corner by the wall, Grischa and Täwje were earning the bread of holiness. And even the Captain of the Kommandantur, though he neither knew nor cared about such things, reaped the prayers and intercession of the dead.

Chapter 3

PORTRAIT OF AN AUTOCRAT

THE only touch of brightness in the lofty room was the pale blue of the walls, on which square patches, where pictures had hung, were not yet faded.

Major-General Schieffenzahn sat at work in a blue civilian jacket, and his front view was most impressive: a straight tall forehead over a pair of small grey eyes, the manifest nose of an autocrat, beneath it a moustache trimmed in the English manner, a shrewd, subtle mouth, the whole face set squarely upon a majestic double chin above the red collar of the General Staff. Broad-shouldered and tall, he sat enthroned at his writing-table, looking quickly through some newspapers, and marking them in blue and red pencil. But seen in profile, from near the great tiled stove, his appearance was far less imposing: the whole magnificient effect was strangely and sadly marred. He had the sagging cheeks of an old woman, his shoulders were too round, and from the oval outline of the weak receding curves of chin and forehead the nose stood out sharply like the beak of a parrot, with two ominous wrinkles at the nostrils and the bridge deeply marked by the spectacles he wore for writing. And when he got up, as he did now—to put a sheet of paper covered with bluish writing on a pile of other such sheets—his appearance seemed to shrink. His legs in their black red-striped trousers were too short, and he had small hands and feet, so that although he could pass for a giant when seated, when standing he was revealed as no taller than a man of average height.

The public knew little of Albert Schieffenzahn but what was conveyed in phrases such as: "the illustrious colleague . . ." or "the devoted comrade-in-arms . . ." followed by a certain famous name. It was, in fact, the truth that in that cropped skull was the directing brain of the whole area between the Baltic and the Carpathians. It was not, indeed, a mind that worked in darting flashes of inspiration; it was far more like a brightly-lit central exchange in which consciousness, judgment, and purpose were organized and controlled. Behind that brow of his was a vast system of ordered knowledge. Whether it had been decided to erect a new depot or hospital, or lay out a new road or field-railway, he would make the scheme his own and ponder over it with loving care. He had the constructive imagination of the artist in planning and carrying out great works.

His creative will was embodied and made manifest in that land. Not a single soldiers' club or cinema was started, not a plank was laid for a munition depot, without his consent. The railways in his area, their time-tables, their carrying capacity, their engines and rolling-stock, moved in his mind like the threads in the action of a play. If any new tasks were laid upon him, he calmly called up such of the resources of his mighty brain as were needed to effect them. In the first nine months of the War he had carried out the transport of troops, the organization of offensives, a great retreat across a network of rivers, and finally the conquest of the country; then came the gradual organization of a complete system of civil government, though when he first took it in hand he knew nothing but the strength and position of the fortresses, army corps, lines of communication, and strategic railways.

Suddenly, with unimaginable comprehensiveness and speed, the whole country took shape in his mind: the forests and plains, the nature of the soil, the mineral resources, and the factories. He summoned all manner of experts, who were ordered to lay before him statistics and plans from which he could deduce the possibilities of development in each area. Then he perplexed these pundits with questions which showed that though he knew much less than they, he had a far deeper insight into all the districts and their several needs. A new currency must be introduced; he introduced it. A system of savings-banks had to be established throughout the land according to the needs of urban or rural areas; he established it. An entire system of education had to be set up, and it came into existence. The sanitary administration of this war-stricken region was his especial work. There rose up everywhere institutions for

the "delousing" and disinfection of the population and their clothing, baths, isolation huts, and hospitals.   He enforced a system of
travelling incinerators.   He introduced German book-shops in the
towns, created field-libraries, and continually added to their stocks.
Newspapers in the seven languages of the country were needed, so
paper factories had to be erected, and printing-presses soon were
busy everywhere, printing in German, Russian, Lithuanian, Polish,
Yiddish, Lettish, and Esthonian.   The distances in this part of the
world were so great that he had already thought out and plotted on
the map a scheme for the first regular airplane service of Europe,
to supplement the communication between Libau and Brest-Litovsk;
then with the machines he had to spare, he organized a regular air-
service, which was to ply in all weathers across his broad domain.
The Operations Section of the Staff was indebted to him and his
all-powerful imagination for the most illuminating hints on the
minutest points, but he took no less pains over the erection of mills
on the faster rivers, for he wanted new water-power to provide the
current for lighting his new constructions by electricity, and he controlled the close and far-flung meshes of the telephone-lines from
the Front to his writing-table and thence right across Germany to
Supreme Headquarters.

The walls of his office were covered with huge tables setting
forth, as clearly as possible, the various nationalities of the occupied
territory and the political parties of each one—indeed, he had extended his researches as far as Poland and even Russia proper.   He
had secret notes of the channels by which the various political groups
might get into touch with the appropriate centres in Germany.   By
the agency of his Political Section he kept control over the inter-
course between the population of the area and the civil authorities
of the Empire, the Reichstag, the Government, and the political
parties.   Not a man of any importance could cross the frontier unless Albert Schieffenzahn had scrawled a "Yes" upon his application.   Even the various religious bodies of the country, and their
schools as well, felt his influence, insofar as he admitted, or (quite
illegally) withheld, the money sent them from neutral countries for
relief.

His colleagues worshipped him.   In his husky, high-pitched voice, but always courteously, he gave his orders in the form of requests, or as if the suggestion had come from his subordinates and he was merely giving it expression. Numerous as was his staff, he knew the trend of all their thoughts and the tastes and opinions of the "intellectuals" among them, while his eye rested unseen on the corrupt manœuvres of those who sought to enrich themselves, whether on a petty or a generous scale. He was remaking the country day by day, improving and modernizing it; by ridding the land of weeds, testing suitable manures and seeds, sheep-rearing and bee-keeping, and detailing parties of prisoners of war for various tasks, and requisitioning boilers, machines, houses, and land.

The motive of his action may be stated in a word: he wanted this territory to be in a prosperous state when it came to be annexed to the German Empire after the War; and he had already adapted the railway lines of his area to the German gauge. He was perfectly clear that the Germans were only beginning to play their part in history; to his mind they were the nation chosen to rule, create, and fortify the breed of men. He had never spent a single hour in the west or in the south; he therefore saw the people of those countries in the light of his reading, which was chosen, though quite unconsciously, to gratify his prejudices. At the present moment he was peacefully marking extracts from newspapers and from the reports of secret service agents which were circulated by the Foreign Office for the enlightenment of the initiated; and he accepted as established fact, reports that were solely designed to flatter the hopes of those who shared his view. For agents who dealt in unwelcome news soon fell into disfavour, and lost their employment; they found themselves mysteriously recalled or transferred to the army.

In his work nothing troubled him so little as the wishes, views, and traditions of the population. He, Schieffenzahn, understood what was good for these gentry much better than they did themselves. They had to accept and carry out his edicts, even when they had no notion of their purpose. He looked on them as not yet of age, and in need of guidance, like the rank and file of the army, into whom he hammered his aims, his thoughts, and his political views, by means of his system of "patriotic instruction." It was for him to command; and his was the responsibility. It was for them to obey, to follow and bow down. If they did not they must be trodden under foot. From a great height, as though from a captive balloon poised far above them, he looked down upon his realm, his towns, forests, fields, and scattered herds of men, and saw—nothing.

He said he had no need of honour, fame, or recognition: power sufficed him. He enjoyed a cigar, good food, stories about Bismarck, his daily ride with only one or two companions, a drive in one of the staff cars as far and as fast as possible, and cheerful and light conversation with his personal staff or his guests; and he enjoyed his measureless powers of work. He hated opposition, independence of mind, laziness, the vast incompetence of human creatures; and remorselessly he hated disorder, sedition, the Western chatter about democracy, and the detestable Nihilistic revolution in the East. In those March days when, by a tacit agreement, fighting ceased, and Russians and Germans visited each other's trenches and fraternized, he very soon issued orders in all directions that this deplorable proceeding must be strictly limited to what might be desirable for the purposes of espionage, and when, near Jakobstadt, the commander of a post incontinently made prisoners of twenty-six such Russian visitors, he singled him out for special praise and smiled with sardonic satisfaction when he was informed, through spies, that the news had spread a wave of indignation throughout the entire Russian Eastern Front. He had been waiting impatiently for the beginning of the Russian offensive. His triumph at his last experiment could be read between the lines of his reports to Headquarters. As was expected, they broke through at Smorgon and Brzezany. He merely nodded. Krevo in the north, Konjuchy in the south, were lost—("dear, dear!"). When he heard that the Russians had made a sudden attack on Jakobstadt and in their fury exterminated the whole garrison, he did frown slightly—("how very unfortunate!"). Then he listened with satisfaction to details of the Russian losses at the southern corner of the Front. There the last divisions of the Russians who had any fight left in them, lay strewn in a dreadful harvest of death. Then came the counter-thrust, and the Allied Armies attacked. The general scheme was Austrian; Schieffenzahn had worked it out—and all went according to plan. The advance of the steady German columns into mangled and chaotic Russia proceeded without interference. Only Schieffenzahn knew what he was aiming for—he had settled that long ago—Kieff, Odessa, and the Crimea (corn, ships, and the Black Sea). He meant to cut a slice off Russia, and to cut it where he chose. He smiled at the idea that the Americans could play any part worth mentioning in the West; and as to the end of the war, his mind was easy. The Austrian Commander-in-Chief had drawn up a plan for a joint break-through in the West by an attack in the plain of the Po and an advance on the French flank from Italy. Before that, by September or October, he would have taken Riga, Dorpat, Reval, perhaps Petrograd, and certainly Dünaburg.

On this radiant morning he was receiving a representative of the Naval Staff to discuss with him the possibility of combined operations by land and sea. Outside the door of his ante-room hung the red light which meant that no man on earth was allowed to enter. When the officer in his blue and gold tunic had left him, it was understood that, in a few months, the Fleet would attack and take the islands of Ösel and Dagö and gain command of the Gulf of Riga after breaking through the mine-field. This was an essential preliminary. The Baltic fleet had paid dearly for an attempt on the coast: eleven destroyers had been detailed for a night-bombardment of a perfectly innocuous railway station, formerly the scene of a decisive interview between two Emperors, and only four ships silently returned. Mines . . . five hundred drowned.

He then proceeded to telephone to the Political Section about the next visit of German Members of Parliament to his area. He impressed on them that they were responsible to him that not one of these gentlemen should be allowed to move a step except in the company of an officer specially attached to him.

"Feed them well, stable them well, and keep them well in hand," he said, with a laugh of satisfaction; he was the man to ride those Parliamentary war-horses.

An orderly brought him tea and sandwiches. Still chewing, he discussed with Captain Blaubert, the Head of the Press Section, certain unostentatious measures for preventing the troops and even the civil population from seeing the less reactionary journals, which were read in spite of the censorship and martial law. This could be done by special arrangements for circulating newspapers and by making a man's promotion largely contingent on his orthodox opinions—but it had to be done with a certain discretion. If a man preferred to buy a democratic paper some days late, rather than the morning's issue of a conservative paper, he was free to do so. At the same time, Schieffenzahn took occasion to point out to Herr Blaubert that one of his lance-corporals, the Rhineland poet, Heinz Flügelig, displayed beneath his tunic a high white stand-up collar; which was contrary to orders. Finally, the General reminded Herr Blaubert of the order that puttees were only to be worn by men suffering from injuries to the legs. Then the Liaison Officer of the Operations Division arrived with his report on the recent severe fighting near Trembovla, setting forth the exact losses of the Russians in killed, wounded, and prisoners; and he received detailed orders for the immediate adaptation of the captured artillery park with a view to the storing of German ammunition there, for the instruction of German gunners in the use of the guns, chiefly of Japanese or American manufacture, and lastly for the construction of depots for brass shell-cases.

After this, at twelve o'clock, Schieffenzahn gave a long interview to Deputy Schilles of the Ruhr. This pale politician, with his short, pointed beard and Mongol eyes, attired in a loosely fitting suit, was the greatest industrialist on the Continent, king of coal and iron and many ships, and the leader in the fight for the annexation of the ore of Lorraine and the mines of Northern France. He sat in the only comfortable chair in the room, his delicate hands lying limply on the arm of it. They spoke with mutual respect but considerable caution; there were long pauses while they sucked at their cigars. Though they had common interests, they suspected each other of divergent purposes. While the king of commerce, nodding his head from time to time with gentle emphasis, was really implying that the subjection of the whole State to the interests— he called them the necessities—of Heavy Industry (by which he meant himself) was essential, if the War was to be won at all, Schieffenzahn smiled secretly at these "bagmen" who tried to use their money to set themselves above the State. He meant to go with them as far as suited him, and shake them off when the time came.

For in the last resort, power lay with the sword. He did not know that this pale, and probably unhealthy, wearer of a bowler hat had been reckoning for the past year on a serious weakening of the State, which he had been expecting confidently since the loss of the battle of Verdun. To the mind of such a man, this diminution of power and prestige would naturally take the form of a fall in the currency. Never again would the German mark go back to par, or even the rate at which it now stood at Zürich. For he understood why, on this neutral Bourse, it immediately rose a few points whenever there was a prospect of an early peace, but at once began to fall when German victories, victories though they were, made it probable that the War would be prolonged. Accordingly, for the past year, he had been borrowing more and more marks from the Reichsbank. He was sure the War would end in a cash victory for him.

To-day he was softly debating with Schieffenzahn—all for the good of the Fatherland—the transference of twenty or thirty thousand civilian workmen from the occupied territory, since General Headquarters had kindly consented to relieve him of the care of his turbulent and embittered malcontents, and the fellows had been called up. Moreover, by replacing them with Jewish, Polish, and Lithuanian robots, he would save a good third of their wages: and finally (still pursuing his financial theories) he was anxious that the Ober-Ost savings banks should allow the dependents of these new workmen a substantial advance upon their wages; after the War, the account could be easily settled. The mark had, in fact, fallen to not much more than fifty per cent of its par value, so that the war material continually pouring out of his factories—guns, shells, rails, equipment, and trucks—debited in gold or in Swiss francs, yielded a hundred and eighty per cent above the normal and agreed profit.

With these schemes still lurking in the background of his acute and sensitive intelligence, he inveigled the General into admiration— genuine admiration—of the astonishing scope of what he was attempting. They talked sagely enough of all these possibilities, and concurred at last in a proper detestation of Schilles's colleagues in the Reichstag, and their plans for overtures of peace: in this, and this alone, they were heartily at one. The Chancellor, a moralist and a metaphysician, though he wore a major's uniform when he read speeches from the Throne, who had caused and was still causing incalculable damage by his statement about Belgium on the outbreak of the War, was just about to retire into outer darkness. But there were swarms of deputies of the Centre and the Left who seemed to yearn to form a peace-cabinet: and only the military caste stood staunchly behind the resolute programme of the patriotic societies which, for the sake of Germany's future, would have nothing to do with any statement that involved the surrender of Belgium. Of course internal politics must be left alone and, in particular, there must be no suspension of the existing Prussian franchise, as a result of which, based as it was on three classes of taxpayers, Albin Schilles possessed about as much voting power in the State as three million soldiers in the field. So they agreed upon a series of red-hot articles in the Army newspapers, urging that it was an insult to the Army at the Front to offer it any sort of bribe for its heroism and degrade the inborn political rights of man to the level of the small change of the parliamentary cattle-market. A fleeting smile crossed their faces as they looked at each other—the pale, gaunt, black-bearded man with his heavy eyelids, and Schieffenzahn so plump and rosy—and then they went to lunch.

Schieffenzahn ate, as his custom was, with the gentlemen of his Staff, who were not allowed to wait for him. It was half-past two: so long had their discussion lasted.

Their footsteps echoed down the desolate-looking mess-room, which was a drawing-room in what had once been a small palace belonging to Count Branitzky. At the end of the table sat the Kriegsgerichtsrat, Dr. Wilhelmi, gloomily attacking his roast beef.

Until a quarter of an hour ago, in the sultry office, always deserted in the middle of the day, he had been waiting for Fräulein Emilie Paus, little Paus with her charming legs, who since the release of so many clerks for active service, had shone as a star of minor magnitude among the lady-typists. Wilhelmi was courting Fräulein Paus. As the bold minx soon perceived that the fat Wilhelmi really meant to marry her, she bewildered the old gentleman with teasing glances and coy denials, while she diverted herself light-heartedly with one of those lieutenants whom a kindly Providence had provided for the entertainment of the girls at Bialystok. (It was true that she had turned him down, so that she might one day be called Frau Landgerichtsdirektor Wilhelmi. She had promised to bring some papers to Wilhelmi's door at half-past one, but she had already made up her mind to send in her stead an unwelcome messenger in the person of Sergeant Barenscheen, who had also dared to pay his addresses to her. Punctual to the minute, she took down from the shelves the first file she saw, carefully dusted it, and with a melting glance pressed it into his hand, saying that the Herr Kriegsgerichtsrat wanted it before lunch. It was the "Paprotkin *alias* Bjuscheff" dossier. The great man rapped out an infuriated oath which made the messenger grow pale. But the dossier was now lying open on Wilhelmi's table. Quivering with wrath at the little wretch, but still faintly hoping that he might hear her giggling outside his door, he waited till lunch-time in his office-chair, studying, at first with indifference, and then with more attention, the dossier that Dr. Posnanski had bequeathed to him. The case was not without interest. He could easily telephone and find out the proper court to deal with it. The legal procedure had been perfectly correct: old Lychow had Divisional Martial Law at his finger-ends. Wilhelmi had a taste for niceties, as, indeed, was proved by his passion for the slim and dainty Emilie. There were many larger ladies in the various sections who had gone there in the hope of adventures, and would soon have come to terms with a Kriegsgerichtsrat. "Officers' mattresses," the soldiers called them. Finally Wilhelmi emerged, and walked over to the mess in gloom and solitude, determined to console himself after lunch with a few glasses of cognac. What was the creature at? She often made eyes at him, let him take her in his arms, and then fobbed him off. Perhaps she was playing the lady; very well, then, if nothing else would do, he would take her to the Registrar's office and get her that way. Besides, after the War, a bachelor would not be so likely to get on. His Majesty had urged his illustrious Consort to show especial favour to married people—for the Emperor always needed soldiers.

Wilhelmi was overjoyed when he saw what table-companions his ill-luck had bestowed on him—Schieffenzahn and Albin Schilles, two of the most influential men in Germany at that time, and both of them joined him in a meal of soup, fish, roast beef with fresh vegetables and a cream rice pudding. He listened humbly to their laughter as they exchanged anecdotes. When the black coffee came, he had the chance of saying a word, and he made a pointed and amusing story out of the dossier—a man's fate in a file—that had been referred to him from the Lychow Division.

"Ah, old Lychow," said Schieffenzahn, nodding, and he grinned a little: "the soldiers' daddy!"

"Yes," said Wilhelmi, with an obsequious laugh, "this time he's writing whole pages about a Russian prisoner."

The lord of a hundred thousand workmen raised his eyebrows and gazed ironically at the lord of nearly a million men. Wilhelmi seized his opportunity, and told the tale with neat and humorous turns of phrase: a deserter, who had been caught by the police, after he had been duly condemned to death (in accordance with Order No. So-and-so), had revealed himself as an escaped prisoner from a German camp. The Division had had him identified, and it had now become the business of Ober-Ost to discover which was the proper court to try him. Schilles marvelled at the delicacy of the military machine which, notwithstanding its tremendous burdens, could seize on such minute occurrences. Schieffenzahn, with his cigar in the corner of his mouth, and his hands on the arms of his chair, looked from one to the other: then he yawned slightly, begged pardon, stretched himself, and observed—that he might be mistaken, but in his opinion this was a political matter.

"I should be much obliged, Herr Kriegsgerichtsrat, if you would bring me the papers to read this afternoon, and I will decide the point. Shall we say four o'clock?"

Wilhelmi, quite overcome by the prospect of such close collaboration with the great man, bowed ecstatically three or four times. This was indeed luck! After all, Schieffenzahn was worth five Fräulein Pauses, and such glory was perhaps the best way of enticing her to share his lonely bed.

Book Four

THE FULLNESS OF TIME

✡

Chapter 1

THE OLD LOVE

A RUSSIAN shopkeeper in Mervinsk of the type of Mr. Veressejeff
has so much to endure from regulations and from his fellow-men
that he is always half choking with suppressed irritation. So if he
shouts abuse at any miserable sponger who comes into his shop, not
of course to buy bacon, but to borrow a bit of string, or ask the
way—some unorthodox Jew, for instance, or some peasant woman—
he is only fulfilling a natural human function; for a man cannot
always be consuming his own smoke, he must have a chance of
belching it out sometimes. There stood Vladimir N. Veressejeff
behind his counter, worn with age, wearing a fur cap on his bald
head though it was now midsummer, pouring forth a foul stream
of contemptuous ribaldry upon the ill-favoured woman who was
standing patiently in the doorway listening to his insults with a
quizzical smile.

"Get out of this! You look like a sow in woman's clothes. The
way to the prison, eh? Is that what you've got me out for? Did
they rub groats in your eyes when you were a baby, so that you
couldn't see anyone in the street to ask? Oh, no, you had come
into my shop to sell your dirty raspberries. But Saint Eudoxia or
Afanasia, or whatever guardian angel was cursed with the charge
of such a filthy soul, has led you wrong, if you're coming to beg
here. I'm a beggar myself, even if I do look like a respectable trades-
man. All I've got left is time to pay my taxes, and you and your
dirty friends want to steal that from me. Out with you!" he shouted.

He had worked himself into a genuine passion. The brandy
monopoly, the railway administration, the post, the military police,
had all contributed to this outburst. The fact that he had launched
it now, and on this particular woman, was rather due to human

nature in general than to the immediate circumstances. Then the woman opened her mouth, lifted up her basket again, and said:

"Why are you so angry, little Father? I am only bringing you a message from Fedjuschka, your little son, your darling little treasure, and perhaps a letter too, from him to his little father. But as you are so bothered, Vladimir Nicolaievitch, I'd better take it to the police, and the message too. They're sure to be civil and say thank you."

As if his beard had suddenly grown so heavy that he could not raise his lower jaw, the testy old gentleman stared at the woman who was smiling into his eyes with bold derision.

"Yes, I'm Babka, little Father," she said, nodding familiarly. "Why shouldn't I come and see you for once? Wasn't your boy my guest and friend for many months? Still—uninvited guests— I quite see that! I suppose I must get used to the way to prison, you hard-hearted old ruffian. Wait till they put Fedjuschka in, and you'll learn it all right, little Tsar of all the Russias."

Then Veressejeff did the wisest thing he could. He laughed loud and heartily, stretched both hands out to Babka, and appeared enraptured at her visit, though he made little impression on her cool ironical attitude. However, she consented to stay with him, and report herself to the police as the aunt of his long-suffering wife. Soon she was enjoying a piece of bacon with bread and salt, and a glass of schnapps in the back shop, from which she could see, through the barred glass door and the dirty little shop-window, the sunlit square, above which towered the cathedral, yellow-tiled, glittering with its golden roofs in the rich radiance of that summer day.

This meal meant more than mere eating and drinking; it meant reconciliation, and for a special purpose: alliance against an enemy whose name had not yet been mentioned. Even one of Veressejeff's own pickled herrings could have guessed that Babka's coming was connected with the recent appearance of the soldier prisoner. She therefore showed that she was as deeply compromised as Fedja's father by asking him quite openly for news of the youth whose name, Paprotkin, Veressejeff now heard for the first time. Then she explained how the man had come to be imprisoned. Veressejeff listened. He knew the Bjuscheff affair from hearsay. The fact that the man now bore a different name, seemed to him, who had had some experience of the Germans, to make the case hopeless. None the less, he thought it very remarkable that the soldier was still alive. Babka made no secret of the fact that she had not come all this way on an idle visit. She was ready to risk her all, to save this man from death.

"I must tell you, my friend," said she, as she sat chewing, and eyed the square, across which he might pass at any moment, as if she were looking down the sights of a rifle, "I must tell you, he's as innocent as a fly. He was a soldier, and a Russian, and he had been a prisoner. He wanted to get home, through the lines, and he thought they would simply let him through. We found him in the forest and took him with us. Then I gave him some advice; and I think it was bad advice. Now I must see what can be done to help him."

Veressejeff could, when he liked, hear more than was said, and when he liked, he could hear less. He said politely that it was of course not pleasant to get a man into trouble by good advice. He would soon know as much about the affair as anyone in Mervinsk, for it was not for nothing that he had all that good vodka in his cellar, and the German signallers often came in to exchange cigarettes for schnapps. He asked whether Babka thought of rescuing him from prison in case of need.

And Babka half closed her eyes, let her head sink sleepily on to the shopkeeper's shoulder and said:

"In case of need a woodpecker can split the side of a mountain."

Veressejeff felt a certain admiration for this woman, who had ventured all alone into a strange city, bent on nothing less than snatching their prey out of the very fangs of the Germans. Certainly he was so completely convinced of the hopelessness of the attempt, that he found it impossible to put much heart into it. But he did not say so: he merely assured her that he was there if she wanted him, and that, in any case, he would find out all about the Grischa affair in the next few days. He liked a little excitement, and if she would only take reasonable care, he was inclined to look upon her rather as an acquisition than as a menace; though indeed, at first, she had made him feel very uneasy.

Then she left her bundle and shoes in the shop, and set out for the prison, restless as a she-wolf prowling round the cage of one of her whining whelps; and this time she had been told exactly where to go. . . . Many such women go hawking berries all through the summer in the streets of the open town; and no one pays any attention to them.

Notwithstanding this, a woman like Babka could not keep walking round a public building of the importance of the Ortskomman-dantur without being noticed. The sentry at the gate had so little to amuse him that he would notice anyone who passed him once, let alone three times, with that downcast look, like a girl at her first communion. "Naturally," he ruminated under his iron helmet, "those peasant-women are afraid to sniff their way into such a crazy hole as our orderly room, simply to sell their berries. On the other hand, the clerks and guards are very fond of cheap raspberries; and nobody can beat the creatures down like the police, we all know that." So the third time he shouted out: "Hullo, grandma!" and "*Malines*," which, being interpreted, means raspberries. "Come inside and you'll be able to sell the lot."

Babka's heart stood still. Confronted by those menacing walls, she had ground her teeth and given up all hope of success, for that day at any rate; and when the sentry called to her, she was on the point of weeping in her fury and despair: Grischa was so near and yet so far! That shout was like a call from Heaven, for she knew at once that, if she could pass unsuspected in and out of the prison, selling fruit to the soldiers, the hardest part of her task was certainly behind her. And with a triumphant smile, she passed under the gateway with its crown of barbed wire.

In those days Grischa was working independently, knocking up coffins out of planks in a corner of the second yard, behind the kitchen buildings of the Kommandantur, where the glue-pot reeked and boiled and bubbled over the portable brazier; for Täwje was no longer entirely occupied with the provision of receptacles for the dead. He was now making some for the living—good, handy little boxes, neatly grooved and glued together, to be used by the soldiers mainly in carrying eggs. Grischa, with his canvas trousers stuffed into his boots and a flannel shirt wide open against his bare chest, bent over the long trestles with the air of an expert. His mind was at peace. To his own surprise, his soul was no longer harried and tormented by unrest. He realized that his life's centre of gravity had shifted far above him, that the decision lay with the old General, and was therefore in good hands. What could have been the use of eating his heart out? Besides, he had complete faith in each of those three different faces, the young lieutenant, the Kriegsgerichtsrat, and His Excellency. Besides, his comrades over yonder had made another attack, Russian fashion, so brave, and yet so hopeless. The men of the Landwehr, among whom he still had his quarters, though they laughed at him, were very willing to lend him extracts from the newspapers, and tell him what they had heard from the wounded as they came through.

As for the delay in deciding his case—well, God had made His creatures that way. They needed time. They wrote everything down on bits of paper and sent them in all directions. That was called legal procedure. At the moment, so the clerk had told him when he came back in high spirits from his journey, his papers were now elsewhere. Sometime, a decision would be reached; he need not worry. Life was pleasant. There were plenty of cherries and strawberries, and for the last two or three days a raspberry-woman, so he heard, had been coming into the prison. Täwje and Grischa would have liked to taste those raspberries, and they confided as much to the Landwehr guards.

That morning Grischa at last saw the raspberry-woman coming through the wooden door of the carpentry-enclosure, with her finger on her lip. Her burning eyes were fixed on him. In his astonishment, he very nearly fell across the table with his face on to a heap of nails. Fortunately, Corporal Hermann Sacht was close behind her. Grischa pretended he had been overcome with joy at the sight of the basket of fruit. He stretched out his hand towards it, saying: "Thank God for raspberries!" The Corporal told him not to overeat himself, and went off laughing to tell Täwje, who at that moment was choosing planks out of the pile of timber. So the two stood alone and face to face, half in the shadow of the chestnut tree, in the July dust; and above them was the canopy of burning blue. Grischa shook Babka by the shoulders and said hoarsely: "How the devil did you do it, my dear? You fly in all of a sudden like a witch, and kiss me." And he caught her to him, and kissed her. Her limbs were almost paralysed, and her consciousness grew dim; she would have fallen had he not held her up, and now for the first time she knew all the power of her passion for this man. She would gladly have given herself to him there upon the ground, on the heap of tumbled fragrant shavings, in the shadow of the leaves.

But they would not long be alone; she had urgent things to say to him which must come before all else.

"Here I am," she said hastily: "Yes, it's me. I'm staying with Veressejeff, near the cathedral. You can find me there any time. I got your letter in the spring, and I've come to make up for what I did. I'll get you out of here. I've managed harder jobs than this. I'll send for Fedjuschka and Koljä, and I'll do all I possibly can."

Grischa let go of her shoulders, and she sank down limply on one of the finished coffins.

"You needn't do that, Babka," he said, stepping back. "We don't want any further mess-up, thank you. My business is all right: a General has taken it on, and we must just wait." And he added, with an awkward smile, "As a man sins, so he is punished. I could not wait in the Navarischky forest, in the camp where I was better off than here. So I have got to learn to wait now; but I'm not so badly off either. I've got food, work to do, and a place to sleep in, and now you're here," he said affectionately, so as not to disappoint her too much. "So now I've got another friend to help me besides Täwje the Jew, who is a good man. They're a good lot here, I tell you, Babka."

Babka sat down and stared at him, as he stood there with his tanned face and bare chest, and cheeks which still bore signs of Sunday's shave. "He doesn't want to get away," she thought. "A good lot, are they? It'll cost him his life if I don't look out." But she only said: "That's all right then."

"Why, Babka, you don't know what's been happening. I'll tell you the next time, or perhaps now, if Täwje's not there. Now sell us some raspberries: you can't think how my mouth's watering." And he dug her gently in the chest with his elbow and winked. Though she was tired, and her feet and forehead ached, she could not help smiling. Now she could take things easy, for she had found him. Like the she-wolf, she forced her way into the cage where her cub was shut up. Murmuring, "Let me sleep for five minutes," she sank back against the chestnut tree, and while still under the spell of her overwhelming exhaustion, she noticed that another man had come into the enclosure; but her eyelids dropped, she felt her eyes turning in her head, and in a second, she was asleep. In her body, something living and growing throbbed and quivered. She had meant to tell Grischa:—another time. The slight barrier of estrangement which had risen up between them must first be overcome.

Grischa's heart went out to the sleeping woman. Täwje walked softly through the dust in his heavy boots, and whispered:

"What a pity; now we've got to wait till she wakes up. It's very hot: but he who steals from the sleeper shall come to a worse end than Dathan and Abiram," and in whispered tones, Grischa asked him to explain who these two gentlemen were.

Babka, with a kerchief knotted round her head, her hands lying before her on her lap, sat breathing deeply, her heavy-curtained eyes upturned and yearning through the leaves towards the sky.

Chapter 2

STAFF CELEBRATIONS

THERE were not half enough orderlies, though they kept scurrying about the lawns. On August 4, von Lychow invited the officers of his Division, so far as they were accessible, to a "beer-evening" that began with luncheon. After lengthy negotiations he had extracted from the Bavarians in the northern sector of the line, a barrel of beer, dark and sweet, frothing and creamy, blending the bitter hop with the mellow barley, a drink for men, more precious, and in these days rarer, than the wine that flowed so plentifully from the cellars of Northern France. It was on the fourth of August, the day of England's entry into the War, and not the second, the date of our own declaration of war against Russia and France, that the feast took place, for as von Lychow said, with a twinkle in his eye, it was only then that History really got into her stride. He explained, as he cut off a neat square of yellow cheese and laid it on the glossy black surface of his *pumpernickel* bread, that he by no means underrated the military strength and training of the French and of the Russians. "They are old fighting races, like ourselves—I mean the Prussians," he said with a chuckle, leaning back comfortably in his arm-chair, to Major-General von Hessta, his artillery-commander, who was sitting on the left: "and to fighting races a war does not mean much: they win one, lose another, and then start a third. There's no hatred in it—I mean the genuine hatred that goes on to the bitter end. But with those English, it's quite another story: their warlike days are far behind them, they send their fighters to the Colonies, and give them the choice of God's earth—and goodbye to them. But once the English have been really tickled up, they're off like a mad bulldog, and then it's serious: it's us they're after this time, and we've got to go through with it—or smash. If you're going to war in an age of democracy, when Tom, Dick, and Harry are asked quite seriously whether they don't mind being killed, it's not until we're driven to the very last sausage that our German lads will show what they're really made of. So let us drink to England, for having forced us, and for still forcing us, to fight it out to the end. On the second of August it might have been 'seventy all over again; but on the fourth we knew what we were in for. *Prosit, Herr Kamerad!*" Major-General von Hessta smiled, and took a deep pull at his tankard.

A long table had been set up in the garden of the General's villa, parallel to the paths, and stretching across the lawn. At the far end a smaller table was laid at right angles, at which sat the lieutenants, as many as could be got together, over whom Winfried presided. The rows of profiles, two long indented lines of brown and pink, above their green high-collared *Litevkas*, on every chest a strip of brightly coloured ribbon, stood out against the blue sky like the edges of a trough, whose living sides were the two rows of officers enclosing the long white tablecloth, with all its knives and glasses. Scattered among the junior captains were pale blue Austrian uniforms—and the long head of Count Dubna-Trencsin, the Austrian liaison officer attached to the Division, overtopped the parted hair or the close-cropped brush-like pates of the Prussians at his side. Behind the chairs stood orderlies in white drill-jackets. They trotted round with empty glasses to the tapsters, who filled the tankards with the precious liquid, and the orderlies carried it warily back to the tables beneath the trees.

It was now midsummer, and the heavy foliage of the walnuts, maples, and limes overhung the tables. The endless babble of voices resolved itself into separate conversations: the company was at the cheese stage. Now that His Excellency had undone the top buttons of his tunic and loosened his collar, they all felt at their ease. Their necks and foreheads glistened in the summer heat, which would have been unendurable indoors; but here the wind rustled in the leaves and fanned their faces, tempering the fires of noon. Every one of them wanted to throw off his tunic and sit in his shirt-sleeves. They had got through their oxtail soup, with marrow dumplings floating among the drops of fat, heaped dishes of giant pike out of the lakes, haunches of venison with cranberries from the forest, and grey Silesian rissoles made of raw potatoes. Then came cheese from Allgäu and Edam, after which the orderlies went round laden with brightly labelled boxes of cigars and innumerable cigarettes. Out came the clicking, sputtering lighters, but Grischa hurried down the table with tapers, in case any might be needed. There were lighters of every kind, but the benzol was too strong, and they all smoked foully. A Captain of Engineers was loudly extolling the mechanism of his, which he preferred to all others: it was shaped like a lady's revolver, and every time you pressed the trigger, it flared up. Nearly every one was longing for His Excellency to rise from the table; they knew the coffee must be ready in the kitchen, and they wanted to drink it standing up, for they hoped to stretch their legs in the great park of the Tamshinski villa, to make room for more beer.

Grischa stood with the tapers, behind His Excellency, who was examining his cigar with the attention which he devoted to every detail. It was a large dun-coloured *Vorstenlander*; he moistened it with his lips, carefully cut off the tip, blew through the opposite end to make sure that it would draw, and finally turned half round for a light, prepared to smoke in peace and comfort. Grischa lit his cigar with grateful care. The General did not look up: he did not know who had done this for him. He turned again to his neighbour, who was freely discussing the subject of officers' pay. When England's health was drunk, von Hessta had taken the opportunity to observe that no officer should neglect to honour those days of August: it was only since then that they had enjoyed a decent income. Their pay in peace-time would just about provide the cat's dinner. But now a man could save a bit. He had two sons serving, and a third was under the ground at Ypres. "Yes," answered His Excellency, "we don't do badly now; and later on if all these peace-mongers get their way, they ought to begin to treat us soldiers as those cunning Chinamen treat their doctors," and he puffed out his smoke with the slow enjoyment of a connoisseur, luxuriously distending his long narrow nostrils. Von Hessta confessed his ignorance. "Why, the Chinese," explained His Excellency, "so I have heard, pay their family doctors well and regularly until their illustrious health is pleased to depart from them; then the doctor's fees are stopped at once, and don't start again till the patient recovers. So, of course, they're out to cure you as soon as possible; and they do, though I suppose they sometimes fail. For I've heard that even in China people die occasionally. What they do with the doctors in such cases, I don't know, but I've no doubt that medicine-men know how to get themselves out of the soup. Your health, Herr Geheimrat!" And he raised his glass to the Surgeon-General, who sat smirking on his right, embodying all the dignity of Medicine.

"Death has ceased to impress us," he said with a laugh, "so that threat won't frighten us. When a man gets hundreds of deaths reported to him every day"——and he wiped his thick bristly beard, as white as the froth upon it from the beer he had been drinking.

The fourth greybeard at this end of the senior table, with his eyeglass cemented between his eyebrow and his cheek, positively bleated with amusement: "Do you mean that our pay should be stopped till the end of the War? Do you think I look like one of our intellectuals in the Reichstag? That cock won't fight. They'll have to do a good deal more blithering before they get *us* to give up what we've got." The speaker was a Brigade Commander, a man of the middle class, of the name of Müller, who had belonged to the cavalry, and now through political influence had at last found means of entering a society to which he felt he really belonged. "Well, good afternoon, gentlemen," said His Excellency, as he finished his glass, pushed back his chair and rose—rather abruptly as it seemed to the last speaker, who was always ready to suspect a slight: but as the host's genial smile was evidently meant for him, and everyone was glad to get on his legs again, he dismissed the idea from his mind.

The guests got up with such alacrity that some of the chairs were knocked over, and in some places the cloth was perilously near being dragged off the table. A bluish cloud of tobacco floated among the rustling green leaves above their heads as the company broke up into little groups. The orderlies rushed at the table to clear away. They tossed off the half-empty glasses of beer as they hurried behind the huge jasmine and privet hedges where the great barrel was enthroned. Each of them made a flying visit to the kitchen and fell upon the fragments of the banquet. They grabbed them with their fingers, wiped away the gravy with their napkins, and rushed out of the steaming kitchen back to their work. The tables had to be laid for coffee and liqueurs, and later on for beer and wine, and perhaps there would be champagne; the time had also come for plates of sweets and cakes of the country.

"Now then, Russky, you can eat till your belly bursts," said grey-haired Wodrig encouragingly to Grischa. The old man liked the prisoner's bright eyes and air of gaiety, and he stuffed a handful of cigarettes into the pocket of his jacket. The orderlies, all brushed and tidied, looked their best in their spotless drill-suits. They were brand-new, for the Ordnance had issued them on loan for this solemn occasion; Grischa, however, had merely received an old tunic with somewhat fewer patches. There he stood, his bright eyes sparkling in his sunburnt face, ecstatic from the dregs of beer that he had poured down his throat, replete with choice morsels, steeped in the taste of cream sauces, cranberries, licked fish-bones, pike-broth with parsley and the marrow dumplings from the soup—flavours which his tongue had never known either in the days of his imprisonment or in his earlier life—and dazed by the presence of so many smart gentlemen, whose necks made a man's fingers tingle to be at them. He liked them for the time in his own way. He was suddenly aware that he was eating up their leavings, just like his poor German comrades; that it was shameful to accept such crumbs, and that the shame was not his nor theirs. Images were sharply cut upon his brain; as he shut his eyes, they flashed into life: below were men in drill-jackets hurrying blindly to and fro and snatching what they could, while above them sat the masters at their lordly table, whence fell the crumbs which those below them grabbed, bustling about like orderlies at table, but with empty hands and blind eyes. The unaccustomed fumes of fresh-brewed beer, quite different from the acrid reek of the familiar schnapps, unlocked new chambers of his imagination whose existence he had never suspected. There they sat upon their chairs, those men whose privilege it was to bestow on him their leavings, and he, and he only, felt that it was shameful to throw scraps to a man as to a dog! Perhaps all the others also understood this, the orderlies, his comrades and those like unto himself, but they did not show it. They took advantage of the opportunity of escaping for once from the dreary monotony of their daily food, as they gobbled, and licked their fingers, and wiped them on the napkins, which they flung furiously into a corner, delicate white damask from the mess-stores, as if they had been the whitewashed souls of those who ordered them about, which, if they durst, they would have crushed out of their throats. Grischa leaned against the wall outside the kitchen; he felt slightly faint, rubbed his forehead with the back of his hand, and looked about him. All at once his inmost being filled to the brim with the joy and onrush of existence. It was good to be alive; it was fine to rush around and hand lights or liqueurs to these brown clear-cut faces, with their bright eyes, and hair of every colour; it would be no less fine to hurl them out of the way with a kick or a rifle-butt, and send them to crack their bones and smash their skulls against the wall like eggs; and then to run home free as a naked savage. They were keeping him shut up—him, Grischa— they had nailed him fast, and that vast murder, that maddening hail of shells, ten thousand in an hour, had begun again, from Dvinsk down to the country through which he had marched in the early days when the Austrians had driven them back. There was no place in the world fit to live in; but he would notice all these things and later take a red-hot awl and one of his smooth coffin-planks, and burn into it all that he had seen. But he must wait till then; now, at any rate, all was bright and happy. . . . Grischa enjoyed the sight of them, his heart went out to them all, young and old, close-cropped gentlemen with monocles that made them look like caricatures. He felt that something must be going out from him to them, there was so much love and so much hatred seething in his breast.

The vast garden of the Tamshinski villa, once part of the surrounding forest, and now skilfully cleared and replanted, echoed with laughter and conversation. Some matrons and nurses had been invited and had already joined the officers. These dowdily dressed, but undeniably female, women had been introduced by way of dessert. They chattered volubly as they walked about, red-faced women whose contours were obscured by their white and blue summer dresses, striped like servants' bedspreads—Prussian countesses indistinguish-

able from the daughters of petty officials, and the matron's harsh
bass voice would have been equally at home in the lodge of the Porter
Piesecke and in Count von Kleinigen's castle. Some junior officers,
headed by Winfried, had made a circle round Sister Bärbe, who was
leaning against a mottled plane tree, talking to them all at the same
time; she was more than a match for them, and to her friends'
delight kept them all good-humouredly at a distance. Sister Sophie
nodded to her from her exalted position on His Excellency's arm,
with Kriegsgerichtsrat Posnanski on her other side. She had been
standing so since they got up from the table, and felt herself to be
in very good company between her two cavaliers. His Excellency
addressed her familiarly as "My Child," and the Kriegsgerichtsrat
called her "Comtesse," and "Gracious Lady"—both of them protecting her from the mob of captains and lieutenants whom for some
time she had only been able to look at through Bertin's eyes. He
had just appeared for a moment from behind a bank of fragrant
"La France" roses. Indeed, she saw Bertin everywhere, for since
his return from Dahlem she had given rein to her feelings, and he
too had begun to recover from the numbness of his stricken
humanity;—his wife's influence, also, had suddenly changed him
into a most marvellous lover, and there began to be appointments
in the forest, and nightly meetings in his or her room, which showed
that there was place in his heart for his love of Lenore, and a love
for Sophie, so long as the two spheres of life were so utterly
divided as in his present time that seemed so like Eternity. Sophie
asked no more. For the first time in her nineteen years of life she
had met a man with a truly tender heart, and felt his power; and
Bertin's strong character, in which there was nothing of the uncompromising hardness of her brothers, her relations, and all the men
of her clan, found an immediate response in her sensitive yielding
nature. She was in love with him. Unless a miracle occurred there
would be a catastrophe after the War—for her, of course. And yet
miracles of that sort could easily occur if that unknown Lenore
should prove to be as original in character and disposition as he was.
Why not? For her there were no obstacles in the way. In her
hospital she had learnt to work much harder than a servant, and
do with much worse food: but without love she could no longer go

on living among the highly bred bloodstock of her family. So she turned to Lychow, who was telling her about Bismarck's furious dispute over the trees in the Chancellery garden, and said with a charming daughterly expression: "Please tell it to me again, Uncle Lychow. I suddenly began to think about something else."

But she soon had an opportunity for testing her self-control; for from behind the late copper beech, near which a weeping willow shed its green tresses almost across the path, appeared Bertin himself and deferentially asked for two words with the Herr Kriegsgerichtsrat. The beloved! But she did not betray herself, and with half-closed eyes made him so slight a sign of greeting that only he was aware of it. How distinguished he looked in his plain private's tunic! And full of the joy of her secret alliance, she let von Lychow lead her away to where, on a semicircular garden seat under the crude moss-grown torso of a fawn, three officers sat talking in low tones about the madness of the Verdun campaign: they had withdrawn from the company to enjoy a quiet discussion, but they sprang from their seats as His Excellency came up with a lady.

Posnanski looked hard at Bertin. "You among all these Generals? Something serious must have happened." And Bertin reported that a courier had arrived from Ober-Ost with a locked bag containing a large bundle of papers, and he was to deliver the key to the Herr Kriegsgerichtsrat personally. Posnanski and Bertin understood each other in an instant.

"The dossier back already?" asked Posnanski. "What can have happened? Come along, Bertin," and they walked across the level lawns up to the house.

The afternoon wore away, and a soft golden light filtered through the leaves. The orderlies brought round the coffee in large cans, and the officers and ladies drank it standing. A sister from a surgical hospital was stuffing her mouth with cake while a staff-colonel in the Medical Service, cup in hand, was discussing with a junior colleague the excision of ulcers from the walls of the stomach, of which he had had twelve or fourteen cases among the "material" recently delivered to him. His remarks were peppered with technical terms such as "jejunum" and "resection." "The case healed perfectly, and was sent off to the Front again," he added, as he dipped his cake into his saucer to sop up the coffee he had spilt in it. Near by were three or four groups of laughing men and women, and the tobacco-smoke rose up in a delicate blue cloud through the golden summer air. Major Grasnick, Lychow's chief of staff, dipping his finger in the coffee and drawing a line with it upon a tray, expounded the meaning of the recent operations, with a copy of the latest report in his hand. The Russians had passed the Zbrucz in full retreat. They would oblige the Austrians by clearing the whole Bukovina for them. But certain importunate gentlemen insisted on asking where the devil "we" came in. The Major laughed. "The Operations Section at Brest-Litovsk will see to that," he said. "You may be quite sure Schieffenzahn knows what he's about. They say it'll start in the north, not quite yet, but all according to his programme. At the end of the month or perhaps in the beginning of September. No, not at Jakobstadt, nor Dünaburg neither—right up north."

"Riga," said Captain Dombrowski.

"Ösel and Dagö," the Major blurted out, then he smiled and put his finger on his lips. "I've not said a word, remember. You didn't hear anything, did you? We shan't advance till then. How far? As far as we choose. All Russia is open to us. Since Schieffenzahn approved that bright idea of the Chief of III B to inoculate the holy Russian with the plague bacillus of Lenin and Co., and sent it across Germany in sealed compartments . . . everything in confidence, gentlemen, of course." And the name of the Colonel in charge of the Espionage Section, that all-powerful weaver of plots, came into the minds of all the staff officers present. Was it possible those fellows at the Front knew nothing of these things?

All these military politics left the captains and lieutenants of the fighting troops excited or incredulous. Herr von Hessta came and stood in the centre of their little circle. He said he was watching the effect of the German victories. "The face of Germany is turning eastwards, gentlemen"; the policy of Henry the Lion, too long discarded in favour of Hohenstauffen dreams of the south, was coming into its own. They would create a vast Baltic province. Prussia would then take all Germany in tow and show the world what a great colonizing nation could achieve. And bursting with excitement he drained his cup and roared: "Where Alexander came to grief and Napoleon crashed, Albert Schieffenzahn will bear his fluttering standards. England is ours: the road to India lies open. . . ." And the conversation turned abruptly to a discussion of the *Kulturmission* of the German banks on the model of the Bagdad railway.

From behind the great rose bushes a fanfare rang out. The band of the Engineers, whose base was in Mervinsk, drowned the conversation with the *Torgau* march from thirty instruments. His Excellency, who had no love for music at the table, and stigmatized it as the wretched expedient of fellows who can't appreciate a good dinner, had not let the band come till four o'clock, and carefully limited their programme—nothing but Frederick the Great's marches, good rousing Prussian music, and a few little potpourris from the old operas: Donizetti, Lortzing, Weber, the *Weisse Dame* and the *Gazza Ladra*. It was to be a promenade concert with drinks all the time, and plenty of orderlies running about with smokes and lights and biscuits.

Sister Bärbe, leaning on Lieutenant Winfried's arm and accompanied by two other sisters—good-natured and accommodating creatures—was thrilled with the music, and asked if they could dance. Winfried laughingly shook his head. It was too early; they must wait: the General would be angry. He suggested children's games, "Puss in the corner," among the birches on the great lawn, which stretched between the old fence and the jessamine bushes. In the young officers there was, luckily for them, enough of the boy left to enjoy these frolics. So, of course, they must also play "Third," or "Who's afraid of the Black Man?" and "One two three and you catch me." They were all formed into a procession and marching solemnly on the lawn, as in a polonaise, when Sister Sophie appeared at Winfried's side, and he kissed her hand as he welcomed her into the circle of young people. "Yes," she said in her soft, clear girlish voice, "I will stay here, but Lieutenant Winfried is requested to go to the refreshment-table for five minutes. Bertin has some business with which he is afraid he must trouble him."

"How long will it take?"

"Five minutes—perhaps less."

And Winfried, clicking his heels together, and cursing the lot of all aides-de-camp—probably Lucifer was A.D.C. to the good God, which ought to have been hell enough for him without going further—and went away. Bertin stood by the refreshment-table; the expression of his small mouth and black eyes looked ominous. Would the Lieutenant be so good as to bring the General for ten minutes' talk with the Herr Gerichtsrat, who had taken the liberty of receiving the courier from Ober-Ost in the waiting-room, as he wanted to see the papers before he dealt with them officially? Their contents were so unintelligible, that he wanted to report them to His Excellency at once. "These lawyers are all cracked," thought Winfried. "It's ten minutes now, is it?" he said with a smile to Bertin. "Didn't you know His Excellency was giving a party to-day, my dear fellow?"

Bertin replied that the Herr Kriegsgerichtsrat was, in fact, aware of that. A quiver in the man's voice roused Winfried, who had probably drunk less than any of his guests, from the delicious haze that came over him in Bärbe's company. It was so charming to be able to go about with his beloved openly before everyone, as though they were already married in the sight of the world. "That was compensation for everything," he thought. "Of course," he said, "Lychow always has time for business if it is very urgent."

"It's incredible," murmured Bertin with trembling lips. Winfried rinsed a tumbler in a large glass basin, which had once held Madame Tamshinski's gold-fish, and poured out some schnapps for Bertin. "Drink it up, Bertin," he said, "and let me make a suggestion. Leave His Excellency out of this, for the present. He's having an argument at the moment with Schlieden, probably about tanks or gas-attacks." (Major Schlieden, divisional gas officer, was considered one of the keenest engineers and ablest men on that Front.) "You seem to have got something unpleasant on hand; why shouldn't I give my opinion first, before we push it on to him? I believe you legal cards have a proverb that no case is so urgent that it doesn't become more so by being let alone." He flicked the ash off his cigarette with a sigh, looked across to where he could see Bärbe, among the trunks of the huge maples and birches, walking away on the arm of a smart lieutenant of artillery, and said to Bertin:

"Wouldn't you have liked to join the party? Sophie's playing about over there."

Bertin shot a quick look at him in reply and said: "Yes, a quarter of an hour ago perhaps, at least to look on, for children's games were, unfortunately, never in my line—but now this order from Headquarters—Oh, what a foul place this world is!" And he ground his teeth. "Come along," said Winfried, and they hurried across the lawns. "The Paprotkin case?" Bertin nodded, "Yes, the Bjuscheff case."

At that moment Grischa had appeared, though they did not notice him; he was carrying a tray, and had come to fetch the coffee-cups to wash them up in the kitchen. "They're in a mighty hurry, bless their hearts," thought he. He had always had a kindly feeling for Bertin and Winfried, but to-day—he felt so riotously gay that he could have flung his arms around them and clasped them to his coffee-stained drill-jacket. A child of his by Babka was on the way —how splendid! She bore a little Grischa in her belly, now about the size of a button, or perhaps as big as an apple already. How strange was the birth of man: he and she and this new thing that he had planted. Life was good—trees grew, and men grew. And he ran into the garden in a burst of eagerness to do all he could for the service and pleasure of the guests as they strolled up and down between the skittle-alley on the eastern walk of the garden and the alluring-looking buffet near the house; the atmosphere was growing more and more unconstrained, and some of the officers were already in their shirt-sleeves. Von Lychow missed his A.D.C. "Lieutenant Winfried," shouted some officious bystanders in a comical sing-song. Whereupon Sister Bärbe said that he had been called away; and a flying officer mentioned he had seen him going away through the bushes.

He soon appeared, a gallant figure in his elegant riding-breeches, smiling and swinging his arms, his tunic half-unbuttoned, and walking with the gay confident stride of one whom all the world loves, and who waits, with his hands in his pockets, for good luck to come his way. He shaded his eyes with his hand for an instant, looking across the heavy rays of rich sunlight towards his uncle's guests. Then he heard someone say: "There he is." His name was shouted, and a certain dapper little Lieutenant Hesse ran across to him, laid his hand on his shoulder, and hurriedly said that His Excellency wanted him.

(Six months later Lieutenant Hesse's arm was hanging in the fork of a beech tree, and his head had rolled into a bramble-bush; though this can hardly have troubled him, as the handsome boy's body was already pierced and torn in half-a-dozen places.)

"Wants me, does he?" said Winfried, lighting another cigarette. "Well, I want him." Von Lychow was sitting astride a garden chair, beating time with his iron-shod boots as he crunched them on the gravel. He asked Winfried when he would be due for leave, for he wanted to go on leave himself. "The fact is that d——d old scalp-hunter the Senior Staff-Surgeon wants some footling decoration or other and I suppose I must get it for him: if I can't I'll have my old epaulettes pickled and eat them with parsley for lunch. Why, ever since I commanded the garrison at Detmold," added the General, "I've been quite an influential person." Winfried laughed. "I don't know how Your Excellency stands on the leave-roster, but certainly, Uncle, it's eight months since you've been in Berlin or at Hohen-Lychow." Of course, the excellent Friebe was there all right, and Aunt Malwine would be getting along splendidly with him and the other servants and the twenty-seven Russian prisoners; while his staff at Mervinsk would be left fatherless, when His Excellency was away, and it remained to be seen whether the sun would observe Divisional Orders, according to which it was to rise at daybreak, or be twenty-one and a half minutes late for parade.

The pack of young officers, headed by Bärbe with her arm round Sophie's waist, ran up to recapture Winfried. He took refuge, laughing, behind the General's back, and whispered: "You're wanted in your office, Uncle Otto, quick! Slip away quietly!"

With a characteristic gesture von Lychow threw his head right back upon his collar, screwed up his left eye, and stared at his nephew through the eye-glass in his right, with a glance which changed in the tenth of a second from blank amazement to understanding and consent.

He pushed Winfried artfully towards the youthful company,

who were clamouring for a dance, and saying, "Please excuse me,"
he turned upon his heel and marched into the house. Everyone
supposed he had gone to the lavatory.

When he opened the door of his office, he noticed three things:
coolness, silence, and a strange tense feeling in the air. In this room,
leaning back motionless, in deep thought, sat Kriegsgerichtsrat
Posnanski, with open collar and legs crossed, gazing at the ceiling,
sucking with pursed lips at his cigar. "Looks comfortable," thought
the old man. He begged Posnanski to remain seated, sank heavily
into the soft leather padding of the couch, and breathed deeply.

"It's nice to be here," he said. "It soothes my old nerves like a
bath in a quiet pool."

At every breath the two men felt less constraint; and now a
deep and solemn peace possessed them.

Posnanski had quite forgotten the noisy party—all its laughter,
sunshine, gleaming paths, garden-lawns, and music: this whole parody
of peace had gone, drawn aside like a pictured velvet curtain, and
showing the truth behind it. And now Lychow too breathed freely,
drinking in this atmosphere of repose. Suddenly he felt very tired;
the eyelids of his wrinkled, shadowed face dropped heavily, his chin
hung limply down from his half-open mouth, and his temples
throbbed for a moment with the exhaustion which was just fading
from his brain. Half-mechanically he closed his teeth on the quill
tip of his cigar holder. A few seconds more and he would be asleep.
His slightly sunburnt hand with its slender wrist and strong blue
veins lay stretched on the buff leather of the couch, like a hand in
a portrait. Through the closed windows, which opened on the street,
not on the garden, even the brass band could not be heard.

Posnanski was not for one moment conscious of his unmilitary
conduct, for his mind was moving in a realm of mighty resolutions
far beyond that conditioned sphere where times of war and uniforms
had any force or meaning . . . and he turned from these high
musings to look down on the stiff old man who had to make the
great decision. A line of Hebbel came into the lawyer's mind—
"Trouble not this sleeping world"—and he resolved to act upon it:

here was the man from whom he must presently wring a yea or nay, whose every effort he must soon engage, and whom he would perhaps entangle in endless complications.

After a very long nap, as it seemed to him, though indeed it was only two minutes, the General drew a deep breath, sat up stiffly, looked about him, and was fully awake to his surroundings.

"Excuse me," he said.

Posnanski bowed slightly.

"It's done me good," Lychow went on. "I had a little snooze. An old stick like me mustn't overdo it; if I peg out, the Division'll —but, of course, you didn't send for me to hear this sort of talk." He rang for coffee, but no one came.

"They're all outside," said Posnanski. "May I send for something myself for you?" He went to the door and called Bertin. The clerk was standing in some confusion by Sister Sophie's side at the door of the ante-room; they both promised to return with coffee. Posnanski shut the door again. When he returned he saw Lychow bending over the dossier with his arms propped on the desk.

"Shall I explain it to Your Excellency in a few words?"

"It's Paprotkin's case—the Russian prisoner?"

"Yes. Your Excellency seems to remember it."

"I remember the whole business. A good fellow; reminded me of—someone or other. If I'm not much mistaken, I've seen a face like that on one of the orderlies."

Posnanski rose to the height of incorrectness.

"Right," he said; "just a moment," and snatched the dossier from the General's hands. "It was a clear case," he explained. "We condemned a man named Bjuscheff as a deserter, and he was subsequently identified beyond dispute as one Paprotkin, an escaped prisoner. His dossier was sent to Ober-Ost to decide what court was competent to try him. Here is the decision of the highest judicial authority in the country."

He took up a sheet attached to the file and covered with bold typescript. From this he read aloud.

"Contents noted, and returned. After consultation with the Chief of the General Staff the Commander-in-Chief requests that the sentence of the Divisional Court Martial be upheld, and that for the execution of the death-penalty the prisoner be handed over in the customary manner to the Ortskommandantur, Mervinsk.

"Even if the identity of the condemned man Bjuscheff with a certain Paprotkin, a prisoner of war, who deserted from the Navarischky timber-camp for prisoners of war, has been shown to be to some extent probable, higher considerations make it undesirable that such identity should be successfully established, inasmuch as the Commander-in-Chief, in full concurrence with the Quartermaster-General, is convinced that the legal aspect of the case is of very slight importance compared with the military and political interests involved. In order to maintain the prestige of our courts and in the interests of military discipline, it is necessary that the proposal to revise the condemned prisoner's sentence should be rejected as unwarranted and further as prejudicial to the interests of the State. The execution of the sentence, which was legally imposed and is hereby confirmed, is to be officially reported here. For C.-in-C., Ost: on behalf of G.Q.M.G.: Wilhelmi, Kriegsgerichtsrat."

"Full stop," said Posnanski, and after a pause: "And I see that it is marked in pencil 'Seen: Sch.' which is unusual but, of course, perfectly in order."

The old man left his corner of the couch and walked over to Posnanski, who politely vacated his chair as the General took the paper from his hand. He glued his monocle into his eye and read the decision through again, sentence for sentence, moving his lips the while. Then he remarked with a cold composure that was almost English:

"Indeed an edifying document," and muttered under his breath: "Good God, what filthy rubbish!"

Then followed an oppressive silence which was broken by a sudden knock at the door.

Sister Sophie, with flushed cheeks, and all the bewitching radiance of happiness in her grey expressive eyes, brought in two cups of coffee on a tray, looked with a smile from one to the other, but when she realized that there was something in the wind, the smile fell from her face like a garment; and with a murmured "Excuse me," she hurried out.

While the old gentleman was sipping his strong and highly sweetened coffee, Posnanski, in a somewhat exhausted voice, began:

"We are not boys. We must not act upon impulse. It is quite clear that in times like these Schieffenzahn regards the life of the individual as of about as much importance as that of a black beetle. If you question the justice of this point of view, you strike at the very foundation of the War, which would be an odd proceeding for a Court-Martial Officer and a General on active service in 1917. For thousands of years thinkers have expressed strong views on the meaning, or rather the meaninglessness, of war. War has been demonstrated to be madness, and in proof of it here we sit in our uniforms, and on the ground-floor Siegelmann sits tapping away at the latest report from Headquarters. A man who says you can't change human nature must be in favour of war."

"Certainly," said von Lychow. "I am in favour of it myself. All we Conservatives are."

Posnanski continued in a steady voice:

"But I hope on the same grounds you support cannibalism, the exposure of children, matriarchy, polygamy, religious prostitution, club law, and slavery, for no man can dispute that these things are on the same logical footing as war, and if you insist that humanity never changes, please be thorough."

"But you must admit," said the General, "war is in the Bible."

"Yes, but it isn't glorified," Posnanski went on unperturbed. "I admit nothing. You can't mix up the Pentateuch and the Sermon on the Mount with the glorification of war, as you mix red wine and champagne; or rather, as in the metaphor, you can, but you will have an unpleasant shock if you do. So the wise man can keep himself aloof, and confuses the issue with obscure speculations as to what might or might not have happened so long ago. But here"— and his voice began to shake with fury—"quite apart from war and peace, is an innocent man sentenced to be solemnly murdered with the help of the judicial machine of Your Excellency's Division. That is the essential fact. The military setting is a detail of no importance."

Von Lychow took up the document to study it again. The rare dark green opals on his sleeve-links clinked, for his hand was a little

shaky. Posnanski felt he had been a trifle previous in coming down
to these broad, fundamental principles. He cursed his own folly
inwardly. Opinions mattered very little: the life of an innocent
man was at stake, and he must save it with the help of this old
gentleman. His passion for argument had needlessly obscured this
simple issue, and his intellectual honesty and force had merely
courted doubts and difficulties. Suddenly there happened something
which the excellent Winfried had long dreaded, and not without
cause: to the lawyer's horror, the chair in which His Excellency sat
fell back with a crash on to the floor behind the little round table,
and the General stood up, purple with rage, stiff as a fencer, holding the paper in his hand, and roared:

"These swine! I won't have such interference. I'll teach them
to mess about with my courts martial. The decision was perfectly in
order and perfectly just: that's all I care about. The Court Martial
of the Lychow Division will not take any orders from these dirty
blackguards. If Schieffenzahn doesn't know that, he'll find it out
now."

Posnanski recovered his composure and smiled with relief. Thank
God for Lychow's good sense! History, indeed, was much this kind
of thing, questions of legal competence, all manner of disputes
and quibbles over claims and precedence. A man's fate may hang
upon the proper reference of a document: and why not? Has it not
often enough depended on another man's digestion, on whether he's
had a good dinner or a good night, or whether he has slept with
some lady or other? One road's as good as another if it leads to
justice. His mistake had justified itself.

Lychow pulled himself together and, remembering his guests,
shook hands with Posnanski.

He said he would telephone to Schieffenzahn to this effect to-
morrow or the day after. No, to-morrow. A thing like that couldn't
wait. Posnanski bowed gratefully, and sat down to draft an appropriate reply.

As the General walked down the staircase and through the garden gate, the pillars of which were topped with moss-grown cupids,
he noted with pleasure, as he always did, the rich iron-work which,
at the beginning of the nineteenth century, the artist Abraham Frum,

grandfather of the author Nachum Frum, now at Odessa, had cast
with his own hands for Mr. Tamshinski's grandfather—noble,
lozenge-shaped panels worked with leaves and arabesques in a style
that had far more in common with the rococo of old days than with
that imperial age. As he passed on, von Lychow, who had just made
a decision, stood for a moment at the entrance to his garden, tapping somewhat absently on the iron with his riding-whip, so as to
prepare himself to rejoin his guests, now scattered in animated
groups. But, alas, misfortunes never came singly, and he was soon
to find himself involved in further trouble.

Of course he did not wish to attract notice. Hosts should not
be away so long, yet he was in no mood for the courtesies which
the occasion demanded. He would rather have been alone for a
short time, sauntering up and down in the mellow evening light, feeling the soft breeze against his temples, watching the moths come
out, and the bumble-bees and wasps and the swooping swallows flying home, hurrying through the golden haze. Along the wall which
enclosed the whole park and garden, ran a narrow, almost disused,
path. Between the creepered wall on the right, and tall bushes and
a hedge of blue firs which had been artificially planted, on the left,
it stretched like a green gorge, for the gravel was almost covered
by tufts of grass. At this point the sound of many people reached
the General's ear—laughter, shrill cries, the vague murmur of a
multitude, and the noise of hurrying feet—and he decided to com-
pose himself for a minute or two and reappear from an unsuspicious
quarter. The skittle-alley seemed to him the very place. . . . With
short strides, his head a little on one side, and not without misgivings, he walked slowly on. War with Schieffenzahn! That was no
light matter, and would make any sensible man hesitate. . . . The first
step would, as always, be decisive: the alternatives were to do nothing and give in—or make a stand now and see the thing right
through. Was this Bjuscheff affair worth a series of vexatious
disputes with one whose extraordinary talents Lychow realized as
much as anyone? Albert Schieffenzahn would thrust out his lower
jaw, and hold on like a bulldog. And he, Lychow, was more than
seventy years old and would be glad of a rest. But in an instant
he had dismissed all such speculations from his mind. The will

of another had dared to impugn his judgment of right and wrong, and within his own domain. Either Germany stood for justice as her rulers saw it, and the conscience of the man responsible, and his sense of law, were the only absolute guarantees of the correctness of his decisions—or else every sort of interference was possible. Anarchy, however disguised, would break forth and rear her hideous, ruthless head, show her bared teeth and grinning nostrils, and eyes swollen with triumph. His Excellency took a deep breath as he realized that here was a responsibility which he could not escape without the surrender of his self-respect and the betrayal of his honour. He mechanically broke off a sprig of jasmine, breathed its sweet Arabian fragrance, and put it in between the second and third buttons of his tunic. War with Schieffenzahn? Why should there be war? He comforted himself with the thought that it might all come to nothing. The General, who had a dozen different things to attend to every day, must have signed for once without proper enquiry. It was as clear as daylight that even the Quartermaster-General at Ober-Ost had no right to butt in on the legal administration of von Lychow's Division. This sort of mistake could be corrected by a word in season, and Otto Gerhard von Lychow, who was seventy years old and Schieffenzahn's senior on the Army List, could put even him in his place without being reprimanded in his turn. But he must sleep on it. To-morrow, perhaps in the morning, or better, after dinner, he would have a friendly talk on the telephone with the Major-General and fix up the whole affair. Of course the man at the bottom of it all was the Kriegsgerichtsrat at Headquarters, that pettifogging old fox. What did they call him? Hadn't he got some fiddler's name? Joachim?—no, Wilhelmi, that was it. An old man like him might easily confuse that long-forgotten prince of fiddlers with Joseph Joachim. More composed, but still plunged in thought, the General turned the corner and came upon the skittle-alley.

It was built of fresh timber. The path had been slightly broadened, a sort of gravel bastion had been constructed, and lightly roofed in. The entire length of the path itself had been levelled and floored with planks, leaving a sloping groove of boards on the left side—and the skittle-alley was ready for the players. At that end of it where the wall bent round at right-angles, the skittles were clattering against each other on the wooden floor.

The shingle-roofed pavilion, which had been neatly constructed by the carpenters of the Kommandantur, under Sergeant Pont, who had acted as architect and master-builder, displayed the exotic and graceful lines of a new style, faintly resembling the lofty wooden synagogue of Mervinsk with its pagoda-like pinnacles, which Pont or Winfried were not the only people to admire. Lychow, as he approached, surveyed with satisfaction its gaily-coloured pillars, and the tapering curves of the roof. He would really have preferred a thatched roof, but the needs of the horses made that impossible. They had just begun the work of tarring and painting it in a chequered black and white design, like a Japanese drawing; the buckets of tar and the huge paint-brush were still standing behind the bushes.

The sun had made two-thirds of his mighty journey across the arch of Heaven. Under his slanting golden shafts the trees rustled in the freshening air and the great yellow marguerites and the sunflowers on the wall now lifted their jagged golden shields towards the west, and glowed like copper. Here and there a Chinese lantern began to glimmer over the distant paths. In the pavilion elderly gentlemen stood in their shirt-sleeves bowling at the skittles, all of which had names: cheers greeted the fall of Lloyd George, Nicolai Nicolaievitch, or Clemenceau, shouts of laughter the overthrow of Wilson, and there were roars of indignation when Bethmann, Erzberger, or Scheidemann went down. (Liebknecht's name was beyond all mention: his proper place was jail.) Herr von Hessta, balancing one of the balls in his hand, was holding forth upon a re-partition of South America upon Pan-German lines:—a vast German Crown Colony clean across the Continent—the possibility of an alliance of Mexico for the conquest of Canada (his geography had grown a trifle rusty). He hinted at the blowing up of American factories and ammunition depots.—"Yes, these were the days of glory for the mightiest race on earth."

His Excellency was not too well-pleased to hear these boastful, pompous, rasping tones. He had hoped to slip across the grass towards the left, and suddenly appear among the gay crowd of the younger guests. But he decided to join the players. An officer of

such high rank must not be allowed to go on pouring out such gossip
of the servants' hall. The broad red stripes on his breeches flashed
in the sunlight as he emerged with a friendly shout of: "Bravo!
All nine of them!" Everyone got up, and von Hessta held his
tongue.

Lychow, with a few cheerful words, pulled out the report from
Headquarters, which he had asked for as he passed the office, and
read it aloud: The Western Front was at last quiet, there was no
fighting except on a small scale near Leintrey. But here in the east,
on the other hand, there was something worth hearing: North-east
of Czernowitz, Böhm-Ermolli's troops had crossed the frontier; under the personal command of the Archduke Joseph, imperial troops
were marching into Czernowitz. (The officers from the fighting-
line grinned knowingly: they all remembered those glorious occasions when Princes and Royalties had not ridden before them to victory.) In the Bukowina the Russians were retreating on the whole of
the long line, Czernowitz—Petrouc—Bilka—Kimpolung. They were
again trying, unsuccessfully, to get possession of Mt. Casinului. On
the lower Sereth, on Mackensen's front, there was increased activity.
Success and victory glowed in the delighted faces of these men
whose business it was to lead other men into battle, with all the
risk of being themselves left dead upon the field.

"We'd do anything for our good allies," croaked von Hessta.
As if to re-enforce his opinion, the band suddenly struck up the
Austrian march, the anthem of the two Teutonic peoples; its broad
emphatic rhythms blared out across the slanting rays of sunlight.
They all stopped and listened as a sound of singing approached.
They walked out on the grass to see what was happening, and from
where they stood in the shadow of the skittle-alley they saw a procession of young people—marching four abreast, led by the pale blue
Austrian uniforms, with Count Dubna-Trencsin at the head of the
lieutenants and nurses, attitudinizing like a drum-major in front
of his drummers, whirling his cane in the air like that functionary's
staff. His eyes looked slightly glazed and vacant as he bellowed out:

*"Mir san vom K. und K. Infanterierägiment
Hoch- und Deutschmeisterr Nummer vier—aber stier."*

and he repeated the popular couplet, and drew up right in front of the laughing, clapping group of skittle-players, while the band, near by, sank into exhausted silence. At this moment the rasping voice of Herr von Hessta was heard finishing a sentence: "Unless those infernal Czechs betray us. . . ." This utterance, though quite unwittingly, was made right under the nose of the Austrian Captain.

Had Count Dubna been sober, the Prussian's unintentional insult would have had no immediate consequences; but he was in an excited condition and had been devoting himself whole-heartedly to his host's refreshments. He started back, like a rearing horse, drove the point of his stick into the grass, bent his tall form over it, and, flushed, speechless, and menacing, he glared into the Major-General's eyes. An A.D.C. must hear everything, and Lieutenant Winfried, with Sister Bärbe close behind him, was on the scene in a second, and by way of a diversion, called out:

"What does '*Stier*' mean, my dear Count?"

"*Stier*," repeated the Count, without taking his eyes off his enemy, who was smiling foolishly and rubbing his chin on the open collar of his tunic, "*Stier* means bare. Empty pockets. All Austria cleaned out to the last man. 'The Czechs betray you'? What the hell do you know about it? Who are you, anyway? Have you seen them lying in heaps on the Isonzo, at Doberdo and before Przemysl, and anywhere else where they fought your dirty war? And what about the men from Eger, Salzburg, and the Tyrol? And the poor Serbs of Bosnia—the real Serbs they are. We're *stier*, that's what we are! And you're still crying out for more dead bodies, more and more dead bodies!"

These words were followed by a silence through which could be heard the rustle of the leaves, and the hum of the bumble-bees, even the whirring of the cockchafers who were just preparing to fly into the sunset, into the great golden gateway of the west. At a signal from Lychow, Winfried laid a hand on Dubna's shoulder, so as to lead him away; but the tall, gaunt officer shook him off, as a football-player fends off a charge.

"Drunk as an owl—don't rile him," said a Major calmly and clearly to Herr von Hessta; but the latter stuck out his chin, and furious at the thought of being challenged by an Austrian, rapped out:

"Yes, my dear Count. Who are we fighting for now on the Eastern Front? Haven't you read the latest Bulletin? Were all the heroes Austrians?"

The Count burst into a laugh, which showed how little he was aware that this was a social occasion. He stood alone on the Planet, leaning forward, championing the cause of Austria against the Prussian Spirit, and yelled his accusations into the General's face:

"What do you think? Galicia and Bukowina are no good to us. We'd have given them up long ago, and glad to do it. But you won't let us. Austria's done for: Mozart and Schubert, Hapsburg and Vienna—all done for. All our pretty little girls left homeless. I suppose you think we're your colonial troops, your dirty niggers. But you're the niggers, you damned bastards. You go about spouting Schiller, but there's nothing in your heads but 'Where's my baby?'—You mongrels, you pack of heretics, you godless, devilish riff-raff. Austria's done for."

And just as he was pulling his stick out of the grass so as to bring it down in God's name between the horns of the Prussian devil, gouge out his hyena's eyes with its iron point, and fairly rid the world of him—his face streaming with tears, his chest, his throat, and his whole body shaken by convulsive sobbing, he fell face downwards in the grass. Then he lay weeping at Lychow's feet, who rapped out hastily:

"Take him away: pick him up." He was himself too much taken aback to touch him. The Austrian had been eight months on the Isonzo and been shell-shocked before he was relieved and sent to von Lychow's Division; so they carried him away with much sympathy and not without some qualms of conscience. "Poor Count," everyone said. "What a pity! It has rather upset the party, but never mind." His Excellency stood biting his lower lip with annoyance. The day was not ending auspiciously; but there was a cheerful evening yet to come. "Carry on," said the General curtly.

Most unfortunately, but with the best of intentions, Captain von Brettschneider, thinking to create a diversion, pointed to where some celebrations were evidently in progress, though they could not yet be seen. He trotted to where the path turned off some twenty yards ahead, and with a broad smile on his face, beckoned to them all to come along. They came. They heard shouts of "Hail!" *"Hoch Gambrinus," "Bacchus lebe"*: a rumbling not unlike the roll of a drum, singing, and the shrill laughter of women.

Along the main avenue, under the coloured paper lanterns, a marvellous procession was drawing near, surrounded by a bevy of young lieutenants and nurses—Sisters Emma, Cläre, Traute, and Annemie. There sat, enthroned on the empty barrel, borne on the shoulders of four orderlies, Grischa-Bjuscheff, his white tunic open showing his bare chest, his head crowned with ivy leaves, and an empty wine-glass in his hand, roaring out in his loud, harsh baritone, the great song of the Revolution which had accompanied his escape from the timber-camp. . . . He sang it in Russian and nobody understood, especially as his right foot was beating thunderous time on the belly of the cask, while the splinters of a wine-glass clinked in his hand in unison. His skin had been cut by one such fragment, and blood was running gently down his neck, but he did not mind: he was inwardly celebrating a festival of his own, as a perfectly free man, Grischa Iljitsch Paprotkin, Sergeant of the 118th Regiment of Infantry, Knight of the Cross of St. George, hero of many fights with bayonet, hand-grenade, and rifle, a man who had not seldom slipped through the fingers of death and was not to be deterred from making his speech, his mighty speech about a pardoned prisoner.

"Eylert Lövborg with vine-leaves in his hair," quoted a literary engineer, and His Excellency, with a dangerously friendly smile upon his lips, which was belied by the glitter in his eyes, asked in a hoarse voice: "Who's responsible for this?" The lieutenants laughingly explained that Captain von Brettschneider had told them the Russky's story. As a reward for his pluck in not giving up the game, but joining in this festival, although he had been condemned to death by the Divisional Court Martial, they had poured two cognacs into his glass of beer, which contained the dregs from many glasses spiced with a little cigar ash. Thereupon he had made a speech in Russian, which no one could understand, and had been decorated with the Iron Cross in tar upon his back.

"Squad, about face!" some one shouted.

The four orderlies, with a drunken leer on their flushed faces, carried out the order, displaying a back view of Grischa—a broad black cross from his collar to his hind-quarters and from shoulder to shoulder.

"God bless my soul," cried His Excellency in amazement.

Grischa, with the confident adroitness of a very drunk man, swung himself round as he sat astride of his high, curved throne, and, facing his hearers, he addressed them thus:

"There is so much forgiveness in the world," he cried in Russian, "that there's enough for everyone, even for the Germans. There are good fellows among them. I have seen my comrades, Russian prisoners, scrounging potato-parings from manure-heaps, and croaking of hunger-typhus all the same. For even that there's forgiveness. I have seen men with their hands bound together and wire nooses round their necks, marching till they dropped; we'll say no more of that: all forgiven now. They were only Russians, and prisoners—but it's all forgiven now. And even if some of them drowned themselves in the latrine—it's all forgotten, and wiped out—we're brothers now. Life's so simple. I've found it all out. It's not evil and wickedness that rule this world. It's all bright and good and friendly, and war's just a huge mistake. We'll turn our rifle-butts into hammer-handles—the steel and iron can be used for tools. Even Paprotkin and Bjuscheff shall embrace, and poor Babka . . . but not a word about her." He struck himself so hard upon the mouth that he reeled, and gazed curiously at the blood upon his hand. The speech and the subsequent blow were accompanied by bursts of laughter. This tone of lofty forgiveness and goodwill, this flight of rhetoric punctuated by loud belches, could hardly be taken seriously. But luckily this interruption stopped the flow of his eloquence. He sank forward with his chin on a hoop of his barrel, saying:

"Täwje, you've got some rum notions, but no one's going to die for them, you little Jewish fat-head": and with that he was sick.

"Take the brute away," shouted His Excellency, in a burst of indignation, shared by all his Staff, against the dirty Russian.

Chapter 3

THE TELEPHONE

I⊤ was ten o'clock at night. The Intelligence Section of the staff was working at high pressure. The windows were wide open and the whole firmament was glittering with stars. Currents of elemental force vibrated all unheeded round the planets—but one of these forces men had mastered. Wires had been made to carry words. The humming waves of electric ether flashed from ear to ear with incalulable speed; for that instant they cease to be words; then, in a moment, they are words once more and bear the purposes of man.

With both receivers pressed to his ears, like the flaps he had worn over them through that long winter in the Vosges, sat the operator, Lance-Corporal Engels, listening to a conversation. Whether this was contrary to Regulations is not certain. He could hear every word. Lance-Corporal Löwengard was leaning up against him, and such was his excitement that he could scarcely keep his pipe between his teeth.

"I say, old man, is he giving it to him hot?" he puffed out amid clouds of smoke. "Has he slopped him one? Can't you speak, old man?"

They liked to call each other "old man" in this most inhuman of all ages. His companion only waved his hand impatiently and went on listening. What he heard was evidently of tremendous import, for he crouched in his seat like a pianist whose hands had been lashed to the keyboard of his instrument. The very room was listening; not a sound was heard. So deep was the silence that the loudest noise on earth seemed to be the early serenade of the nightingale which was pouring forth a stream of marvellous flute-like warblings from the depths of a lilac bush some distance from the open window. Far away on the horizon could be heard the throb of a motor-car.

"I say," said Engels, turning to his comrade, as he laid his hand over the mouthpiece of the telephone. " 'Damn it all, do you want to make a murderer of me?'—that's what the old boy has just said to those swine."

"But he wouldn't dare say that to Schieffenzahn?"

"You don't know Lychow."

"Still, he must do the thing in the usual way, and what's the sense of barking at Wilhelmi? He's only Schieffenzahn's office-boy."

The talk subsided and they fell to listening once again. The two operators, and anyone who had overheard the General's words, would have understood the Bjuscheff case in all its simplicity. A man had been condemned for an offence which it was clearly proved he had not committed, and instead of re-opening the case they wanted to shoot him. And Lychow would have none of it.

"It's quite clear that the old man isn't having any."

But Engels, as an experienced veteran of twenty-two, snapped his fingers in the air, and after a pause he asked in the prescribed formula that ensures that no private shall, even by accident, address a superior officer in the second person:

"Is the conversation finished, please? Then I'll disconnect." And drawing out the plugs he cut off the General's office from that of the Kriegsgerichtsrat Wilhelmi at Bialystok, so many kilometers away. Then he lit a cigarette and said:

"Of course the Boss isn't taking any, so he thinks, at least— but I wouldn't give the price of a fag for Bjuscheff's life."

"Yes, but that's murder," said Löwengard; "the fellow's innocent."

"Look here," answered Engels, "when they send you to crawl out of the trenches in front of the wire to dig up the A telephone and listen-in to the Frenchies, are you guilty or not guilty? But there'll be a murder right enough if you're unlucky. What's the good of talking to the Prussians about justice? I wouldn't give the price of a fag for the whole of Bjuscheff, from head to foot."

"What! don't you think the old boy will hold on?"

"Of course he will, you fat-head," said Engels, "but if Schieffenzahn gets a good hold on the other end, the rope'll break, and the old boy will find himself with the short end in his hand and his

—— on the office floor. If Albert likes, the man will live—but not otherwise."

"But why has Schieffenzahn got a down on the fellow?"

"No one can know, old man. What's at the bottom of his mind is more than any old sow could root up. Perhaps he don't care a blast and it's just Wilhelmi swanking. Then you'll hear no more about it."

"Well, I shouldn't be sorry, I can tell you."

"Or it'll be like two dogs after a bone. If so, I prophesy Albert will get nasty."

"Poor old Bjuscheff!"

"You may say that. On these occasions it's the bone that gets the seediest time of it."

"Perhaps we'll get peace before it's settled," said Löwengard, with a puff of smoke. He loathed to think that his Division, or, indeed, any part of the German Army, should have anything to do with such a cool and barefaced bit of brutality. He was twenty years old and had once been an art student. "I wonder if Bjuscheff knows what a lucky fellow he is?" he added reflectively.

"Why, his name isn't Bjuscheff, it's Paprotkin, so they say. I've known the story a long while."

"And told me nothing about it?"

"I promised Bertin not to, old man."

"When he hears about it he'll be surprised—Paprotkin, or whatever his name is."

"You can call him Bjuscheff safe enough. He'll never get rid of Bjuscheff any more."

The switchboard began to click again and the work of the night went on. Outside, the nightingale had long been silent.

Chapter 4

THE END IN VIEW

A PEDLAR can easily get on good terms with German soldiers. So this raspberry woman, whose name was Babka, had for some time been permitted to ply her trade in the men's quarters at the prison and even in the guardroom. And as it soon got about that she liked or perhaps knew this Grischa—Bjuscheff—one can never be quite sure of such things with people who are speaking quickly in another language—she was sometimes allowed to have a chat with him in his cell, with the door open, of course. In any case discipline had been somewhat relaxed for Bjuscheff, since the soldiers, and even Grischa himself, had heard the incredible rumour that Schieffen-zahn demanded his head. Night was drawing on, and summer-lightning throbbed and flickered across the sky like the mighty quivering eyelashes of a terror-stricken god. Grischa sat crouching with his elbows on his thighs, clasping his aching forehead in his hand. His face looked sunken, and no wonder; there were black shadows under his eyes, his forehead seemed swollen, and his chin was thrust forward beyond his upper teeth like a man chewing something with a bitter taste. Babka, seated on an upturned bucket, was leaning against the wall, and watching his mouth with yearning anxious eyes. She wanted him to speak and he would not. High above her head stood the window of his cell, like a purple jewel on black velvet. From time to time the bright wings of the lightning flashed across it.

Babka was speaking to Grischa with the coaxing voice she would have used to a young and frightened animal. Nothing serious had happened, she said. It was true they had made him drunk, and mixed cigar-ash or something of the kind with his schnapps, which makes you drunk quicker than toadstools do, and painted his back, and dragged him round on a barrel, but there was nothing in all that. It was their disgrace, not his.

"Don't sit there as though you were dying of shame."

No answer; and while she waited the lightning came again, and every corner of the bleak room stood out for a moment in its brief flickering radiance. So she tried once more: he had made speeches, and been sick, but no one minded what a man did when he was drunk. There was no shame in that. And suddenly, in the hope that a little roughness might be more effective, she clenched her tense and quivering hands and shook her fists at him, crying:

"Grischa, this won't do: you can't sit here saying nothing, as if I wasn't here. I won't stand it. I'll go": and in the hope of conjuring up the memory of days gone by, she tried to charm him into speech by her old uncouth endearment:

"You silly soldier man!"

This time Grischa did wake up. He had heard and understood every word that she had spoken, and from the depths of his bewildered being, wrestling with a world he could not understand, he said gently to her:

"Go, Babka, you'd better go. Somebody's after me," he added mysteriously, as he pointed to the window through which the lightning had at that moment flashed and vanished. "It's not safe to be with me," he said in the strange, weak voice of exhaustion and convalescence.

Babka, who had at last got a word out of him, felt that this was something like salvation and that the worst was over.

"Have they sentenced you again? How many years have you got?" she asked him abruptly. And he, impelled to seek comfort from his only true friend in the world, other than Marfa Ivanovna, who was so far away that she could only pray for him, answered:

"There's no new sentence, and that's what I can't understand. It's the old sentence, Babka. The Bialystok people mean that Bjuscheff shall die, and by Bjuscheff they mean me. They don't believe in Paprotkin, no matter what you tell them. Some people think that the truth must be believed, but it isn't so."

For a moment, Grischa was sorry he had spoken, for Babka, quite forgetting where she was, laughed as heartily as she would have done in her own hut in the wild wood.

"Sh!" he hissed sharply at her. But from her belly and heart, throat and mouth, burst a defiant shout of laughter that shook the foundations of the world. It mattered little; at the moment the prison was almost empty, the guards were sitting outside on benches writing letters home or reading: all the windows were open, but indoors they would have had to use electric light, which of course must be economized. So at length this laughter won the day, and Grischa, too, smiled.

"Yes, it is enough to make one laugh. Everybody knows who he is. A horse doesn't mistake himself for his plough, nor the hammer for the nail. Fritzke and Birkholz have been here to prove it, and it was written down all complete. There's something behind it, I tell you."

Babka nodded slowly several times, tense with silent fury.

"All right, then," she said at last hoarsely. "Now I'm sure of it. So the Devil's come back again, has he? Haven't I felt queer since you came, as if the world were upside down? It was so peaceful in the forest: it seemed as if Satan had gone to sleep up there on God's throne. Oh, he's cunning, he's laid his trap very well—he's got at you through me. . . . Now spit at me! Tear my hair out. . . . No, don't or you might hurt your little one inside me."

"Be quiet," said Grischa, with a natural dignity that sat well on him. "Not so loud, not so wild—you needn't yell like a cat in a basket. If I die to-morrow, or the day after, that's an end of me; better than waiting till Monday morning, I dare say. I'm dead sick of it all," he went on in level tones, with an earnestness that frightened Babka. "Leave it as it is." And he stretched himself full length on his bed, with his hands clenched behind his head, and looked up at the window. "You might dip a towel in water and put it on my head," he said wearily. "Even if a man's going to die he doesn't want a headache."

Babka quickly did what he asked. She wrung out his towel and, although it was no longer clean, he soon felt the delicious coolness against his neck and his aching forehead. Then she brought the bucket up to him and begged him not to talk like that about death and wanting to die. But he asked her to let him sleep, and if he could not sleep, to let him lie and dream.

"Look," he said, and pointed to the window in a way that made her feel afraid: "Look, there's that lightning again—how bright and sudden it is. I can lie and dream when there's lightning."

"Now I'm certain of it—they've given you poison; you're giving up, you won't pull yourself together."

But Grischa said: "You don't suppose I think it's all up, do you? Of course I don't; the General and his people wouldn't let me be killed. That won't happen. There are people here who believe me, and who know the difference between Paprotkin and Bjuscheff well enough. They stand between me and the other man, and the one that's nearest gives the orders. And yet," he added, "there are all sorts of new things that have grown up in my heart, more than I've ever noticed before."

Babka began to feel a cold fury boil within her against all these forces that were weakening her friend from within, and harrying him from without.

"These devils!" she thought, "these loathsome worms! they'll eat him out hollow as a worm eats away a plank. Soldier boy, soldier boy," she groaned, "remember: the man who's furthest off hits the hardest. A bullet's better than a rifle-butt, a field-gun's fiercer than a rifle, and the lightning's deadliest of all. A General might take some trouble over a soldier once or twice: then, if it was no use, he'd let it drop. That's as clear as mud in a bottle. Only your own legs will get you out of this. . . . Grischa," she added, with an earnestness that concealed a certain fear that he might refuse, "you must escape again."

In reply, he merely sighed and said drearily: "Go to bed, Babka."

Babka understood him well; she felt the reproach all the more because he murmured it so gently, and she went on urging him: he must escape once more. But for her advice, and but for her cursed silly cunning, he would have got away the first time; he must try again. Nothing worse could happen to him than what was going to happen already. Better be shot running away than against a wall. If he followed his own plan, his luck would turn. He could break out, and wait somewhere in hiding—whatever he thought best. She'd help him, but she'd only do exactly as he told her: she'd promise and swear that he'd get home as sure as, but for her advice, he wouldn't be lying there to-day.

"Please go away," he answered with closed eyes.

She called out his name piteously, then she said: "All right, I'll go. Have a good sleep."

At the doorway of the cell she stopped, and gazing with a sad and kindly look at his face, which, like all faces seen from above, had the hard and bony look of a skull, made up her mind what she must do. It was she once more who would have to act. At least she could open the door for him. Those people had put poison in his drink. Now she would make a brew of schnapps for the Germans. She had seen plenty of herbs and toadstools near the city; she could make a fine, powerful brew out of them, and the General would certainly give her time to do it in. Then she bent over him and whispered: "Sometimes I feel quite weak, Grischa; that's the way with women in my state. A bottle of schnapps would do me good. You can easily get it through the soldiers from the canteen: I can't."

He yawned, and said listlessly: "Schnapps? All right. Now go, Babka, they're shutting the gate." And immediately afterwards, as though to prove Grischa's instinct for time, and how completely he had become a part of the prison organism, Corporal Hermann Sacht appeared in the doorway of the cell and suggested she should go home, telling Grischa that he couldn't sit talking all night; and he took the "old lady" away with him. They nodded slightly to each other, as common people do who like to hide their feelings, and the key turned in the massive door.

Grischa had never dwelt for long on the idea of another escape. He lay there almost contentedly in the stillness, after Babka's existence had passed away into the unknown, and listened to his thoughts. After all these troubles, he loved to lie there and breathe deeply, all alone. His eyes were open and he was staring at the window. The lightning flashed again and again. Grischa thought someone was aiming at him.

"He's shooting in at me," he thought. "I wish I knew why he should want to shoot at me, a common private soldier, neither good nor bad; but he keeps on at it. If only I understood what it all means. It would be better," he thought, as he lay there drowsily musing and feeling easier in mind, "to take cover before I go to sleep: cover, that's what I want."

The thought of doing anything, or escaping, soon dropped out of his mind as he began to fall asleep, but to take cover was only common prudence. One could sleep better under the bed than on it: in that way he would have another good inch or two of beech-planking over his head. And as he was thinking of rolling up his blankets and sleeping on the floor under the bed, his consciousness faded. As he lay snoring, stretched out at full length, he saw in his dream a lieutenant, a general, and an endless line of German soldiers passing before his eyes, with their backs towards him, and the lightning flashes, like the quivering eyelids of a brooding God, flickered across his pallid face. His upturned nose actually cast a sharp-edged shadow over the corner of one eye.

Towards morning came a thunderstorm which cleared the air for many miles about. Seldom at this season did a day break as fresh and gay and silvery blue as this eighth day of August, whose first bright hours found Bertin at his desk, composing poetry. In those early morning hours, while he was fresh from sleep, his brain still alert and his style not yet subdued to the army pattern, he wrote his comedy in verse, labouring to give it formal coherence, but otherwise leaving it to take its course, almost as though he had little hope of achieving a complete success. It would serve to get his hand in for more serious work, and he was almost aghast at his own invention which seemed to him too potent, when, towards the end of the first act, Cæsar appeared, so striking, so vital a figure, and of such human significance, that he threatened to put the whole drama out of gear. So he now turned his attention to the broader aspects of the action as a whole, and equally to the essential theme and purpose of his drama; and he grew very busy indeed. Soon after nine a knock came at the door and an office orderly stepped in with a file under his arm, a man like himself, a well-groomed, flaxen-haired, spectacled lance-corporal, who sat down, helped himself to one of Bertin's cigarettes, and began to talk of the most important topic of the day: they were threatened with a new "murder commission" and a general comb-out. Bertin had no qualms because he, as belonging to the staff of a fighting unit, had nothing to fear in his position even from a "K.V." * It was quite otherwise with his comrade, Lance-Corporal Langermann, who had scribbled his way up from the orderly room of his obscure Kommandatur to the office at Mervinsk; he had to shiver in his shoes, while Bertin sat serenely on his hind-quarters, protected by his Regimental Sergeant-Major as obviously indispensable.

"Can't you do something, old boy?" he murmured dolefully. "Don't you want any more help? If ever I have to go back to the Front again, I'll cut my thumb off."

Bertin expressed his hearty sympathy. Then he asked what else he had come for. Langermann raised his head slowly like a man awaking from sleep.

"I've come to fetch the Sentence."

Bertin understood him at once. His mind was still unclouded, and with the cool sardonic vision of the common man he saw the image of Schieffenzahn rise up before him in the likeness of a peasant, brutish and very evil. Without giving the Division time to protest, somebody had informed the Kommandantur, and now here was Corporal Langermann—indeed, without knowing it, he had had some little influence in the Grischa case—come to take formal receipt of his documents so that the sentence might be carried out. Something of this sort was in Bertin's mind as he gazed reflectively at Corporal Langermann. Had he come in the afternoon Bertin would perhaps have betrayed himself by his anxiety and embarrassment; he would have said more than he had a right to say, involved the Kriegsgerichtsrat quite unnecessarily, and generally behaved in a far too emphatic and high-handed manner, which would have been disastrous. But as it was, he said to himself: "What fools we were to bring in Lychow so much too soon; now we have got no trumps left." It flashed through his mind that indirect methods are always better than direct ones, in art as well as in affairs; a sweeping blow is far more deadly than a short straight thrust. And so he began quietly to think out a course of action. In the first place he made

---

* Fit for service.

up his mind that Corporal Langermann knew nothing. Bjuscheff's sentence—that was all. So Bertin decided to be mysterious. Hadn't he heard that this Bjuscheff business had been going on for a long time? His Excellency himself had been mixed up in it: he'd talked to the Bialystok people personally about it and whoever got into His Excellency's way over this business might get an unpleasant shock. Had Langermann got any enemies in his office?

And Langermann began to feel nervous. When a Corporal of Kommandantur has G.V.* against his name and a comb-out is in prospect, it is unhealthy for him, however much he may be within his rights, to get up against a General, as it would be to take a wild-elephant calf away from its mother. So when Bertin proposed he should postpone this ticklish question, not for long, of course, but for two or three days, he heaved a sigh of relief.

"There must be mistake," Bertin suggested. "As far as I know this sentence will not be carried out. You can set your mind at ease: if necessary, the Divisional Court Martial will send across the sentence and the instructions for carrying it out."

Langermann thought this looked like a way out; no names need be mentioned even if further enquiries were made for the documents, and on the other hand nobody could suspect him of failing to obey his "old man's" orders.

"Very well, then," he said, getting up. "Of course you'll see that this case will be properly dealt with?"

Bertin reassured him.

When he was alone, he thought over his plan of action. No orders had been given to withhold the documents because no one supposed that Schieffenzahn would make such a diabolically direct and unsuspected attack. In this matter he had therefore acted to some extent on his own responsibility. But, after brief reflection, he came to the conclusion that he was quite safe. For the present, Schieffenzahn's attack had been averted by the pawn Bertin. None the less he paced uneasily up and down the room. His verses had suddenly lost their savour: between him and his image of Cæsar came that pallid parrot-profile with its sagging cheeks, and the two

---

* Fit for garrison duty only.

deep wrinkles round the upper jaw, which distinguished all Schieffenzahn's portraits.

After a few moments' thought he telephoned to the Kriegsgerichtsrat and told him what had happened. Posnanski, who was just
having breakfast after a ride in the woods, shouted irritably: "That's
Schieffenzahn all over," praised Bertin's diplomacy, decided to go
without his violin practice, and ask Lieutenant Winfried to get an
assurance from the General that he would stick to his guns.

Winfried opened his eyes wide. Of course His Excellency would
stick to his guns. The Kommandantur had better not make fools
of themselves, the matter was still pending, and there were some
people who had something more to say about it. And they agreed
that those fellows over the way should not get hold of the sentence
or any authority to carry it out, unless signs and wonders fell from
heaven.

Half an hour later Posnanski rang up the Kommandantur and
told them, in a polite and friendly voice, that there must have
been a misunderstanding, even Section VII B could sometimes make
mistakes, the Bjuscheff case was not yet fully investigated, and if
any confirmation of this was needed they might apply, of course
through official channels, to His Excellency, as the supreme legal
authority.

Corporal Langermann whistled thankfully to himself, and he
did not know that even mightier machinery had been set in motion
to relieve him of his cares. For, in the last resort, only vast
mysterious forces could suspend for a while the law of cause and
effect, in military affairs so rigid and so ruthless, and leave the
matter in abeyance.

For meanwhile in Berlin and Great General Headquarters, the
Pope's effort to end the War had taken a more concrete form.
Nothing, indeed, had been said of Alsace-Lorraine or of the Eastern
Provinces as yet, but a feeler had been put out concerning Belgium;
and this was quite enough to bring the smallest and most powerful
party in the Empire, the party of the Generals, Industrials, and
Professors, hot upon the scent of treason. As the Papal Nuncio had
been encouraged to intervene by someone in the Emperor's entourage
(perhaps by the Kaiser himself!), the salvation of the Fatherland

had become an especially difficult and urgent task, so that Albert Schieffenzahn, whose political tool and assistant the successful and ambitious Wilhelmi had become, had to give his attention to considerably more momentous moves in the game than the question whether the Lychow Division was to regard the Bjuscheff case as still in suspense or as a *causa judicata.* Moreover the Operations Section at Brest-Litovsk, cigarette or cigar in mouth, was intently following the German conquest of Courland, Livonia, Esthonia, and half the world. Germany had got her teeth firmly into these Eastern lands: vast movements of troops were taking place, units were brought from the quieter Western Front and linked up with naval forces, mainly with the object of securing the islands of Ösel and Dagö, small useless heaps of sand, at the cost of hundreds of young lives. Schieffenzahn wanted to give the King of Prussia a little more room to move by presenting him with the ducal coronet of Courland—and Courland was next to Finland—and thereby set the German Emperor against all this interminable babble about peace.

Only a slight change revealed the increased importance attached to Grischa by the Kommandantur. They gave him an A.D.C. in the person of Corporal Sacht, who, outside the prison, had to accompany him everywhere with a loaded rifle—an extremely welcome change of duty in the lovely summer of 1917.

So Kriegsgerichtsrat Posnanski said many times, either to himself or to Bertin:

"If only I knew what Albert had up his sleeve: he's a devil for keeping his mouth shut"—while Bertin, who was enthusiastically absorbed in working out his "Cæsar" play as a result of having lost his heart to a young Athenian lady called Pericleia who had unexpectedly appeared in the plot, maintained that only an idiot could expect the Divisional authorities to carry out a sentence which they themselves had cancelled as being null and void. Posnanski replied with indistinct mumblings indicative of doubt, chewed his cigar, and looked worried, though he could not tell why.

Chapter 5

NOT UNCONCERNED WITH SCHNAPPS

BABKA lived in Veressejeff's house like a free and independent cat, that comes and goes when it likes, and no one can tell where it will wander off to next. She was no trouble to the old shopkeeper, though he often cast a suspicious look at her girth which, after the fashion of women, seemed in a few months to have increased. But before he could make sure, she was off again, a grey and silent figure, with a deep furrow between her brows.

She felt too much respect for Grischa, with his ups and downs of mood, to laugh at him for his faith in the General, but she simply ignored it. The Devil was taking a malicious vengeance for her many insults, by entangling her in an unreasonable passion for a passing stranger, making him the father of her child, and now bringing him to his end in an execution-trench smeared with quick-lime. Sometimes she would admit that he had so far succeeded, as she clenched her teeth in an access of rage, which she at once suppressed for the sake of her unborn child. Besides, she had other things to do than to indulge her feelings. Her plan for helping Grischa to escape was simple and comprehensive, and presented no difficulties. She had made friends with many of the soldiers and intended, late one afternoon just before the guards were going on duty, to drug or kill these German friends of hers with a strong sweet dose of poisoned schnapps. She would then throw open all the doors right under Grischa's nose and then, perhaps, when there was nothing in the world to stop him, he would deign to walk out of the prison.

The thorn-apple has whitish, funnel-shaped blossoms, fruit like chestnuts, and beautiful dark green indented leaves; it grows on hedges near great towns, and on manure heaps—not from any romantic preference for places where poison feels at home, but simply because men will not let it grow elsewhere. So much for the *Datura stramonium*. The deadly nightshade, again, *Atropa bella-donna,* and the black nightshade, *Solanum nigrum,* with their russet bells and little white stars, delight to keep it company. The poor poison plants, which have not the luck to support great industries, live a forlorn existence, and one must be a practical naturalist bent upon special studies, even as Babka was, to give close attention to them.

In the warm August nights, people who want to be together can scarcely bear to sit indoors. So it comes about that sometimes friendly pairs of lovers go out to watch the shooting stars which bring so many omens and fulfill so many wishes. On nights when the moon hangs steeped in light like a round fruit between the leaves, the outlying gardens near the town find special favour among lovers. Two such pairs, who were lying on tarpaulins in the moon-shadow under the thick lilac trees, in front of Lieutenant Winfried's house, could see the stars moving like glow-worms between the branches. A rustling noise of hedgehogs after their prey, the sudden movements of sleeping birds invisible in the darkness, a soft invitation to a glass of wine or a cigarette—these were the only sounds. A gentle dew was falling on the blankets that were spread over them. Oh, the deep, drowsy joy of summer! Oh, those nights when human hearts seem to soar upwards in fulfillment or desire to those dark domes of foliage above them. There lay Winfried and Bärbe, in the deep contentment of that hour; Bertin and Sophie, happy in the friend-ship of their bodies and their souls: his soul was turned towards the west, towards Lenore, while hers was wholly given to the man, though she knew full well that he was not hers for long. And through the warm air between the bushes and the grass hovered happiness, the easy-hearted tender happiness of youth, far above all the despair that filled the world, and its vast yearning for deliverance. The four lovers lay so quietly except for a few soft, whispered words of affection, that no one on the moonlit road beyond the hedge would have guessed their presence. Opposite them, on a kind of deserted slope, grew a wild and tangled mass of weeds and herbs; and thence there rose strange, pungent, heavy odours.

Through the silence of the summer night a step was heard approaching, bare-footed but unmistakable. Bärbe heard it clearly enough, and Sophie too; but the one was lying in blessed peace with her head on her friend's shoulder, while the other was slowly running her fingers through Bertin's hair as he rested his head against the hollow of her hip—and all men find it hard to move when they are so comfortably disposed. Babka was coming up the road, making straight for the tangle of bushes and the plants with their thick stalks and fat leaves. She had taken careful note of the spot during the day; but hers was no harvest for the sun to shine on. Adepts tell us that poisonous herbs should be gathered when the moon is up and on the increase: both going and coming the gatherer must refrain from worldly speech, and if he meets with anyone on the road, he must devoutly murmur a Paternoster or an Ave Maria. He must also start upon his journey with the right foot, and return with his left foot foremost, being very careful not to change his step. And if he does all this, no evil spirits can meddle with his undertaking. So, muttering as she went, the woman plodded on towards the bushes. There she plucked off the blooms and leaves and little berries—she had a use for all of them—working quickly, and her basket was soon full. As she stood up to return, a shooting-star traversed the sky slowly and majestically from right to left. This happy omen made her certain of success. If a gendarme met her now, he would certainly take her for a moon-struck woman and let her go home unmolested. On the way, she would pass by the back wall of the prison, and sit down and close her eyes for a moment under the window of a certain cell.

In these days anger against Babka was slowly rising in Grischa's heart. Until lately, this raspberry woman, who had promoted herself to the sale of pears and cherries, though she occasionally brought back from the woods a basketful of fresh blue bilberries, had only visited him in the afternoons and evenings; she would set down her basket, and they would sit, sometimes saying little and dropping into silence, sometimes bursting into a sudden flow of animated talk, while the corporal, with his pipe in his mouth and his rifle between his knees, sat near them, on a block of wood, a barrel, or an upturned wash-tub, or sometimes actually on a bench. During the last few days, however, she had almost been lying in wait for Grischa in the early morning, slipping past him with a few brief words of greeting; and in the evening, when he ceased work, she was in her place once more. In the morning her eyes were fixed hungrily and beseechingly upon his, and in the evening she came as if to claim fulfillment of a promise that had never been given. Grischa knew that it was all for him, to save him, and to set him free. He ought to have been thankful to her; and yet at last she so angered him that he began to curse her softly, but with all the brutality of a man who can only vent his fury in the language of the people. He upbraided and reviled her, calling her a bitch, sniffing round his legs and asking for a kick, and he mimicked her cringing ways:

" 'Bottle of schnapps, please, for the old woman!' You didn't whine like that in the forest, did you? You pushed us all about properly when we were your soldiers. Go and talk like that to Max of the canteen."

And as she stood motionless and silent, with the same obstinately imploring look upon her face, he changed his tone and hissed at her impatiently:

"It's no good thinking I'm going to escape. Do you want to know why? Because I'm sick of it. You can't keep dipping a man in hot water and then ducking him in cold. They don't do that at the baths. First hot water, then cold, and then a lay-down—that's the way they do it. I tell you I won't stand any more of it. I'm fed up with being hunted about all over the country, and shaken like a rat in a dog's mouth. That's me! I'm tired of it all, I tell you—all the chasing and worrying and hoping and fearing; it takes some doing, escaping, but I did it, and then I got caught and sentenced and let off and sentenced again—and I'm through with it." The tone in which he dismissed the subject should have warned Babka that her scheme was hopeless; he fell into a brooding silence and then, with the harassed look of a man confronted with some matter that he can hardly express, much less explain:

"What's the meaning of it all? Old Täwje says that for God everything has a meaning, says he, and as its God's meaning, it's a good meaning, and yet, you see, there's somebody shooting at me, and if he hits me and lays me out, where does the good come in? That's the devil of it," he added. He had long forgotten Babka, his anger, and the bottle of schnapps. And yet it was written that she was to get it.

Among the more important institutions of the Kommandantur was the huge canteen, the soldiers' bar and restaurant, in which (as is well known) three-and-fifty pfennigs, a larger part of the soldier's pay, was extorted from the heroic sons of the Fatherland for the benefit of the Kommandantur. And as nothing weighs so terribly upon the soldier as the monotony of his humiliating and barren existence, in which a cigarette is something of an event, and a glass of schnapps a gift of fortune, and a meal is as good as a love affair, when chocolate or plum jam—even sausages and cheese—have an emotional appeal far beyond their nutritive value, it will be readily understood that a well-conducted base-canteen will show an excellent balance at the end of the month. True, this money was to go back to the Kommandantur, but when? And who was the Kommandantur for this purpose? And if Captain von Brettschneider and Sergeant Halbscheid, Sergeant-Major Spierauge and the factotum known as Max of the Canteen, choose to agree together about the disposal of the canteen funds—that they should, "for the time being," be applied to the "extension of business"—who is to come forward and say: "Stop, this is our show, and we demand an account"? A company of the Landwehr that has no wish to be transferred elsewhere, are very ready, however much they may curse in private, to see the canteen turnover steadily increasing, though without any tangible advantages to themselves; and they are quite prepared to be mulcted on the first of every month in a certain sum for canteen funds.

This particular canteen had been established in the extensive shop of Refuel Samichstein, after the owner had been evicted under a requisition warrant. This was a document which restrained the occupier of a house or shop, on pain of imprisonment, from taking a single one of his own towels or washing-basins away with him, though it guaranteed, of course, on the faith of international covenants and the German Imperial Eagle stamped thereon, to restore to him all his property after the War. Until then, Samichstein with his wife and five children inhabited two rooms in a wooden house in the Brötchengasse, and when he passed his shop he had the satisfaction of observing what architectural improvements the Germans had made in it. The hall and the large front room now contained a bar, with tables and chairs for the guests. The room beyond, once a shop, too, was a high vaulted chamber which had belonged to a late eighteenth-century house, built by the great-grandfather of the last occupier, and was divided down its length by a barrier, and used for sales across the counter; immediately behind this barrier were kept the stores which spread into various parquet-floored rooms beyond, once the sitting-rooms and bedrooms of a great family. Barrels of herrings, great round tins of *Rollmops,* pickled cucumbers, boxes full of candles, drums of petrol for filling lighters, electric torches, and spare parts, square blue packages of sugar, tinned fruits and jams, preserved milk, and sardines in oil, artificial honey—all these treasures towering up among mountains of tobacco, where once had stood the beds of the children and their parents. (The latter had been neatly packed up and relegated to an unfortunately damp cellar, and after a series of requests spread over a period of three months, and nineteen formal petitions and personal applications, Refuel Samichstein was permitted to remove his now mouldy and moth-eaten beds to his new quarters. Until then, he had full authority to sleep upon the floor.) And from the ceiling of this once Jewish house hung strings of pork sausages, sides of smoked bacon, and fragrant hams.

For some time Grischa had been familiar with these rooms. He helped in the unpacking of fresh consignments, rolled casks of beer into their places, stacked up the various goods, washed the plates, glasses, knives and forks—in fact, Max of the Canteen had found someone to take his orders, and thus became a man in authority. His fat, red, boorish countenance with its scrubby red beard and prominent ears was wreathed in gratified smiles. Now he was no longer last: although he belonged to the small, but respectable, class of German soldiers that could not sign their names, there was now another at his beck and call. A cheerful fellow was Max of the Canteen with his fat paws and sausage fingers, and if all things came to an end fifteen months later and the army was no more, he would be the only one

who would manage to keep the canteen going in the altered times to
come. Many cushy jobs would come to an end then: Max of the
Canteen might not be able to write his name, but he wasn't worrying.

There he stood, chewing a quid, and loading up Grischa with
tins of tobacco. Sometimes he joined in the work, sometimes he
stood looking on with his hands in the pockets of a large leather apron
that smelt of many things, but especially of pickled herrings. Grischa
in his drill jacket and his peakless cap, or *Krätzchen*, pulled down
over his right ear, against which he was steadying the tobacco tins,
stowed away his burden with the patience and composure born of
experience. When he returned after much arranging of the stock,
he found Max in conversation with a certain orderly he knew: it
was the Chaplain's orderly, who had again been sent to buy a special
sort of cheap cigars which were only supposed to be sold to the
rank and file. The men get plenty to smoke, thought the Herr
Pastor. These admirable little dark brown weeds, so absurdly cheap
because they had come from the requisitioned Belgian army stocks,
were well worthy to soothe an hour of pastoral leisure. For in
many a chaplain's home there flourished five children, great or small,
and their father must economize over his own indulgences. So he
hoped to get hold of a box. Now according to the regulations an
individual purchaser might only have a maximum of six cigars a
day, and Max explained at length, in his rasping Low German, that
his request was inadmissible. He pointed out that the reverend
gentleman did belong to the Division and not to the Kommandantur,
and His Excellency von Lychow would be the last to support
his officers, or those who ranked as officers, if they applied for
goods only issuable to the rank and file. Max knew this as well as
the orderly, and the latter departed, fully determined that if the man
of God wanted anything else he should go and fetch it himself.

The two brown cart-horses drooped their heavy ears and necks
dolefully over the trough of hay which had been put in front of
them, and chewed meditatively. They knew it was going to rain: it
was in the air: they realized uneasily that they would soon be wet
and miserable and not be able to move. But Grischa, as he unloaded
the supplies, hoped, looking up at the grey sky heaped with clouds,
that his drill jacket might yet be spared. The Samichstein house

stood in one of the twisted streets of the old town of Mervinsk, near
the great Bes Medresch, called in the official plan of the town,
"Chief Synagogue." These tortuous alleys were to-day almost deserted; for it was Sunday and this was the only sign of it.

The institution of Sunday, largely obliterated by the War, as
if to prove that the world had returned not merely to a pre-Christian
but to a pre-Judean era, had to some extent survived in Mervinsk
under the Protestant garrison, which provided at least one church
service and gave the staff and the personnel of all the various offices,
hospitals, postal services, and the like, the chance of enjoying a
real Sunday—diversified, certainly, by church parades, but at least
the afternoon was free. The fact that the Jews were presented with
a second day of rest, since on their own Sabbath the little wooden
shops were closed and silent behind their iron bars and padlocks,
was due to a philanthropic attitude towards minorities. "Well, well,"
thought the Jews, shivering as they drew long, dusty, black cloaks
tightly across their chests, "this is better than the time when the
Kommandantur compelled us to profane the Sabbath and keep our
shops open."

About a quarter past eleven the streets of Mervinsk were transformed into a camp: the men in field-grey stamped about the streets,
all the shops were open between eleven and two, and in a quarter of
an hour the canteen was full to overflowing. Three minutes later
the ceiling had disappeared behind a cloud of smoke, and a clatter of
cries and laughter hung like another cloud about the bar and counter,
while in quiet corners games of skat had started. The horses were
right: it had begun to drizzle—a persistent, penetrating rain, which
soon soaked its way quietly through to the skin. Luckily for Grischa,
a sergeant who had just entered the canteen and was wise in the
vagaries of the weather, had thrown his ground-sheet over his
shoulders like a cloak, and after a word with Max, not unaccom-
panied by a glass of schnapps, he lent Grischa his red-brown canvas
sheet. Now Grischa was protected from the rain and, as the cases of
tobacco had to be kept dry, he worked in most un-Sabbath-like haste.
At regular intervals his huge form, bearing, Atlas-like, a case on
his right shoulder, would appear in the storeroom, which, as has

been explained, was part of the shop, bend beneath his burden, set it down, stand for a moment or two to get his breath and hurry back once more. Meanwhile Max was selling pocket-knives, small batteries, candles, chocolate, carbide for lamps, and much tobacco in all its forms. The doorway between the two rooms, from which the door had been long since removed, gave a glimpse of the front room and the hall where the men were drinking and playing cards. Behind the bar, with its rows of glass and its shelves of bottles at the back, Sergeant Halbscheid officiated like a priest selling salvation. Through the grey light of that rainy afternoon, and the blue tobacco-smoke under the vaulted ceiling, from the right wall, the Emperor, and from the left, Field-Marshal von Hindenburg, looked down upon all these soldiers, who were sitting on stools at the bare deal tables or on benches against the walls, with their beer-jugs beside them or on the floor between their feet. For the past ten days the hutments round the station at Mervinsk and on the outskirts of the town near the railway where, shortly before, two new ramps had been built, had been seething with troops of all arms. They came and went every few days, and through the delousing centre, a complicated wooden structure, a thousand men passed daily. Thus these transient multitudes swept through the garrison of Mervinsk, taking with them their memories of the town on their journey to the north or west. They all came from the south or from the east, they all knew that Russky was down and out, and said so, they were bursting with all manner of fables about Japanese and French artillerymen, firing from the rear at the retreating hordes of infantry, while German and Austrian shells hurtled after them to speed them on their way.

"No, my boy," said an artillery sergeant, recognizable by the black badges on his *Litevka*, and the grenades on his shoulder-straps, "do you think that if we're ordered to we won't fire on our own infantry? Why do they want Frenchmen and Japs to do it for them? Them as wants to go on living had better obey orders as long as there are any of them left."

"Yes," said a young machine-gunner to the artilleryman who had volunteered this information, "you'll fire at us too, and it won't be for the first time either, you b——y fools. You can do that with us all right," he added gloomily, "because you can always get two sergeants and ten idiots to do anything, even shoot their own comrades. And as long as you can, the War will go on."

A young orderly corporal who, with two other men from the Base-Office, was sitting at the same table as the two speakers, found this conversation disagreeable and disquieting. He solemnly examined his cards, found he could do nothing, and passed. But his two companions were not attending.

"Look at the Russian," said one of them, pointing at Grischa, who, with his case of tobacco on his shoulder, was marching through the doorway like an imposing stage super. "Look at him, that man's as good as dead."

"That's him, is it?" said the corporal. "But so are we all. *Prosit*, Karl."

"Yes, but not so far gone as that," insisted the transport man; "he's got his pass for the next world."

It was now the third man's turn; he had been considering his card, which was not a very good one, and wondering whether he might venture to declare green solo.

"Rubbish!" he said. (A man in the black leather of the lorry drivers can say what he likes.) "Old Lychow won't have it, and so much for the Kommandantur. He's not afraid of the Brass Hats either. Never you mind who I heard it from—but he has properly told off Schieffenzahn's old ape of a lawyer."

Then he looked thoughtfully at his card, which interested him much more than this unprofitable conversation, though he quite believed what he had heard, and having decided that green solo was too risky, he too said he would pass, and this led to a "*Ramsch*," in which the one who makes the fewest points is the winner. But now the corporal who had been first to play looked more cheerful. He certainly had the worst card and became eloquent as he played it.

"*Kreuz!*" he said, slamming down a card. "And talking of crosses, I've seen the cross on that Russian's grave already—what do you suppose the telephone clerks know about it? Emil the carpenter and the sign-painter have got a bet with the A.D.C.'s

orderly that the man's for it, and I've got that straight from a fellow in the Kommandantur office."

"The Russky's looking pretty queer, certainly."

"I'm not surprised," said the other reluctantly taking the trick, for he'd got a fine ace, a cross-ace in his hand. "The whole thing's been on the mat since May. Is his name Bjuscheff or is his name Grischa?"

"That's as clear as my a——," said Max, suddenly breaking in. He had left the counter with two bottles of schnapps under his arm, to take them to Herr Halbscheid behind the bar, and have a look at the cards of his friends from the Base-Office. "There's no such person as Bjuscheff: the fellow came here for a drink with two guards from the Eberswalde prison-camp who had known him for a year and a half." So saying, he stamped back to the bar and stood the bottles on the perforated tin top of it.

Grischa was just having a rest, leaning in the doorway and surveying the room, which was full of German soldiers and a pleasant reek of tobacco and schnapps, not to mention beer. On his way back Max met him. A strange feeling came over this Hamburg dock-hand, who was enjoying his soft billet here, as he looked at the changed and apparently careworn face of the Russian. As undisputed master of all the stores in this huge canteen, Max knew that no one would ever look after them like Grischa, and if he wanted to give anything away, the Russian was the man to keep it dark. "Have a drop of schnapps, Grischa?" he said, and they disappeared together into the two storerooms at the back, which were always shuttered and in darkness, so that no unwelcome stranger should spy out the treasures.

"It's raining like hell," said Grischa, panting; "a schnapps will go down very well," and he blew in his hands. "I was cold enough in bed last night." And Max, as he poured him out a kümmel and another for himself, observed:

"Look here, Russky, you're a quick worker. It's a long time since you chewed a quid of tobacco: here you are, and I'll stick a bottle of schnapps in your trouser-pocket later on, eh? We may get some more cold nights; strictly against the rules, my lad, but never mind. Don't let anyone see it, will you?"

Grischa slowly and thoughtfully sipped the marvellous kümmel, thinking to himself: "A bottle of schnapps! There's somebody after me. The Devil's in that Babka." He resolved at once to refuse it, but in such a way that no one would be offended. He winked knowingly at Max and clapped him on the shoulder.

"Thanks," he said. "You're a good fellow, Max, but I'd rather not have it. I'd rather have a drop here from time to time, you see. I can't very well hide it under the bed: they turn it up every morning. Put it behind there on the herring-barrel." Max grinned assent, "Right you are," and put the newly opened bottle away as directed, under a paper bag. Grischa shook him by the hand and smiled, and the wrinkle between his brows deepened as he went out to continue unloading the wagon. Meantime the game had been ended, and the cards shuffled and dealt again; but the conversation about the Russian had spread to the onlookers. There were now two other soldiers of the garrison lounging behind the players in their Sunday uniforms: one of them from the field-bakery and one from the mounted police, both cavalrymen. The baker had once been a dragoon and wore yellow collar-badges; the other a hussar, who was in a grey coat covered with grey braid, and had blue stripes on his breeches and his cap.

"Yes, but look here," said the hussar, while all the bystanders, who had been asking each other about the man's story, listened intently, "there's more in this Russky affair than you fellows seem to think."

"Yes, a deal more," echoed the baker. "It means that there's no more justice in this world. What's going to happen to him might very well happen to you or me."

"There must be courts and judges," said the machine-gunner slowly, and with bitter emphasis, "but they must be just, or else we can't trust anything or anybody. The State ought to be like a balance," he went on meditatively (he was a Silesian, of the 58th Regiment from Glogau), "with the goods on one side and the weights on the other, properly balanced. There must be justice," and he looked round at the others; what he said seemed so obvious that not one of them even nodded.

"We don't see much of it," said the artilleryman contemptuously, and a trench-mortar man with his badge on his sleeve laughed so much at this that he had to sit down.

"Leave, and rations, and so on, eh?"

" 'Were our food and leave the same, war would be a jolly game,' " quoted an infantryman, whose shoulder-straps were folded over (to conceal the regimental numbers of the units that were being shifted)—a long-forbidden, but significant couplet, and the corporal, who had a "grand" with three in his hand, though he was hardly yet composed enough to realize his good fortune, observed:

"Yes, there's a lot in this affair. I'm keeping my eye on it."

"So are a great many other people," agreed the lorry-driver. "Paleske in our wagon-lines has written to his brother about it; he's at Borsig, you know, so they'll have something to talk about while they're turning out shells."

The artilleryman nodded. That would be something for them to think over: it wouldn't hurt them to know what was going on here.

"Yes," said the man in the middle, who had again turned up a bad card: "let 'em know all about it. This afternoon I'm going to write to my brother-in-law Pawlik who's working in the Cleophas mine with the Poles in Upper Silesia. They're stuffed up with lies just like we are. Who's that over there?"

A red-bearded sergeant in the threadbare tunic of the fighting-line, with his cap on the back of his head, a glass of schnapps in his hand, and a cigar between his fingers, stalking to and fro behind them, suddenly stopped and looked around at the beer-drinkers and card-players, and two men who were writing field post cards in the midst of the hubbub; he was slightly drunk and therefore a trifle irritable. What had caught their attention was the Iron Cross of the First Class on his tunic, which in the case of privates and N.C.O.'s was always an exceptional distinction.

"Don't you quarrel with the rain," he snapped out in a Frisian accent to one of the artillerymen who were arguing about the weather. "We want rain badly; it keeps the boys in the trenches and dug-outs up to the mark. Fine weather stops the war. But the rain makes them sit up and take notice." And in a voice that was hoarse from over-smoking he began to sing: "The Captain's dog's a fat old beast, bow wow."

A group of soldiers burst into roars of laughter. They had the same threadbare tunics and evidently belonged, like him, to the infantry, who bear the burden of war.

"Come on, let's have *'Buntje's Sturmlied'*; out with it, Hermann."

A corporal asked in an agitated voice whether they were all mad to sing that song here under the noses of the Staff: did they want to get into clink? Whereupon the sergeant called him "a bloody sh——." "That's our special song: every officer in the regiment knows it. Come on, friends, everyone join in the chorus, please," and roaring like a mill-race he began the song of the Captain's dog until the others, catching their leader's recklessness, sang the chorus to an old, old, Berlin air. The first stanza rang out:

"Unser Hauptmann, der hat einen fetten Hund, gick gack,
Und von Kohlrüben bleibt uns der Arsch gesund, kick kack!
Und die Töle frisst krachend ihr Kotelett,
Und der Landser wird lachend von Lause fett"——

and then, still timidly, the Chorus joined in, half-aloud:

"Na, da stürm' wir mal, stürm' wir mal,
Jufifallerassassassa,
Stürm' wir mal, stürm' wir mal,
Jufifallera."

"Und der Urlaub ist für den Bauern da, fick fack,
Und der Landser bleibt gerne im Graben ein Jahr, zick zack,
Und die Holzwoll' wärmt ihm das Bettgestell,
Und wenn ihn mal friert, so spielt er Appell."

"Na, da stürm' wir mal, stürm' wir mal,
Jufifallerassassassa."

The refrain burst forth yet more loudly from the bar-counter through all the rooms; the men sat, horror-struck, or jumped up nervously, or tried to hide behind each other. The voices of the singers rang with the fury in their hearts. It was not only the sergeant, with his flaming beard and glaring eyes, who was singing, but the little knot of infantrymen belonging to that regiment whose shoulder straps were rolled back to conceal the numbers. The whole room bellowed out the last verse:

> *"Und krepierte Landser, die tun ihre Pflicht, pick pack,*
> *Und morgen stehn wir im Tagesbericht, schnick schnack,*
> *Und der Kriegsgewinnler wird madenfett,*
> *Und im Drahtverhau klappert das Landserskelett:*
> *Na, da stürm' wir mal, stürm' wir mal."*

There was not a man, not even a "Base-hog" (except the two assiduous writers of post cards), who was not carried away by the fury and the despair of the refrain: *"Jufifallerassassassa."* They yelled till the windows rattled: and when the last *jufifallera* echoed up to the vaulted ceiling, the smoke-laden air of the canteen rang with the tumultuous joy of men who had eased their souls of a great burden.

Sergeant Halbscheid, who had no wish to lose his comfortable billet, turned his back on the guests throughout the proceedings. If there should be any awkward enquiries, he could say he had not seen a single one of the singers. As for a sergeant with the Iron Cross of the First Class and a red beard, a Rhinelander or Frisian perhaps, who had come to the canteen on Sunday—no, he could remember no such person. As the uproar died down into a harmless buzz of talk, he turned slowly round, and but for his native Thuringian sang-froid he would have been horrified: for he was confronted by a broad-brimmed felt hat perched on a long narrow head, a tunic with lilac facings and collar, a small silver cross at the neck; it was the Divisional Chaplain seated at a table. He had evidently come in quite unnoticed in the midst of the uproar, and was now smiling benevolently and praising the singers with ingenuous good-humour.

"Splendid fellows," he said: "that's the stuff. I admire such gallant martial spirit. 'Come on boys'—that's the old *furor Teutonicus*. Let's hear the rest of your song."

With a friendly grin the sergeant explained that he was sorry but the song was over. The Herr Pastor, with his bearded boyish face, expressed his regret that he had not heard it all—then he turned casually to Halbscheid. He had, he said, sent his orderly for cigars, and there must have been some misunderstanding. He had wanted a small box: the name of the brand was—and he peered shortsightedly into his notebook stamped with the Iron Cross—"Forest Murmurs," six pfennigs each.

Under any other circumstances Sergeant Halbscheid would perhaps have winked to the reverend gentleman and invited him to come outside, in spite of the rain, or to come back at a more convenient moment; but another song seemed imminent, as he saw the drawn, weather-beaten faces of the trench moles crowding round, and eyeing curiously the smartly cut pastoral tunic of this reverend seeker after cheap cigars. . . . And with the deprecating voice of an old innkeeper, which indeed he was, Sergeant Halbscheid expressed his deep regret, but the Herr Pastor must surely be aware that he was only allowed to sell cigars to the troops and only six at a time. The Herr Pastor could be served in the Officers' canteen or mess.

The customer blushed slightly; he said he could not get that brand there; and he added nervously, "But I'm practically one of the troops myself."

The soldiers who heard him—the real troops—only smiled tactfully. They grinned not, neither did they roar, but their Heavenly Father understood them; so Herr Halbscheid merely nodded and explained that he could not go beyond the regulations.

The reverend gentleman gnawed his underlip with his great tobacco-stained teeth. At that moment Grischa reported to the landlord that he had finished his work and asked if there were anything more to be done.

Herr Halbscheid hoped that the man of God would avail himself of this diversion to beat a dignified retreat. Halbscheid liked a quiet life, and had no wish to try conclusions with an educated man and one who dined at His Excellency's table. So he turned hurriedly to Grischa and told him in a confidential voice to go inside again and open the cases of beer—Max would tell him how many—and have them unpacked by noon, put the tobacco on the shelves, the cigars in the drawer underneath, and the cigarettes on the table.

"Very good, Sergeant," said Grischa, glancing coolly at the Chaplain, and letting his eyes rest for a moment on the silver cross beneath his collar, as he turned to go.

"Who's this wretched object?" squeaked the padre at Grischa. "Don't you know an officer when you see one? Has the fellow been here all these months without learning manners? They'll teach you soon enough at the Kommandantur when I report you. What's the fellow's name?"

Grischa was silent. He could not take his bewildered eyes from the Herr Pastor's cross. It was not a Russian orthodox, properly consecrated cross, but still . . . Suddenly a voice broke in from behind, the good-natured voice of Max of the Canteen, dock-hand and illiterate:

"General's Orders, Herr Pastor, no saluting on fatigue."

And Grischa thought: "No, there can be no second life after death. If people like that pretend there is, don't believe them," so he answered in Russian, not in German:

"The fellow's name is Sergeant Grischa Iljitsch Paprotkin; he has been unlucky, very unlucky all his life, though he has never done anyone any harm. Grischa Iljitsch Paprotkin, prisoner, awaiting sentence," he added gravely in German.

"We can produce witnesses to that," said Max from the doorway in his deep quiet tones. "Isn't there anyone here who saw the Russian at work?"

But Herr Lüdecke had done enough to satisfy his pride.

"We shall meet again," he said with a pompous wave of his hand, gathered himself together, turned on his heel, and strutted quickly away like a potentate breaking off an audience.

Meanwhile Grischa sat on a bench, trembling. He was everybody's doormat, anyone could wipe his dirty boots on him. Had he committed a crime? If not, why did they treat him like this? And while the soldiers expatiated in picturesque language on the purpose of a chaplain's existence, or tried to soothe Grischa by explaining that the padre would soon drop it; that he probably had half a dozen kids to feed at home; that Wilhelmi (i.e. Halbscheid) had only to keep his mouth shut; and that the little parson was always trying to scrounge a bit;—the meaning of what had happened was gradually taking shape in Grischa's mind. He rose and dragged himself slowly off.

"Don't be afraid," Halbscheid shouted after him. "I shan't report anyone to-day."

Grischa went into the storeroom and carefully stowed away his bottle of schnapps in his long baggy drill trousers. Though the neck of the bottle was sticking out of his pocket the paper bag concealed it. He had changed his mind, he explained to Max: he would take the schnapps back to his cell after all, and Halbscheid agreed that such liquor was a specific against the plague of parsons. "But you've got a thick skin, Russky, like me," and he gave him a resounding slap on the shoulder. Grischa smiled at him, while in the next room the corporal declared a *"grand ouvert,"* and the man from the transport opined that in the army everybody pinched whatever he could, and added, "So much for your bloody 'grand'," as he slammed his victorious card down on the table.

Chapter 6

CERTAIN MATTERS ARE MADE CLEAR

In those days strange secret forces were brought to bear upon the German Generals. Dark rumours were about that perhaps the Fatherland could only be saved by turning Army Headquarters into a dictatorship. Perhaps one day the voice of the Mighty One would declare for or against it. If the Reichstag, with a majority of the Electors behind it, demanded a solemn undertaking to restore Belgium, then they would have to send the Reichstag home. They would show those gentlemen how much better they got on without them. To induce a Protestant Empire to renounce her peace-terms and her conquests would indeed be honey on the Pope's bread. Besides, the Spaniard was getting busy and bleating pompously about Alsace-Lorraine, and an immediate peace. Moreover, there was trouble brewing in Austria. Army Headquarters alone felt the responsibility for Germany's future, realized the need of a great State to expand, and replied to the whinings of the peace-mongers by great new victories in the east. His Majesty had unfortunately let himself be bullied; but, on occasion, one must be Prussian, much more Prussian, than the Hohenzollerns.

Exzellenz von Lychow was furious against all these military intrigues. "Monstrous, I call it!" he would shout at Winfried. Of course, Belgium must be given up. The "Flemish movement" was mere eyewash, and they must not let anyone mislead them into adding still more doubtful elements to the Prussian population. They'd snaffled enough land in the east, in all conscience, so why the devil should a pack of swashbucklers like Schieffenzahn, who had the time—and the cheek—to interfere with his legal decisions and defy his sense of justice—why should they make the name of the Army stink throughout the Empire? Didn't they know that the real Army wanted peace, and the sooner the better? Von Lychow dictated a long letter in this strain, addressed to someone in the immediate entourage of the Emperor, for his hearty, bluff old Prussian ways had procured him many friends among the War-Lord's military advisers.

"Better cross out the bit about Schieffenzahn, after all," said the General, when Winfried read out to him what he had written. "He seems to have dropped that Bjuscheff case, so if he likes to play the fool in politics, I'll leave it to somebody else to punch his nose for it."

At this Winfried shrugged his shoulders with a rueful smile and protested: "Do let it stand, sir; Schieffenzahn's a wily old bird. I don't think he's played his last card yet." But the letter was sent, as Otto von Lychow had directed: without the blessing of the A.D.C.

Only the day before, Kriegsgerichtsrat Posnanski had taken Lieutenant Winfried aside after dinner and invited him into a corner to drink a cup of coffee. In his hand was a letter, typed on a sheet of common copying-paper, unsigned and incorrectly spelt. A Military Postman had brought it to his house that morning; and Posnanski asked Winfried to read it now. It ran as follows:—

"Sir,

I am only an orderly and dare not sign this. But I have something important to tell you, Herr Kriegsgerichtsrat. Please don't think the poor Russian's case has been put in the waste-paper basket. A high official is going to bring it up again. I only want to warn you, Herr Kriegsgerichtsrat, that a very important gentleman is interested in it. I beg you not to give me away. I don't want to get into trouble, but my conscience won't let me rest. I got to know about it all by accident and I can't help telling you. Please don't give me away."

Winfried reluctantly glanced through the letter, then he read it more carefully, stared into Posnanski's spectacles, and waited. The lawyer nodded. The letter did not surprise him, but what the consequences would be Solomon himself could not have prophesied.

"If Schieffenzahn wasn't so uncommonly busy nowadays, we should have been favoured with his attentions long ago. But I can easily imagine what his head's full of just now. In ten or twelve days we shall read about it in the *Bulletin*."

"You can't imagine anything of the kind," thought Lieutenant Winfried, "and he'll take good care you don't. If the doings of the Committee of Seven, the Government and the Generals, got about before the Government was ready, the bomb might burst."

It suddenly occurred to him that it was funny he should compare the conclusion of peace to a bursting bomb. It would be a long time before his mind was rid of these damned military metaphors.

"Why so pensive, my young hero?" Posnanski's voice broke in; he recovered himself in an instant and asked:

"Can the sentence be carried out as long as you've got the papers locked up in a drawer?"

Posnanski gave him a sly nudge: "You may well ask that," he said. "Of course not. Nobody can wheel that barrow any further as long as we sit tight on it."

"Very well, Herr Kriegsgerichtsrat. I shall now hand you His Excellency's official order not to part with the Bjuscheff dossier and execution-warrant without His Excellency's express written instructions. I hold you responsible," he added, with the utmost gravity, "that this order shall be scrupulously obeyed."

The lawyer jerked his hand up to the place where the peak of his cap should have been, and said: "Very good, sir."

Then they both laughed and said with one voice: "That's that."

But Posnanski carefully folded up the orderly's letter, and tapped it briskly. "Now Wilhelmi can scribble reams if he likes. God bless the art of writing, my friend. But it's a pity that honest fellow didn't sign his stuff. We might have set his fears at rest. I expect it's one of Wilhelmi's clerks."

"No," said Winfried, after taking another look at the letter, "I'm sure it's from a genuine orderly. A clerk would have put a lot more typing mistakes in, to make it look more real."

Posnanski found this convincing and agreed that an orderly must have done it. Who would have suspected that it was Milli

Paus, Wilhelmi's little darling, whose fingers had fluttered over the typewriter to the great peril of her master's peace of mind? He was trotting about with the fatuous air of an accepted suitor, he felt that she was his already; and change keeps a man young. That she chose this particular way of giving him some wholesome mental exercise, testified to her kindness of heart. She thought it shameful that this unhappy Russian should be done to death to please the arrogant Schieffenzahn, and she knew well enough how bitterly Wilhelmi had resented a certain telephone conversation with Lychow's people. Why should not her hand avail to save an innocent man?

As he embraced her late on that August evening, Wilhelmi found her in a skittish, teasing mood. "Don't scream like that," he said irritably.

At that season the fruit of the chestnut trees had grown to the size of cherries; darkness came sooner, and swarms of shooting stars swept over the wide sky about the eastern plains, in the coolness of the early September nights. But the days still broke fresh and radiant: just the right weather for the advance and very refreshing for the wounded. At Mervinsk, as elsewhere, new field-hospitals were being erected, and Täwje, the little goat-bearded carpenter, was again in much request; he was engaged with Grischa in making doors of fir or pine planks with a broad cross-piece and a hole for the lock. They were working as before in the backyard of the Kommandantur prison, and while they talked freely in Russian, Corporal Hermann Sacht sat on guard beside them with his rifle between his knees: which was something quite new. It was Rittmeister von Brett-schneider's quiet way of showing that he still had some say in Mervinsk. He hung, as it were, a rifle above Grischa's head; and in that highly cultivated brain of his there moved vague memories of a phrase, he had surely read or heard in some novel or some play—no matter where—describing how someone had hung a sword over some one else's head: a thrilling moment. It had hung from the ceiling by a single horse-hair, he seemed to remember, while the man stood there unsuspecting, so that when the sword fell, it would pierce his skull just where it was thinnest.

The first appearance of Hermann Sacht, who while engaged upon this duty, might smoke, or read or write letters as he chose, when he was not joining in the conversation, led to one of those discussions, full of dark suggestions and significant silences, that lasted for days. Täwje, that yellow-skinned, grey-bearded old goat, whose wrinkled eyes betrayed the humour that could prevail over an empty stomach, showed that he and his people knew Grischa's history. With Grischa's help he sawed planks of equal length on the block under the chestnut trees, planing them on a special table made of heavy boards and thin wooden blocks, and set up in the open air; then he glued and nailed them together in the shed. Grischa, who had been gradually trained in every trick of the carpenter's trade, was helping him or working away by himself, while Täwje was loading his pipe with the cheap canteen tobacco, which was part of his wages. They understood each other very well. They were both of them despised and half-starved, they both disliked their German masters, so their sympathy was securely founded. Täwje, indeed, looked with the indulgent eyes of a grandfather on this young nation, which had learnt nothing from the failure of all conquests from Achaschwerosch (Xerxes) to those of Bonaparte, whereas a carpenter of the name of Täwje, or perhaps Towja or Towiya, had already wielded sword and plane in the days of Alexander. Grischa, on the other hand, was merely indignant at the pompous and stupid way in which they had treated him. Of course the Germans were soldiers. There was no harm in that. A man felt very fine and fierce, when he raised his rifle to his shoulder, or hurled a hand-grenade, or, bristling with rage, flung a charging enemy aside with the point of his own bayonet and broke the fellow's neck as like as not while he kept a watchful eye on the danger that lurked in the barrel of a rifle or the muzzle of a gun. But for the present he had had enough. He had shown his mettle; now it was time to make peace. Thinking was a wearisome job, and he spent hours every night puzzling out the cause of this long, futile, suffocating agony. If he could not trust his officers, he couldn't trust anything or anybody. A man must obey his officer—or else, in the good old Russian fashion, lay him out with a rifle-butt for not knowing his job, and find a better leader; he must follow him blindly, or else watch his every movement from the very start. During these discussions, Grischa sometimes noticed that Täwje was looking, not at his lips but at his eyes. Täwje, indeed, had a vague feeling that Grischa's eyes expressed much more than his mouth. They had a restless, searching look, those eyes of his, changing sometimes to a vacant stare, which revealed the yearning soul of the man to the old carpenter.

"Never mind all that, my lad," said he. "It does not matter very much. What matters is what is written."

He was thinking that what is written is, "Thou shalt not kill," and even before that, it was written: "Whoso sheddeth man's blood, by man shall his blood be shed." Of course, the Book was full of stories of killing and the shedding of man's blood. And it was for the wise ones of the earth to reconcile these things. But perhaps, if he uttered his thoughts, it would only offend the Russian, or unsettle him; he could see by Grischa's eyes that a great deal was going on within him, of which perhaps Grischa himself knew nothing. Täwje, who was deeply interested in the man, drew him out to talk about himself, and discovered how the General had stood up for him, how the people of Bialystok wanted to shoot him, and all the rest of Grischa's story.

"You can take my word for it that I'm all right," said Grischa. "The General promised they shouldn't touch me. It's absurd they should try to pretend that Bjuscheff's still alive, when his bones are rotting in the forest, hundreds of versts away, beyond many rivers, when they've sent for witnesses to prove I'm Grischa, and a court martial and a lot of judges and lieutenants and dozens of Landsturm fellows know the truth, God's truth, about it all. And now they put this corporal with his rifle, to stand sentry over me as if I wanted to escape again. Do they take me for a silly idiot?"

Twice in succession, at the words "escape" and "silly," the name of Babka came into his mind and he shook his head angrily. Täwje smeared the smoothly planed edges of two planks with glue, and pressed them into the vise to hold them steady until they dried.

"That's not the point," he said thoughtfully. "The Captain knows that there's someone behind him who wants the sentence carried out, whether it's just or not; it's your blood he's after, not the truth. And that man has never seen you—the great Schieffenzahn, I mean—who signs so many orders and whose face you can see on everybody's wall. 'Thou shalt not make to thyself any graven image,'" he quoted to himself in Hebrew.—"There's something behind it all. We must try to understand the meaning of it. I'll search the Gemara, and we're sure to find it out."

"Somebody's after me," said Grischa heavily. He cursed inwardly at the thought that Täwje would laugh at him, but the carpenter, who had been brought up in another spiritual world in which he lived and moved when his work was over, merely replied:

"I dare say. It's a queer business: it's like two dogs tugging at a lead, and you're the lead. The stronger dog pulls the other off his legs, but the other may have sharper teeth and bite it through. Or you're like a bone two dogs are quarrelling over: the stronger one tears it away from the other, but the one with the sharper teeth breaks the bone. There's meaning in everything if you look for it."

So saying, he plunged the brush into the seething glue-pot and began to fit the edges of two more planks together; his curved wooden pipe hung from his draggled tobacco-stained moustache. "And if you want to understand the meaning of anything, you must find out who's going to be affected by it. If two men throw dice, the result is important for one or the other, but not for the dice."

Grischa listened eagerly. "I'm not a die or a dog's lead. Christ died on the Cross for me too." And Täwje, as he passed his hand over the smooth surface of the two planed edges, answered:

"That may be, but what says the kopeck? 'I've no right side or wrong side either; just an eagle and a date: and I too have come out of the minting-machine.' And yet man does what he likes with it."

"Yes, that's what a man does with a kopeck, but a General can't treat a man like that."

"True enough," answered the carpenter composedly, taking his dripping brush out of the pot and twisting it round to get the glue off it, "very true: but who's talking of Generals? Perhaps it's a matter for the mighty ones; perhaps for the peoples of the earth. It may be a very great matter indeed."

And he told him the old story of our father Abraham, how he

pleaded with God. "He did not speak with him, he strove with words for Sodom; he said: 'Why wilt thou destroy this great city? Peradventure there are fifty just men therein,' and God consented: if there were fifty just men he would not destroy it. Do you think he didn't know there were not fifty just men in Sodom, and when Abraham could not find them, and bargained with God, offering forty-and-five, and afterwards thirty, that the lives of the people might be saved and the great city of Sodom spared, do you think he didn't know all the time that there were not ten just men in Sodom? God cared nothing for just men and how many there might be.

"God wanted our father Abraham to show whether he was a man or no: and didn't he show himself a man? Very well. Now consider these just men for a moment. (He was gradually dropping into the rapt sing-song voice in which the Talmud is recited in the schools, and swaying his body to and fro.) Had there been ten righteous men in Sodom the city had not perished. It lay with them whether they would be just or no; they knew what God requireth of men—a very simple matter. He had not given them six hundred and thirteen commandments to keep as he had to the Jews. They had Noah's seven commandments and they did not keep them. Well, then, suppose there had been ten righteous men in that city, or nine, and one that was doubtful. If he had resolved to be just, do you think he would have been just merely on his own account? No, he would have saved the city. The justice of the just men of Sodom was a sign, Grischa, for the whole city, so it seems to me. Fifty just men would have been a mighty sign; ten just men is a poor sign, but no just men at all, that was an evil sign indeed. I tell you our times are more wicked than those of Sodom and Gomorrah, as it seems to me. Now consider. Here is a man condemned to death, and it is quite clear he's innocent, and many people know he's innocent. And if his innocence prevails, then, as I see it, there will be ten just men in Sodom, and the city will not be destroyed. But if his innocence does not prevail, and they carry out a sentence which they all know is wrong, then, Grischa, there are not twenty just men in Sodom—nor ten, nor five, and the wrath of God shall rain down fire and brimstone, and the mighty city of Sodom with her Emperors and Princes and Generals shall be destroyed: mark well my words," and he was silent.

His cheeks were flushed, and his eyes—those crafty little eyes of an elderly Jew—flamed with passionate zeal to see the Kingdom of God established on this earth. But he said no more, for sight of Grischa's face broke in upon his reverie. The sergeant said nothing: he stood with his mouth open like a man being choked, and stared aghast at his companion.

"That's enough," he cried out hoarsely, "that's enough. I'm done for."

Täwje was right. Somebody was after him, but not because his name was Grischa. He had always thought that a louse like himself—how should anyone trouble his head about him? But what the Jew said explained it. A single drop would make the saucepan overflow, a single match would set the steppe on fire. And Täwje, though he could not take back a word of what he had said, tried to reassure him.

"Done for? Of course not. Why should not justice prevail among the Germans? There's a General, a court martial, a lieutenant, and a whole division on the side of justice. You can't say it's settled. For the present the scale of life weighs heavier than the scale of death. The Germans have a great deal of good in them. And they're winning victories again. Do you think the Judge of all the Earth cannot see small things and great things and his whole great creation at one glance? But I'll tell you this: what happens to you, whether it's good or bad, is much more important to the Germans than to you; you must see that the Empires and the great peoples of the earth, the Germans and the Russians, weigh more than one sergeant in the balance."

Grischa saw his company, his regiment, and the lines massing for the attack, he heard the scream of the shells, whining and shrieking hideously as they approached; he heard them burst, and again he saw his comrades, torn and mangled, with half an arm, or with their faces blown away and spurting blood from many wounds. He beheld whole regiments, divisions, fields black with the heads of marching men, and behind them stretches of broad plough-lands, cities, and forests, spread out as on a map, the whole vast countryside full of men and women cutting corn, children on their doorsteps playing marbles, and dribbling greybeards—with a strange exaltation he saw, and saw clearly, the Empires and peoples of the earth; Täwje had convinced him and he answered:

"Of course I am a louse, but Russia stands for something."

"Yes," answered Täwje cheerfully, "and Germany stands for something too: and possibly the Jews too. And didn't God make the Poles? Very well, then: you needn't worry. Whatever happens to you will be for the best. I soon found out there was a meaning in your story. Look here, we must finish this door by midday. Go and get some more nails, Grischa. There's a packet of two-inch nails inside on the bench. They may be a bit too long, but we'll use them, and for why? If the ends are bent they'll hold better."

Chapter 7

GOING ON LEAVE

OTTO VON LYCHOW was not in the best of moods when he returned
to Mervinsk from the new front line. He was full of suppressed
irritation; as a General he cursed the necessity for moving his Division more than two hundred kilometres forward without any fighting
in which it could distinguish itself, and as a man he hated having to
ask his men to advance through the mud and rain of early autumn
now that the War was nearly over. As with all simple natures,
mental conflict paralysed him physically, though he had no notion
of the cause. The Staff-Surgeon came, listened, and measured the
General's blood-pressure; but as the patient could give him no clue
the oracle was dumb. And if a Staff-Surgeon cannot diagnose a
General's disease, but merely finds him tired, he does not threaten
him with arrest, and shout at him till the plaster comes off the walls;
on the contrary, he pronounces him in urgent need of leave, and, in
the interests of the Army, orders him away at once. When Lychow
confessed this to his nephew about midday, Winfried felt uneasy.
He did not want to worry the old gentleman before he went away,
but did want to get authority to act against certain persons who
were making themselves objectionable. He gaily agreed: his uncle
looked like a baby with diarrhœa and must be wrapped immediately
in warm flannel and given weak cocoa in a bottle. It was a pity he
should have to go away for a cure just now when the Russky's case
was looking lively. However, so long as his uncle would leave him
the necessary authority to carry on the game of chess with this poor
pawn, he hoped to manage very well without the General. Lychow
did not answer; with bloodshot eyes, not unlike those of a falcon, he
stared absently at his lively nephew. He envied him that un-
trammelled youth which he had kept intact all through the fighting

round the Souchez sugar factory, and before that, among the ruins of Ypres. They had been through something—all these German soldiers . . . and every day came reports of new victories. In the process of forcing the mine-barrier in the Gulf of Riga only four mine-sweepers had been sunk. Our losses were naturally understated in the official bulletin: but none the less, after Riga was captured, shell splinters, sharp and edged like crystals, some as long as a cigar, some as tiny as a shot, had changed and marred many a human body. But none the less Riga was now in German hands. The left wing, so it was reported, drove the Russians before them in their steady advance. God had smitten them, and whole brigades slung their rifles and marched eastwards. Not otherwise had German divisions marched by whole brigades, eastward also after the Marne, now almost three years ago to the day, till they dug themselves in beyond the Aisne. The Russians would never dig themselves in again, so it was written in the stars; Schieffenzahn was pressing at their heels. And as for peace . . . Lychow meditated, passing into a sphere of thought where there was no such place as Mervinsk. It was right and sensible to put aside all question of peace if new victories could give them better cards to play. But he dreaded the insolence of pride, the *hubris* of Belshazzar. The history of the great Empires flitted through his mind. They had all burst because they had blown themselves out too far. The true Prussian policy was not to gamble on futures, but to pocket small and certain gains at once. To unprejudiced eyes, the partition of Poland under Old Fritz had entangled Prussia in a net of difficulties, and God had shown favour to Germany in ridding her so soon of South Prussia and the Grand Duchy of Warsaw. Certainly the country was now called the German Empire, and perhaps had learned a little of what it could digest: though to look at Alsace, to say nothing of Lorraine, you wouldn't think so. In Metz twelve years before he felt he was in a foreign country. . . .

Winfried noticed with sympathy, though not without a touch of alarm, the old gentleman's sudden absence of mind, though he could guess the drift of his thoughts. "Certainly," he thought, "he must go on leave. He goes to sleep while he's talking to you."

"What about that Russian fellow?" asked His Excellency abruptly.

"Oh, just the same old row. Five days ago Wilhelmi favoured us with twelve typewritten pages on the subject ending with a short questionnaire. He's insisting that the sentence must be carried out."

"Out of the question," growled von Lychow.

"Of course," said Winfried. Posnanski had shown the patience of an angel in the "exposition of the Divisional aspect of the case," as the lawyer christened it in his delightful jargon. But it seemed that Schieffenzahn stood by his own people no less stoutly than Lychow stood by his.

"The fellow's got no respect for grey hairs," muttered Lychow angrily. "The thing is so ludicrously clear that if he had a spark of decency in him, he wouldn't have the face to say another word. But he'd better leave me alone, and not butt into my backyard with his puffy cheeks and parrot's nose. Do you know what he looks like?" he asked jovially. "He looks like Old Queen Victoria in a *Simplicissimus* caricature. Exactly like," and he laughed heartily, thoroughly pleased with himself.

"Then perhaps," said Winfried, "you won't mind if Schieffenzahn goes for you personally over this business?"

Lychow gathered his legs round the stool like a rider at a fence: "Does he mean to?"

"If legal German is German, and really means anything, I fancy we shall soon get a pretty stiff letter or a request for an interview."

"Much I care," said Lychow, with calm contempt; and Winfried, who had suddenly had an idea, laid a friendly trap for the General. If Lychow was really going on leave, he must pass through Brest-Litovsk, where Schieffenzahn was pumping inspiration into the Operations Section, and only good could come of thrashing out this wearisome affair in a personal interview.

"Not a bad idea."

Rittmeister von Brettschneider did what the name of Rittmeister implies: he rode forth one day. He was mounted on a beautiful silky-white mare and his bulbous congested countenance with its pudgy nose loomed portentously above Syra's arched neck and small

nervous head which betrayed Arab and Trakehnian * blood. Rittmeister von Brettschneider, who was sprung from a family of rich
West-German manufacturers, could treat himself to such a notable
horse. And while the laborious nags of the artillery and wagon lines
in that autumn of 1917 had for a long time past had more chopped
hay than corn in their bellies, and their kindly masters looked
forward to the winter with alarm, the Captain felt quite easy about
Syra. The Kommandantur at Mervinsk could well provide the means
of keeping the Captain's charger in excellent condition. The Captain
himself, a hussar from Krefeld, was now talking with half-closed
eyes, from his exalted height, to a creature who was standing on his
own feet, as motionless as the rifle which he held close against his
side, in strict accordance with the drill-book.

The Captain rapped out a brusque monosyllable.

The other, who understood him immediately, having served under
him for some time, answered: "Corporal Sacht."

The Captain nodded to imply that he knew it. Then he cast his
eyes over the man's uniform, for any irregularity in a uniform may
be used in various ways to humiliate the wearer. But he could find
fault with nothing. (His men knew what was the most important
thing in war.)

"Stand at ease."

Corporal Sacht obeyed by slightly relaxing his limbs. He was
standing near the gate, between the horse and the wall of the prison
yard; and he gazed up at his officer with a faithful and expectant
look at this Olympian personage's insignificant nose.

"Look here," croaked the mighty one, "you've been put on guard
over that Russian. That's not the job for a smart fellow, but I can't
help it. I shall hold you personally responsible that the man does
not escape from justice. I fancy someone is trying to get him out.
Now I warn you," he said, suddenly lowering his voice, his small
menacing eyes gazing coldly and pitilessly into the wide-open eyes
of the soldier, "don't you get yourself into trouble. I shall hold
you to it, Corporal," and he added, half to himself, "it will be only for
a few days longer." And with a vague salute, as the Corporal brought
his boots together with a clatter, the Captain touched Syra lightly

---

* *Trakehnen:* A famous royal stud in East Prussia.

viction. He flattered himself that he knew how to deal with a foolish affair like this. . . . Wilhelmi's reminder should not have been
needed. He would ride up to the court martial office and, without
dismounting, shout a few words through the open window or knock
on the window-pane with his crop, and depart with the death sentence
in his saddlebag. That was the stuff to give 'em. He really must put
an end, once and for all, to this eternal dispute between the Division
and the Kommandantur. The General was indeed an exalted personage, but behind Brettschneider stood Schieffenzahn—and even heavy
objects, once their weight is known, can be made very easy to handle.

Twenty minutes later a horseman galloped home. His face was
livid and set and deeply flushed, his prominent ears stood out more
than ever, and there was an ugly glare in his cold grey eyes. However much he sought to control himself, his hunched shoulders betrayed the fury of a defeated man. What a waste of a lovely
September morning!

Every week and every day brought fresh triumphs. But every
day German youths and men fell in their thousands; scraps of falling iron pierced and tore the wholesome flesh, blood gushed forth,
men spun round and fell shrieking to the earth or plunged forward,
silent, on their faces. Moreover there was news of serious out-
breaks in the fleet at Wilhelmshafen, and it was reported that in
Berlin there were many deputies trying to stop the War before the
next winter of famine came upon them. Yet thousands upon
thousands of square miles were being added to vast domains soon
to be ruled by German overlords—"right up to Finland, gentlemen,
and even including Finland." The claim to world-dominion is felt
by every nation, and the Germans were now drinking deeply from
that cup. Albert Schieffenzahn was hard at work. The new territory from Reval to Dorpat would be administered by Ober-Ost, new
ports were being opened to German enterprise: besides Libau, they
now controlled Riga, Windau, Reval, and Dorpat—centres of ancient
German culture, full of splendid buildings, churches, and town halls.
No one could say they had been annexed by force, if it was the wish
of the population to come under German rule. Of course the Letts

would not be asked, and the Esthonians' minds would be made up
for them—but who in all Europe cared for that? Hadn't they always
printed their newspapers in German characters? . . . The Major-
General plunged greedily into this glorious new task with his usual
restless energy . . . garrisons, communication lines, and civil administration! The Courland barons were glad to have German soldiers
billeted in their castles—though they were rather taken aback when
their new lord and master, a sergeant-major or a fat lieutenant, shot
down in an idle or drunken mood the stork which had been the
sacred bird of the household for five or six generations. But
Schieffenzahn saw only the general outline, the structure of the new
German map and of his new domain. So weeks flew by like days.

The summer apples were being picked: the pears had been
gathered some time back, the red service-berries heralded an early and
hard winter, though that does not need much prediction in these parts.
The year was falling. Our little earth went rolling and spinning
along her narrow orbit; she sailed through the autumn equinox;
fierce winds and gusts of rain burst from the atmosphere and beat
upon her continents. The early October sun looked down, pale and
distant from its encircling mist, and every morning the world was
glittering with hoar-frost, white and velvety, and blue with the stain-
less blue of heaven. Every morning, baskets full of rustling leaves,
green, wine-red, and brown, were swept out of the prison yard,
from under the maples and chestnuts.

"Little mother's getting properly fat these days," said one of
the guard approvingly, and without any notion of a joke, to the
white-haired basket-woman as she trotted through the gateway,
bringing all manner of supplies to the prisoners and soldiers. She
now looked after their washing, and for a few pfennigs brought their
things back to them clean and mended; but she chiefly dealt in apples,
a glass of schnapps when she could, tobacco and cigarettes always,
sewing-thread, needles, and what a soldier always lacks: darning-
wool. Yes, it was undeniable that her figure was filling out. She
was getting fat on the good food that was handed out to her nearly
every day from the kitchen. The soldiers were sick of their monotonous diet. "Calves' teeth" (pearl barley), "blue Henry" (groats

soup), dried vegetables, potatoes, peas and beans, and a meagre meat allowance which was slightly increased on Sundays. "Glad someone likes it," thought Corporal Sacht, and clapped Babka on the back.

Brettschneider was wrong, the affair was dragging on, and a good thing too. For the turmoil of the advance had overwhelmed even the Kommandantur at Mervinsk with work; there were troops to be moved, fresh quarters to be found, continual bickering as to the responsibility for cleaning out the men's hutments and the stables; contributions to be spread over neighbouring villages, the countless requirements of arriving or departing troops, and constant care was needed to see that these latter did not take away any of the furniture which had been made for them by the Kommandantur, or provided from the houses in the city. It seemed likely that the purely military history of this region would soon be over, and a civil bureaucracy might spring up overnight. The military authorities would have to give some sort of account of their stewardship, and the Jews began to display singular ideas on the subject of the rights and property of private persons. In the west, American troops were landing, a remarkable sight. Even Guatemala had managed to ship over a life-size commander-in-chief, with his staff and a full twenty thousand Sammies and Jimmies. There was no talk of peace that side, but something surprising was perhaps going to happen here in the east. There was no denying it: these defeats had given a mighty impulse to those who wanted to end the War at any cost, those worthy people who abused each other as Bolsheviks, and who, if they could only be kept at arm's length, might prove exceedingly useful.

Babka saw Grischa every day, talked with him, and listened to his discourses. She felt comforted and almost cheerful when the child began to move within her. It was growing. Probably it would be a boy, but she would have been quite pleased to have a girl: she could have made something out of her. All was well so long as her soldier man, her Grischa, walked about with his silent, brooding air, and sat on the edge of his bed every morning feeling more and more sure that he was safe. She knew he thought a great deal. The world on which we live is mysterious. Life, which goes its own way, gives few opportunities for explanations. What was waiting for us after death the priests could tell you well enough, but it mattered little. It was pretty certain that a man who was likely to have a hole blown in his head, or be burst into whirling fragments by a mine, had little cause to believe in a new life. In the great beyond there could be no room for so many innocent dead. Still, the fate of man was surely very strange. He explained all this to her as they were resting after the end of the day, or in the midday interval. She would listen with an air of attention, so as not to irritate him, but she had little doubt that what was really needed was a bottle of poisoned schnapps and the assistance of the Devil.

"You see," he said, as he drew his finger-nails across the wooden surface of the table, "it's no good putting thoughts into a man's head when they won't fit it. Would you give a man a key which won't fit the lock, let alone open the door? I am a poor man and a hand in a soap-factory, and away in Vologda, on the edge of the steppe, sits Marfa Ivanovna looking after her child and perhaps another one too. Very well, then: and here are you and I, and you, too, are carrying a child of mine: you may be sure there's some meaning in all this. That Jew Täwje has told me a lot of things, and nobody knows more about God and the world than the Jews. You had better wait and see what happens. I want to get home, and I shall get home. But don't think any more about escape, please. You're a sensible woman and you're saving up nicely for the little one. How many months is it now?" And he sighed gently. "I never knew till now how much I enjoyed those days in the forest, when I was marching eastwards through the snow; and the rabbits and the tree-cat—it was all so jolly! And Fedjuschka and Koljä and all the boys and Otto Wild. Still, it's not so bad here. I've learnt to do all kinds of work, and when I get home I can earn my living as a carpenter."

Babka looked at him, then stroked his hand gently once and said: "The child that will never have a father will be born in December."

"No father!" laughed Grischa merrily. "Why, it will have you!"

Towards the middle of October, when the thin layers of ice over the ruts and puddles crackled in the rays of the rising sun, the ground was hard of nights, the twittering of the birds grew less and less. Bialystok at last gave utterance. It was an uncompromising document, in three sections, each of which fell like a hammer-blow: the first was an enquiry as to why Headquarters had not been notified of Bjuscheff's execution, although clear instructions had been issued to this effect; the second was an answer to the representative of the Divisional Court Martial, expressing Ober-Ost's extreme astonishment at such an attitude, and the request that they would forthwith withdraw their opposition; the third was a threat to give the Kommandantur at Mervinsk a direct order to carry out the sentence: His Excellency would be answerable for this departure from the usual official procedure. The Kommandantur had been advised of the position; were authorized, if necessary, to take immediate action.

Winfried sat opposite His Excellency looking pale and excited. Lychow said, stroking his moustache:

"Impossible: Schieffenzahn has been misinformed. In a week I shall be going on leave and shall have to see him in any case. Telephone this evening, Paul, and say I'm coming, and we'll discuss the case then."

Lieutenant Winfried threw an anxious, searching glance at the General, who nodded confidently.

"Good," said his nephew, with a sigh of relief. "That's the only thing to do. You'll soon put him in his place."

"It is unthinkable that he should behave with such brutality to a man older than himself, with forty-seven years' service, not counting his time as a cadet," said Lychow emphatically. "Besides, over both of us there's the Emperor, and I'll give you my word of honour . . ." he rasped out, flushing deeply: "I won't give in. I'll take the matter up to the Emperor!" And he crashed his fist upon the table.

That week it grew colder every day. Winter underclothing had to be hurriedly issued to the prisoners and guards, though the men in the trenches had long since been carrying it about in their packs. Every morning the sky looked dull and grey, as if snow was coming, and every evening twilight fell upon frozen roads, when the mud had hardened into stony ruts, and the puddles into smooth surfaces of ice; but still the clouds did not break. Winfried duly telephoned and easily secured a week's postponement of the question.

Grischa knew nothing of all this; all that troubled him was the cold at night. In the early morning, on parade, the sergeant looked at him with a new, strange interest.

On October 31, 1917, before Exzellenz von Lychow climbed into his reserved compartment with its red cushions, mirrors, and carpets, with affected cheerfulness he reassured the two gentlemen who, among others, had come to see him off, saying:

"I'll talk to him. He won't bully me, I fancy. In any case I'll wire you the good news, or get someone to telephone it; and it will be good, you can take my word for it, because after all we do wear Prussian tunics, you see, and not Tatar sheepskins. By the way," he added, stepping on to the footboard, "in case you should need to take any action in this business, Paul, I'll back you up—within reasonable limits, of course! Do you get me? I think it's going to snow at last," said he, "I'm shivering all over."

The train, which would have to stop a few hours in Brest-Litovsk, before being connected with another going west, was full of men on leave, both officers and other ranks. At last, with a grinding clatter, it moved away from the wind-swept platform. Grey morning light; tall arc-lamps; wooden buildings; and officers saluting.

"There's a General on board, old boy," said the fireman to the engine-driver, blowing his nose in his fingers.

"Is that so?" the other answered. "Well, he won't make this old coffee-machine go any quicker."

"I didn't think he would," answered the fireman, "but I think God will spot him, and won't let us break down this trip."

"I wish, Karl," said the engine-driver, as he put the lever over to full speed, and closed the valves, "I wish we had the old days back when we used to run the freight trains to the Front—hay cars and lumber cars—through the forest all the time. I used to like that. Do you remember how you were always seeing deer when there were hay cars on the train?"

But the fireman had forgotten.

"I think it will snow to-day, and it's no joke getting stuck with the rotten coal we've got and our fire-boxes made of anything except copper. And if we get stuck with a General on board, that'll be the end of us."

The engine-driver spat:

"Oh, sh . . ." he began, bending out. He did not finish the word, but his comrade understood what he meant to say: it was the most popular word in the whole War.

Book Five

RETRIBUTION

✡

Chapter 1

A VICTORY

SCHIEFFENZAHN rose from the table, and with a smile at the white-haired civilian opposite him, remarked:

"It's a pity, Herr van Ryjlte, that you're not a German: I should immediately put you under open arrest. What cigars! What coffee! You're corrupting our Spartan habits!"

The grey-haired Dutchman, with his ruddy, placid countenance, answered with equal courtesy:

"If I were a German, I should be patriotic enough to consider it a privilege to let you shut me up."

And they both laughed. The three officers of the Operations Division—this conversation was taking place at Brest-Litovsk—were delighted with the old gentleman's retort. They knew that Schieffenzahn's good-humour meant that he was full of bright ideas and things would go smoothly. Dr. van Ryjlte, who was more than seventy years old, sat calmly in his chair. He was waiting for the above-mentioned coffee which he had brought with him—fine strong Java coffee;—and he and his hosts each lit one of the offending cylindrical imports which he had also brought. He smiled peacefully as he looked round at the company, cracking walnuts in his bony hands, and did not betray his deep disappointment. He was a Delegate of the Red Cross who had been sent to Germany to inspect certain camps in which deported Belgian men and women had been interned, and to see their grievances redressed; he had also come to warn the great Schieffenzahn quite frankly about America. He could not get over the General's icy unbelief, his impenetrability to new ideas. "America's all bluff and humbug: they're getting above themselves." That was all he could get out of him; and indeed this was what the yellow press had incessantly dinned into its millions of readers, and the General and his grocer both believed it.

Nevertheless he had approached his task with care, and to avoid any suspicion that he was some malignant fellow, trying to paralyse the German will to victory at one of its great poles of energy, he had begun by reminding the General of how, in the year 1914, the world at large had foretold Germany's imminent defeat. "You don't know Germany," he had said to his South American business friends, when they had prophesied that she would soon be lying with her back broken under Russia's heel; and now he had come to the Germans with his message: "If you haven't been in America, you don't know what sort of bloodhounds you've got after you." The United States were not to be compared with Roumania, or Italy, he explained, although the latter had standing armies. America would cover the Front with engines of destruction, and behind each one would be a team of smart, hawk-eyed fellows all spoiling for a fight, fellows whose spirit had never been broken by a drill-sergeant.

But at this point, the words died on his lips, as he observed the General's smile of polite superiority: and he said to himself, with full assurance in his heart: "With open eyes ye rush on to your destruction, and there shall be great lamentation over you." His thoughts had wandered far from the occasion and the moment; as he looked through the window to the westward, he seemed to be speaking to a multitude of assembled Germans—a vast expanse of upturned faces—who listened to the old man's hoarse entreaties. He had sunk into a deep reverie, and his fingers trembled slightly, as he held his long cigar.

Schieffenzahn, with others who shared his views, had recently contrived to baffle the Pope's peace efforts, and he now thanked the Dutchman politely for his pains. He had quite different information from America, backed by statistics and borne out by expert evidence. Herr van Ryjlte greatly underestimated the striking power of the German Army, which was the result of long training, and which had had no equal for the past half-century. Of course, he was particularly grateful for this frank and friendly expression of opinion, and if his Dutch friend wished to do a much-needed service to the nation in its hour of trial, he might use his influence to destroy the prejudice which was felt in neutral countries against the annexation of Belgium to the German Empire. Belgium itself would be much better off: she would be an independent Federal State, like Bavaria or Saxony, and a part of the greatest of the European Powers. What could she possibly want more?

Van Ryjlte's arms dropped helplessly.

"How about freedom?" he asked. "The freedom of a people?"

Schieffenzahn laughed. "Little peoples can have but little freedom. Within the German Empire, Belgium already enjoys more liberty than she did before the War. The stronger the army, the greater is the liberty it guards."

"Perfectly conclusive," agreed the Dutchman, and promised to do his best. But he meant something quite different. . . . He saw it was useless, and his hands gripped his thighs beneath the table as he resolved to sell every sort of holding he had in Germany, as quickly and quietly as possible: currency, Government loans, shares and debentures of the great Schilles works, and his credits with German firms.

"When a ship is certain to sink, a rat that did not leave it would be a fool, and deserve to drown," he reflected, grimly trying to dispel his gloom, as he put sugar in his coffee. The familiar proverb, which laid aspersions on the rat, had no doubt been invented by Insurance Companies or skippers full of whisky. For as the rat went on board of its own free will, on the assumption that the ship would float, as any reasonable ship might be expected to do, it was justified before God and the world, if it left the ship before it had to bear the consequences of the Captain's incompetence. . . . He genially apologized for his interference in matters of policy, which came very ill from a guest. "But," he added, with a faint smile, "do not consider me as a guest, but as a troublesome and unwelcome relative, who has come here with the best intentions, to warn—say, a son-in-law—against a risky business transaction."

"I like 'son-in-law,' we'll leave it at that," said Schieffenzahn with a laugh, and they sat down to talk. . . .

The city of Brest-Litovsk, beyond the railway station and the great blue-towered cathedral, lay ghost-like and silent as death at the foot of the citadel, where the Operations Section and its infrequent guests were housed in a collection of hutments and barrack-

buildings. During the fighting which had led to the capture of the
city, it had been gutted by fire, and was now a desert, and a habitation
of ghosts. Along the grey streets the windowless façades stood up
apparently undamaged, but behind them was nothing, or a mass of
crumbled ruins. Broad desolate stretches traversed by roads and
lined with heaps of debris from which chimneys protruded, marked
the sites of wooden houses, of which only the brickwork of the fire-
places survived. Above it all the snow was drifting, for the snow
had come. Since midnight it had been falling in heavy silent flakes,
sometimes caught and driven by the wind, downwards through the
white air. The sky, yellow and lowering, gave promise of much
more snow to come, when in the middle of the morning van Ryjlte
had been fetched from the station in a small sleigh. He had
stopped several times on the way, and in the company of the young
Lieutenant who was with him, whom he immediately presented with
a magnificent cigar, promising him some more as soon as he unpacked, had peered through the doorways of the stone and brick
houses in this city where an Imperial garrison rubbed shoulders with
an ancient and famous Jewish community. Brest, as it is called in
Lithuanian, or Brisk, as the Jews have it, was the home of the
Brisker Rabbinim, he reflected, and as a collector of Hebrew manuscripts, he had hoped to find much spoil. . . . Cats ran mewing up
broken staircases; tall grey twisted shrubs were growing in the
ground-floor rooms, and on the copings or the gutted floors of the
upper stories brown weeds and grasses shivered in the wind. Everywhere warnings were posted against entering these ruined houses.
Men had built them, van Ryjlte reflected, and probably men would
build them up once more. In this way Corinth and Jerusalem,
Alexander and Rome, had all passed and come to life again; war and
peace were the ebb and flow of humanity's tide:—it was good to live
behind a dyke, he thought.

The day had begun successfully with the Dutchman's visit, but
there were some awkward hours ahead and Schieffenzahn would
need all his wits about him. He clenched his fists. He wouldn't
be taken in by this plausible rubbish: he would go straight on,

and people in the way had better mind their toes. He stamped
genially up and down the room, in the darkest corner of which
was a camp-bed; there he worked and slept all the time he was
at Brest. Old Lychow was the next item: "Lychow 4.30" was
written in red ink on the calendar. Another of these grey-haired
fools who waste the best hours of the day with their tedious im-
portunities. Oh, these Generals! If he ever said what he thought
to one of them, it would get about that that brute Schieffenzahn
could not be decently polite to senior officers. It was already three
o'clock, and after that strong Java coffee he could work with a will.
He had first to reconsider Ober-Ost's proposal for the administration of the newly-occupied Ukrainian territories. The document was
already adorned with a number of Austrian protests and counter-
proposals; all the fault of that confounded Lychow, with his staff
celebrations, where Count Dubna had made his drunken speeches.
Thank God, the man had now definitely become a hospital case, and
was being treated at Baden-Wien. But that did not affect the difficult relations between Austrians and Germans which were becoming more serious every month. A large-leaved atlas of the occupied
territories was spread out with the documents on the white deal desk,
the centre of which was covered with green baize. There must be
a way out of these difficulties, and Schieffenzahn was the man to
find it. But first he must polish off this fellow Lychow, this nar-
row-minded quarrelsome pedant, this old dug-out from the depths
of Brandenburg; the whole clan of them had always been prating
and plotting on the wrong side, i. e. against Bismarck. "Let him
come," he said softly to himself as he arranged the papers; "he'll
find his business settled already." He took down the receiver and
said to the sergeant who answered the telephone:

"Matz, wire as follows at once to the Kommandantur at Mervinsk: 'Settle Bjuscheff case according to instructions already received, and report duly carried out within twenty-four hours.' Bring
me before half-past four a notification from the telegrapher on duty
that the order has gone."

The sergeant answered: "Very good, Sir," repeated the message, and Schieffenzahn hung up the receiver. As he gave the order
he felt for an instant an oppression at his heart, but at the same time

a sense of grim satisfaction at the thought that Herr von Lychow was coming to waste time over an affair that had long since been settled. For a few seconds he was conscious of this feeling of constriction, and realized that it was due to the strong coffee he had drunk—coffee of a freshness and purity to which they were unaccustomed in blockaded Central Europe. The room seemed dark for three o'clock in the afternoon, and he went to the window. Courtyard No. IV lay deep and silent beneath its soft covering of white. There were great ridges of snow on the roofs to the right of him, and on the casements, from whose chimneys the yellowish smoke of burning wood swirled merrily upwards. The room was pleasantly warm, full of the pleasant fragrance of cigars—a man could sit there comfortably, with plenty of light, and do his work in peace. He switched on the electric light, and its yellow glow beat down from beneath the green shade of the office lamp, and the window turned into an opaque square of blue in the semi-darkness. He leaned his head on his fleshy hand and studied the memorandum of the Austrian authorities, drawn up by the Foreign Minister, and liberally bespattered with notes and comments. If only the Austrians would consent to a German General being appointed member of the new Ukraine Council, with a casting-vote, wherever the new capital might be—in Kieff or Odessa—a great deal could be done to meet their views. There was a certain Hetman Skoropatzki who made himself very prominent; he could be titular head of the new State, just like one of those horses' heads that used to be nailed on the gables of barns. "O Fallada, do you hang there?" suddenly came into his mind from a memory of Grimm's fairy tales: he probably had not thought of it for fifty years. However, he put everything else out of his mind, and concentrated on the text before him and the interplay of political and economic claims involved by it. He paid little attention to questions of nationality, which were set forth at length, such as the claims of the Poles against the Ukrainians, and their demand that the Cholm county should be assigned to the new Polish Kingdom—he was much more interested in the acquisition and transport of the Ukrainian wheat. He suddenly realized that the control of the harvest was the key to the whole position; on this point he must be firm: everything else hung on this. At the end of

1917 it was no easy matter to form a correct estimate of the economic factors of the situation.

Punctually at half-past four the faint clink of Exzellenz von
Lychow's spurs was heard at Schieffenzahn's door. At five minutes
to five he departed. Their interview was noteworthy in many
respects; both men spoke their minds, and the result was what might
have been expected.

Lychow had left his cloak outside, as it was covered with snow.
The old gentleman sat, with his gold-laced cap on his knees, a glove
on his clenched left hand—he had politely taken off the other to
shake hands with the enemy. At first he missed something—of
course it was his long straight sword that stood so comfortably between his knees, and was so convenient to hang his cap on; a man
cannot express his feelings so pointedly without the support of the
long piece of steel which has swung at his side for nearly forty years.
Schieffenzahn, in a loose *Litevka*, which he liked to wear unbuttoned, so that he could put his hands in his trouser-pockets, had the
advantage of him, thought Lychow.

He began by asking whether the Quartermaster-General was
aware of the position: there had been unwarrantable interference
with the judicial authority of the Division, and a perfectly regular legal decision had been treated with contempt. His tone had
already become rather acid; but Schieffenzahn, with the genial
propitiatory smile of a younger man humouring an old man's whim,
reassured him:

He had read through the papers himself once again during the
last few days and he could not understand what objection His Excellency could have to the decision which the court martial officer
at Ober-Ost had recommended to him after mature consideration,
and which he thoroughly approved.

Between the two antagonists was a broad expanse of writing-
table; on it was an inkpot made of the cast-steel base of a hand-
grenade, a flattened brass shell-case for an ash-tray, copper limber-
rings for paper-weights, and some unpleasant-looking shell splinters,
such as could be picked up everywhere in the lines. On the right was
the telephone, on the left the Ukraine papers; in a black papier maché
bowl with little golden stars on it lay the fountain-pens, copying-

pencils, large coloured pencils, red, green, and blue, and ordinary lead pencils with blunt points adapted to Schieffenzahn's well-known marginal scrawls. It seemed to Lychow that the table was getting broader and broader, as if each of them was at the edge of a continent, a flat plain peopled with pigmies, tiny specks called men; and he and Schieffenzahn yonder, swollen to the stature of colossi, crouched or glared in hatred on the confines of this world. He felt he ought never to have come here. His baggy-cheeked junior opposite made him feel that he was certainly the weaker man, perhaps only to-day because he felt unwell, or perhaps just because he had justice upon his side. A man who recognizes justice, must also recognize that it imposes limitations, he thought, already absorbed in his own reflections before the battle had fairly started. To a man who respects justice, his neighbour's flower-beds are sacred. A man who does not respect it, may perhaps live three stories lower down, but with his thick skin and tough skull, he plunges about in forbidden regions: it is nothing to him if they are forbidden. "I have made a colossal blunder: a man can fight better at a distance. . . ." He began to grow angry with himself at these meandering reflections, took out one of his own cigarettes and tapped it on the case, and asked, with an appearance of unconcern, what was the Major-General's view of the situation as a whole: was he going to abolish completely the independent legal authority of the Divisions, and introduce a new military code, according to which justice might indeed be sought for, but when found, was to be thrown into the waste-paper basket at the caprice of a higher court, or even one of equal jurisdiction, which might happen to think differently?

In reply to which Schieffenzahn growled out that nobody could have more respect for the jurisdiction of so experienced a soldier and one who stood so high in His Majesty's favour, but matters of policy were not everyone's business. Apparently the members of the Divisional court martial had missed the most important aspect of the case, which it was his duty to take into account.

Lychow felt that he must keep calm: this was the core of the dispute between them. But he did not want to plunge rashly into such fundamental issues. So he said quietly: "But, my dear Schief-

fenzahn, how is my court martial officer, who is a capable man—
as I think you will admit—to find out which is the court competent to
deal with a given charge? If you thrust your more enlightened views
on us in this way, we shan't be inclined to refer our cases to you."

Schieffenzahn was becoming annoyed. Did the old figure-head
take him for a child?

In spite of his irritation, he answered in a matter-of-fact tone
that if an explanation was due to anyone it was due to him. It was
intolerable that a man sentenced to death as a seditious person, a
slinking Bolshevik, should have been allowed to survive so long, and
he had clearly and unmistakably intimated his wish that the sentence
should be carried out. And instead of obeying a plain order, they
came to him with quibbles about jurisdiction and legal competence.
He, Schieffenzahn, was responsible for seeing that nothing should
endanger the German victory, at least on the Eastern Front. He
had to keep the army well in hand. When such issues were at stake
it was no time to be splitting hairs about justice and injustice. He
would be the last man to upset the authority of a General. (That
sounds quite Fritz-like, thought Lychow scornfully.) But His Excellency von Lychow was the last man from whom he would have
expected to have to endure all this stuff and nonsense about courts
and jurisdictions.

Lychow bowed slightly, and he thanked Schieffenzahn for his
good opinion. He said that the matter had gone far beyond a mere
question of jurisdiction. It was a question of plain justice—whether
in Prussia there was to be equal justice for every man, as the Bible
says: "One scale, one measure, and one weight shalt thou have for
thee and for the stranger within thy gates. I the Lord have spoken
it." He was quoting at random and his legs quivered as he spoke.

Schieffenzahn made a polite gesture of agreement. There must
assuredly be justice, and therefore no exceptions. As every day a
thousand men fell as a sacrifice to the German victory, he supposed
that a Russian deserter, who had so disgracefully abandoned his
post in the prison-camp, might well fall with them. And he smiled
amicably, delighted at the cunning with which he had caught the old
gentleman in his own trap.

But Otto Gerhard von Lychow smiled too: he had got Schieffen-zahn now; he had managed to lure him on to ground where that laborious intellect was hardly at its best.

"Certainly, Herr Kamerad," he said, "you have put the case very well. Throughout this War, at every moment of the day and night, innocent men have gone to their deaths, all honour to them. But the responsibility for this rests with all the generations that have built up the State, and also with the men themselves. They agreed to take part in the pageant of history, and their children and grand-children must reap the fruits of their sacrifice. Of course, it was to some extent imposed on them; still, it may be considered voluntary, as long as the country is ready to obey the decisions of its responsible leaders. But now, Herr Kamerad, I am sorry to have to point out a slight flaw in your argument. Let me finish what I have to say," he exclaimed, as Schieffenzahn prepared to answer. "Do I send my men into action with the intention of getting them killed? If I had a voice in the matter they should all come back alive, every one of them, sir! If that is impossible, I submit sorrowfully to the in-evitable—as long as war is the ultimate means of making a nation great. But you, on the other hand, are proposing to sacrifice against his will a man well known to be innocent, because in the furtherance of your purposes you think merely to do the State a service. The soldier always goes into battle with a certain degree of willingness, for he thinks there is a shadow of a possibility that he may return; in the last resort, he puts his life in God's hands, for the sake of his home, his country, and his Emperor. But this Russian—the ma-chinery of justice is to be used to put him to death unjustly. Do you dare to compare him with a German soldier?"

"I do," said Schieffenzahn nodding. "Look at the facts. How long does this degree of willingness last? If the German soldier refuses to obey orders, he is shot. And as for that shadow of a possibility of returning—if he's lucky this time, he'll be for it next time. Consider, Exzellenz. Phosgene shells, and gas attacks, are gradually reducing the scope of the Divine Mercy that you men-tioned. The art of war, looked at from the technical point of view, seems to be intended to put God in His proper place. I prefer—though I am afraid I shall offend you—to take the plain blunt view of the situation: the State creates justice, the individual is a louse."

Von Lychow leaned back in his chair and said softly: "If I thought that was true, I should feel no better than a dog. The State creates justice, does it? No, Sir, it is justice that preserves the State. I learnt that as a boy, and that alone gives a meaning to life, in my view. It is because justice is the foundation of all States, that nations have the right to tear themselves to pieces in their defence. But when a State begins to work injustice, it is rejected and brought low. I know, as I sit here under your lamp fighting for the life of this poor Russian, that I am fighting for something greater than your State—I mean for mine! For the State as the instrument of eternity. States are like vessels: and vessels wear out and break. If these cease to serve the purposes of God, they collapse like houses of cards, when the wind of Providence blows upon them. But I, General Schieffenzahn, know that justice and faith in God have been the pillars of Prussia, and I will not look on while her rulers try to bring them down."

The small dark room, in which the sole illumination was the circle of light from the green-shaded bulbs in the centre, seemed to stretch away to infinity round the two men who sat there contending for a man's life. Outside in the vast silence the faint sound of snow could be heard eddying against the window-panes. Von Lychow got up and, absorbed in his reflections, absent-mindedly drew the curtains in this room that was not his. Schieffenzahn looked at him quizzically. To think that an old stick like this should come to him with quotations from the Bible, as if Haeckel's *Riddle of the Universe* had never been written. Did such superannuated old dug-outs think that they could guide and preserve the German Empire? At last, as he toyed with a paper-weight in the shape of a Roman sword, made from the limber-ring of a heavy mortar and inlaid with copper, he asked if His Excellency was prepared to take his oath that Prussia had grown up in obedience to God's commandments. Maria Theresa and the Polish nation had expressed quite a different view on several occasions, and the proletariat had the most singular notions on the subject. And, smiling down on von Lychow from the superior height of the nineteenth century, he began cautiously to pull to pieces the old gentleman's political theology : touching upon the franchise, the rights of property, and the distribution of land.

But Schieffenzahn's superior attitude was lost upon von Lychow. Might must not be divorced from Right. If Schieffenzahn's objections were more in accordance with reality, yet he was well aware that all human institutions were imperfect, and the influence of the people still counted for something in the formation of the future. But nothing in the world could justify a State setting in motion the mighty machinery of the law against the innocent, and so destroy a nation's sense of justice. The national sense of justice, he said, quivering with emotion, was the symbol of Divine justice, and if it is thrown on the scrap-heap on political grounds, no one could tell whether, as a result of such an outrage, in the eternal spheres of the Divine justice sentence might not be passed on the State itself : *Mene, tekel, upharsin* might be seen faintly glimmering on the wall of a room in which a General was using his pitiable logic to bring God's commandments into contempt.

"Pitiable logic," indeed ! Albert Schieffenzahn started in his chair. He had borne with the pious old dodderer and kept his temper, so long as he had remained polite. But this he could not stand, and in a harsh imperious tone he requested von Lychow to moderate his language. He must remember he was not at Herrenhut or at a mothers' meeting.

Von Lychow slowly drew on his glove. He was familiar with that sort of talk, he said. The Lychows had tried to get rid of it after Saalfeld and Jena, but half Prussia had been swamped by it. "No doubt the Schieffenzahns think it extremely up-to-date," he added. "However, there's no more to be said," and he flicked the cigarette-ash off his trousers.

Albert Schieffenzahn breathed heavily, and thrust out his lower jaw, bulldog fashion, though it was by nature somewhat receding. He thanked von Lychow for his observations : he had enjoyed the lecture on Divine Providence, and now he proposed to make some remarks in return. He flattered himself he knew all about discipline and the best means of enforcing it. He had therefore telegraphed orders to the Kommandantur at Mervinsk to the effect that the sentence should be punctually carried out by the following afternoon.

He saw Lychow start, and grip the back of the chair. Yes, he went on, he had done so without the slightest hesitation. His Excellency might, of course, appeal to the Emperor afterwards. Then he, Schieffenzahn, who was so unpopular and had already taken so much upon himself, might get into hot water again: but he did not mind. However, he now wanted to make the difference between them perfectly clear. In His Excellency's opinion the execution of the Russian would be prejudicial to discipline, but in his own, it was in the interests of discipline and was, in fact, demanded by political necessity. Their views were diametrically opposed. Very well, then. As His Excellency declined all responsibility—"Of course I do," said Lychow emphatically—he had better give up his leave and let the 5.20 D. train go off without him. He could go straight back to Mervinsk by the next train, or by a car which would be at His Excellency's disposal, and personally prevent the Ortskommandant from carrying out the order of the Q.M.G.—in other words, of the Commander-in-Chief. If he, Schieffenzahn, then sent a lieutenant and ten men to take the Russian, dead or alive—and he leaned forward and smiled insolently at his visitor who, with his cap in his gloved fingers, was staring at him, motionless, from behind his chair —His Excellency had better place himself at the head of his Division, and with full understanding of the consequences, resist him by open force, and, with his Bible in his pocket, return blow for blow in defence of what he conceived to be right. "Don't you agree, Your Excellency?" he asked, as Lychow opened his mouth to reply, but merely swallowed and said nothing. "As you decline all responsibility, and are quite sure that you have the interests of the Empire and of justice on your side . . ."

The room was strangely still. The silence that surrounded Lychow was like the silence of an Arctic waste, cut off from all the world.

"God help me," he said at last: "I'm a Prussian General . . ."

"So Your Excellency will proceed on leave, and not declare a private war on me, but yield to my poor logic after all?"

Lychow nodded: he had come into the room pale and determined, but now he turned to go with bowed head and heavy footsteps. Schieffenzahn got up politely, and pushed his chair back sharply and exultantly—the noise he made echoed against the wooden walls like the slamming of a hundred doors. As he stood there, he pushed up the green-shaded electric lamp, the better to illuminate his triumph, so that its yellow glare lit up the battlefield as far as the door.

Lychow walked to the window with his spurs tinkling, just as if he had been alone, pulled the curtain aside, stared out vacantly for a moment, then turned round and looked steadily at his victorious antagonist.

"I am only an old man, Herr Schieffenzahn, nobody can jump over his own shadow, however small it is: and I've cast my shadow for seventy-two years."

Then he laid two fingers on his cap and went.

Major-General Schieffenzahn, standing with his legs apart, watched with a sardonic smile the door close behind a beaten man.

Chapter 2

A DEFEAT

But this was not the end of the matter. Schieffenzahn was forced to realize that he could not switch his attention off as he was usually able to do, and give his mind to the question of the administration of the Ukraine. Now he understood why primitive races believed that there were many souls housed in a single body, and any one of them could easily break loose from it and remain after the body had departed. Below in the street he heard the car that was to take the General to the station, approach, and then depart. But Lychow's soul still stood yonder near the writing-table. Schieffenzahn felt no thrill of elation at his victory. The feeling that at the end of the interview had brought him so squarely to his feet did not last: it shrank and disappeared. The matter was not settled. Schieffenzahn almost cursed himself aloud. Damn these nerves of his; he knew what he wanted—more sleep. To-day was Reformation Day, and he was to dine with the Saxon officers. It would be a late night and he already felt jaded and worn-out; and he longed to go to bed. There was a feeling of dull exhaustion round his heart and his eyes twitched. He yawned convulsively two or three times, opened the file on his left, and let it fall again. "I'll have a cigar," he thought. So the champion of justice had departed, and Schieffenzahn hoped he had taken his shadow with him. He would not find it so easy to kick against the pricks. Strange how these Biblical tags would haunt a man. "Oh, damn it all," he said with a laugh, picking up a bottle of brandy from a table near the foot of the bed, took down a small glass from the shelf, filled it, and swallowed the fiery contents with relief. He felt at once exhausted and excited. In his unbalanced state, after an interview like this, it was unfortunate that he should have caught sight of the lid of the cigar-box, on the under side of which was a picture and some printed words: ... A cheerful manufacturer had chosen as a cover design for these large, excellent, almost black, Brazilians, a picture of a knight in blue and brown, helmeted and in full armour: on his shoulders were plates of steel, and his ominous, romantic eyes gazed steadily into Schieffenzahn's weary face. Against his breast he held the pommel of an uplifted sword, and across it was written in Gothic characters, "Retribution!" so that Germany's enemies might see it and tremble. Albert Schieffenzahn was momentarily taken aback, but at once recovered himself, carefully selected a cigar, and clapped down the lid with a laugh: " 'Retribution!' An excellent title for Brazil cigars." Then he cut off the end, lit it, and walked up and down, enjoying its fragrance. He could not help realizing that the word had irritated him. Retribution indeed! A cigar ought to be called *Kamerun, Kronprinz Wilhelm,* or *Farm and Fireside* perhaps. The idiocy of these arm-chair warriors sometimes took disturbing forms. It was a shame to let such boxes get into the hands of tired men.

By this time Lychow was slipping off in the train. He was not going back in a fury to Mervinsk—not a bit of it. He opened the window and took a breath of air. How cold it was, and what a stupid lot of snow. But the D. train would get through: it would be pretty thick, though, by the first of November. After all, the War could not be fought under cover although it was winter, and snowing. Man had conquered nature.

Schieffenzahn began to feel he would like to lie down. There was too much to think about. The ghost of that conversation hovered round the table and awaited deliverance. "To err is human," he remembered from the book from which he had learnt shorthand. When all was said and done, he was but a man, and a man placed in a position in which errors cease to be merely human but may produce the most appalling results. Perhaps the old gentleman had infected him with his own fear of Hell. The dread of retribution! Everything seemed to be conspiring against him. But he must not give way to this, he must think; thought would drive away such fancies. All human systems must be inspired from time to time by a breath of superhuman intuition, for whether a matter is important or trivial, or will have any consequences or no, can never be decided until after the event. What, in God's name, looking at the circumstances now, could have induced Napoleon to have Enghien shot, or made him think, at Waterloo, that the salvos of artillery were from Grouchy's Division, when in fact they foreboded Blücher, and defeat?

Humanity was tainted with superstition. People were loath to admit, though it was an established fact, that any event might influence any other. We knew hardly anything. Fools knock their heads against a window-pane like wasps, though they can easily get out elsewhere. What a man like Schieffenzahn might do, he thought, as he sank down on the creaking camp-bed, spread a newspaper under his feet, and stretched himself out at full length, had far-reaching consequences. No act of a man in his position could ever be casual or isolated. The wise decisions that emerged from that shaven pate of his would be part of the life of many generations yet to come. Their weal and woe was already tingling in his nerve centres. In his dreams, at table, or at stool, a voice within him whispered that this power of his was all-pervading, unshakable. His mental life had become part of the Empire's destiny, and could never be shaken. "And to achieve all that, Your Excellency," he said to himself in contemptuous mockery of that invisible presence that still hovered behind Lychow's chair, exactly where Lychow had stood and stared at him before he turned to go, "to achieve all that, I have not needed your God or His Heaven." And furthermore: this hard entity that was Schieffenzahn, that too was unshakable. He was the centre of that vast network of authority, and wrong decisions, however trivial, could be cancelled somehow or other. After all, why should he crush this poor devil beneath the engine of the law, with open eyes?

It wasn't worth letting the old man threaten him with Death and Judgment over a trifle like this. Quite right, Exzellenz, a General who sent Divisions into action had on strictly practical grounds the best reasons for wanting them to come back safe and sound: but if he stood this Russian in front of a firing-party, he would be simply kicking the man into his grave. And "Why, oh why, dear swan?" Really the whole affair was not worth troubling about. . . . After all, he could do as he liked, thank God: he had but to wink an eye and the Russian died or lived.

And if he let him live, he would be left in peace. He had only to issue an order of the day to Lychow's Division, to the effect that this man Bjuscheff was not, in fact, the deserter Bjuscheff, but an escaped prisoner, who must be brought before the proper courts and suffer the penalty for this serious offence. Why not? Only because he did not want to put von Lychow in the right. Who was this von Lychow, anyhow? Where would he be if Schieffenzahn brought his concentrated forces to bear on him for a single evening? He got up with a groan of exhaustion, felt his way to the desk without his spectacles, took down the receiver, spoke to the sergeant-major on duty, and told him to get him put through immediately to the Ortskommandantur at Mervinsk. And he added in the gentle voice of a tired man: "You must ring loudly, Matz, I may be having a short sleep."

"That's settled," he said with a yawn, stretching himself out again, in the dark quiet room. The lamp was pulled down low over his desk, and gave out only a faint green glow; the snow beat gently against the window. Schieffenzahn felt better: Lychow would be surprised, he thought, when he heard about it. It couldn't be helped, but he rather grudged him his little triumph. He looked like Captain Abert of the Military College, giving a geography lecture. "A good General," Captain Abert would say, "always secures his retreat in proper time": a very important rule, this, never to let your retreat be cut off. As he fell asleep, memories of the immediate and far-distant past mingled and rose up before him. He thought of the retreat of the Grand Duke, which could not be avoided, and his own retreat, now—and there stood Captain Abert; he looked with his big reproachful eyes at Albert Schieffenzahn, who did not know where Sofia was.

Sofia . . . the word brought to his mind Sofie, his mother's maid, who lay in bed, and laughed, as the door opened, a low musical laugh, and the little boy's face was thrust inside the door. But very soon the bell would ring for him to be dressed. Then he would run clattering down the stairs, and rush round the courtyard with his fists clenched. . . . An undersized, sensitive boy, with a knowledge of the world beyond his years: his impressionable brain grasped objects and ideas in clear-cut outlines; he was gentle, susceptible, acute, easily moved to tears, and fond of his mother's company. He played with his soldiers; in his picture-book he loved a certain drawing of the baby Frederick II, in long clothes, performing on a drum; his two uncles were lieutenants in the reserve: and to be an officer was the only way to win that social position which the son of Schieffenzahn, the miller, so much needed in the country town, in his dealings with the sons of the Junkers who sent their corn to him to be ground. So his father and mother decided that their clever Albert should become an officer: he should go to the *Kadettenanstalt* as soon as possible. The lad knew he would be unhappy, but agreed to go, delighted at the prospect of wearing uniform so soon: he would have a blue coat, black trousers, with a red stripe, and perhaps Guards' badges on his yellow collar, and yellow or even white shoulder-straps, gleaming brass buttons, and at his side a real steel dirk, or at least a belt, which would certainly suggest one to his boyish imagination. So his inner self was split asunder: a secret half of him knew that a young ambitious lad must soon begin to bow before the wishes of the great, so he set his foot on the lowest step of that endless stairway and began to climb. The boys would ill-treat him because he knew too much, and he did not yet realize that, besides that, he would have to yield up the fruits of his cleverness and youthful agility of mind by doing the stupid bullies' work for them. And how they tormented him nights! He whose brain absorbed so much of his strength, was horrified at the excesses which their gross bodies could endure: but he could not betray them, for nothing more terrible could happen to him than to be expelled from their society; or even sent home in disgrace, because he could not bear the stern traditions of the *Kadettenanstalt*. Nobody would believe what orgies of lust and torture went on in the dormitories, courtyards, and passages. If a boy was physically weak he needed a protector, and a protector was only to be had at the price of a surrender of body and soul. At eight or nine years old only a coarse mind could fight its way through the despair of a little desolate child-soul which sits and cries under some spiritual stairway, cries to go home, cries for a woman's love. Still, the nearer one gets to manhood in the waking world of men, the less time one has for women; a man must work, go forward at all costs, increase the powers of his mind, acquire knowledge—history, German, geography, railways, Army organization, map-making. Old von Lychow's prototype, Abert, stood by the wall, in front of the map of the German Empire, a conglomeration of many-coloured States sprawling across Europe shaped like a bear. The boy looked up sharply: "Please, Sir, I know." Abert was a rotten name, and the shameless young ruffians quickly changed it into *Abort.** Schieffenzahn was a rotten name too: how often did he have to open his mouth to show whether his teeth were really crooked. (Still, that would at least teach him to show his teeth. Albert, again, was too like *Albern.*† The world is so full of humiliations for people with such names, that it is impossible to rise high enough to escape such ignominy. He wanted to become the greatest man in Germany: but that ambition was un-Prussian, for he would still have to do the work of the fools with a "von." He would have to train himself to put all his achievements, all his ideas, and all powers of work, ungrudgingly into the service of a "von": he would be too proud ever to accept a title himself. Even if he became a great man: he dared not confess to himself how early and how fervently he had worshipped this "von." He would always have to be the second, working behind the back of a larger, more substantial "von," who would presently be growing moustaches and bask in the glory of Schieffenzahn's achievement. Would that change when he joined a regiment? It would not change. It was best to keep his deeds as anonymous as possible. Yet he must climb this stairway, if he had to go up it on hands and knees, this endless stairway, with its brown banisters painted with stripes of yellow, flight by flight, towards Heaven, beneath those rafters where lust and torture held sway, up to those dark and dreadful attics. And all his sufferings came from his low birth. He had been born at the foot of the staircase. He had sat on the lowest steps, where they had taught him to look with awe upon those above him; as a result, he must look with contempt on those below, and woe to those of them who dared to question the sacred character of that stairway and that climb. For, otherwise, the whole agony would have been without sense and reason. Such sceptics must be crushed beneath

---

* *Abort*: Lavatory.   † *Albern*: Silly.

the boots of the von Brekows, von Smorschinksis and von Bellins. Woe to those who maintained that a free man could hold his head high if his foot was not set upon that stair. Such fellows must be rooted out. . . .

There he lay, a great fleshy bulk in his camp-bed, sunk in a deep sleep; and as he lay he saw a little boy, clad in his shirt, dragging a cadet's trousers up the stairs behind him, up and up, to where there was no escape, only lust and torture, nothing to hold on to, no landings, and no way back, for the way was barred by a horde of grinning school-fellows, long since mouldering in their graves. His arm hung down over the edge of the bed, and in his fingers was a cigar which had gone out. The telephone bell rang sharply. "The bell for the morning break," thought the child with a sigh of relief. Abert, the geography-captain, could not keep on asking where Sofia was, for as the class had decided to torment him because of his middle-class liberal ideas ("We'll soon get rid of that little bounder: he's only fit for a sapper"), now no one could put up a finger and say that Sofia, the great Church at Constantinople, was on the Golden Horn, and was built of light grey brick striped with red. (*His* Sofia was in bed, and laughed when the door opened and little Albert did not dare to go in.) Captain Abert's face was yellow and his hair white and he looked with his wise, kind, searching gaze deep down into the soul of Albert Schieffenzahn, where the tears were always lurking, too ready to burst forth from those childish eyes, in the early days before he had learnt to turn his moods inside out like a stocking which he must get on his foot. It was the bell: the class was over. Outside were meadows, and streams in which he could cleanse himself of all this foulness, reedy retreats where he could be alone at last, away from this mob, whose slave he must be so long as he was weaker than they. And Albert Schieffenzahn lay on the warm sand, watching the darting dragon-flies, far away from Lichterfelde, thinking of holidays, and his soul yearned for death:—he longed to be gently swallowed up in the warm, clear, tawny waters of the Krummen Lanke, in which he used to plunge, among high hills covered with birches, oaks, and grey-green pines stretching up towards the sky. But he was a good swimmer, and he must swim his best. His father and mother were waving from the shore, running beside him and urging him on. He swam with long steady strokes, his head half under, and instead of drowning himself he never swam so fast.

The door opened very gently in the half-darkened room. Sergeant-Major Matz, with a sheet of paper in his hand, tiptoed reverently up to the writing-table and, in the circle of light shed by the lamp, put down a copy of the telegram which Schieffenzahn had dictated before his interview with Lychow, together with the usual form, initialled by the operator on duty, and confirming its despatch. "What a man!" said Matz to himself as he looked with awe upon the sleeper. "I can't disturb him. After all, I don't get up so very early: but he's been at it since eight this morning. I should be a swine to wake him, just to tell him that the snowstorm had messed up all the lines beyond Bakla, so that there's no communication with Mervinsk, and the signallers won't have that section right before to-morrow afternoon or evening. He's fighting for us, and sweating his head out for us: let him sleep. The world won't come to an end, and Germany won't fall into the sea, just because he hears the news an hour later."

Whereupon he extracted two of the large Brazilians from the cigar-box, as a reward for his forbearance, and shaking his head with honest admiration, he took a last glance at the sleeper and slowly closed the door behind. Albert Schieffenzahn noticed a change in the current of his dreams. He stirred in his sleep, and turned to the wall; he began to slip backwards even further to the time when he had played with balls of wool and bobbins under his mother's ironing-table—he remembered her apron, white as apple-blossom, the pure penetrating smell of freshly ironed shirts and the laundry-baskets of table-cloths and napkins—he saw it all again. . . .

The wind drove the great white flakes softly on to the black window-panes. From the distance came a whistle. It was the despairing shriek of an engine struggling against the snow.

Chapter 3

SNOW

SNOW on Western Russia! Somewhere above the forests lay the
pivot of the storm. Round it, like the spokes and rim of a mighty
crystal wheel, whirled legions of white flakes above the silent earth.
The air was rent in pieces by the frenzied gusts. The storm swooped
down lashing and shrieking upon tree-tops, hedges, and roofs—on
all that stood up before it, and across the stretching plains that
cowered beneath the blast. Myriads of flakes had begun to melt but
the cold laid hold upon them, and in a few hours the slush was
covered with a solid and enduring robe of winter. The world was
changing her face: it was becoming white, and black, and grey. The
forests between Brest-Litovsk and Mervinsk were seething and
howling with the storm. Flakes fell in the rivers and were drowned,
but elsewhere they conquered. They swept over that vast land,
falling thick and heavy among the tree-tops; the pine-needles were
soon matted with their covering of snow, and in a few hours they
would strain like sails beneath the storm. The stout sixty-year-old
pines creaked in the wind like masts; they shuddered, bent, and
swayed, but their roots held fast. The good months were over and
the bad time had come again. . . . The beasts crouched in their
lairs and hearkened to the onslaught of winter: badgers and hamsters,
who are always careful to keep a well-filled larder; foxes, bold and
fearless—the snow does not spoil their hunting;—but the hares with
quivering ears and the rabbits would come off badly in the next few
weeks. Mother lynx with her now strong and healthy brood sniffed
fearlessly at the icy wind: once again there would be chances of
pulling down young deer whose long legs had got caught in the
undergrowth. In the plantations, where the old trees had been
cut down, the roe-deer huddled side by side, and the stag, his

eyes mournful with presage of the lean months to come, raised his steaming nostrils to the sky, and laid back his branching antlers. Winter had come upon the world. The men out yonder in the interminable trenches and dug-outs that war had made, watched drearily and grimly the beginning of yet another winter of war, drew gloves over their numbed fingers, piled wood into their stoves, and stamped savagely through the slush that squelched about their feet. "We shall be home for Christmas," said they, and they knew that they were lying; while above their heads the spirit of the snow danced a wild dance over the desolate places and the forests, and strove with all his might to entangle the branches of the trees together, and strew the ground with heaps, drifts, and swathes of snow.

From Brest-Litovsk there stretched over the land a network of black lines in all directions: wires, flexible and coated with rubber, soaked in protective solution, and covered with twisted thread. Like thin black nerves, they coiled over the earth in shallow ditches, just beneath the surface, or traversed the air on tall poles. They accompanied the telegraph wires along all the railway lines; they crossed the forests on straight paths decreed for them. The telephone wires of the army hung high above the earth in the forest tree-tops; their course was marked on the map and the line was carefully secured wherever necessary. In the summer no one paid any attention to them, but in the winter they paid dearly for this neglect. The forests, where the wind-spirit waved his snowy hands, took little heed of these black rubber-coated wires. Suddenly the tree-tops and the branches would break under their great burden of snow, and bring the wire down with them. Sometimes it caught in the fork of a branch a little lower down, stretched taut like the string of a violin; and a wire that had been laid loosely across the trees now had to stand a strain and the contraction of the cold. If only it were made of copper which is so tough and elastic! But for a long time past steel wire had been used for all the army telephones, except for the Imperial Section between Mitau and the Palace at Berlin, which was of pure copper; so the wire, in obedience to the laws of physics, broke. It stood the tension stubbornly and then snapped: one of the parted ends whistled through the air and curled round a branch like a lasso, tangled among the slender birch twigs; the other sprang back, caught in the undergrowth, and lay there in loose folds: in a few hours it was buried beneath half a yard of snow. At the edge of the forest, snow-drifts a yard high were heaped up before nightfall; the wind was the master-mason of this wall. Roaring and exulting he laid his snow-bricks against trunks, undergrowth, and tree-tops; the swirling air, like a solid thing, served him both as trowel and as mortar. To the right or left of the railway lines, according to the direction of the wind, there rose silently or in tumult, slanting dunes of snow, which could engulf a man up to his chin. Twilight fell, and winter howled and laughed and moaned.

Throughout the land, in corrugated-iron hutments, the timber houses of the country, and cabins of tarred pasteboard, were scattered the signallers, the telegraph-companies, repair-parties, and labour-companies. They knew there would be plenty for them to do next day, so they sat listening to the spirit of the snow as he clapped his hands and drummed and beat upon their walls, and they watched the cracks which had let in so many draughts, getting gradually blocked up, so that a genial warmth began to spread about the room. There were some pleasant trips before them in the morning, but they would not think about that now. This evening they would play nap under the lamp or sleep in their bunks. It would do no harm to grease their boots again, oil the soles, and hold their puttees up against the light to see if there were any holes in them.

Snow upon Mervinsk. . . . The city, on the slope of its low hill, was protected from the weather, and some distance from the centre of this whirling storm. But at nights the street grew full of snow. Winter had begun. It was now time to see whether there was wood enough stacked up in the courtyards, so that at least they might keep warm. The Jewish and Polish cab-drivers were polishing up their little Russian street-sleighs. Over the open spaces on the outskirts of the town, between railway buildings, platforms, hutments, store-houses, and over the town itself, blew an icy wind with flurries of snow, a faint image of the storm that roared and revelled in the forest. But no one minded the windy tournament in the sheltered streets of the town that was their home. This time the snow was falling heavily. It had begun the day before, and now it was lying two feet deep. Electric light had been newly installed, and a sturdy little dynamo made the wires hum with throbbing life. Would the snow bring them down?—that was what everyone was thinking about. If they held, they held. If they broke, offices, hutments, and prisons would be plunged in darkness till they were repaired.

When, early in the morning after Lychow's departure, an order was received from the Kommandantur that the prisoner Bjuscheff was not to leave his cell that day, the corporal on duty whistled through his teeth and merely said:

"So soon?"

Daylight was slow in coming. When they crowded into the yard for parade, some rubbed their eyes and thought the snow looked very comfortable, others hoped for a little snowballing. But the sergeant-major detailed the men for duty and kept them busy supervising the gangs of civilians who were sweeping away the snow; after which, quite casually and without any explanation, he gave the order about Grischa: and so Grischa was allowed to snore in peace.

He slept on in happy ignorance, and as the day was dark, he slept till late into the morning, and the guard were not disposed to wake him. As compared with Lychow, he was but a mole, he could not know what was happening in the kingdom of his gods, that his protector had gone on leave, though he had left Winfried with full authority to represent him in the matter. When Grischa at last awoke about midday, much refreshed by his sleep, but hungry and chilled to the bone, he had a somewhat uncanny feeling. The sense of time, which never entirely forsakes a man, told him that several hours of the day had already gone. He was amazed that nobody had opened the door, that he had not been called for parade or breakfast. Under his bed was a secret and forbidden store of cigarettes and bread, all sorts of odds and ends and a little money. The stove would want stoking up to-day, he thought; he felt terribly cold. Unfortunately he had given Max's bottle of schnapps to Babka. He had, however, such profound confidence in his friend the General, that he merely thought some detail of the daily routine had gone wrong; he never guessed that his own life was at stake. He drew

his stool up to the window; a thick cushion of white snow lay along
the narrow projecting ledge in front of it. Snow lay everywhere.
Grischa's heart rejoiced. Snow meant home: snow meant Vologda,
and the little sledge in which Grischa raced over the steppes drawn
by his grandfather's solitary dog. Snow was an infinite playground:
snow was so clean that a boy might eat it, snow was so soft that a
boy might roll in it; it was warm and it was cold. A snowfall in
Mervinsk might well have surprised him: but it merely gave him
intense pleasure. For in his home at Vologda, towards the end of
October, the great snowstorms had already begun to sweep over the
long since frozen steppe, and with the snow came sledges in which men
travelled all the faster to their friends. "This snow," said Grischa to
himself with a smile, "is blowing in the Germans' faces." As he was
hungry, he lit a cigarette and smoked with tolerable contentment
though he was shivering with cold. He unfolded his cloak which
had served him as a pillow, and put it on. "Ah, that's better," he
thought with satisfaction, "now I don't mind what happens." And
something did happen. He had not smoked a third part of his yellow
cigarette when a guard hammered on the cell door.

"Russky," said a voice, "you're smoking. Don't let anyone catch
you; I don't mind, but if anyone comes I'll let you know."

"Come in, open the door, comrade," said Grischa, astonished.
"What's happening in Mervinsk?"

"You may well ask," said the other.

"It's snowing," said Grischa, by way of a reply.

"You may say that," said the other.

"Is there no work to-day? Is it a holiday?"

"You may say that, too," answered the voice, gruffly. It was
Arthur Polanke of the Landwehr, from the Choriner Strasse, Berlin
N., who was talking to the prisoner. "Yes, it's a holiday. To-day's
Reformation Day; but that means nothing to you, you're little better
than a heathen."

"It's all so quiet," said Grischa. "I shouldn't mind a bit of
breakfast."

"Of course it's quiet when the company's away on duty: but you
can have some coffee, though if I were you I should wait till twelve
o'clock. It won't be long: it's nearly half-past eleven now."

"Company away on duty?" said Grischa in astonishment. "Then why have I been in bed so long?"

The man outside was silent. He seemed to be reflecting for a moment whether he should speak; then he said in a low voice:

"I'll tell you. The old man went on leave yesterday."

"Who?" asked Grischa innocently. "Brettschneider?"

"Lord, no, he's there all right. I meant your special old man, Lychow. And we've had orders that you're not to be let out of your cell. It's a summer cell too, so they must have their knife into you again. And as your case isn't settled and you haven't got into any more trouble, you may explain it if you can, because I can't."

Grischa listened, and laboriously reproduced these words and images in the terms of his own thoughts; then with a short laugh he said:

"Beasts! they're revenging themselves while the General's away. Afterwards they'll say it was a mistake, or somebody's orders."

As the prisoner could not see him, the guard grinned ominously and muttered: "I'm glad you take it like that. Now I'll open your cell, and you can clean it—that'll let some warmth into it. There's no work this afternoon, the stoves will all be going strong, and if the corporal on duty will look the other way, we'll leave the door open all the afternoon, so that you'll at least have company, and it will be nice and warm for you."

And Grischa thanked him.

And when the dried vegetables and tinned beef were brought round at midday, Grischa's mess-tin was filled very full, and he thoroughly enjoyed his dinner.

Then he left his cell, which they had actually forgotten to lock, and went into the guardroom, where the men of the Landwehr were just lighting their pipes, and the barrack orderly was carrying off the empty mess-tins to wash them out with warm water and wood-shavings. When Grischa came in some of them glanced up from the cards which had just been dealt, others from their letters, or their books, and then turned back to what they were doing, with rather too noticeable an unconcern. Grischa filled a pannikin with hot water from the great iron cauldron on the stove, and was about to go and empty his mess-tin in the common trough outside—that invaluable trough that provided food for three pigs. And as Lychow lived near by, the men might rely on the fact that these animals would be fattened up for ham and bacon, and not wasted as mere pork, as happened to so many pigs behind the lines; strict orders were given that these valuable animals should have free access to the kitchen refuse. But when he had got to the door, Corporal Hermann Sacht walked up to Grischa and said:

"Half a minute, Russky: you go and wash that out in your bucket."

"But what about the pigs?" Grischa answered with a smile.

"We won't bother about the pigs to-day, old man," said the corporal very gravely, "you mustn't be seen outside. You're to exercise in the yard from two to three, with the others; you'd better curl up in your bunk."

From this, and from the strange deathly stillness that followed the corporal's words, Grischa understood. He stood motionless, his mouth and eyes grew a little pale, as he looked at the man who was almost his friend.

"Now you know what's up," said the corporal contemptuously: but the contempt was not for Grischa.

"Yes," said Grischa, "I do." And he cleared his throat sharply, then, stiffly and with measured steps he crossed the room, followed by the looks of all that sat there, and passed along the dark passage to his cell; it was one of the first, on the right hand, against the outer wall. Hermann Sacht watched him go, and then went after him.

"Leave the door of your cell open, Russky; you must keep warm, and if you want to smoke—well, we're smoking and no one will notice you."

And Grischa thanked him.

About this time the snowstorm burst in full force over Mervinsk. The cell was full of smouldering twilight. Grischa stretched himself out on the bed, with his hands under his head, and covered by his two blankets. He reflected that a mattress, stuffed with wood shavings, did not give much warmth in winter. At first the shrill icy blasts of wind whistled through the window-frames cleaving the tobacco smoke into whirling clouds, but in a few minutes that same wind had blocked up every crack with snow, and the air in the stone-paved cell gradually grew warmer.

"Now it is finished," thought Grischa, "and I must go."

Only a few minutes before, he had felt himself secure, sheltered by a protecting hand, and now the certainty of death was upon him, swift and inevitable, death while his limbs were strong and wholesome, and he turned over in his bed as if he felt the walls of his coffin against his body, and all were at an end. A bitter taste mounted to his palate from his throat, and he thought: "Well, I shan't be sorry when it's finished; now, at least, my troubles will be over."

He sank back in utter exhaustion and despair, his mouth opened suddenly and as the pipe dropped from his hand he fell into a deep sleep, though, indeed, his heavy meal and the oncoming darkness had as much to do with it as the numbness at his heart. Men who have known something of life, and have had to bear a hand in tasks that they have hated, have no great need of telegrams and official instructions in order to grasp what is going on. Grischa, who was to be shot, and the company who were presumably to shoot him, alike knew what was to happen, even before Schieffenzahn, far away at Brest, had taken down the telephone receiver to send a certain order on its way along the wire.

Shortly before two o'clock Hermann Sacht, who had passed quietly by the open cell, said in astonishment to the corporal on duty:

"Russky's asleep: do you think we'd better leave him alone?"

"I don't mind," said the corporal, "but orders are orders: he must go out for exercise."

"Yes, his health is very precious," said Hermann Sacht in grim irony, as he snapped the padlock on the cell door, "but perhaps he would like to have another look at the snow coming down, and hear the doves cooing up in the roof, and the sparrows fluttering through the drill shed, which is the only place you get a breath of air in this sort of weather. Who do you think will have to do him in?"

"We shall, of course: it's our job."

"That's right enough," said Hermann Sacht, with a laugh, as

he slung his rifle over his shoulder, "he'll be shot with the rifles he's cleaned himself."

"Oh, well, he'll be sure there'll be no dirt on the bullets," said the other, nodding, "and we'll have our cartridge-cases to remember the Russky by, until we throw them away again."

"Perhaps it would be a good thing to dig his grave soon; if we wait till the ground freezes it will take twice as long."

"And perhaps there'll be one of those coffins left which he and the little Jew sweated at for so long."

"Of course there will," said one of the company, looking up from his game of draughts, "there are at least five in reserve and two extra big ones. He'd certainly fit one of those."

"Two minutes to two," said the other with a whistle of surprise as he glanced at his watch, "wake him up, and a pleasant afternoon to you."

Under the drill-shed, which was well enough suited for parades and physical exercises, though it was hardly large enough for drilling, the wind blew wafts of snow, tiny icy crystals or gusts of frozen rain, right under the roof almost to the inner wall. Little spectral eddies of dust arose from the ground, twisting like dervishes till they dropped and gave up their transient ghosts. The sparrows chirped busily in every corner, pecked about for seeds, or sat, puffed out like little balls, upon the rafters. From their safe, warm lodging in the roof came the contented cooing of the doves.

"It's hardly weather for a walk even here," thought Hermann Sacht as he stamped about patiently by the side of Grischa, whose hands were thrust deep in his overcoat pockets. His woolly, khaki-coloured overcoat (one of those which Sluschin & Co. did so well over), and his ill-assorted German boots, kept him warm. He tramped along, inside the row of wooden roof supports, from one end to the other of the shed, ninety-three paces in all, and back again. And Hermann Sacht saw that he was thinking. But he was not exactly thinking: as he walked up and down, he watched the snow in the air, his eyes wandered over the dust on the ground, the wooden beams, the nails, the nests in their several corners, the dark nooks where the beams joined the rafters, spiders' webs, and fluffy little sparrows; and he listened to the cooing of the doves and the creaking of his guard's leather belt. And as he took all these things in, he asked himself:

"Will these things last?"

The keen air did him good. "How long," thought he, "shall I breathe this air?" He must try to understand how the air entered his lungs: man is blown out like a ball. He frowned, and stared steadily before him as he tried to imagine what it would be like when a man could no longer blow out this ball. After about twenty minutes he turned to Hermann Sacht, who, so as not to disturb his prisoner, was walking quietly up and down in the opposite direction; but his cloak was much thinner and he was pitiably cold, and he was burdened with a rifle weighing nine pounds, not to speak of a supply of cartridges.

"Shall we go in?"

It was not really a question, but a kind of friendly command. Grischa was changed, though he had not noticed it. In a tone of voice that he had not used since his escape, and with the quiet assurance of a seasoned soldier, he had suggested what he knew was best for him.

Hermann Sacht looked at him doubtfully. "This sort of breeze takes a bit of getting used to: and you've got the right to a full hour, Russky."

Grischa nodded: "I know," he said, "but we'd better go in all the same."

"If you weren't a decent sort," said Hermann Sacht, with a sigh of relief, as they hurried back to the building keeping close to the wall and carefully avoiding the storm-swept yard, "you might have kept me hopping about here for a good forty minutes, though I want to pack up a parcel and write a letter with it. But you are a decent sort," he reflected, as his eyes wandered over his prisoner, apparently seeking some solution: "a really decent sort, and yet everything goes wrong with you."

"Oh, what does it matter whether I'm a decent sort or not," said Grischa, in a voice that showed his complete indifference to such distinctions. "When did the sentence or the order come through?"

"Sentence?" said Hermann Sacht, as they walked through the covered passage which connected the main building and the second yard, or drill-ground, with the guardroom. "You've made a mistake. It hasn't come through, nor yet an order. Nothing has happened at all."

"Then how do you know that they are going to . . ."

"Oh, come, old boy," said Hermann Sacht, meaningly, "it's pretty clear, isn't it? They've had their knife into you for a long time, and have made up their minds to carry the sentence out, and as soon as the General had turned his back, they lock you up. That's as plain as your face. If the Divisional Office ask for you this morning the people here will say you're ill, or they'll have the cheek to say straight out: 'nothing doing.' Meanwhile they'll telephone to Schieffenzahn. 'Lychow's away,' they'll say, 'shall we do it now?' What more do they want? I may be wrong, but we're both old soldiers; we've been a long time in this line of business. And, O Lord——" he suddenly stopped, "here's the War going on for another winter."

These last words were uttered in so hopeless a tone that Grischa realized that here was a man who envied him—who would certainly sooner live than die, but if he had to die, would rather be killed now than next spring.

"True, comrade," he said, "the grave is dark but at least it's quiet," and a wan smile flickered round the corners of their dark unshaven lips and their despairing eyes.

Chapter 4

NEWS

THE telegraph room of the German Field Post Office at Mervinsk echoed with the tapping of Morse instruments, and there all manner of cables came to rest. Higher Staff Officers usually telephoned messages to be sent by telegraph: they were then written down on the proper forms and dispatched through the usual channels, when copies had been taken and filed, so that if a message was ever questioned it could be verified. The telegrapher, Manning, who at the moment was engaged in receiving messages, had a great admiration for Sister Bärbe, and she too liked the astute Berlin business man; he was genuinely devoted to her in his off-hand way, and his attentions brought to Mervinsk something of the fragrance and gaiety of the great city. Moreover, he waged constant war with his superiors, because his uniform fitted him far too well, and his cap was much too smart, so that in the half-light even a major would often take him for an officer, and salute. And every one of his adventures, faithfully retailed to Sister Bärbe, brought a moment's cheerfulness into the ghastly typhus hospital, where the poor soldiers of the Austrian mixed battalions lay writhing in delirium, and were cured or died. Just now they were Czechs; they seemed to talk much like the others, but they were fairer and the cheek-bones and noses more noticeably Slav. . . .

Corporal Manning knew all about the Bjuscheff case. He also knew that His Excellency von Lychow had gone on leave, so that he felt a sudden shock, like a blow in the stomach, when, about four o'clock, he received the telegram from Brest-Litovsk signed by the Quartermaster-General. It was his duty to enter it on the prescribed form and send it on; he knew that in three-quarters of an hour it would reach the Kommandantur. In the hall, some of his comrades, who were off duty at the time, were discussing the use of War Correspondents, and after he had personally dealt with the telegram in question, he jumped up, opened the door, and signalled to them and to his friend Schaube.

"Take my place for a minute, will you? I've got to go out."

"Oh, I dare say," answered Schaube, clapping the receivers over his ears, and the other disappeared into a telephone-box. Everyone knew whom Corporal Manning wanted when he asked for the field hospital.

He was told that Sister Bärbe was engaged, but that Sister Sophie was coming to the telephone. (At that minute Sister Bärbe was sitting with the morphia syringe in her hand at the bedside of Jaroslav Vybiral, a tailor's assistant from Prague, to relieve his last agonies.) The poor fellows were taken to the hospital much too late, the excuse being that the roads were bad. (Indeed they were: our own men knew all about that.) Manning gnawed his lips with impatience and waited: in his thin hand, encircled by an elegant wrist-watch, was a cigarette which he soon threw away, as he had no light. At last there was an answer:

"Sister Sophie here."

"Never mind who I am, Sister"—he did not want to give his name.—"Look here: in less than an hour, the Kommandantur will get a bit of paper, with a first-class signature, requesting to be notified that Bjuscheff has been shot within the next twenty-four hours. Have you got that, Sister Sophie?"

From the other end—the telephone was in the Secretary's office on the second floor—came a voice.

"Yes, thank you," and he could tell by the tone that she had indeed understood. She too had the presence of mind to mention no names.

"Somebody," Manning went on, "might be glad to hear the news, as His Excellency happens to be on leave." "I'll see to it," came the reply, suddenly in quite a cheerful tone:—somebody's come into the room, thought Manning, or else the sister on duty was trying to overhear—"May I invite Bertin too?"

"Good idea," said Manning, and he heard Sophie laugh heartily.

"You know how to laugh, Sophie: give my love to Bärbe. I must go back to my work. Good-bye."

"He might have said 'Sister Bärbe,'" thought Sophie half-unconsciously, astonished at this unaccountable and most disquieting piece of news. As she ran up the little flight of steps to her ward, she knew she must act, and act with decision. Generations of officers and men in authority stirred in the brain of that charming vivid creature. Before she got back, she knew exactly what she would do. So she turned round, went down the stairs again, through the hall and round the corner and stopped at the door of that important personage, the Chief Surgeon, who was then on his rounds. Of course, as in all offices, there was supposed to be no admittance, and the great man was only approachable through two or three underlings. But Sister Sophie simply lifted the latch and then, noticing that the door was locked and the key on the outside, she boldly opened it. Then she drew the curtain across the entrance to the next room; if she were caught here it would be by either the Chief or his Deputy: in the former case, she would merely be cursed, and in the second, kissed. Or if any unauthorized person, like herself, should intrude, she would coolly ask him what he wanted. She was no longer Sister Sophie, Bärbe's assistant at the hospital; Fräulein von Gorse had burst into life once more, the humble disciple of that bold and destructive young gentleman Bertin with his high cheek-bones and his fiery eyes, and she knew that she was confronted with something like a crisis and one that deeply concerned her friend. For a moment she hesitated at the telephone: she was wildly anxious to speak to Bertin first and tell him at once the monstrous thing that had happened—she wanted him to hear her breathless voice and throbbing heart together with the dreadful news. Then, however, she reflected that it would be quicker and safer to get on to Lieutenant Winfried than to ring up the Kriegsgerichtsrat's clerk, especially as the call was made from the Chief Surgeon's room. So she asked to be put through to His Excellency's A.D.C.—Down in the basement, Lehr, the telephonist, was abstractedly putting the plugs in and out, for he had just received a letter from his wife at home full of bitter complaints about her separation allowance—and thus it happened that Lieutenant Winfried was informed, in a few agitated sentences, of

Schieffenzahn's order, half an hour before the message reached the
Kommandantur. No one came in. In that silent room, papered a
dull brown and green, the twilight deepened; across the window
passed a wall of moving snowflakes: and Sister Sophie ventured at
last to ring up Bertin, at the court martial office. Lehr, the much-
married, below in the basement, turned over the third page of his
letter, and absently put through her second call. In a flutter of fond
excitement, and with a torrent of hurried words she whispered into
the ear of the beloved what had happened. She at once heard his
hoarse voice in reply, saying again and again: "What? What?" in
a more and more menacing tone. She explained to him that Winfried
had already been told—yes, she had told him herself. But she had to
speak to Bertin at all costs that evening.

"Good God, woman," he groaned suddenly, "we are dishonoured;
this is the end of us": and she understood him. He meant the end
of Germany as a moral entity, as a civilized community—or a
Christian society, as she represented it to herself. To-day at the
Soldiers' Home there was to be a small celebration for the Saxon
Protestants, but equally for anyone who cared to come, in honour
of Reformation Day and in commemoration of the great act of that
Man of God, Martin Luther. The Evangelical Sisters had a day off
for the purpose: their places would be taken by their Catholic and
Jewish colleagues so that on one of the two following days, All
Saints' Day or All Souls' Day, the Catholics might go off duty. The
ceremonies at the Soldiers' Home did not begin till nine: and Bertin
promised to be there without fail.

Lieutenant Winfried was much absorbed in some figures on a
sheet of paper before him. He was sitting at his uncle's writing-
table and calculating whether the interview with Schieffenzahn could
possibly have taken place already. He considered it impossible, for
he remembered that Lychow had said something about half-past
four or half-past five. This hopeful thought had flashed into his
mind and deadened the impact of the monstrous news. He called
for the time-table. The D. train for the west left Brest-Litovsk
shortly before half-past five: "Half-past four, then," thought Winfried, "and it takes three-quarters of an hour to get there. . . ."

And with that reflection Winfried screwed up one eye and sighted an imaginary rifle with the other (if the expression may be allowed). People who are not quite sure of themselves, he suddenly realized, like to confront stronger persons with a *fait accompli*. Schieffen-zahn's afraid of the old man: he heaved a sigh of relief and the awful strained expression faded from his face. If Lychow had given little Albert a proper dressing down, then the Devil and all would be in it if the order wasn't cancelled. After all, Prussian gentlemen still got their way, and, besides, any other result was, humanly speaking, inconceivable. After a few minutes, Posnanski rang up and asked in friendly tones whether Paul Winfried would do him the favour of "crossing his unworthy threshold forthwith." He had some news for him. And Winfried said, with a laugh, that it had already reached him too. It was not so very serious, really. Of course he would gladly come over at once, though he was "up to his eyes in work": still, as there was a war on, he could find time for one more job. Anyhow, he must have a talk with him about what to do in the next few days, so he would "chuck work, and blow along at once."

Whereupon Posnanski sniffed characteristically, and then with his usual persistence politely asked the Lieutenant to ring up the ser-geant-major on duty at once and ask him whether Paprotkin had reported this morning, as he always did, for duty at Divisional Head-Quarters.

Winfried snapped the fingers of his free hand and said:

"You think you're very clever, don't you?" He would run over in a quarter of an hour, and might he venture to ask for a cup of tea. Then he walked through two empty rooms, entered a third, said good-evening, and sat down on the corner of a long table, at which Sergeant-Major Pont, who had drawn the green-shaded lamp down low over his head, was studying two large photographs of the Mervinsk synagogue—his work was as good as over, and, besides, who would have dared to question the actions of a Staff-Sergeant-Major?

"No," answered Pont, as he looked at his chief in surprise, the Russian had not reported to him that day; he had probably reported at the court martial office.

"No, he hasn't," said Winfried.

"Do they think we don't exist, because His Excellency is away?" asked the sergeant-major. "Somebody must have put them up to treating us like that."

"When the cat's away, the mice will play," said Winfried, laughing.

Pont shook his great close-cropped head, which already had patches of grey about the temples.

"I beg your pardon, sir," he said, "I'm sure someone must have put them up to it. 'Don't like the looks of it,' as my eldest boy would say. He's two years old," he added, as a sudden yearning for his son filled his heart.

"Then he ought to know what he's talking about," said Winfried. "We'd better ring up those fellows across the road."

The office of the Kommandantur confirmed Winfried's suspicions: No, they said, the prisoner Bjuscheff had been kept in his cell to-day by Captain Brettschneider's orders. There were special reasons for it, and besides, a telegram had just been received from Brest-Litovsk, the contents of which the office had no authority for passing on to the Division.

"Yes," said Pont, derisively in answer. "You'll be too proud to know us soon. May I ask what you are going to do with him?"

Corporal Langermann, at the other end of the telephone, could restrain himself no longer (ever since he had got his second stripe, three weeks ago, he had been burning with departmental zeal): "Shoot him within twenty-four hours," he blurted out.

Pont started back in horror: "Are you daft, man?" he said, slipping into Rhenish; and Winfried realized the situation.

"We know all about that," he whispered into Pont's other ear: "they want to finish him." Then he took the receiver out of Pont's hand and calmly announced himself.

He spoke with that quiet composure which he had always maintained through those dreadful days at the Souchez sugar-factory and in Pozières cemetery on the Somme, at the first tank attack.

"I must inform you," he said, "that at half-past four His Excellency had an interview with the Quartermaster-General in connection with this matter, and that any hasty action may involve even the most important personages in serious consequences."

Langermann, student of philosophy, who was seated in his office not far away, spasmodically clicked his heels together, but answered in a triumphant voice:

"The order mentions twenty-four hours, Sir: you may rest assured that no hasty action will be taken before then, Sir. Quartermaster-General's orders, Sir," he added, with the relish of a card player who takes the winning trick with a long-reserved ace of trumps.

"Right you are," snorted Lieutenant Winfried contemptuously, as he hung up the receiver.

Grischa felt cold in his cell. He wished it had been next to the semicircular guardroom, from which the three rows of cells projected, trident-wise, into the main building. But the passages were dank with the cold air of the last three weeks, which would probably remain there till the summer. Grischa, who was stamping up and down the cell, up and down, from door to window, stopped: it suddenly occurred to him that he would be a queer object by next summer. He had seen men who had lain in the earth throughout the winter and the spring and then been brought to light again in the course of trench-digging, or by some other accident of war: they still looked like men, but they were not beautiful. Yet why should he turn away from them, when he too was destined to become just such a shrunken mouldering corpse himself? He had had to face much: why not this horror too? His beard would have grown long on his cheeks and on his chin where there was skin still sticking to it; he would have no eyes worth mentioning; his tongue would either have rotted away or be protruding from his mouth like a bit of dried leather; he would still have some hair, but there would be no stomach under his tunic, if, indeed, they let him keep his tunic—here the native decency of his class came out and he determined that he must at least be buried in his shirt and trousers. He knew what was right and proper. A last request was always granted: he would ask to be buried in his uniform and boots, fully clothed, in one of the coffins which he had made himself; not flung into a hole like a poor wretch killed in battle half naked or without a rag on him, like a dead dog.

At last the cold became intolerable; he opened the door of his cell and appeared at the entrance to the passage, surveyed the long room that he knew so well, under the friendly light of its three electric lamps hanging high up in the roof, one at each end, and one in the middle over the writing-tables. A genial warmth streamed from the stove, and Grischa gave a grunt of satisfaction. Then he moved a stool near the entrance, sat down with his back to the wall, and waited to see whether anyone would drive him away. After a few seconds' hesitation the corporal on duty decided to do as the others had done; he might get into a bit of trouble over it, but not much, for the Russian had for so long been looked upon as one of themselves: he could pretend to be stupid and say that he could not understand why the man should now be flung aside like a dirty dish-cloth.

Grischa liked warmth and light: but he was in no mood for company. He seemed to have a great deal to think about, and he could have thought more easily alone. Then he reflected that he would soon be quite alone, and miss his friends: so he resolved to sit down and, as far as he could, pursue his thoughts among them all. Tobacco he had, which was the main thing, otherwise he would have had to borrow or buy some; he would not have liked to have had to buy it, as he had been saving up for Marfa Ivanovna and his little girl and for his future stock-in-trade, so as to start business free of debt. He had learnt much in the War. He could make little ornaments of metal, such as rings, and paper-weights in the form of swords; he was also an excellent wood carver; using an ordinary knife he could make salad-knives and forks from lime-wood, with roses and foliage carved in relief upon their handles; fish-knives, with handles representing a long, scaly, curving fish, or walking-sticks with a snake twined round them. He had learned many and various trades, last of all the carpenter's, and he could earn money by them all: so he was never likely to have starved. The German authorities had charge of his possessions: sixty-three roubles in paper money, saved out of his pay, and sixteen German marks.

They would have to give him all that back, or, if not, send it to
Marfa Ivanovna. He knew it would be sent through Sweden. They
were sensible people there, who kept out of the War, and they
undertook such small services as these between the two mad
warring hordes, so that the memory of human fellowship should not
entirely perish from the earth. He thought how he had meant to
get home, and sighed: he had set his feet upon the way to peace,
so that at last he might sit down in quiet by his wife and child; but
the War had caught him in a trap, in a trench that had no outlet.
He saw himself as an imprisoned wolf, ensnared into a defile—
or some quarry with sheer sides, and at the end a towering, slippery wall. After him came the pursuers, strolling at their ease,
as they watched the furious beast twisting his head to right and
left, preparing for a desperate leap, determined to defeat that terrible
wall. Leaping and scrambling it reached the top, and once again was
free. Grischa saw all this as in a vision, vivid and clear-cut; he
was not greatly astonished, for he took it as a sign from his inner
self warning him to escape. But he shook his head wearily. He
would only escape from these pursuers to fall into the hands of
others. Between Mervinsk and the Front the country was dotted
with camps, hutments, rows of tents, and all the roads were seething
with despatch-riders on horses or motor-bicycles, patrols of military
police, leave-parties marching to the station or returning. It was
quite clear: only an idiot would think of escaping. And with a deep
sigh of deliverance Grischa confessed to himself that he did not want
to escape. The bone was tired of being wrenched about by dogs.
It occurred to him that this vision had been present to his eyes once
before when he was stamping along with Corporal Sacht in the face
of the pelting whirling masses of snow, and the phantoms of the
wind. Sacht had given him to understand that he was a good fellow.
Was he a good fellow, he wondered? And he looked out into the
room. The Germans lay in their bunks, on bedding stuffed with
wood shavings or paper, and mattresses made of garden wire, reading books or newspapers. Others sat at the table in the centre,
writing letters, playing cards, and they were all chattering and smoking. The room was filled with grey acrid fumes, and the twice-
breathed air of many men. Were they bad men? If he, Grischa,

were to go to the door and open it, Corporal Sacht, who lay back there with his boots and belt, would creep up behind him with his rifle. Then, if he ran away, along the passage, through the first courtyard and the door on the right, he would hear voices behind him shouting: "Stop!" And then he would hear the well-known crack of an infantry rifle, or several of them, behind him. As luck might have it, a bullet would smash his back in, or it wouldn't. If he got any further, in a few seconds these friends of his, when they heard the shots or most likely before, would come rushing up with bayonets flying: and then, with expressions varying between anger and amusement, but all glad to have the matter settled, they would find him lying on the ground, writhing or motionless, but certainly soaked in blood, with his face on the stony, muddy pavement, or in the snow—why, in the snow, of course.

They were not bad men. He knew them all. They were neither good nor bad. They were men who could and would behave decently in any given circumstances. But upon their necks was the heel of those above them, and them they feared far more than they feared to take a human life. At the moment twenty million men were doing this, and four hundred million men and women considered it right, proper, and natural. Grischa was surprised at his own re-flections. He pursued his train of thought: if a man gets away, because he does not want to be shot in a few days, he is shot for doing so; not by bad men, not by evil men—nor is he a bad man or an evil man. That, at least, was sure; whether he, Grischa, was a good man, he who was sitting here with his curved brown pipe glowing under his nose, nobody could decide and it was nobody's business. But he wasn't a bad man any more than the others. As he had done no harm and yet was to be shot, a blind man could see with his stick that being good or bad had nothing to do with being shot or left alive. It wasn't God who settled such matters now, but that Devil of Babka's. He might ask the Jews, who would have it all written down in their books, but if he was to be shot, and pretty soon too, there was not much point in that. At any rate, the world was now so ordered that here was an innocent man going to be shot, and that smelt more of the Devil than of God. . . . Grischa was not at all surprised to find himself absorbed in such meditations. "Why

not?" he asked himself: a man who must die has plenty of time to
think about God and the Devil. It was just like this vile world to let
an innocent man be murdered: for there was a difference between
being killed in battle and being solemnly shot down for no con-
ceivable reason. What that difference was Grischa could neither
express nor reason out; he simply saw that the two things were as
different as an apple and a cherry. The cherry stood for death on
the battlefield, which was one kind of thing; the apple for the shooting of an innocent man, which was quite another. And suddenly a
mood of bitter black revolt came over Grischa as he thought of
this deed of violence. He didn't so much mind being shot, but what
he did mind was being shot in this senseless stupid way, having
done nothing to deserve it. It was enough to drive a man frantic.

But suddenly, as he closed his eyes wearily, and bent his head in
meditative enjoyment of his injured innocence, pictures began to
rise before his mind—memories, this time, of his past life. He had
been a hero—a mighty soldier. He saw a man fling up his arms—a
man in pale blue uniform—a bayonet thrust between his shoulders,
and the blade stuck so fast, that he had to put his foot on the man's
ribs before he could drag it out of the spitted body. Then he flung
him, dying, into a shell-hole, and the hero charged ahead, with a
sinking at the stomach, but he had not time to think of that. . . .
He merely made up his mind to do his job more neatly: why on
earth do people have stomachs?

Of course he was a hero. He had learnt to shoot, and not for
fun either; he had learnt to press his gun firmly against his shoulder,
to breathe gently, to keep the fore and back sights in a line, and
fire without a tremor, whenever he caught sight of a man's head
or shoulders, or a glimpse of chest or back: and whenever, at short
or long range, a scrap of grey or pale blue cloth was visible, between
trench and trench or on a hill side above the woods, he had been
taught to make sure that one German or Hungarian should not get
back: to wound him was something, to kill him better still. He
knew, too, how to throw a hand-grenade. Another scene came before
his eyes: he saw four men with bayonets, running breathlessly for
cover, a boyish young corporal at their head; he had carefully aimed
and thrown his hand-grenade, and he saw it burst among them like

a great stone among five sparrows. Not one of them escaped—they were all dead men. That's what they called a Russian retreat, did they? These scenes of his soldier life in that famous regiment to which he had belonged, were imaged in his mind in tiny, vivid pictures: it was true that he had not killed men every day, but he had done so more often than he realized, in the encounters of attack and defence. He, Grischa, was certainly not a bad man: but such feats were not exactly pleasant to recollect. He had blindly accepted the tradition of the regiment: to fight bravely for his Tsar and for his Country, and to do the whole duty of a soldier—Christ would quite agree to that. But experience had taught him otherwise. Täwje had been sure of one thing. "Whoso sheddeth man's blood, by man shall his blood be shed." And he saw it: it had nothing to do with good or bad. The Bible did not say: "the bad man who sheds man's blood shall have his blood shed by good men," nor does it say "the good man who sheds man's blood shall have his blood shed by bad men." It simply said: "he that sheds shall be shed, he that smites shall be smitten," and Grischa's whole face lit up with surprise as he grasped, with infinite satisfaction, the conclusion of this brief meditation. He was glad to find that the matter was in order; his anguish passed away. The case of Grischa Paprotkin no longer seemed to him a thing foul and unnatural: it was quite in order. All that mattered was that something should be in order. This whole generation had shed man's blood: and now the whole generation was to be poured forth in vats or buckets or drops of blood, no matter how. Justice must be served.

And so, at peace with himself and now strangely cheerful, Grischa asked Hermann Sacht for leave to go out to the lavatory as an excuse for getting a little fresh air. How blue the twilight was! As he hurried across the yard he noticed with astonishment how much clean white snow had fallen since the afternoon, and how deep it lay on ledges and roofs, and even on the nails on the wall. The wires of the electric light were sheathed in white, and the supporting poles wore thick white caps of snow. The night air surged against the men's faces and hovered round them like a haunting presence. Grischa took a handful of the white flakes and thrust it in his mouth.

"Tastes nice," he said to Hermann Sacht, smiling.

"Makes you thirsty," answered the German, who had known the agonies of snow-thirst in the Serbian campaign.

"Doesn't matter," said Grischa with a laugh, "but it tastes clean in the mouth, and makes a fine bed for a man to lie on."

Then he said thoughtfully:

"If that old woman—Babka—comes, I'd like to see her."

"Right," answered the corporal, "I'll arrange that. There's nothing in my orders against your seeing visitors. But she never comes before six. She's afraid of meeting the 'old man'."

During the lunch interval that afternoon, Posnanski was sitting at his table, Winfried was perched on the arm of the settee and Bertin was pacing up and down.

Winfried was explaining:—"Albert must have sent off that wire before Lychow could get at him—like a frightened schoolboy. His ukase was issued at three-thirty, but he was not to see the General till half-past four. And if the old boy's given him a good lecture he'll think quite differently and take it all back. I'm as certain as I stand here that this cable will be countermanded—and before dinner to-night."

It was one of Posnanski's gloomy days, which always had the effect of making him express himself in quotations:

"Thinkest thou thus? why then we may endure."

He thought of what followed but kept it to himself.

Then, shortly before his departure, Winfried rang up Corporal Manning, told him where he could be found in case a telegram from his uncle should be telephoned on to the Kommandantur or to him; he would be in mess in the evening and later on, until about eleven, at the Soldiers' Home: "There's some sort of a Saxon Protestant function," said he laughingly into the receiver; "come if you feel like it. Some of the nurses will be there: we shall have a little music, and it will be quite a pleasant evening." And after that he could be rung up at his house. And he expected some flippant and amusing reply from that affluent youth, one of those cultivated business men from Berlin, without whom the literary stage could hardly exist. But a voice replied in grave tones:

"I'm afraid it will be only too easy for me to get away, Sir. I should ordinarily have been on duty. But all communications with the west have been held up by the storm. We're just sitting twiddling our thumbs."

"What!" shouted Winfried, in such dismay and so loud, that the terrified Posnanski dropped his cigar on the table. And Manning gave him the latest information of the damage done by the storm. Communications with the west had been completely cut. The great forest territory between Bakla and the boundary of the Province was just a mass of tangled wire. No repairing parties could possibly get out before early next morning. "The last message from the west came in at half-past four. We've got no wireless: and if we're cut off much longer I expect Brest will send airplanes."

"Good God," stammered Winfried, "then the fellow's done for"— and he wiped away the sweat which had suddenly started from his forehead.

"What's happened?" said Posnanski eagerly. "For Heaven's sake, tell us."

And Winfried explained.

The three men stared out in anger or despair at the snow which beat softly on the square black windows, and which to each and all of them had been such a welcome deliverance from the drab greys and browns, the dust and dirt, of Mervinsk.

"Then it's no good," said Posnanski; then suddenly recovering himself, he added: "One of us must have a word with Brettschneider. If the man's got any sense at all he'll wait for a further telegram. If His Excellency has not stretched out his hand, there will be plenty of time for Herod to murder the poor innocent."

"No," said Bertin with a sad smile. "Somebody else is playing Herod."

And they saw the Tetrarch seated on his throne, mitre-crowned, heavy-jowled, with Schieffenzahn's parrot-nose and "Pour le Mérite" ribbon.

Book Six

RESCUE

✡

Chapter 1

BABKA PREPARES

AFTER the blind fashion of mankind, Babka suspected nothing. That afternoon she entered the peaceful, busy, smoke-filled guard-room, where Grischa sat by the wall enjoying the warmth and following his thoughts, and greeted her acquaintances, who shouted "Hullo!" to her as she entered. They were grateful for any break in the monotony of prison routine, and eager for any news of the city that lay hidden beyond those walls. She now sold many things; she always brought fruit, especially apples, and of course cigarettes; but above all, Russian pastry—appetizing little cakes made with herbs or grated cheese, and mixed with cheap suet and smuggled flour, though there were strict orders against such composite confections. The soldiers would often make fun of her, but the little brown-faced woman had a sharp retort to every jest. Her figure was noticeably filling out: but no one would have thought that she was seven months gone with child. The soldiers no longer took her for an aged woman but still less for a young girl, and in her soldier's boots and rough clothes she hawked her wares among them like any pedlar; besides, they were so used to calling her "old woman" that they could not think of her as young. Then she crouched down beside Grischa and gazed at him intently. His face seemed to her to have grown longer and strangely peaceful; he told her in plain rough words what had happened—the arrival of Schieffenzahn's telegram was not discussed at all in the guardroom, but the atmosphere of the place was so heavy with doom, that though there was nothing to bear out what he had said, Babka sat silent and overwhelmed. That was the way of the world, she said. She had known it for a long time. No one could teach her anything. She felt as though a hand was gripping her heart, and a feeling of horrible oppression made her gasp for breath. She passed the back of one hand hurriedly across her forehead, and with the other she rubbed her neck and the back of her head. In that moment she knew that the time had come for her to strike, and that she must now save Grischa even against his will. She breathed deeply several times, and felt herself again: and that little dawning life moved gently in her womb. Of course it would be as little use to tell Grischa of her purpose as to tell the unborn babe within her. They were both behind a prison wall, and both must be set free, whether they liked it or not. She quietly cast her eyes over the guards and tried to count them. Her bottle of schnapps which she had spiced and tasted with the tip of her tongue, that rich green liquor cooled with snow, would fling open all the doors, unlocked as they were, and give her fifteen minutes' grace. She did not reflect that the slightest symptom of poison in the first man who showed it would bring scores of others running in from all sides. The whole complex and delicate organization of a military prison was quite beyond her experience. She only saw the short passage from this guardroom through the hall, across the second yard to the gate; thence she would keep close to the prison wall and plunge into some dark alley of the city. Then let the Germans hunt for Grischa. She stroked his hands that lay nerveless on his thighs and asked him:

"When?"

And he answered:

"Look here, Babka, I'm happy now. A quiet woman is better than an acre of land. No one knows when it will be. There are all sorts of formalities to be gone through. Certainly it won't be to-morrow morning, so I shall get a night's good sleep; and it won't be to-morrow afternoon either, because that would upset the work of the prison. They could arrange it for the day after to-morrow: then the sergeant will be told of it to-morrow morning and have his men ready for the following day. I tell you what," he said, getting up, "I could do with a bit of sleep. It's stupid, I know, but I suddenly feel dreadfully tired. If you could sit by me I should sleep much better. You've got a child of mine in your belly, and Marfa Ivanovna's child is scrambling about in the kitchen, and I shan't see either of them, yours or hers. There'll be peace one day," he added;

and he laid his hand on her head as she crouched there beside him:
"then you had better go with your child to Vologda. It's a long way
off, farther than you think, but you can get there by railway. Then
the two children can meet, yours and hers, and you can both black-
guard me together:—here he smiled, pressed her hand, and moved
off. "Come earlier to-morrow," he said over his shoulder, nodded
again, and disappeared down the gloomy passage, and was swallowed
up in the cold and darkness.

She stared after him. Was that her silly soldier boy? What
were these strange thoughts of his? She could not understand.
What if he refused to walk through the open doors? She shuddered
at the thought. That was her fear, and was indeed the only risk of
failure. But then she reflected: he won't think like that when the
time gets nearer; to-morrow he'll begin to feel it, and he'll go off
with me right enough. To-morrow was the day of All Saints, a
festival for her as well as for the Catholics; the next day would be
All Soul's Day and candles would be lit over the snow-covered graves,
in memory of the dear ones who had been taken away. A solemn
time, and a favourable one. The Devil would certainly have less
power when all the Saints held sway, and when the tribute of a tiny
magic flame was paid to all the souls, in purgatory, in bliss, and
even to the luckless ones in Hell: at any rate it seemed likely. Then
she heaved a sigh, for her mother's heart pitied the soldiers who were
to drink her sweet green schnapps and get such deadly stomach-aches.
But she comforted herself with the thought that perhaps the draught
would not be strong enough for one glass or two to kill a man. She
had mixed in with it plenty of thorn apples and henbane, deadly
nightshade and belladonna: but a man could stand a good deal, and
it would be quite enough if they only vomited or fell foaming and
rolling their eyes in convulsions on the ground, for then she could
pull Grischa out of the prison by the scruff of his neck like a helpless little dog. When that was done they were welcome to recover.
And if she made a good job of it, they might get some sick leave into
the bargain. . . . And with a faint smile she nodded to them as she
went out. "A rum old girl," thought the soldiers, as with her basket
on her arm she passed out into the darkness and the snow, through
the hall, straight across the courtyard to the gate, leaving the shelter

of the walls under which a path had been trodden. The snow fell
steadily, with a menacing, almost fateful, persistence. The air was
still and therefore much warmer. Wherever there was a light the
great falling flakes showed up against it, white and lovely. The
lower branches of the chestnuts were bowed under their snow burdens, and the wires of the electric light were taut and tense. The
sentry at the gate stood huddled in the shelter of his box. Babka
exchanged a few words with him, as she used to do with all the
soldiers, and wished him good night. Then the man was left alone
once more; his gaze wandered wearily up and down the wires and
he reflected that if it went on snowing much longer they must snap
somewhere or other. They had not been made of copper for a
long while; they were merely steel wire, and if his luck was out the
damage might be done while he was on duty and all the lights in
that vast jail would be puffed out as if by some giant—and he
amused himself for a while with these reflections.

In the meantime, Grischa's soul was roving through the many
ways of the labyrinth of sleep. He had flung himself down and
gone to sleep as sound as a boy in a bundle of hay that steeped his
senses in its fragrant intoxicating breath. The wind was no longer
blowing against the window, and the general warmth of the building spread in through the passage, and there was a warm layer of
air in the lower part of the room up to the height of the bed. Clad
in his cloak, with his boots off, like a butterfly in its chrysalis, with a
spare shirt and ground-sheet rolled up to make a pillow, the doomed
man lay within those four narrow walls that reeked of smoke and
stone masonry, and slept: he slept away his living hours and lived
in the calendar of dreams. Death was stirring within him. His inmost being was upturned, as the earth is turned up by a mole, laying
bare new seams of thought, burying the old ones beneath them, and
as he sank deeper and deeper into the toils of sleep, a sort of smile
was limned on his stern grey sunken features. He was drinking
"*Bruderschaft*" with those he had killed. They sat at long tables
supported on rough balks of timber driven into the red and spongy
earth, tables such as soldiers drink at; they were sitting on benches,
toasting one another with tumblers full of coffee which they scooped
from great bubbling cauldrons: but that coffee was blood. There

were Germans in their grey cloaks; Frenchmen (whom he had seen
when working on the Western Front) in their sky-blue tunics, and
steel-blue ridged helmets; Tommies in khaki with small faces and
snub noses, then the Austrians, and the Russian hordes, and among
them was Grischa himself. They had killed one another, and now
they were drinking each others' healths in the soldiers' Heaven and
perhaps the soldiers' Hell; how should he know the difference. . . .
The blood shed for their several Fatherlands, collected together in
one huge cauldron, tasted sweet, like punch. The mighty draught
coursed even more riotously through Grischa's heart and veins than
what he had drunk at the General's party. He stood on the bench,
with an arm outstretched, gripping the hot iron drinking-cup by its
two handles, and shouted exultantly in Russian to his comrades:

"Friends, this is our great hour! At last we drink together, each
one of us has put off the accursed garment of life; but it did not
fit us, it was not made by a tailor, it came out of a factory, and the
contractors must have made pretty profits out of it. Now our tunics
sit well upon us, we have room to stretch and there's breath between
our ribs. Good health, comrades!" He drained a joyous draught
of the sweet warm blood, sent the goblet round the table, and rejoiced to see that all the company leapt to their feet and drank to
him, Germans from the Carpathians and Novogeorgievsk, Austrians
from the great battlefield of Lemberg; but now they were all together and at one, this great company of the blessed dead. Only the
rank and file: not an officer was there, not even a sergeant-major,
all of whom were probably bestowed in some other department of
that Heaven or Hell; these were N.C.O.'s and privates of all arms,
and when they sang, that great song burst forth that had fallen on his
ears, centuries before, when Grischa cut the first line of the wire
fence, in the blue-grey light of the snow on that freezing and tem-
pestuous night, as he stole across the white and empty space. There
it lay, stretching before him, pale with the blue pallor of a corpse,
with silver-grey tints like those of peeling skin. There was a smell
of almond-blossom, a soft odour of decay, and with giant strides
Grischa, his whole earlier life packed in a bundle on his back, hurried
through the stages of decay, gliding as if on skates, over an endless
plain. The wind tore the uniform from his body shred by shred,

over him, like huge cloud-shadows; the passionate F sharp, and the *Moonlight* with its rippling cadences and its long yearning, as of a soul in agony. He must play something brilliant and dazzling, if he wanted to get the two inquisitive beasts out of their lair. He saw in Bärbe's bright insistent eyes that she wanted something of the kind, and he did too, if only to shake off his depression . . . he'd got it; and through the clatter and the smoke, there rang out suddenly the great deep chords with which Beethoven bursts through the bonds of daily life and clears a way through to the world within: *The Waldstein.* After the first seven bars, there was still a hum of conversation in several parts of the room, and men in shabby grey tunics who wanted to listen, said "Hush!" Then they were all silent, except for the Countess in the neighbouring room who went on babbling tirelessly in her gentle voice with endless twitching of her thick black eyebrows. At last she began to prick up her ears. Life had so ravaged her soul that she was always in quest of something to fill the emptiness within. She would not have been content merely to listen; her restless eyes needed to be satisfied as well. She left her seat of honour on the sofa, hurried to the door, and none too softly either; she was eager to see the pianist, and the fingers that flickered and danced across the octaves, as she had heard tell of, but not seen, at the concerts of Hans von Bülow, Rubinstein and Rosenthal; and Pastor Lüdecke followed her meekly, seeing and honouring in her the embodiment of that great world which had deigned to take notice of a little parson out of Mecklenburg. It had been well burnt into the bones of Sisters Emmi and Nettl that they might not continue seated after the Countess had left her place. They stood in the doorway behind the backs of their two superiors, who, with their fingers on their lips, hastened as softly as they could over the creaking floor to the pianist. Manning smiled to himself out of the corner of his eye at having hooked his fish so successfully, and then, rapt in a soft sadness, and in an exalted mood that made him little inclined for courtesies, his soul soared upwards into the fastnesses of the spirit. In the next room a whispered Council of War began.

"I shall make a pilgrimage to-morrow morning to Brettschneider. He must put off the execution until there's been time for a telegram," said Posnanski in a low and troubled voice.

"Suppose he doesn't?" Bertin put in. "What then?"

"His Excellency left the man in your charge," said Sister Bärbe to her friend. And a look came into all their eyes, which meant, "we are too young to dare to meddle with such great matters."

"There's nothing more any of us can do," answered Winfried slowly.

"You won't give the poor man up: you can't do that!" cried Sister Bärbe, with a passionate movement. "If I were a man in your position—Oh, I feel like saying 'Shame on you!'"

Lieutenant Winfried raised his eyebrows.

"You must remember," he said sharply, "that there's an order of Schieffenzahn's on the table."

But Bärbe, with a menacing, searching look at him, said: "Does that matter?"

"It matters if I am sent to the Western Front," said Winfried with a smile.

"His Excellency would take the responsibility," said Posnanski, thoughtfully.

"But what could we actually do?" asked Sister Sophie.

And Bärbe, bending low over the table, whispered: "We could rescue the poor man from those beasts at the Kommandantur till Lychow comes back."

"And hide him," Bertin added.

Winfried broke one of the hard oaten cakes between his fingers. "That means kidnapping him."

"Helping him to escape, at least," Posnanski explained, "or in plain language—snatching him away from certain crooked teeth the way the what's-his-name bird gets a bone away from the hippopotamus."

They were all silent: near by thundered the great rondo, the cadenced chords with their runs and syncopations. Bärbe stared so hard and so steadily at Winfried that bright steely rays seemed almost to flash from her eyes to his; and she fired that young head, half-gay, half-serious, to a train of practical reflections.

"We've got plenty of depots and labour-companies in the trenches and the advanced posts, outside the Kommandantur area. . . . We could put the man as far out of Brettschneider's reach as if he forced them, as good Catholics, to work like this on All Saints' Day, was a personal injury and a piece of calculated Prussian chicanery. So they glided forward, and their water-bottles, knives and mugs, and the rolls of wire and tools on their backs clattered as they moved; all the while they were unconsciously scaring away the wild animals that had spent that night of storm in the thickets to the right and left of them, and were now taking their morning sleep.

"Good Lord, look at those pines," said Corporal Mittermaier, pointing ahead of him.

Across their path a tall tree, with its top almost twisted off by the storm, stood bowed and shattered: ten long hours of snow and driving wind had almost brought it down. Another, already withered, lay bent and broken, a lopped and splintered stump along the snow. Following a path which had been lately cut they went forward into the heart of all this devastation, or at least into those parts of the forest that had suffered most. Under the boundless covering of snow stretched a tumbled barrier of torn, crushed and uprooted trunks marking the path of the blizzard that had fallen upon the forest like an avalanche from the sky.

"Good work, that, *Mordssakrament*," said Toni in amazement.

"Ah, there we are," said Alisi, pointing to the wire, that he had never let go out of his mind any more than a gun-dog ever leaves the scent.

From a birch tree, a few yards away, hung something like a black whip-lash. This was the first break . . . ten miles or so inside the forest on the edge of which the other signal-parties were still raking and floundering about.

"That's a good beginning, as the worm said when he dragged the willow leaf into his hole," said Alisi. "Now we can have a bit of food."

And they discussed how little work they would do to-day. For running ski-races and fetching up in a muck-sweat at the far end of the wire, just to please that silly swine Schieffenzahn, was rank blasphemy on a holy day like this.

"First we'll light a fire, and then we'll see better what to do. We'll have a look at the damage later on."

They moved on into the ravaged forest, gliding cautiously forward to avoid the branches which lay like snares about their feet:

tree-tops snapped or wrenched off, shattered branches, a tangle of bushes, creepers, upturned earth, and stripped trunks bearing the marks of their martyrdom. Hans, who as corporal might be supposed to know more about snow-storms, stated his views. It was hopeless to try to get any further. The fellows far at the other end were welcome to fish up the wire if they had the ill-luck to find it—and patch up the old line with new material. Afterwards gangs of navvies might come along and clear the ground for a permanent repair. They determined to light a fire in some sheltered spot and have breakfast as soon as possible, and then, some time later in the day, they might look round the damaged area—or they might not. There was the end of the broken wire on that birch tree, let it stay there for a bit. They twisted some branches together to form a roof and covered it with snow: they made a comfortable camp fire with the petrol from their lighters, brewed some tea with snow-water and drank it mixed with rum, toasted their bread and ate it with some tasty bacon which the man from Allgäu generously shared with the Penzberger, and then spent a whole hour in following the tracks of an animal which they took for a wild pig. For a wild pig would have been much appreciated by their detachment, especially by the N.C.O.'s. They might, indeed, have found the other end of the wire, which was not far off in the matted branches of an oak tree, before it was quite lost beneath the snow. But conversations over wires like these nearly always meant unpleasantness for common men, so they decided that their time would be much more profitably employed in hunting for pigs than for wires, that their day's work might be reasonably regarded as ended at the above-mentioned birch tree, and that to-morrow would be an excellent day for continuing the search. So they settled down comfortably in the keen, cold air—red-cheeked lads with sparkling eyes; alas, this time the wild pig was careful to keep out of range of Mittermaier's Parabellum pistol.

So Sergeant Matz at Brest-Litovsk was right: no Major-General could get a word through to Mervinsk.

Every sergeant carefully distributes his work for each day, like a man drawing up a menu, which he submits to his officer for approval. The latter, to preserve his own dignity, sometimes makes an alteration—crosses out or adds some item, then he signs his name to the document, and each of them can bask in the sense of duty faithfully performed. But on that day, All Saints' Day, nineteen hundred and seventeen, which broke grey and misty here, too, in the city of Mervinsk, Sergeant-Major Spierauge had not ventured to draw up any scheme for the duties of the day. The shooting of a man was an affair of ceremony from the very beginning, rigidly regulated, from the promulgation of the death-sentence, and the restitution of the prisoner's property so that he might leave instructions for its disposal, until the time came for the civil experts to appear: the man of God, who is to save the prisoner's soul, and the doctor who is to certify the death of his body. And punctual and solemn instructions must be given to the executioners, so that they may turn out as smartly as possible—though there was little opportunity for smartness here, as the Landwehr men had only one uniform apiece—and wash the mud off their boots before they march to the appointed place, where a man could be shot with the greatest safety or buried with the most convenience. If the execution were to be carried out that afternoon while the light was still good, say about three o'clock, the order would have to be issued at nine o'clock at the latest, at company-parade. At the moment the office was temporarily idle, as owing to the interruption of communications, no messages were coming in from working parties in the neighbourhood, or from troops about to pass through and in need of billets, so that the stalwart, red-faced, flaxen-bearded sergeant-major was inclined to give the matter rather more particular attention.

Rittmeister von Brettschneider sat in authority in the State-room of the old official residence of the Russian Police Commandant in Mervinsk. It was a house with huge white arcaded walls, an imposing entrance staircase in the Russian manner, and windows six feet tall. A glass door in the front wall of this sumptuous room opened on to a balcony, the delicate trellis-work of which resembled that on the park-gate of the Villa Tamshinski, and came from the hands of the same artist. It was a lofty room with a carefully-laid parquet floor, and the figured yellow and white damask tapestry on the walls, and its general air of splendour made it look like an apartment in a palace. For this reason Brettschneider kept it for his own use though it was uncommonly draughty and made his feet cold. Three blankets had been hung over the door, three army blankets, one on top of the other (the men slept all through the winter with two), and it was not until there were at least twenty degrees of frost that the Captain showed any desire to move into a room next door which was smaller and simpler but where he could keep his feet warm. The stove was a magnificent creation in the style of the First Empire, on a bevelled stand of glazed china, and supported by four griffins of the period: it gave out plenty of warmth, but unfortunately far above the level of the Captain's feet. Half-way up the wall, opposite the writing-table, hung two life-size portraits in huge gold frames: they represented the Tsar Alexander the First, in close-fitting buckskin breeches, with handsome delicate features, insolent moustache, green frock-coat blazing with decorations, and under his arm a truly sublime cocked hat as big as a window; and Nicholas the Second, who now had little say in the Government of his Empire, but was very imposing here in his long trousers and sword, as his pensive bearded face, with its high cheek-bones, looked irresolutely down on his admirers. The two Tsars, painted in pleasing colours by good artists, had been presented to the commandant of police by the manufacturer Tamshinski, on the occasion of a long since forgotten anniversary in gratitude for a volley or two of ball-cartridge fired at his strikers in May, 1905; and after a long period of obscurity these imperial figures had been restored to honour, ever since the elegant Brettschneider and his friends began to use the apartment as a club-room. The strong light of an electric lamp glittered on the gilded backs of the chairs, covered with yellow and white damask fabric like the walls along which they were ranged; and shone on the long, manicured nails of the Captain and Commandant, to whom the perplexed Spierauge, who stood with drooping shoulders in an attitude of profound apology and obsequiousness, was submitting the paper which his chief called "the menu for the day," and on which there was as yet no mention of any arrangements for bringing the Bjuscheff case to its conclusion. On the margin of the blank sheet the Sergeant had written the word "Bjuscheff" followed by a note of interrogation, to remind the Captain of the exceptional business of the day. It was nearly eight o'clock. The company would parade in half an hour, so there was plenty of time. . . . Herr von Brettschneider filled his pipe with Dutch tobacco, which was not indeed of the best quality, though pleasant enough to smoke, and brought his whole mind to bear on the one word "Bjuscheff."

As long as this man had been an object of contention between the Kommandantur and the Division, Brettschneider's self-respect had revolted fiercely against the humiliations which were inflicted on him by men who were much more powerful than he, namely a General and his officers acting on his instructions. A Russian, as such, Brettschneider considered quite beneath his notice, a creature on whom he would not waste a single thought. If he was left alive, well and good; if he was put out of the way, that was an end of him—nothing could be less important. He smiled to himself in the quiet assurance of his triumph: after all, it was he, Brettschneider, that had played the winning game and not His Excellency. Of course, a certain Schieffenzahn had been in it, a fellow who was not to be trifled with; he was like the queen in a game of chess, standing at the end of an empty row of squares and exerting her power from a distant corner of the board. Her mere presence always sufficed to arrest the movements of the other pieces just at the decisive point. He, Brettschneider, had reckoned on this queen and she had not disappointed him. Now he (or she) was taking the pawn, round whom this exciting game had centred for so long. Brettschneider wrote down the number of the section—section 1 of No. 2 Platoon—that was to carry out the execution; he fixed the time, at about half-past three, when the light would be good for musketry, but not too bright; and finally he gave orders for Bjuscheff's property to be fetched from the drawer where it was locked up and taken to him in the prison. There was no need to promulgate the sentence as this had been done soon after the man's trial, and he was to be shot now in obedience to an order which had merely been suspended; ignoring for the moment the question of spiritual ministrations, he instructed Sergeant Spierauge to ask the Staff Surgeon to send him one of the younger surgeons, and to apply to the Red Cross delegate to see that Bjuscheff's effects were sent via Sweden to his widow: for all the correspondence (if such it could be called) between relatives on either side of the line went on this slow and laborious journey through Sweden. It so happened that the Swedish delegate himself, Professor Count Ankerström, was spending a couple of days at Mervinsk before continuing his (strictly conducted) journey to the new Front Line in the southeast. Outside the windows of the Kommandantur hung one of the seven or eight great arc-lamps that brought light to various places in the dark city of Mervinsk: the cable on which it hung and the connecting wires were taut with frost, and on the reflector above it was a great cone of snow. The powerhouse had just rung up, asking for assistance in knocking down or sweeping away the snow from the telegraph-poles, wires, and lamps: they were showing signs of collapse under the burden, and steps must be taken to avoid a short circuit or a break in the wire or something of the kind. Brettschneider allowed his attention to be diverted for a moment and instructed Spierauge to rearrange the fatigue duties and detail the necessary eight or ten men for this important work; if garrison troops were not available, convicted prisoners or men awaiting trial must be used.

Then an orderly appeared, and standing stiffly in the doorway, reported that Kriegsgerichtsrat Dr. Posnanski—he said in his excitement Dr. von Posnanski—wished to speak with the Herr Rittmeister. Brettschneider settled himself in his chair, smiled quietly, fingered his short, English moustache, and, looking up, as his custom was, to Alexander the First, whose white breeches and cock's feathers shone faintly in the half-light, fell into a comfortable train of reflection. His first thought might be represented by "Aha!" and in that word was all the triumph of a victory. It was quite obvious that these people had some favour to ask of him in connection with the Bjuscheff case.

But immediately afterwards he saw that although at present he held all the trumps in his hands, in four weeks or so a General, an "Exzellenz," namely old von Lychow, with his white hair and imperious eyes, would be backing those who were now coming to beg favours of him, and that General Schieffenzahn, an extraordinarily busy man, might some day, in all good faith, forget all about the Ortskommandant at Mervinsk, just when the said Ortskommandant needed him most. He therefore immediately gave orders for the Kriegsgerichtsrat to be shown in, and said to Spierauge, who had slipped quietly into the next room: "Wait."

Dr. Posnanski entered, his cloak unbuttoned at the top, carrying his cap and gloves, very clean-shaven, and showing by the red circles round his eyes that he had not slept well; he shuffled in, leaning sideways and with an absent look in the eyes behind the thick spectacles. The two men shook hands, and Posnanski began the conversation by expressing his regret that it was so long since he had seen the finest room in Mervinsk. The stucco ceiling, explained the lawyer, looking upwards as he leaned back in the rococo chair, was a first-rate piece of work. He said that he was convinced that the same Italians who were responsible for the marvellous work in St. Michael's Church at Vilna had moulded that magnificent roof.

"You don't say so!" said Herr von Brettschneider, who had hitherto not found time to notice this masterpiece, and, as a matter of fact, the silver-green ceiling was fretted with the graceful network of myriads of whitish spider-webs, long since tarnished by smoke.

"Yes," said Posnanski, clearing his throat. "You live in style, you gentlemen of the garrison: our furniture is of deal and made in Mervinsk, while you can put your feet up on carved walnut writing-tables."

Whereupon Brettschneider remarked dryly: "I have to, there's such a draught on the floor." Then with an awkward gesture he offered his guest a cigar.

Posnanski politely accepted one of those stumpy cigars which suited his Silenus cast of countenance so well.

"I've come, of course," he said with affected unconcern, after a few puffs, "about this Russian, who's been giving us so much trouble."

"You may well say that," answered Brettschneider, remembering one September morning when he had ridden forth, and silently applauding his own sagacity.

"You surely don't want to make an enemy of His Excellency," said Posnanski insinuatingly.

This was a tactical error, for he had got the entirely false idea that Brettschneider was a murderous sadist, to use his own uncompromising words.

"I do my duty and take the consequences," answered the Hussar Captain, raising his eyebrows.

"Of course," agreed Posnanski, "who could doubt it? But when His Excellency went away, an interview had been arranged with Schieffenzahn at half-past four. Your telegram came at half-past three, didn't it?"

(Brettschneider wondered if he had got this information from the telegraphers.)

"It must have been dictated at least two hours before His Excellency could have seen Schieffenzahn," pursued Posnanski. It was of course possible, he proceeded, that the Major-General might have given such good reasons for carrying out the death-sentence that His Excellency had had to give way. But there was little ground for expecting this result, for the merest glance at the papers made it as clear as daylight that the verdict was based on false assumptions and therefore invalid, a consideration which in his opinion must override all the military and political objections that the Quartermaster-General could bring forward.—(Here he suddenly grew pale as he realized that this verdict had been his. "Who," he thought, "expounded it so wisely to the General? Who took the responsibility in the sight of God, and was not ashamed of it? I did, alas, I did!") "His Excellency promised," he went on, in a sudden sweat of horror, "to wire the result of the interview. But the wires are all down and all telegrams are stuck in the snow for the time being."

Brettschneider lifted the receiver and asked Corporal Langermann, who answered, to find out how long it would be before the wires were mended. Then he turned to Posnanski:

"In point of fact, that's no business of mine," and he drew hard at his pipe and made the Dutch tobacco glow: "for my telegram reads, 'report execution within twenty-four hours,' and Major-General Schieffenzahn takes full responsibility."

"Of course," said Posnanski with a nod, looking at him with a friendly and appealing expression in his great round eyes: "but when all is said and done, a man's life depends on these same telegraph-wires, and if it turns out later that delay was possible and desirable, the consequences might be unpleasant.

"You see, Herr Rittmeister," here he leaned forward confidently, "His Excellency will take this case up to the Emperor, as he is anxious it shall not create a precedent. The Military Cabinet will call for the papers, and as we have them, they will get them. The last document but one will be a telegram from His Excellency: 'Postpone all future steps till my return,' with the comment 'could not be done because, on the authority of the preceding order of the Q.M.G., the Kommandantur at Mervinsk had refused any further postponement and had disposed of the case of Paprotkin or Bjuscheff. . . .' "

"Let us call him Bjuscheff," said Brettschneider lightly, "and leave other possibilities alone. I understand the position entirely. I see no reason to oblige His Excellency, since he has several times been very offensive to me. Why should I? At the moment he is dressed up as a General and I as a Rittmeister: but when we take our tunics off, as we shall do some time, he'll be a little country squire on his Brandenburg estate, and I shall be the junior partner in Brettschneider & Sons, a large concern which he has certainly heard of, in control of a couple of thousand workmen, turning out my iron tubes and girders. ('Brettschneider Sons, Inc.!' thought Posnanski, mentally striking his forehead with his hand, 'fancy not realizing that!') My patent of nobility is recent and not of much value, while his dates back to the misty past: but really, Herr Gerichtsrat, need you and I attach much importance to that? If I had been my father I should have accepted it too: why not? It is a great help in Germany just as baptism is to a Jew—I beg your pardon!—but it doesn't mean that we were born on different hemispheres. And if I had been stupid enough to take up soldiering as a profession—the Brettschneider works at Münster is a much better proposition, I can assure you—I should have reached the rank of Excellency myself one day. It's quite clear," he said. "He's a Conservative, and I'm a National Liberal, which is nearly the same thing. On several occasions he might well have been politer and more amiable with me than he was. But that's the great difference between us: he stands for the landed interests and I for industrial interests—very well. Since the memory of man his crowd has been playing the first fiddle in Central Europe, Russia, Italy and especially at home in Germany. A man of such ancient family, of course, can allow himself to champion a poor Russian in this off-hand, generous way. So far, so good. But now mark what I say, Sir: the War has proved for the first time how shaky these ancient landed families are. England puts on a blockade, and suddenly there's not enough of anything—meat or bacon, vegetables or corn, and not a sign of a potato anywhere. In spite of tariffs and contributions, the exemption or temporary release of farm labourers—nothing does any good. But industry's all right, Sir. Agriculture's come unstuck. I tell you, the squires won't rule Prussia much longer. Now you'll see how these kind and honourable gentry will defend themselves—people like Lychow, I mean:—good Lord! with tooth and nail, and every weapon they can raise. Just wait a bit: there'll be the devil's own shindy when you least expect it." And then, leaning back in his chair and coolly ignoring Posnanski's astonishment, he returned to the point at issue. "You're asking me to postpone the business, and why not? Why shouldn't I give you the chance of getting your own way after all? Well, my orders are that the execution is to be carried out by this afternoon at half-past three. Can I do it? Of course I can't. And as my excellent Corporal Langermann has not reported yet how long this breakdown will last, you can be quite sure that the line won't be working to-day. Perhaps we'll be able to get through to-morrow morning, or perhaps even to-night. If your General telegraphs that he's got round Schieffenzahn, then the Russian will be all right. But if I get no news by to-morrow afternoon, I shall have him shot at three o'clock to-morrow instead of three o'clock to-day. If the line is not working by to-morrow and you want further delay, you have only to give me a ring. But if I get through to Ober-Ost first— then what they tell me goes, and I'll let you know, and carry out the sentence sooner or later. That's sure enough to float a company on. Remember, I'm answerable to Schieffenzahn."

Posnanski breathed such a sigh of inward relief that it was difficult for him to conceal with how little hope he had started the interview. He called himself an old fool for only having seen the cavalry Captain, and not Fritz Brettschneider, under the soldier's tunic. The sweat was pouring off his forehead when he rose to go, for, as has been seen, the stove heated the upper strata of air with true Russian enthusiasm.

"We'll keep in touch with one another," he assured him grate-fully, as he took his leave.

Then Langermann rang up:

As yet no one could say whether the damage to the wires would be repaired to-day or to-morrow.

Brettschneider nodded, as though the man were in the room, and then he called Spierauge to his table and told him he wanted Bjus-cheff's execution postponed for at least twenty-four hours. He need only tell off the ten men for special duty with those asses at the power-house, and he'd better be off quick—here he glanced at his watch—for the company must have fallen in already.

Spierauge vanished. Brettschneider screwed his eye-glass in his eye, rose from the table, took his gloves and cap from a chair, picked up his riding-crop and prepared to stroll off leisurely to his duties in Prison Yard No. 2. Before he left the room, he waved his hand gratefully to the portraits of the two Sovereigns where they glittered in their heavy gold frames, so bland, so brilliant, and so inspiring. He thought he could read in their faces praise of his wise and royal treatment of the matter, and as they were only painted figures and he a living man, he gave them a half-humorous salute, bringing his gloved hand to the peak of his cap as he looked up at them. His spurs clinked gaily on the polished wood of the parquet floor.

Before the Rittmeister's arrival, Sergeant-Major Spierauge strode up, gracious but terrible, walked behind the first platoon, to the leading file of the second, which was the fifth section of the company, and the first section of the second platoon, and said to them in low tones:

"You may be put on extra duty to-morrow afternoon: mind you turn out smart. Extra duty with rifles and ammunition. Clean up your rifles as though for an inspection, have your helmets and leather equipment all in order, and boots ready for marching in the snow. You must do the battalion credit." And he expected grins of ap-proval. But every face in that row looked stiff and forbidding, and even somewhat graver, stiffer and grimmer than before. "Aha," he said to himself. . . . Then the corporal who had been posted as a look-out came up at the double and reported the approach of the com-pany commander.

"He's in a jolly good temper," he whispered to the sergeant.

"What's that b——y well got to do with you?" replied the sergeant-major genially. No, it was clear that the Landwehr men weren't looking forward to doing Bjuscheff in. That was what was the matter.

At that moment, swinging his riding-crop gaily and whistling softly what he could remember of the *Fledermaus* overture, the Rittmeister strode through the gate. The sentry presented arms, bringing his heels together with a crash.

"Attention!" rang out across the snow.

Chapter 4

GOD'S WORD AND MAN'S WILL

It was the first of November, 1917, and the day of All Saints was dawning at Mervinsk. The sky lowered thick and grey, as though it were hung with weather-stained tarpaulins, and through the atmosphere beneath it drifted a sluggish mass of chill damp air from the swamps and steppes of Russia, to melt, like a glassy iceberg, on the Western Plains. It had begun to dissolve, and the currents of cold air seemed like clammy icy tentacles that threatened to lay hold of Mervinsk soon after noon. But otherwise the day began as usual.

When the men returned from parade, Grischa asked, as he was having breakfast in the guard-room, whether there was any news about him, and Corporal Schmielinsky, who was in charge of the guard, first platoon, fourth section, could honestly say that he had heard nothing.

Moreover, Corporal Sacht, who was still personally in charge of Grischa, for the simple reason that he had hitherto avoided being put on to other and more laborious duties, had no news either. Whereupon Grischa said that he would not stay in his present cell, he wanted a warmer one—he would have the big one by the passage, and he also wanted a thorough wash. He would heat the water himself. The soldiers looked at one another without answering, and the corporal of the guard was equally embarrassed; they were wondering whether any prisoner, even if he was preparing for death, should be allowed to speak with such freedom—for of course he had no right to want anything: at the most he might ask a favour. The fact was that Schmielinsky, who was expecting promotion soon, could not say what he thought: but looking at Grischa's eyes that seemed to grow hourly more sad and more bewildered, and his narrow lowering forehead, he consented, saying:

352

"All right, my lad."

He was a member of the Social Democratic party, with strong political convictions; and the field-post brought him not only the *Vorwärts* but also special pamphlets—the so-called *Letters to the Troops*. He finally sat down, a lanky figure with haggard cheeks and restless eyes and, gathering his long limbs together, read his newspaper.

Grischa first scrubbed the bed in his new cell. He took a handful of soft soap, sluiced the brown suds and fresh hot water over the floor of his new abode, and scrubbed it clean with an old mop and towel belonging to the guard; then he washed everything, even the stool under the window, with several more pails of water. He would make sure there were no bugs about. As for the lice on his own body, he could keep those within limits: they were as inevitable as getting wet in the rain. He had a sullen look as he did all this, but he enjoyed it, and he felt—so far as he realized his state of mind— much as he used to feel in former days, or, strange as it may seem, even happier. The perpetual suspense, and ever-renewed uncertainty, and this eternal slavery was coming to an end. . . . While the water was drying off the floor of his cell, he asked leave to go and see Täwje the carpenter, if he was in the building. He was, in fact, there, engaged in putting together window-frames for the new hutments at the station for men passing through on leave. He hailed Grischa with eager friendliness. His Adam's apple and his beard— the light grey pointed beard of one who had once had red hair— positively quivered in excited emulation. Grischa had come to get Täwje to help him choose his coffin, and Hermann Sacht, gnawing at his pipe, went with them into the store-house where there were no less than five of these sinister receptacles. Täwje had clearly already heard what lay before Grischa: his eyes, the cunning little eyes of a wise elephant, never left the face of the broad-shouldered Russian. Täwje was not surprised at Grischa's air of surly self-possession. . . . Then they walked through the great timbered shed towards one of the five coffins which each of them had privately and independently decided was the right one. It was the biggest and broadest and Grischa smiled as he said:

"That one will be nice and comfortable."

"Yes," answered Täwje: "even a man as tall and broad as Grischa could manage very well in that one."

Grischa said he would try it: and just as he was, in his long cloak and with his cap on his head, he stretched himself carefully in the abiding-place that was his own handiwork, crossed his hands over his chest, and touched all four sides of it. Then, forgetting the presence of the two onlookers, he closed his eyes, sank back, heaved a sigh of relief, and found—Peace. If a man did not need to breathe, he could manage very well below ground. In that narrow dwelling he would certainly go on living, another sort of life, but there he would be—it was surely better than to have been blown up by a shell, so that only a fragment of one's body could be buried. It was disgusting not to be a complete corpse: in common graves it must be a matter of anxiety lest a head might be stuck on to a body that it did not belong to, or lest a leg that was left hanging on a branch might find its way into the wrong grave or even be carried off by the creatures of the air and the field. Resurrection was self-evident. A being that once had been so strong as he could not be struck dumb by death. In his own words and in his own way, he was certain of eternal life: the indestructibility of the living organism, and the timelessness of the moral laws, both of which conceptions are mirrored so clearly in the human spirit, was thus borne in upon his consciousness. The heathen, he thought, must be mad, and the people who live in cities, and burn their dead: it seemed to him an atrocity. "Leave the covering over me," he thought inwardly, "let the earth be trampled more and more above my head. I shall be alone. No one will break in upon my rest with an order, with the programme for the day—nine o'clock this, and ten o'clock that. Oh, I shall be happy then. . . ." Hermann Sacht felt faintly uneasy as he saw the man lying on the smooth shavings smile gently to himself. Täwje, on the other hand, was in no way astonished. He said something. And from far, far away there fell upon Grischa's ear the question whether he could lie there comfortably until the Resurrection. He let himself be slowly drawn out of the racing tide of words and thoughts, opened his eyes heavily, as if he had to shake the earth off his eyelids, and said:

"I can wait there very well. That's my coffin right enough. I made it myself, I know, because at the top end of it, rather down low, there's a knot in the wood that looks like a large prune.

Hermann Sacht bent down and found the knot. "That's queer," he thought: "this fellow has measured himself for his own coffin without knowing it." Then he told Grischa to get up as they would have to go back to the prison.

Grischa said he did not want to go yet. He sat up in his coffin with his legs hanging over the edge, and talked with Täwje about the Resurrection. On the Last Day, which could not be very far off now considering that innocent men were being shot, it would not be hard for him, Grischa, to come forth from this house of his once and for all and stand before the Judge. But what would happen to the other poor devils, whose bones had been scattered to the winds, and rotted into dust?

And Täwje explained to him that these too would not be al-together lost. When God created man's body He put in a little bone called *Lus*. This bone was indestructible: from it, if need be, the whole man could grow once more, body and soul, when the angels blow their ram's horn trumpets on the Last Day.

And Grischa was comforted.

Hermann Sacht, leaning on his rifle, asked him with surprise, if he believed in God. He, Hermann Sacht, did not. Nobody could ex-pect him to do so. If life was so unjust and this ghastly war lasted so long that millions of men were killed leaving many millions of widows and orphans, and so many innocent men destroyed, what was God doing? Besides, creation was quite different from that. It was all nonsense to say that it had taken place six thousand years ago. The earth was millions of years old, as science had clearly proved, and man was nearer to the ape than to God. Nobody could persuade him, Hermann Sacht, that man had once lived in Paradise, and had been driven out of it by a good God simply because he wanted knowledge. Those were fairy-tales, in which people had once believed, but were no use to grown-up men who travelled in railways and sent telegrams.

Grischa listened in amazement. What had all that to do with God? Of course he didn't believe in God, he said. He believed in the Resurrection, which was a plain fact, but that had nothing to

do with God. Once a man was born, he was born, and would go
on living; Grischa did not know how, but he would soon find out.
The priest and the ikons and the saints and the Trinity and all the
rest of it meant very little to him now, and if he met them all after
he rose again they could not be offended at his unbelief, since he had
found everything in the world so different to what the priests had
told him. Every man who had ever planted a seed in the earth and
watched a blade of corn grow out of it must believe in the Resurrection. At this point Täwje could no longer contain himself:

"Well and good," he said, "but who makes the seed grow? Do
you expect me to believe that the seed grew of itself? Who
so wisely ordained that out of a grain of wheat there should come
forth a long jointed stalk with an ear and who knows how many
grains of wheat just like the first?" And indeed, if he was rightly
informed as many as seven or eight such stalks, each of them with a
full ear of corn, could grow out of one grain.

On this point, however, Hermann Sacht and Grischa were at
one. That, they said, was Nature. Nature grew and caused to grow,
and if man did not understand all her ways he would understand
them later.

Täwje laughed. Later indeed! As if men were not always getting more and more stupid. Let them deny it if they could. As if
Moses wasn't wiser than all the professors, and even the Prophets a
little less wise than Moses, and the Tanaïm a little less wise than the
Prophets, and the men of the Great Assembly a little less wise than
the Tanaïm, and so on, down to the Chief Rabbis of to-day who said
themselves how little they knew compared with the Patriarchs. Were
not the holy scriptures of the other nations wiser than the nations
themselves, with their World War and their conflicting factions? "I'll
tell you something," he announced triumphantly: "there were giants
once, bigger than Og the King of Bashan, and Og the King of
Bashan was bigger than Goliath, and Goliath was bigger than Alexander, and Alexander than Pompey. Wasn't Pompey much bigger
than General Schieffenzahn? It's all quite plain," he said, getting a
little breathless, "the race of men is going downhill. The kings don't
know the thousandth part of what King Solomon knew. The judges
are not to be compared with Gideon. The women are gossiping fools

compared with Deborah, and the mothers contemptible compared with Rebecca and Rachel. That's as clear as daylight. And yet you say, 'we shall know more later on'? If men would turn to God and change their hearts, and so continue generation after generation, they would once more be wise, and then the Messiah would also come, and there would be deliverance for many Jews and for all humanity."

The German and the Russian listened in astonishment to the Jew, who believed in the truth of the old stories just as firmly as they believed that the sunrise would bring daylight. It was no use disputing with him. He was only a carpenter, and Hermann Sacht gave Grischa his hand to help him to get up. But as Grischa shook the shavings off his greatcoat, and began to put them carefully back into the coffin, for he wanted his bed to be as soft as possible, Täwje, looking meditatively at the ground in front of him, went on:

The question simply was, how far they had descended in the course of time: whether the present generation was not perhaps the generation of Sodom, and after a punishment like this War, better times might perhaps come and men might begin to change their hearts. And as nobody answered, he walked behind the two of them, as they left the store-house with its moist reek of timber; and the smell recalled to Grischa's mind a long-forgotten journey, in times long since past, in a timber-car. But Täwje decided to lay this question that evening before his fellow-travellers on the road to knowledge. They happened to be holding a small festival in the Bes Medresch. That night they would conclude their study of the entire Talmud, he and some other Jews even older than himself, and with the assistance of cakes and brandy they would celebrate this memorable event, which makes an epoch in the life of a man, and many knotty problems would come up for discussion. Why should he not raise this question—a tremendous question, as everyone must admit? For if this innocent man, whose innocence was universally acknowledged, lost his life by the will of his judges and after an illegal sentence, it might well be asked whether this generation were not the lowest since Abraham. And when Grischa asked him to come and say good-bye to him, when it came, to-morrow or the day after that, he shook Grischa's hand with both his own, looked at him affectionately, and promised that he would come when Grischa liked. The two soldiers went peaceably back to quarters; as they crossed the yard, they sniffed in surprise, and said: "It's got colder." The snow, which had already got into that slushy condition which precedes a thaw, had formed a crust upon the surface, and they held on to each other, so that they should not slip in their hobnailed boots.

Lieutenant Winfried sat at the General's writing-table. Sergeant-Major Pont stood near by, leaning against the back of a chair. His eyes looked tired; he had to-day received by post a number of technical publications dealing with his former trade of builder, and had been following the development of the new ideas about building and the latest styles of architecture at home. Some of these innovations, he reflected, were the work of his own pupils, and some of colleagues of his own standing, while he himself was in danger of being quite forgotten. After this war there would be a shortage of houses, as there had been after the campaign of 1870, owing to the great number of early marriages. "The building problem should be attacked at once," he read. And he thought how wise those fellows had been to stay at home and what good work they were doing for civilization. This active, enterprising man felt the dull tyranny of routine like a crushing weight upon his heart.

"We mustn't throw up the sponge, Herr Pont," said Winfried, who was also in low spirits. "Yesterday some of us came to the conclusion that we may have to get this man out of the Kommandantur and keep him out of the way till His Excellency comes back."

Pont gave his mind to the question. "I do not think that would be wise, sir," he said. "And at any rate you could get no official authority for taking such a step."

Winfried nodded. He knew that.

"The case has got beyond what may be regarded as official or legal, that is quite true," he answered with a smile.

But Pont objected.

"Beyond what is legal, perhaps, but not beyond what can be officially justified from our point of view. It is they, not we, who are in the wrong at present. That is the only point which makes our position unassailable if there should be any inquiry into the case.

It is quite in order that the Russian should be in the custody of the Kommandantur. If we get him out, that will be an act of violence and may bring serious consequences."

Winfried showed signs of impatience. He explained that Posnanski was drafting a treatise with a terrifying number of sections and sub-sections on the desirability of extending the jurisdiction of the Division within its own area, so that the administration of justice might not be interrupted. If he, Winfried, attached the Russian to a certain labour company, not very far from Mervinsk, but outside the garrison area, this would, at a first glance, hardly seem an illegal act.

"But it would at a second glance," said Pont, still unconvinced.

"Then why do you suppose I've got the Divisional seal and the famous green pad?" said Winfried with a boyish laugh.

"That would only be legal eye-wash," Pont persisted. But Winfried asked if he would accept such an authority as justifying him in detailing the Russian for duty in the usual way?

Pont reflected for several moments. He would be protected by the A.D.C.'s signature and seal. He had no fears for himself, but he could not advise the Herr Lieutenant to do this. Schieffenzahn would certainly look for a scapegoat, and he would be powerful enough to send that scapegoat into the wilderness, or, in other words, to the Front.

Winfried laughed. One who was in danger of the law himself, would not be likely to get another man court-martialled. Schieffenzahn must know that he was acting illegally, and besides he, Winfried, did not care to look too far ahead. He had the seal, he could sign his name, and he wanted Pont to tell him first, where the man was to go, and, secondly, who would help to get him away.

"I can easily get into the prison," he said. "I don't need any chit for that. I shall take the clerk Bertin with me: he is one of us. But someone must be at the steering-wheel, and the fewer in the plot the better. Will you drive for us? You will get yourself into a horrible mess, my dear Pont, but you'll do that anyhow if you post the man to a labour company. You're in it anyhow, so I think it will be better if you take a hand in it rather than one of the regular drivers, whom I could cover for a time, but they're only privates and someone might make it nasty for them one day later on."

Pont came from a race of Rhenish smugglers and adventurers, and he felt their blood stir within him.

"Thank you, Sir," he said. "I may as well get some fun out of it."

"So you'll drive?"

Pont nodded.

"Where shall we take the fellow?"

"That's easy enough," said Pont. There was a certain redoubt on the right slope of a spur at the foot of the hills east of Mervinsk: the men called it "Lychow's bunion"; it had deep cemented dug-outs, and a road-company was working there. He knew the way, the roads were good, though they might be a bit slippery at the gradients.

"Lychow's bunion!" said Winfried, with a laugh. "I like that! It's called F.S. 5 on the plan, but that's not half so expressive. Well, then, you will attach a Russian prisoner for road-duty at F.S. 5, as from eight o'clock to-morrow morning. I will stamp and sign the order and at five or six o'clock we'll fetch the man. The sentry will let me through right enough, when he sees who I am. You can get a greatcoat and a cap for the Russian, out of store. You might see that they're ready in the car by this evening."

He smiled with the adventurous zest of a boy playing "Police and Robbers." And well he might, for he was only twenty-two.

"You might type out the order at once: there's my machine."

Pont turned the switch of a green-shaded lamp, put some paper between the rollers, and typed the heading: "Order." It was a dark November day outside and the electric light was needed.

But as he was in the middle of the sentence . . . "to be attached temporarily, as from Nov. 2 of this year, for temporary service, to the working party at F.S. 5 . . ." when he got to the word "temporary," the light silently went out.

"Bulb's gone," said he; he went into the next room, took an electric bulb out of a drawer, and screwed it in. No result.

"Hullo!" he said.

He went back to the next room and turned on the main switch which connected all the lights in the office. Again no result. Winfried had followed him and they looked at each other. Short circuit perhaps? "Excellent," said Winfried in triumph. They would have to go to the canteen at once and get candles. If there was no light in the prison either, then it was plain that the gods were on the side of right.

He took up the receiver, to enquire if that was so, but behold, the current had failed there too.

He raised both hands in the air like a conqueror raising a triumphal crown.

When steel wires have already been straining under a heavy burden of snow, and the temperature suddenly falls seven degrees, the tension is too great and they snap at the weakest point. The weakest point in the network of the electric-light system was on the direct wire that led to the City Hospital, where the side turning branched off from the main street, and a large arc-lamp hung between two standards. At the moment nobody was passing. The humming wire snapped, the ends whipped through the air and struck the telephone cables: at that contact bright blue flames hissed upwards, in the power house outside the town the insulators on the switchboards crackled with scattering sparks; engineer N.C.O.'s were hurriedly fetched: the dynamos had stopped. The men on duty cursed at this visitation: they might have anticipated it from the thermometer. The important thing now was to find the broken wire at once. It was lucky that it had happened in the middle of the day; the damage could be put right before the evening.

After dinner Sergeant-Major Spierauge solemnly appeared in person in the guard-room of the prison. He could see out of the corner of his eye the prisoner Bjuscheff sitting on a bench, eating soup; he felt the burden of all the trouble this poor wretch had brought upon them, and the dreadful issue that must now be faced. All that remained now was to make arrangements for the execution and to inform the condemned man of the time fixed for it. He was relieved to think it would soon be over, but he must steel his heart and go through with it. In his outer active life the sergeant-major was sure he had a heart of steel: but when he looked within he was unpleasantly aware of certain disturbing emotions that might put him to shame. In his practical work he was more than efficient,

but moral questions he was inclined to thrust aside and visit his
irritation on the head of anyone who might be near. He had come
to see Bjuscheff, but not only on his account. It was November 1:
the day of pay-parades, health inspection, and also the day on which
cigars, cigarettes, and tobacco were served out, and the canteen
profits were reckoned up. Of course the electric light would choose
this day to break down. Spierauge spoke with his usual voluble condescension, twirling his thick moustache, with a notebook stuck between the second and third buttons of his tunic, his high-peaked cap
thrust back from his low smooth forehead, displaying a most unmilitary tuft of hair. It couldn't be helped, the guard would have to
bring their carbide lamps with them to the pay-parade.

"Won't you postpone it, Sir?" said Corporal Schmielinsky, and
got a sharp answer for his pains:

"I suppose you want me to postpone the underclothes inspection
to-morrow, and the issue of stores, and Bjuscheff's execution, too,
eh? You're always putting things off. You'll put yourself off one
of these days——" he added in a more friendly tone, pleased with
himself for having thought of the word *exekution*—a good handy
foreign word—which was tolerably vague and well calculated to
relieve a man from embarrassment. And when he saw that the
prisoner had finished his meal, he signed to the interpreter who had
come with him and was sitting on a chair by the door, smoking
languidly, and walked up to Grischa.

"Tell him that the execution is not to be postponed any longer
and that it should have been carried out to-day, but that we have put
it off until midday to-morrow in case General Lychow's intervention
in the prisoner's favour may be successful. But tell him that he must
not build upon this: and that the time for any possible intervention
expires at noon to-morrow; and failing this the execution will take
place at three p.m."

A silence fell upon the long dreary room, a silence so deep that
the men could be heard whispering in the hall outside through the
half-closed door, much to Sergeant-Major Spierauge's disgust. No
matter what the men were doing or wherever they happened to be
they forsook their tasks, and their faces were turned towards Grischa
and the Sergeant-Major as if they were drawn by some unseen

magnet: the very air between those two pairs of eyes seemed tense and vibrating. Bjuscheff, as they had grown accustomed to call Grischa, turned pale, then sickly-green, and then his face suddenly flushed—with anger. But he so far controlled himself that he did not shout at the interpreter but merely turned upon him bitterly.

"Tell him," said he, "that they are shooting an innocent man; tell him I don't care when they do me in; but tell him the sentence is wrong and that everyone knows it: tell him it's a shame and the shame will not be mine."

This was translated by the interpreter, Pavel Dolken—a Lithuanian. But as he had the head of a philosopher—though a commonplace one—on his sturdy shoulders, and had long been meditating whether one race could ever really understand another, he allowed himself to render the Russian word "shame" by the German word "injustice": for what was the use of causing trouble? It never did much good, and Grischa might well relieve his mind without irritating that of the Sergeant-Major. The prisoner's passionate tone was not unwelcome to Spierauge. He said in a cold official voice:

"We can make allowance for a condemned man but he must not go too far"; which the interpreter, by way of compensation, altered slightly by translating the German word "condemned," by the Russian for "a man in trouble."

"If he wants anything special for his supper he'd better tell Corporal Sacht—all the other men will turn out for the pay-parade, of course. He can have what he likes. The officers are having Michaelmas goose and that means there'll be several. He can have a bit, and some red wine to drink, and whatever he likes to smoke, within reasonable limits. To-morrow his effects will be handed to him so that he can arrange what is to be done with them, and if he wants to send them to his wife, the Red Cross will see that she gets them," he added. Then, with a sigh of relief, he said: "That's settled: now tell him to get these silly ideas out of his head. There are hundreds of thousands of stout fellows who'll be killed to-day and won't have the luck to get roast goose for their dinner first. Stop," he said, tapping his forehead just as he was about to leave hurriedly: "I forgot the most important thing. Ask him whether he wants a Russian priest or one of our padres: I don't know whether we've got a Russian priest in the town: if not, he can choose between the Catholic and Protestant chaplains."

And Grischa, who had listened quietly to it all, replied that he didn't much want a priest but he would think it over. If he was to die, he would not make much fuss about it, but he wanted a good bath first, and he would like to have company that night—people with whom he could talk his own language, Babka and the little Jew, Täwje, and he wanted to be buried in the Russian Cemetery, and, if need be, he would dig the grave himself to-morrow morning.

"Certainly, certainly," said Sergeant-Major Spierauge, with a nod. "That's all simple enough." Then he shut his notebook, put it back in his tunic, and wished him a good day and a good night and courage for his last journey; and as he turned to go, he added that things were not so bad as they looked, for who in these days had the luck to dig his own grave and know when and where his bones would rest? This was a damned unsettled time, and not a man of all those that stood there in the guard-room had the least notion when he would get peace and quiet and be paid off once for all. Then he raised his hand to his cap, and went out thoughtfully considering whether he had enough of the cheaper sort of army cigars which he usually served out, or whether he had better draw a couple of boxes of the better quality which were also supplied to the troops, but which he sold privately on his own account. He felt depressed as he walked across the cold and cheerless yard, looked up at the clouds or rather the mist above his head, heaved several sighs of relief, and tried to shake off this most unusual depression—without realizing that it was his own fate that lay upon his mind. . . . For in spite of his apparently secure position, he was not sure that he would ever enjoy in peace the little property which he had scraped together—and, indeed, mighty eater and drinker though he was, and in full health and strength, he was doomed to join that vast procession that the dreaded Influenza was to march off the stage of life.

Grischa, who had remained standing until the Sergeant-Major's gold stripes faded away in the half-light, fell back on the bench with a groan. He felt as though his heart was bursting and that all his blood was rushing to it. Pale and cold, with sweat upon his hair and forehead, he sat there, thinking he might be sick at any moment. He kept saying as he clenched his fists: "I knew it all along! That makes all the difference! I was quite right, I knew it all along." And this comforted him. He managed to avoid being sick, and by breathing deeply several times his heart appeared to shrink nearly to normal size. Then he longed to get a breath of air, and accompanied by Hermann Sacht, who walked by his side like a sympathetic shadow, he strode between two rows of embarrassed faces to the yard, and into the snow, with which he rubbed his forehead and his temples. And behind him rose a confused roar of excited and indignant voices.

Chapter 5

A LIEUTENANT AND A CORPORAL

At about two o'clock the Signal Section reported to the Staff that the damage to the electric light and telephone wires had been located. The telephone would be working again in half an hour; the electric light would take rather longer, but towards evening, about six o'clock, the current would certainly be available.

Winfried heaved a sigh of relief, and asked whether the long-distance wire was working.

"No, sir," said the corporal who had been sent from the Signal Section to report: "not yet"; but the snow in those parts had melted, and that would make it easier to trace the damage. It could not be long before the wire was spliced.

Winfried dismissed the corporal and went over to Pont to ask him when he expected to have finished the pay-parade. The Sergeant-Major replied that he would be ready about four o'clock.

At four o'clock it would be too light for Winfried's purpose. About five o'clock, he thought, would be better, or perhaps later. At any rate before nightfall. In the meantime Pont had finished writing his order to the working-party at F.S. 5. He opened a blue folder; Winfried signed, and said:

"Bring it over here, and I'll stamp it."

The clerks sat busily typing at the windows, and up above, on the next floor, in the Operations Section, could be heard the laughter of the officers amusing themselves till the light was on again. Rittmeister von Badenbach was telling an excessively humorous anecdote about how he had held up a public bath for Jewish women, so as to photograph the bathers, and as he had a very racy style, the story met with great success.

"A regular Christmas party," said Hermann Sacht scoffingly. On the long guard-room table was burning a solitary candle, and another in Grischa's new clean cell, which he had himself made tidy. An intolerable silence brooded over the vast desolate room. The corporal noticed for the first time that the room was, in fact, a vaulted chamber with a curved roof, with shallow arches running up to the ceiling between the windows. As he sat on his bed, with his rifle leaning against the wall just within reach, the network of garden-wire that supported his straw mattress creaked with his every movement: and from Grischa's cell came a continuous sound of muttering. The Russian was talking to himself. He was whispering in his own language. "He's drivelling," thought Sacht, "just slobbering away to himself," and he sighed deeply. Supposing Grischa came and strangled him, now that he had nothing more to fear? Supposing he made a last effort to escape? Very likely there was no one else on the ground-floor. The men had gone over to the main building where they were waiting until their turn came to traverse staircases and passages to the orderly room, where under Spierauge's eyes they would receive their pay from the paymaster, and their tobacco from the store-corporal. A man who had nothing to lose would not let a murder stand in his way if he saw a chance of escape. So, in case of accidents, Hermann Sacht slipped a ball cartridge into the magazine of his rifle and released the safety-catch. Certain words of Brettschneider, flung out at him some weeks ago, had been burnt into his memory. . . . There he sat quaking, torn between his sympathy for Grischa and fear for his own safety; and in the cell next door a man was crouching, staring at the candle and muttering and talking to the flame—a man pressing his clenched fists against his cheek-bones, and watching his own life burn away with the candle-flame. The stove cast a huge cannon-like shadow on the wall. There was a great glowing fire in it, a coal fire, as the guard had acquired, in no very regular way, a quantity of large coal-bricks intended for locomotives. Outside a blue twilight was falling. It was warm enough, but the darkness and that murmuring voice made the place seem strangely desolate. Grischa had fallen into a sulky mood. He was reproaching himself for being afraid, kept telling himself that all his endless troubles were behind him now, and if he escaped with his life they would be before him again: that death would be much easier now than going off to the War, and leaving Marfa Ivanovna. "What have you got to say good-bye to, my lad? Nothing but this bloody prison, and many more of them. It's quite clear if you're left alive you'll be shut up again. You'll have to work, and shiver, and eat muck, and it will always rain. The Russians yonder are not making peace; they're making war, and the Germans don't mean peace, they're forcing them to fight; and what about the French, the English, and the Americans?—there's no end to it all. It's all been very well arranged for you. You've tried your coffin; and it was a fine little house that you measured and made for yourself. You wanted to go home, of course; but they'll never let you. There's a lot of things between you and your little old cottage in Russia— barbed wire, bayonets, mines, machine guns, and barrages. Oh, Grischa," he sighed to himself: "you know you're a fool to be afraid, and yet you are afraid, you silly soldier man. . . . If only Babka would come. She said she'd come soon. She'll be here in a minute. She's carrying your child, and Marfa Ivanovna has another one of yours at home—O God! It's no good always being afraid." At the thought of death a shiver of fear passed through his whole body. Then came a knock at the outer door.

Hermann Sacht opened it, with a gasp of relief to find it was only Babka, wearing her shawl and with her basket on her arm, and her piercing grey eyes wandered over the strangely empty room.

"Yes," said Hermann Sacht, "Grischa is in there. It's a good thing he's got a visitor. You'll cheer him up, and make him laugh a bit. There'll be supper later on and a drop of schnapps."

"Schnapps?" said Babka. "That's nice. I've got some schnapps, too," and she pointed to her covered basket from a corner of which the necks of two bottles of schnapps were sticking out.

Grischa seized hold of both her hands, drew her on to the bench beside him, and said he was glad to see her: he needed a bit of cheering up—it would all be over to-morrow—and as he spoke, his teeth chattered and his eyes almost rolled in their sockets. He hoped what had to be done would be done quickly. He could have wished it otherwise. But it was very well at is was. The sooner the end came the better.

Hermann Sacht at last said he wanted to go out for a moment. He'd have to lock them in meanwhile: but they mustn't mind that. So he went away: it was good to leave this almost airless room behind him for a while.

Babka stroked Grischa's hands compassionately, kissed them, and said: "We'll get away all right—you needn't be afraid. I've got the schnapps here—enough for the whole lot of them—two bottles, a good one and a bad one. We'll drink out of the good one, shall we? —it warms your innards—and I'll get them to drink out of the bad one. Before the poison works I'll go away and wait for you outside, opposite the prison entrance, and you'll find me in the black gateway of the Jew Rothstein's house. They'll all be very sick and perhaps they'll die. You'll easily get past them, Grischa, and we'll hide you this very night where nobody can find you. Veressejeff the grocer is our friend if we keep a tight hold on him. He's got the key of the little side door of the cathedral, and he'll let you in. For the first week you can stay under the altar in the crypt: there'll be bread and schnapps there and a light. It will be still warm enough in there; you'll have a soft bed to lie on, and you'll be able to last out till I come to fetch you with a sledge. I tell you," she added triumphantly, as with an agonized compelling look she sought Grischa's eyes which were staring past her across to the candle on the guard-room table, "they won't recognize us and they can't find us, I tell you. You'll have a fur coat and cap to wear, civil clothes, and a passport, and you'll go with me to Vilna in the sledge, do you hear me? And then old Mrs. Bjuscheff will be able to hide you. However, there's time enough for all that. Let's have a drink, Grischa," and she uncorked one of the two bottles, pushed the glass over to him, filled to the brim or a little over, and he drained it with greedy satisfaction.

"Give me another," he said hoarsely and tossed off another glass. "Won't you have one with me?"

She said she would not, for schnapps would not be good for the unborn child. Every sensible woman knew that. And she would soon be bearing Grischa a son! There was something like exultation in her voice, and her eyes, no longer shaded by her coif, blazed, as she laid her hands on her body where the child moved in its damp warm veil of flesh. And Babka talked to him as a contented wife talks to her husband, and told him how she would lie in at Mrs. Bjuscheff's, who was a midwife; she had already made little coats and baby clothes out of soldiers' shirts which she had bought or bartered; they should have been given back to the sergeant-major— but soldiers weren't such fools and preferred to make a bit out of them. Baby clothes could be made out of pants, and dainty little jackets out of shirts. She had brought him his own rough flannel underclothes, with great patches in them, thoroughly clean, and took them, wrapped up in a bit of ground-sheet, out of her basket.

Then Hermann Sacht came back and Grischa looked thoughtful, but not so pale and forlorn, in the light of his solitary candle. He fancied a smoke. Babka gave him cigarettes, and when he had lit one at the candle-flame, he leaned back, blew a stream of grey smoke through his nostrils, and felt for the first time a little more hopeful. The way to freedom lay open if he chose. He was no longer a beast being driven straight to the shambles with barriers on either side. Once more there was a choice before him, and as he rubbed his left ear, which was itching, with his thumb and first finger, he asked her for further details of her plan and was deeply relieved to find that she had none: only that he was to take advantage of the effect of the poison on the men, to say that he felt ill too, and wanted to go into the yard and be sick: he was then to stand as near the gate as possible, put his fingers in his mouth, and make himself vomit, and if any of the sick men went with him to watch him, he was to give him and the sentry beyond him a good crack on the head and rush out through the gate. It would probably be still open, and if it was not, so much the worse—he would have to draw the bolt. It certainly wouldn't be locked. In the street there would be one moment of danger—he would have to cross it in the bright light of the lamp if it was burning again: but they were fortunate because the Devil had helped them by breaking the lamp. She would be standing in the dark passage, and lead him by the hand through the network of back alleys. As they knew the way, they would have got as far as Veressejeff's along two narrow by-streets before a patrol had so much as reached the main avenue. Oh yes, Babka knew her way about in the city as well as in the forest! There was not much difference, except that here the forest had four walls. They only

needed to keep a good look-out just as on the Grodno moors, and
in the great forest where they had first met. "These Germans are
foreigners here," she said contemptuously: "and no one will give
us away, for anyone who is about in the streets at night is much too
much afraid of being caught." How would they live in Vilna? Why,
just as here in Mervinsk. In Vilna there were whole streets of
houses closed and shuttered in which typhus and enteric had done
their work; and however hard the Germans tried, they could never
catch them there. . . . He could lie safely hidden till peace came
and they could depart, whether they had won or lost the War, and
that she didn't care a hang about. . . .

And Grischa stroked her hand and listened. Yes, that all sounded
very good—he could not deny it. It would be some sort of life to
be in hiding again. All the old terrors would come back once more,
he supposed: he wouldn't see much of the sun and he wouldn't be
really free—still, it would certainly be a life of sorts, he said emphatically, to comfort her. Then he yawned and asked her to sit
down for a while: he was a little tired and would like to lie down for
a bit and sleep, and then he'd wake up again. He wasn't used to
schnapps now and it had made him tired: he'd soon be all right again.
In reality he wanted a little peace and quiet to think things over.
He did not want anything before his eyes when he took counsel with
himself and considered the opportunity that had been given him:—
so he lay down on his bed, drew the blankets over him, turned his
face to the wall, and closed his eyes, while Babka slipped into a lazy
twilit state, full of rich reflection—somewhere between sleeping and
waking, soothed and encouraged by the warmth and quiet, and filled
with the life of the being within her that was so soon to come forth.

Grischa was not really in the least tired: far from it. Wide-
awake and clear of head, he saw his thoughts with marvellous dis-
tinctness in that dark chamber in which a man's thoughts grow
to fullness, when he shuts his eyes. What was the choice before
him? By God, it was a choice between two graves! A grave beneath
the church, with a light perhaps and something to eat and drink,
then a wild flight in disguise, perhaps pursued; after that, life in a
Vilna cellar, out of sight of day and of all men who might be likely
to betray him for a reward. On the other side, a quiet grave in a

fine coffin that he had himself planed smooth, and that fitted him: there would be no light there nor food, but he would not miss them for he would not need them any more; and there would be rest, eternal rest—a deep-drawn sigh of relief that went beyond all the boundaries of being. Could there be any doubt where his choice would fall?—Quite apart from Babka's comical notion that the men in the guard-room would stay on duty after the first moment when they felt ill, or perhaps dizzy and inclined to vomit, there were plenty of men to relieve them. Weren't there nearly three platoons lying about on their straw mattresses, who would curse of course, but go on duty as soon as they were sent for. And what about the sentry at the gate, what was to prevent him shooting? And even if he missed Grischa, of course he'd rouse the whole place. This was just another woman's plan, well meant and well made, and full of wise precautions, but unfortunately it would not work—and here he lay, with only one more trouble to face, though it was a pretty big one, and that not till to-morrow afternoon; and meanwhile he would be untroubled and at peace. Wouldn't he be a fool to rush head-long into all this danger and confusion, with the sole result that his savings would find their way into the sergeant-major's cash-box, because he had had no time to make his will?

How pleasant it was, he thought with satisfaction, not to feel someone grabbing him by the neck and shoving him forward; now he was free to make a choice again, to go where he liked and not where he was driven. Life indeed! He had had enough of worry and struggle. If a man was always forced to go about with wet feet, wouldn't he prefer an easy death, or even a hard one, to all this torture, especially if he were saved the trouble of making up his mind to leap over the precipice or to pull the trigger? And he, Grischa, if he chose Babka's way, would have to expect fifty times worse torments than three months' wet feet. By God, he would not go out into the snow again, into the darkness and the cold, back to the hunting and hiding, the fear of discovery, and, at the worst, to be brought down with a shot in the back like some poor wretched hare. He preferred that everything should proceed in due order, and nothing should disturb his rest till noon to-morrow: but it would be very unwise to tell poor Babka that. All he need do, would be quietly to empty the bottle of poisoned schnapps down the sink when she had gone. He might even drink it himself, if he could not bear the idea of a bullet in him. But, he thought, a bullet soon does the trick, whereas poison works more slowly; it makes a man first dizzy and then sends him mad—which is no death for a soldier. Go your own way, Grischa, now you have your choice once more. Be nice to this poor silly little woman. If she had not given up some of her sense to her little one, she must certainly have seen that no good could come of her plan. And he rubbed his eyes, sat up, yawned, and smiled between his yawns at Babka, who awoke from her reverie with a slight start and smiled back at him.

They made plans of how they would arrange to be together after the War; Grischa might sell his cottage—which, of course, was little more than a stable—and migrate to one of the more friendly neighbourhoods which he had since got to know and where he felt at home. It was warmer here, there were fewer icy winds from the north or east, the soil was better, and one could get a bit of land on the outskirts of a town. Then he could live with the two women, not exactly together, but not very far apart, and if Marfa Ivanovna made trouble at first, no matter: she was a sensible woman and would make the best of it. Babka smiled in a sort of happy trance. Nothing could have been more grateful to her ears: if she had been a girl without a child she might have set her teeth, and let Grischa go where he liked, but now that which was within had nearly come to fullness, it was a pleasant thing to hear that he, the father, was going to live near by, and would like the child in his arms, and punish or reward it as might be called for, and as a father should. There was no reason why the two women should not get on together. There were jealous women, of course—here Babka laughed;—she knew much too much of life—and the tide of it had passed into her blood —not to know that a man must roam, and likes to go his way from time to time, and a woman only destroys herself when she runs after him. She would not inflict that sort of thing on Grischa. She had had her men, she had never thought of children and never had any, but now matters were very different: there was a child within her, that moved and filled her body, and made her so happy that she could have laughed aloud—and Hermann Sacht looked out from his corner, where he was puffing away and reading old-fashioned humorous stories in a volume of the "Reclam" series called *The Rhinelander's Home Treasury*, and noticed that the woman bent down over the doomed man's hand and kissed it as if it had been the hand of a priest or a grandfather. . . . Then Babka, pregnant as she was, had suddenly to run out into the yard, and Grischa, seizing the moment when neither of the other two could see him, picked up the bottle quickly, uncorked it with a nail, which he used for various odd purposes, and poured the green acrid-smelling liquid into the bucket. "What a pity!" he thought, frowning, "that was the Padre-Kümmel," and he remembered the Sunday on which he had been given it. "No," he thought firmly—for what he had drunk had calmed his fears and lit his vision—"never again. No use messing a man about now: you ought to have thought of that before." Then he poured some of his own vodka on the table to account for the smell of spirits, tossed off another gulp of it, filled the green bottle with water, and chuckled quietly at the thought that with Marfa's violent temper there was something to be said against trying to run the two women in double harness. Soon afterwards a canteen orderly brought Grischa some apricot jam, new bread, and a bottle of wine, sent by the Kommandantur, and some cordial with the greetings of Max and Sergeant Halbscheid, and having been treated to a glass himself, the orderly was requested, on his way back, to ask Täwje the carpenter to come round. He was told there would be pickled herrings for breakfast next day—Grischa was to have plenty of everything, and a box of a hundred cigarettes was provided for him and his friends. When Täwje was admitted by Hermann Sacht, and, still wearing his cap, had pronounced a blessing, eaten some of the bread, and tasted his first glass of schnapps with an approving twinkle, Hermann Sacht observed:—

"I'm fed-up with this porter game, I'll stand no more of it—running about like this to open the door has made my legs shorter, and when I fall in on parade to-morrow I shall be too small and they'll move me two or three places down the line. Those fellows are always stretching their legs on the stairs or in the orderly room, while we sit huddled up like Jonah in the whale's belly."

This was Täwje's opportunity and he produced from his treasure-store of the Midraschim strange legends of Jonah, the whale, the sea-dragon Leviathan, and the Paradise in which that same Leviathan was slaughtered by Jonah, and served up, stuffed with herbs and with a rich sauce, at the tables of the blest. And they immediately resumed their theological discussion of the morning—common folk love such interminable arguments—and Hermann Sacht, in the fullness of his western common-sense, denied all immortality; Babka would have none of it either, Täwje in his superior fashion proclaimed his certainty, and Grischa declared that he would put it to the test. He banged his fist on the table in his heated objection to Täwje's exact knowledge of Paradise—for no one could guess what would come after the Resurrection. "If you blow this candle out," he cried, "or it burns down to the end, then it will be dark, you know that, and if you light another one, it will be light again—you know that, too. But what this new candle will look like, and how it will shine—how can you tell that? It may be thick, or thin, and the flame may be yellow or white—what's the use of guessing? You must wait and see."

Hermann Sacht laughed. "Then I know exactly what the Resurrection looks like: I've got your candles here, canteen candles—look at them, they're all alike, made of good paraffin, and if a man's hungry he can eat one at a pinch."

"That's true," Täwje went on. "Poor people's hunger is so terrible that they would eat up their own salvation just to have a good meal for once. Are you going to tell me that it's not the age of Sodom and Gomorrah?"

"It's the Devil's age," said Babka.

When Hermann Sacht, whose pleasantly excited mood had been disturbed by a sudden knock at the outer door, opened it somewhat peevishly, he stepped back, dazzled by the glare of an electric torch. He could not recognize the newcomer until the latter had stepped forward into the light of the solitary guard-room candle, and Hermann's eyes had overcome their momentary blindness.

"Herr Oberleutnant!" he said in astonishment.

"Evening!" said Winfried, casually. "I must have a look at our poor Russian."

"Oh!" answered Hermann Sacht, "he's all right, he's having a cheerful evening with his friends; he's better off than you, Sir, he won't have to go out into the snow any more."

"That's all you know about it," thought Winfried.

Hermann Sacht made a rapid calculation. The General's A.D.C. had of course the right to visit Grischa if he liked, but in that case it would be hardly correct for him, Corporal Sacht, to sit down in the cell at the same table. The presence of even a very friendly officer always made a common soldier feel uncomfortable. Laying his rifle cautiously down beside him, he stretched himself on the bed and shut his eyes. The Lieutenant's arrival had suggested a good idea to him. He too had an electric torch, but as he feared to waste the current, he had only used it once; then, as now, he had done so under the stimulus of example. To-night he felt the need of the thing much more than if he had merely had to make a journey through the open fields or enter a strange house at night. So he rummaged in his pack, the private soldier's cupboard, which hung at the end of his camp-bed, and pulled out the precious torch.

Grischa hailed Winfried's coming with delight. He was over-joyed to have such a distinguished guest. Never in his life, he said, with some exaggeration, had he had such a jolly time, and felt so well and happy as now, when he could open a bottle of wine and treat the Herr Oberleutnant to a glass: he knew the Lieutenant had a kind heart, and had come to tell him that it wasn't his fault if Grischa had to die; he knew that the General had done all that was right and proper to save his life. And no man could do more than was possible. But now the Herr Oberleutnant must sit down. "That's Babka," he said, "a woman, and that's Täwje, a Jew." It was he that had helped Grischa to make the coffin, and it fitted him as if it had been made to measure.

Winfried remained standing, and looked round him ill at ease. Of course, every man had a right to enjoy himself in his own way. It was stupid of him to be put off by Grischa's company, the fumes of alcohol, and the stale air in this narrow cell.

"The first thing we must do is to open the window," he said;

Grischa would not allow anyone else to do it, but himself climbed on the stool and before he unfastened the window he made a short speech to his guests to show that he was still sober; and indeed he only tottered slightly. A stream of fresh cold air poured in upon the combined reek of candle-smoke, schnapps and humanity, the light flickered and the shadows swayed and shifted.

Winfried looked at his watch, and said he had not opened the window for nothing. They could think better with a little fresh air. Täwje must interpret to Grischa what he was going to say. He had come to take Grischa away with him. He would give no explanations—there was no need for them. Grischa knew who were doing their best for him. Now he'd better pack up his things.

Grischa listened attentively to Täwje, who apparently found it necessary to go into all manner of excited explanations; Babka joined in too, and at last Grischa stood up and shut the window.

He did not want to go into any more prisons, said Täwje to the officer, shrugging his shoulders; he did not want to leave this place, he could not stand any more trouble. He was comfortable here, and here he would stay.

But had he forgotten, Winfried asked, what was to happen to him to-morrow? (He thought it better not to mention the possibility of a reprieve, when the wires should be working again: this would only strengthen Grischa's unreasonable obstinacy.)

But Grischa, with a sweep of his hand, waved his guest into a seat, and said grandly:

"I am a poor Russian, and I am very grateful to the Lieutenant, but I don't want to go. I know very well what happens in the end when two dogs are fighting over a bone. There won't be much left of it by the time the strongest gets it. And there isn't really much left of me, thank you all the same. No, I am warm and jolly, now the window's shut again, and the Lieutenant's kindness makes me feel as good as a double go of schnapps; it is nobody's fault but mine —but I will not come. A watch will go till the main-spring's broken: my main-spring's gone and I don't want a new one put in."

Winfried was furious: time was precious, damn it; but he controlled himself, unbuttoned his overcoat, looked at his watch, sat down, lit one of Grischa's cigarettes, and, through Täwje who interpreted, reminded his friend Paprotkin that he had always wanted to go home. Of course, there might be delay, but if he would be reasonable and come along now, all would go well, so far as he could predict anything. Otherwise nothing but a miracle would save him from being shot to-morrow afternoon. He wanted to put him somewhere where he would be safe till the General's return; the case would be retried, and before any sentence could be carried out, the War would be over.

As the General's A.D.C. he could assure him that peace with Russia was nearer than ever. Then the prisoners would be exchanged and there would be general rejoicing and an amnesty; then he could clear off to Vologda, to his wife and child, and all this wretched business would be no more than a bad dream. But only if he followed him now: this was the moment, and if he missed these few minutes of twilight, then no more could be done. Grischa would be merely committing suicide.

Grischa listened to the sputtering of the candle. Then he laid his head on his arms and burst into tears.

"Once you're in the street," urged the Lieutenant, "there's a car waiting for you, and you'll be all right."

Babka shuddered as she whispered quick, imploring words into Grischa's ear, and clung to his arm. This was much the best plan: he must go with the Lieutenant, and save himself. The father of a family must keep his head on his shoulders. Grischa looked up; the tears were still running from his eyes and he sobbed out:

"They won't leave me any peace: I must go into a cage again. Am I never to have any peace? Don't you see, Täwje, how they are tearing me to pieces between them? What can a man do? I shall have to go." He wiped his nose and sat up straight at the table. "All right; more trouble"—and he began to weep again.

"Thank God," said the Lieutenant, springing to his feet. "Leave your cap and coat here, I've got everything in the car for you: come along just as you are," and turned to go, while the other sat and watched Grischa buttoning up his tunic. He had only taken three or four steps when a light flashed in his eyes.

"What's that?" said Winfried stopping short.

A voice replied, and the speaker immediately showed himself:

"Corporal of the Guard; of course the Lieutenant knows . . ."

"Don't hang about there in the dark, man," said Winfried angrily.

"I'm on duty, sir."

Winfried suddenly realized that here was an obstacle, a fence that would have to be taken. "Never mind," thought he:

"You're not going to make a nuisance of yourself, Corporal?" he said.

"That depends what you've come for, Herr Oberleutnant."

Winfried explained casually that he had come to fetch the Russian, as if it was the most natural thing in the world.

"Of course, the Lieutenant has an order?"

Winfried picked up the typewritten paper with its large official stamp, and held it in the light of his torch. They went up to the candle, for it was a pity to use the battery as Hermann Sacht remarked. Then he read it carefully, looked at the paper, and even examined the back, where counter-signatures were often written. There were none. This was an order from the court martial office. What he needed, to hand over the Russian, was the authorization of the Kommandantur signed by the Herr Rittmeister.

Winfried caught his breath; but he said reassuringly that this could be obtained later. The corporal answered:

"I'd rather have it now: there's no time like the present. I can't do it otherwise."

Winfried saw the fence growing higher; he tried a quiet imperious tone. "You hand the man over; I'll take the consequences and the responsibility."

The corporal stood firm:

"That bit of paper's not good enough, sir."

Winfried drew a deep breath. He must try and touch the man's heart—otherwise it was hopeless. He reminded the corporal that after all he was a man: he wasn't a hangman or a hangman's mate. In a friendly and almost imploring tone, he said: "You must let him go, my friend; I shall just take him," whereat Hermann Sacht, with no less friendliness, released the safety-catch of his rifle, and said: "In that case I'm sorry to say I shall have to shoot the Herr Oberleutnant." And while Winfried drew himself up and instinctively fumbled for his revolver as any officer would do in the face of such an insult, the corporal said in a quiet stern voice, as he looked straight into the Oberleutnant's eyes:

"I know all about your responsibility, Sir; at the very worst you'll be sent to the quietest part of the line for a short time; but I'm only a corporal, and should get it in the neck. At the best I should be knocked about and starved and slave like a convict for years and years until I die, or go off quickly, like a blasted hero, with a bullet in my head. No, Herr Oberleutnant. I've got my orders, and I won't go behind them, I'm damned if I do. Nobody cares what happens to us men," he almost shouted. "They make short work of us if we give trouble. The Russian will stay here and be shot to-morrow unless the Rittmeister signs that order. It's been well knocked into me and every single soldier in the Army that a man's his own best friend and must look after himself."

The world of rules and orders that he knew and understood seemed to be collapsing round him, and he leapt at Grischa and seized his right hand in his own, still holding his rifle in his left. Grischa had for some time been standing three paces off; he could not understand what they said, but his eyes told him what was happening.

"You must forgive me," cried Sacht: "I've always done my best for you: but I've got a wife and child at home and I can't disobey orders," and before he dropped Grischa's hand, he added more quietly: "God forgive them who bully decent fellows into behaving like swine." Then he turned round, pushed back his helmet, strode to the door, stood with his back to it, and held his rifle at the ready with both hands, with its muzzle pointing slightly down, and his finger on the trigger.

Winfried, letting the order fall on to the table, was about to make some reply: his heart was thumping against his ribs—then suddenly the current came on and the bulbs in the great room burst into a blaze of light so that they all had to shut their dazzled eyes—and Winfried simply said:

"It's all up."

With trembling fingers, and thrust-out lower lip, he held the order in the candle-flame, scattered the brown ash on the ground, and put the candle out. Grischa, who was standing motionless, rubbed his eyes, turned about and walked without a word back to his cell. Babka, who had been glancing quickly from one to the other of the three men, reminded him in a hoarse excited whisper of her schnapps: "Now's the time," she said. Then Grischa made a blunder: he chuckled quietly, shook his head, and with a word, pointed first at himself and then at the bucket.

Babka almost leapt at the bottle, saw that the cork had been taken out and put back again, pulled it savagely out, raised the bottle to her nose, looked at Grischa in horror, poured a few drops into the palm of her hand and licked it: it was water with a slightly acrid aroma and tasting faintly of schnapps. Then she moaned, but the sound of that moan was choked within her. Something gripped her heart, and though she clenched her claw-like fists, she sank into a chair; the room reeled about her, a piercing stab of pain seemed to cleave her body from its very entrails, and she uttered a long moaning cry. She felt moisture coming from her, and a second wave of pain swept over her body. It is not wise to frighten women much at the beginning of their eighth month; but Täwje, who was a married man, understood at once, after a hurried word with Grischa, what was making the woman shriek like that, and when, with much stamping and clatter the men came in from medical inspection and pay-parade into the guard-room which was now habitable again, they found the woman lying on a bed in a convulsion.

Winfried asked some of them to carry the old woman out carefully. At least the car which was waiting outside would be of some use now, to take her to the hospital. . . .

Now, for the first time, they saw in Babka's flushed drawn face those youthful eyes of hers, and as they gazed after her and talked about how all sorts of strange things happen to people, and how the old apple-woman had got young again, they did not notice that Corporal Sacht, ashen-grey and streaming with sweat, propped his rifle against the bed, lay down and in spite of all the light and noise, drew his cap over his face, and went to sleep like a man who had just done the hardest job of his life. Sergeant-Major Pont, sitting impatiently at the steering-wheel of the car, and Bertin, heard with sinking hearts Winfried's short sharp order: they wondered what was happening, and how strangely Fate seemed to be driving people hither and thither. They took Babka to the city hospital. Then it was ascertained that she was simply in childbirth, but as it was her first child it would be a long business; the civilian doctor, a pale grey-bearded Jew, in a spotless white smock, shrugged his shoulders: no one could tell whether it would last twelve or twenty-four hours. They would let the Lieutenant know.

They were silent as they drove home. "Well, it isn't all over yet," said Winfried, before they stopped at the Divisional Head-quarters. But Pont, summing up what they were all thinking, said: "It soon will be."

Just at that very moment Grischa flung himself on his bed ex-hausted, liked a washed-out dish-cloth. Sergeant Schmielinsky locked the door behind him. As he slept and dreamed, the tears trickled out of the corners of his eyes—perhaps in sorrow for the world, perhaps in pity for himself.

Book Seven

GRISCHA ALONE

✡

Chapter 1

THE MEANING OF IT ALL

In Winfried's house, on the outskirts of the the town, the lamps were burning as brightly as ever: in the powerhouse the dynamo was whirring and thudding, all the wires had been repaired. The great tentacles of cold air had moved slowly past the city and now had fastened on the branches of the mighty forest; there they would freeze and turn into hoar-frost, until they were merged in the mass of the surrounding air.

"I think it will soon be thawing," said Sister Bärbe, regretfully, running excitedly to the window. Then she shut the little inner lattice of the double window, between the inner and the outer panes of which were delicate moss-like traceries of frost. Before she turned round, Lieutenant Winfried whispered in her ear:

"Be patient, dear, be patient."

Winfried's face had quite a new expression, or, rather, an old one—drawn, tense, agonized, and there were hollows under his keen eyes: it had looked like that for months against a background of dug-outs, nests of machine guns, and under his steel helmet in the glare of rockets, on the edge of shell-stricken emplacements and shell-holes. The only difference was that his face was now pale from office life: then it had been brown as leather.

"I'm afraid I don't feel patient."

Posnanski was sitting in a corner on a sofa, smoking a light brown cigar. Bertin was sitting with fiddle and bow before the music-stand; Sister Sophie was at the piano and about to sing. But all this—these five people, the surrounding room with its soft green wall-paper, the bedroom next door with its broad bed—was nothing more than a setting and a complement to the telephone that stood importantly in its corner, gleaming with nickel and black enamel. Sergeant Man-

385

ning, who was on duty that night, was to report any call which might come in from Ober-Ost or the railway station at Brest, which were cut off until now by the snowstorm. Even if the call were meant for the Kommandantur, Sergeant Manning had promised to ignore the usual official secrecy and let Lieutenant Winfried know. To-morrow morning, if not to-night. The stations round the damaged area reported that repairing-parties, taking advantage of the thaw, would have put up new wires wherever the storm had broken them. Moreover, they could pick up wireless messages for Mervinsk if anything important was expected.

"A poor devil of a Russian isn't important," said Posnanski bitterly, from his corner.

These five found the strain of waiting almost intolerable. They could not bring themselves to confess that they had given up hope.

"It's impossible," said Lieutenant Winfried for the ninth or tenth time, "that Lychow should have given in without showing his teeth. We shall certainly hear from him, and if it's too late, then God have mercy!"

"On whom?" asked Bertin, from his music-stand.

"On us all," answered Winfried: "on our honour, on the Empire, on the German nation—who knows what beside."

There was a dead silence broken only by the bubbling of the electric kettle. It was eight o'clock and it was quite absurd to wait up for further news to-night. At that moment the restoration of communications with the east was not so important as to compel the repairing-parties to work at night.

"We are a set of fools," observed Posnanski.

"You may smoke, gentlemen," said Winfried to his guests.

They felt they had been sitting there for hours. On the next day Pastor Lüdecke was to hold a special service for All Saints in the little military chapel at Mervinsk, and Sister Sophie was to sing one of those solemn and majestic arias from a cantata of Bach. That evening she had promised to rehearse it to her friends; but not a note would come. The slow passing of the minutes wore out those five people, and like a thin ash reduced to powder, the seconds of those five lives fell away into the void, which seemed to envelop this expectant house. They rattled spoons in their teacups, which

Herr Ruppel had washed up and laid out, and took great trouble not to provoke one another with any ill-chosen words—while they were still trying to hope for what none of them believed. Posnanski took his spectacles from his weary eyes.

"Let us all say quite candidly what we're thinking about," growled Posnanski.

Bereft of their glasses, the pupils of his eyes bulged out naked and defenceless, red-rimmed in the setting of that Socratic clever face.

"We are hoping that, in spite of everything, an innocent man's life may be saved," answered Sister Bärbe, almost hysterically.

Posnanski shook his protuberant cranium.

"Is this a time to trouble our heads over individuals?" he replied gently: "What do individuals matter, and how can one talk of guilt and innocence now? While we speak, over in the West, or in Italy, our gas-shells are crashing into dug-outs, shrapnel is whizzing from dolomite to dolomite, and on both sides human beings like ourselves are fighting. In all the salt seas round Europe torpedoes are ripping open the sides of ships, and drowning men like ourselves, and all the newspapers and all the governments, all the civil authorities and public departments, are telling us to hold out, while the shortage of necessaries spreads the War into the homes of every one of us. Poor Grischa," he added, shaking his head, "if you enter upon another condition to-morrow, don't think you'll be the only one to suffer."

The light blue tobacco-smoke hung over the table like an evil miasma emitted by his words.

"Then why in your opinion are we really waiting?" asked Bertin abruptly, pressing his fiddle under his arm. "The jurisdiction of the Division is only a symbol to you, and Schieffenzahn's interference is but a parable."

Sophie, who was sitting near Bertin, encouraged him with a warm pressure of her hand which was hidden from the rest of the company.

"You've guessed right, young man," said Posnanski, nodding. "It's all a symbol, and a parable."

"It's all for the sake of Germany we're waiting here," said Winfried, wearily, "hoping that in the country whose uniform we wear and for whom we are ready to face mud and misery and death, the law may be respected and justice done. We can't see our country perish just as she thinks her greatness is beginning. Germany is our Mother, and we will not see her ranged upon the side of wrong. For the nation that forsakes justice is doomed."

Sister Sophie shook her delicate head. She could not express what she felt, but her feelings were rooted deeper than in the destinies of peoples and of nations. Phrases from the Bible echoed in her inward ear. It was the influence of the Old and New Testaments, released by Bach's music, that filled her being. Her heart yearned for justice, not because the soul that throbbed within her, and the divine longings that she had known since childhood, were stifled under the sovereignty of wrong. "An innocent and just man shalt thou not destroy," she thought, or rather heard. "I will not suffer the godless man to triumph." Her heart was weighed down with all the horror of a heathen world.

"Let's start," she said abruptly, trying to shake off her distress; she struck the opening chords of the prelude, and Bertin began. The echo of the little Bach orchestra rose upwards in thin tinkling cadences from the old derelict piano. To-morrow Sergeant Manning would accompany her on the harmonium, which served instead of an organ; to-day she would accompany herself. But the aria was not to break upon that silence in a single lonely human voice: a tenor part was to go before it and shield and uphold it with its protecting spell. Bertin's fiddle was to play it; the slow melody awoke and dissolved in delicate modulations. And now, amid these soaring undulating cadences, and supported by the harp-like chords of the piano, there floated through the room the chant of a soul inspired, grave and very lovely, trembling with the eagerness of exhortation:

> "Be not ashamed, O Soul,
>   To confess thy Saviour's grace,
>   If He is to call thee His own
>   Before the Father's face."

Sister Sophie's pure soft alto banished fear from the room. She sang with the artlessness of a sensitive nature. A longing after love thrilled in the solemn beauty of that deep sad voice, as once in the mighty spirit of the Master when, rapt in a divine ecstasy, he wrote down the aria—the last prayerful outpouring of the German soul. The three listeners were engulfed and lost in the wordless beauty of that music, in which Bach's passionate piety found utterance in Sophie's dumb yearning soul, that only song could release; and Bärbe knew it and listened. At the moment when Sophie was about to begin the second strophe, Sister Bärbe started and turned towards the telephone.

"It's nothing, dear; I'm afraid it didn't ring," whispered Winfried.

At that moment, away in the orderly room at Brest, Sergeant-Major Matz was tearing up a yellow slip of paper with a pencilled note of Schieffenzahn's message which he had not been able to get through the night before. The Major-General had let the matter drop. When it was reported to him that the line had broken down he had merely nodded. "All right then, it can't be done," he had said to himself. The sentence must go forward. Moreover, he could no longer understand the overwrought state of mind which had caused him to commit the blunder of cancelling the order. Surely he had thought it over carefully before sending it. The old man had upset him, and he had been over-tired. But the Russian's case was over, the correspondence would disappear into Matz's record office, thence to pass into the hands of Herr Wilhelmi. He could not afford to remember such trifles and he erased the Bjuscheff affair from his mind. Although, therefore, Matz had had no orders on the subject, he was doing exactly what Schieffenzahn would have wished when he dropped the paper into the wastepaper-basket—carefully picking up two fragments which had fluttered on to the floor—and growled: "there'll be plenty of urgent messages to send without this sort of thing, as soon as the wire is working again."

Posnanski was just then thinking to himself how strangely moving the music was. It wasn't simply Sophie's voice or Bach's music—though "simple" was the word, he reflected. He marvelled at the rich grave sweetness of the theme, the sustained power that could find some new inspiration at every turn of the melody. And with what sweet piety the girl sang. It is not a bad sign, when piety is dissevered from the faith of churches as transfer pictures are peeled off damp paper. Piety is getting independent, and that fatherly old gentleman known as the "Good God," that somewhat insipid distillation of past faiths, would be gradually pensioned off, and make way for mightier embodiments of the Divine. His chin was resting on his hand, and his stumpy fingers held a cigar; from time to time he took a puff at it, and his eyes wandered restlessly over the faces of the two pairs of lovers so far as he could see them.

Sophie stood with her back to him. Her pale, rapt, inspired face was only visible to Bertin, and she had given herself to him long before she had allowed him to be present when she sang.

She went on singing. Strange starry melodies were woven into that music, and above the smooth dark flood of harmony swept the intense clear rhythm of the violin and the girl's enraptured voice:

> "But he that on this earth
> Dares to deny His story
> Shall be denied by Him
> When He doth come in glory."

Lest the crude, harsh world of fact should break too violently upon their silence, the violin accompanied the last verse of the aria in a livelier strain, and returned to the prelude, unravelling its texture, untying the knots and loosening the bonds of the melody. For a long time not a word was uttered. The house seemed to stand on the top of a pyramid, which sloped down into empty space on every side. "We daren't go out," thought Bertin; "we should fall and break our necks." Now that he had heard her sing he loved Sophie for the first time. He would have liked to draw her head down to his own and kiss the lips of her whose breath filled the world with inspiration, but he contented himself with kissing her hand.

Sister Bärbe stared spellbound into the circle of her cup, which looked like the impress of a tiny universe, veined with the dregs of tea. She felt no fear, but only pity for a man who was suffering and whom none could help. "Poor Grischa," she thought, as, to her own surprise, a tear trickled mournfully out of the corner of her eye: "poor, poor lad. . . ." Her sympathy with the sorrows of the world of men had been caught and concentrated on this tiny point, Grischa, as in a lens, and burned into her soul.

Winfried mechanically looked at his wrist-watch for about the sixtieth time, and at once forgot what he had seen.

"Tchah!" said Posnanski at last, clearing his throat. "What was that you said about Germany? What is the sense in that, my dear boy? Whoever rises in the world, and has to act many parts, tramples on his own soul, and therefore sinks inwardly. Germany as a Power is rising like a batter pudding, Germany as a moral force is shrinking to the thinness of a thread. Why should one be surprised? That's the way with States. It doesn't much matter. Not until the thread is broken, and injustice is recognized, finds general approval, and is installed as a principle of government, do matters begin to look very black. There will always be people to intervene—even unimportant people like you and me: and if they take enough trouble they can leaven the whole lump well enough to make life possible. And if not—well, Germany is not indispensable, and if it were to retire from the scene for a short time, the mere fact of having produced John Sebastian Bach will have justified its existence. Humanity clusters round the great earth in little groups: if one of them goes into the shade and sleeps for a while another will jump into prominence. Nobody knows," he concluded reflectively, shutting his eyes, "why man sticks to this earth at all. Certainly not because he is primeval mud, like any other piece of organic life, but because he appears to be a switch-board for transferring the forces and purposes of the universe into terms of consciousness and practical reality. Flying, wireless, and submarines come much more easily to him than doing right for its own sake. Morality is not a pretty word, but still . . . It must be our next task, I think, to try to make the nations feel that justice hangs over them in heaven among the stars, just as the individual feels it when he is not maddened or stupefied by the pursuit of money."

He said no more; his thick rasping voice was silent, and to make amends for his outburst, and especially to relieve his hearers of any sense of embarrassment, he added:

"That's the answer to the riddle of the universe: now for the next."

Winfried looked more cheerfully at Posnanski's shining cranium. Germany would rise once more.

On a bench in the Bes Medresch, at the long table by the stove, sat eight men, none of them under fifty years of age. They were celebrating a great event; in the course of many years they had read the whole Talmud through together, studied it from end to end, chanting as they swayed to and fro, disputing over every verse, and joining in that age-long debate, which perhaps more than any other has sharpened the wits of men for intellectual tasks, for acute judgment, and the drawing of nice distinctions. At the side of Täwje, the carpenter, sat Reb Hersch Zerkleiner, the carrier, and Reb Jacob Hacht, the saddler, next to him Reb David Rothmann who was simply a *"batlen,"* a knight-errant of poverty, with no trade at all, and the watchmaker's assistant, Marcus Abraham of Plotz, who was called Plotzke; and at the top of the table, between the two tailors, known respectively as Reb Mendel Schneider and Reb Isaac Schneider—who taunted each other with trade rivalry even as they read the learned book, though they had lived and searched the scriptures side by side for many years without a thought of serious estrangement—towered the Chief Rabbi of Mervinsk, in his fur cap, with his stick between his knees, Rabbi Nachman ben Reuben of the old family of the Pinchas of Pinsk, the men of which, since the time of the one-day King of Poland, Schaul Wal, had been outstanding spiritual lights in the synagogues of that country. He had come to his own Jewish people, to keep a feast with them, for to keep feasts and to be merry was never so appropriate as now, so he sipped his schnapps and nibbled at the gingerbread cake as he gazed at the flame of the candle which was stuck in the neck of a beer bottle and filled the Bes Medresch with flickering shadows. On a bench half-hidden by the square stove slept Reb Esriel, the beggar, and on the stove lay a boy, whose mother, Fejge, had died of dysentery a few months before, and had had to leave her little Avremele to the care of strangers. The Chief Rabbi sighed heavily. His head was humming with the long sing-song drone of the learners of the Talmud, faintly rising and falling, its plaintive rhythm broken by foreign intonations and constantly recurring "oi" sounds, like the laments of Philoctetes in his agony—lamentations from the Mediterranean shores, and cries of grief from softer climes and souls more lightly moved. A Chief Rabbi is neither an ecclesiastic nor a pastor of souls, but the spiritual head and the central legislating authority of the synagogue, and when he gives rulings on matters of law and custom, or in family and business disputes, or gives decisions on whether food and utensils are clean or unclean, he is in the direct tradition that developed through the Sheikh of a Bedouin tribe and the Patriarch of the clan, into the tremendous figure of Moses, and has since declined again into the office of Chief Rabbi. The Pinsker, as he was briefly called, had reached his seventy-ninth year. His whole life was taken up with the interpretation of his nation's sorrows; and now he was getting Reb Täwje to tell him the story of the Russian which the latter had been talking of when the Rabbi, accompanied by the Dajan, or Deputy, had come in. He was listening attentively, his gaze concentrated on the knob of his staff, to the tale of a man, a Russian, a non-Jew, who was going so calmly to an unjust death.

"Perhaps," Täwje said, "in earlier incarnations he has done much evil—in the body of a Russian. Who can tell? Perhaps under Nicholas I (may his memory be accursed) he had so tormented Jewish boys and lads who had been called up as recruits for the army, that they drowned themselves or jumped out of the window, rather than be baptized. Are not such deeds monstrous? Perhaps he was more fortunate, and (woe and alas!) some poor Jewish child, or children, let themselves be baptized. Or perhaps his soul was lodged in the body of a Minister (cursed be his memory) who gave evil counsel. And because of his former wickedness it was incarnated once more in the body of a common soldier, and so suffered many tortures and must at last be put to death though he is innocent; then he shall be set free to dwell in that part of Paradise in which those who are not Jews may live."

Of all the members of the synagogue, Reb Täwje was one of those who had the deepest respect for, and faith in, the teachings of the Cabbala, insofar as they had been renewed and recreated in the Chassidim. The Rabbi listened with an unmoved countenance and a benevolent expression, and nodded as the Dajan, his companion, who acted as assessor on points of Rabbinical law, replied to Täwje:

It might be so, but again it might not. In times of peace he would have been inclined to say that Reb Täwje's explanation of so dreadful a sin as the killing of an innocent man was not unplausible. But now things were different. There must be some other explanation, because in war God spoke to the peoples, and the deeds of the Mighty Ones always revealed their nature. With the Rabbi's permission he would like to tell the gentlemen what had secretly come to his ears, that they might see in what times they were living: an English General would enter Jeruschalayim within the next few days and give back the City to the Jews, as had been prophesied since the time of Daniel; and no Turk or Russian either would lay hands upon the Holy City.

"You see now in what times we are living. Do you not think that some mighty event is at hand?"

The presence of the Pinsker prevented any outburst of passionate exultation; but this piece of news was followed by a torrent of whispered questions and exclamations. Reb Mendel Schneider clapped his neighbour gaily on the back, and Täwje, who had begun to sway gently in his seat, fell into a sort of sing-song wordless dance-rhythm and his body swung backwards and forwards in his ecstasy. Then the Pinsker began to speak, looking first at the roof and then turning his gaze on his Dajan:

The first Empire was that of Pharaoh, the Egyptian, the second that of Shalmaneser of Assur, the third Nebuchadnezzar's, the fourth Alexander's, and the fifth Empire was Rome. They were Empires with wars and mighty armies and senates of wise men; each of them had its own system of law and many different gods. God's will had been revealed to men in the Torah, and outside the Torah in the heart of every man. But because they did not accept the Torah they perished, and why? It was harder for them than for the Jews. Whoever holds to the Torah must needs follow his inner voice. But whoso does not hold to the Torah has only his inner voice and it is hard for men to follow their inner voice alone. Wherefore, God in His mercy gave Israel the Torah. The peoples of the earth have always said: "Why do you keep these commandments and why do you suffer such hardships?" But if we had answered them saying: "It is much harder for you, for it has been laid down that men shall keep commandments because they represent the inner voice of man," they would not have understood. "Is it not so?" he asked.

His hearers sat motionless and silent, and did not even venture a word of agreement; the truth of what he had said stood so clear before their minds.

"Very well, then," went on the Rabbi with his soft and mysteriously impressive intonation. "The sixth Empire was that of the Emperors, and there were Emperors in ben Maimon's and Raschi's times until the present day; sometimes there were two Emperors, the Emperor of Rome who was the German Emperor, and one at Byzantium who was the Russian Emperor, and both their eagles had two heads. They worship many different gods; they cannot help it, and even if they have only one God in their minds they disperse Him into many forms because their nature is such that they cannot do without such embodiments of God. The seventh Empire will perhaps begin when a Jew rules again in Jerusalem. Perhaps that will be the last Empire, and perhaps there will be an Emperor who lives on an island and worships one God, as is the case in England, so they tell me. In England, so I have heard, they will not allow images and have a great respect for the Torah of Moses. When was the crown taken away from Rome and why was it taken from Byzantium? It is written, 'in those days there were many innocent persons in the prisons and they brought them forth.' The commentary says that the words mean: they brought them forth to death, for otherwise the proper phrase would have been 'they let them out.' When was the crown taken from Alexander? When Antiochus Epiphanes (may his memory be accursed) began to put innocent men to death. Matitjahu rose up against him; and the crown passed over to Rome because it is written: 'They sent ambassadors to Judah and greeted him and wrote it in the tables of the law.' The meaning of which is—they wrote justice in the tables of the law, and thus they won the Empire."

And with that he suddenly fell silent and those seven or eight Jews, his hearers, sat in wonderment, and one and all of them thought out to its conclusion what the old man had said. They

needed no further explanation that Empire must pass from the hands
of him who slays the innocent to him in whose laws are justice; that
the seventh epoch of the world was now to begin and that in some
incalculable way England, of which these men had made themselves
a definite picture on the strength of two or three symbolical charac-
teristics, would be forthwith called to rule over this new world.   They
pondered once more on the changing epochs of time, and as it was
not thought respectful to drink the health of the Rabbi, they picked
up their glasses and drank to the Gabbe (Treasurer) or the Dajan,
politely wishing him long life.   They looked at each other proudly.
It was well with Israel now.   There were judges on the earth again.
They stroked their beards, blinked cheerfully at the flickering candle-
flames, and in the tumult of their thoughts they did not mark the
deep snoring of the two hungry sleepers by the stove and on top
of it.   On the bookstand by the wall stood the mighty volumes of
the Talmud; with their broad black backs they looked like a row of
Jews sitting at table, and, like them, they carried back certainty for
many thousand years.

Grischa slept so profoundly in his cell that even his strangled
moans in the grasp of some fantastic dream, and his hoarse gurgling
snores, did not wake him.   In the corner of that room—so high, so
narrow, that it looked like a coffin set up on end—he lay, a tiny forlorn figure, and the fear of death which he had mastered in his waking hours made his lower jaw hang loose and quiver, and his mouth
worked hideously like that of a man half-choking in some poisonous
fumes.

In the bright and comfortable room in Winfried's house, Sophie
and Bertin, accompanied by Posnanski, were just saying good-bye.

"I wish I wasn't so frightened," said Sister Sophie, breathing
heavily.

They had got Sister Hilda (Cohen) and Sister Lina Bomst to
take their places for an hour or two that evening, on the plea that
they needed a breath of air.

They did not wait for Sister Bärbe, who was standing at the

telephone with the receiver at her ear, trying to get through to the Hospital and find out how Babka was getting on. In this way the three others were able to take their departure in a tactful and unobtrusive way, and leave Bärbe behind with Winfried.

The Matron of the lying-in ward, a woman doctor trained in Russia, was quite ready to tell them all about it: the case was fairly normal, she said, but the child was awkwardly placed and the mother no longer young. The labour might go on for some time. It would be better to wait a little longer if they wanted to avoid using instruments.

In the house of the grocer, Veressejeff, on the second story, Alexander and Dawja, who had got married since the summer, lived in one room and a kitchen. Both of them, though they had no illusions as to their competence as teachers, were employed in the terribly overcrowded State schools, and were thus able to combine what they called "their respective economic bases." Beneath them Veressejeff was striding up and down, and they could hear him through the ceiling. Alexander was reading a book that he had got from a German soldier, dealing with the causes of the general hatred of Germany. As he explained to his wife, he was engaged in studying a new form of bourgeois hypocrisy. Dawja, watching with amusement the rapid movements of his hands as he underscored passages and scattered exclamation marks in the margins, was making cigarettes; she rolled a slip of the thin yellow paper round the end of a thin tube like a tiny gun-barrel, which was filled with finely cut tobacco;—then with a tap on the little wooden ramrod the contents were shot neatly into the *papyrosse*.

"Do you know why he is rushing up and down like a caged wolf?"

Sascha looked up, and nodded.

"Not because they are shooting an innocent man, but because they're doing it without the right sort of medicine-man to see him shot. People like him only care about souls. They're horribly afraid of ghosts."

"He has sent for the Russian priest at Starashelnaja. Don't you think it's pathetic that he should worry himself so much over a stranger and his resurrection?"

Alexander wrinkled his brow and meditated.

"Yes and no," he said finally. "It *is* touching from one point of view, but from another it looks too much as if he were afraid that a claim to soul-monopoly might be endangered."

Dawja sat with her hands motionless for a moment, and stared at the sharp-pointed flame of the petroleum lamp, which was trembling slightly.

"It makes me sad, Saschenko, . . . another innocent man—and there'll be thousands more. Men are devils."

"You'd better go on and say the Germans are devils, and then you'll be as completely wrong as this cunning old humbug of a professor here. His conclusion is that people hate the Germans because they work so hard. No, my dear, people to-day are what they are—a little worse than they need be. It is their institutions, which they did not make themselves but have so carelessly allowed to grow up from one generation to the next—it is those that you must change. Stop forcing people to do things—and you will soon see how much nicer men will become."

"It's the uniform that does it," said Dawja.

Sascha laughed, snatched from her a cigarette which she had just made, lit it at the lamp, and said:

"Uniforms are only the expression of economic force; economic force, my dear, that's what it is, and that's what we must change. And mark my words it will be changed."

He shot a bold and challenging look across the lamp to the opposite side of the room where hung the portrait of Karl Marx with his flowing mane and spreading beard.

"Leave it to the sons of the Rabbis! Why have we learnt to think, and why should we, who can see into things as far as most people, be afraid of anything in the world, especially when we've got women like you to help us? If the Germans stay in this country, then we must fight the Germans, and if the Russians come back, we shall have our old friends the Russians to deal with. Whatever language the enemy speaks, we know his name: 'The Devourer of Surplus Values.' "

"I wonder why," she said, "that isn't the usual translation of 'Capitalist.' It might do some good." (They spoke Yiddish together on principle.)

"Because," he said, closing his pamphlet, "it is just these people who have enslaved the language for their own purposes, and they are not going to let people call them by their right name. It is quite clear that these gentlemen must fill their pockets with all they can find and they don't much care where they find it. Then they're called conquerors or Imperialists. The conqueror needs an armed proletariat: he calls them armies, though they have little or nothing to do with the professional armies of earlier stages in European history. The armed proletariat must be kept in continual fear of those he fights for, and that is called Discipline, and for the sake of Discipline innocent men are shot."

"If all difficulties could be solved as easily as that, it would be simple enough to make people see the truth."

She felt like bursting into delighted laughter at the eager intelligence that shone in his emaciated ill-shaven face: but she could not. The laughter never reached her lips, her heart checked it and changed it into sighs.

And from the floor below rose the creaking sound of the restless footsteps of Veressejeff, who was waiting for a priest.

Chapter 2

THE GRAVE DIGGERS

THERE was a good deal of excitement and whispering until the command, "Attention," brought the Company stiffly into line. Sergeant-Major Spierauge, on this morning of November 2, was detailing his men for their various duties, just as on any other day, and when he did so he found a surprise waiting for him. Among the last men who had reported sick with a view to being released from duty and put under the orders of the Medical Officer, or even sent to Hospital, stood Corporal Hermann Sacht. Although there was little sense in such a proceeding in a garrison town, it was the practice even then, for discipline's sake, to keep an eye open for malingerers. Corporal Sacht looked pale and shattered, and his hands were shaking in the most unsoldierly manner. His eyelids twitched and his eyes were unsteady. His temperature was taken and found to be 104. He had to be handed over to the medical officer on duty, one Dr. Lubbersch, who, to avoid being treated as a Jew, dealt with the rank and file in a very sharp and summary manner. But he did not succeed in sending Corporal Sacht back to duty. The corporal might recover from his fever after a few days' rest in bed, but it would leave him in a depressed and exhausted condition. Then he would be sent away on leave, which does no man any harm.

When they were dismissed, the Company did not know what was going to happen to Bjuscheff. However, they all agreed with those who had hammered on the tables yesterday evening and shouted menacingly:

"We won't shoot him. He's a friend of ours. He's done all sorts of things for us, he's as innocent as a new-born baby, we won't do him in."

Of course, a seasoned and wide-awake soldier like Sergeant-Major

Spierauge had long since taken a sensible view of the situation. In fact, he was quite astute enough to realize that for the time being he must not tell the Herr Rittmeister the real reason why the idea of having the execution carried out by the prison-guard must be given up. If he did so, the Rittmeister could not help taking the attitude that the men must be severely dealt with and told they must keep their mouths shut and shoot their fathers and mothers if they were ordered to do so. A sensible man, thought the Sergeant-Major, guesses the right thing to do and says nothing. And so, before morning parade, he reported to the Base Commandant in apologetic tones, but without moving an eyelid, that the work was so heavy that between three and five that afternoon he would not, unfortunately, have at his disposal the necessary ten or fifteen men to carry out the order of the Quartermaster-General: but that in the three empty recruit depots there was at present housed a battalion sent back from the Front to be "deloused" and re-equipped, etc., and they could easily provide fifteen men if called upon.

Rittmeister von Brettschneider also knew what was proper, and it did not occur to him to regard the Sergeant-Major as a cunning old fox. Not for a single instant did he allow himself to be disturbed by the real state of affairs, although he privately had a pretty good notion of it. Remarking "that's a much better idea," he went on to the next point, and they both understood each other.

"We don't mind potting someone for you," said Sergeant Berglechner in his broad Bavarian, "if you give us an extra round of schnapps for it. An N.C.O. and fourteen men, that makes three bottles of schnapps, and one bottle for me makes four. I'll send you fellows with carbines, they'll do it better at a short distance."

Sergeant-Major Spierauge promised the schnapps and began to discuss the fate of the battalion with the Bavarian so lately back from the trenches; it had once been a regiment of mounted Jägers, but had since been turned into a machine-gun battalion with both light and heavy guns. The Bavarian asked him if he had ever seen lines of gassed corpses that it would take him twenty minutes' tram-journey to pass through. The battalion had taken part in the break-through on the Italian Front, and before that in the great Roumanian retreat at Focsani, and earlier still in the terrible winter battles in the Carpathians; now they were being sent into the Flanders fighting. It consisted of lads of an average age of about twenty who really did not mind what they did. They had a canary as a patron saint; its cage was hung on the limber of the No. 1 heavy machine gun, and the bird was tenderly fed with sugar. At the beginning of the year they put up a pretty good show at the *Morthomme* which was a pretty hot corner: they were all trained snipers, and when the War broke out their average age was seventeen.

"We can't afford to be squeamish," said Sergeant Berglechner: "people like us who've so often wiped the next man's blood off our belt-buckles, and as often as not didn't know whether our legs were on or off; what does your bloody girls' school think of that, you old scrimshanker?

"What do you think we're all going to do when we take off our tunics, if we live to do it? Tell me that, my boy. We shan't suit the jobs we came from, that's sure enough: we've got a bit too big for them, I fancy. Right, then: at two sharp," he said firmly. "I'll send along four squads—a sergeant, a corporal, and fifteen men. As a matter of fact you're a pack of fatheads to go to all that expense. I've got a little scent-spray here"—and he laid two fingers on the brown gleaming leather of his revolver-holster—"that will make two neat little holes in the back of the lad's head and do the trick nicely. But as you will—as Schiller says"; and he nodded and swaggered off resplendent in green puttees, map-case, and his officer's dirk with its silver tassel.

"There, I'm sure I felt a jerk at my heart that time," thought Sergeant-Major Spierauge, as he looked after him: "that's my third cigar to-day; it's this damned smoking; I must knock it off a bit."

In the early hours of the morning the sky had been covered with fleecy clouds that forboded sunshine, and, indeed, about ten o'clock the sun came out. Telephone communications with the West had already been restored by nine o'clock; at first one line only was working, the others were repaired later and were completely monopolized by conversations between the Intelligence Section and the Operations Staff, while Grasnick telephoned the more urgent messages to Brest-Litovsk. The General's A.D.C., however, soon appeared in the major's room wanting to know whether His Excellency had sent any important message to the Court Martial Office; Major Grasnick duly inquired but the answer was: No, His Excellency had continued his journey as he had arranged to do; he had not left a message to be sent or dictated a telegram or anything of the kind: whereat Lieutenant Winfried expressed some mild surprise and went his way, though when he was outside the door he leaned against the wall and wiped his forehead. He felt the need of air so much that he had to unbutton his coat and unhook the collar of his *Litevka*. But the chill of the unwarmed corridors and staircases soon made him shiver, and he had to do up all his buttons again. "Good God!" he thought, and he repeated this simple but impressive formula more than once, what could have happened? What could he do? It was true that there were a dozen different ways of stopping a few files of men marching a prisoner out to execution; he could come upon them suddenly, bring them up short with a definite order, or confuse them with a forged telegram. But he knew that none of these possibilities were really open to him. And even if His Excellency had himself been on the spot and had not gone on leave, Schieffenzahn's open jaws and the general fear of any appearance of disobedience or insubordination would have made him refuse to sanction any further action. Poor lad, he thought, and grew pale; poor Germany—and he called to Herr Wodrig to bring a bottle of brandy and a glass. Then he telephoned to Posnanski and asked him to come and see him, as he wanted to know whether any representative of the Court Martial or the Division had to be present at the last scene. And Posnanski promised to come.

The Russian soldiers' cemetery lay on some rising ground to the east of Mervinsk, an expanse of countless tiny crosses, each with one or two wooden cross-pieces. Sergeant-Major Spierauge had arranged that Bjuscheff, with the help of the cemetery staff—one of the many sub-sections of the Kommandantur—should dig his grave himself. This sounded very cruel; but the sergeant-major was a man of experience and knew that many things that will do a man good look harsh at first. It would be much more dreadful to sit shivering in a cell and listen till the knock came upon the door; so the doomed man had a walk there and back and some manual labour that prevented him from thinking and dwelling on his agony. And Grischa found it not unpleasant. Just as he had carefully inspected his coffin which, though unwittingly, he had put together himself, so he liked the idea of preparing his new dwelling-place. As Corporal Sacht had reported himself sick that morning, two other men from a section he did not know went with him as guards. Picks and shovels were found outside the cemetery. The snow, which had frozen lightly over in the night, was now beginning to thaw: the sun, now half-way to the zenith, came out, as they reached the higher ground, and warmed them. It was with a real feeling of pleasure that Grischa found the place where he was to work, in the further left-hand corner, immediately adjoining a path. He would not have liked to lie among a crowd. All arranged in squares, as the Germans do everything, he thought, when he saw the field of crosses stretching away in front of him, divided into three great groups: the Catholics, the Orthodox, and the Jews and Mohammedans. The Landsturm-men attached to the cemetery, Hamburgers, had, by Spierauge's orders, prepared the place already: and there lay a bare plot of earth, black, damp and frozen. Grischa went to work with a will.

"Gently, gently," grumbled the Hamburgers, as he appeared to be taking too much room for himself. They did not know that he was to be the inhabitant of the house whose walls he was now building, for he did not tell them, and they often had men to help them.

The pick struck crumbling flakes from the stony substance into which the frost had changed the rind of the earth's crust; and the upturned clods revealed a silvery network of soft veins of frozen water.

The two guards, much too sensible to stand and freeze, leaned their rifles against the cross of the next grave, keeping them well within reach, took up two picks and began to throw up the earth at each end of the grave. Soon, a few inches below the surface, they came upon softer earth, first damp, then dry: and they all began to use shovels. Grischa watched the earth, as they dug deeper and deeper, grow lighter in colour: loam, rich clay, veins of sand, and yellow soil once more. Truly, thought he, a clean grave. He must be careful it was not too short or too narrow. With clear, wide-open eyes he looked about him. So his time had come. Beneath his heart he felt a strange and dreadful sensation. He must not look, he must not turn, or something there might leap upon him and chase him horribly over the mounds: it was that black beast he had once seen in the forest, he thought, the hideous tree-cat, which Babka had told him about later:—how it was called a lynx, and could tear a man to pieces if he were only armed with a knife. She crawled along the snow nearer and nearer—he could see her fangs and claws and devil's ears—but here was good earth, warm sound earth—and he thought of the countless times in the War he had dug himself in, when, working breathlessly for very life, they had to dig for cover against infantry-fire or scraps of flying iron. "In you go," he said to himself fiercely, as he drove the spade in with the centre of his boot. With a steady swing he drove it down and flung out the earth; a pleasant warmth spread over him and loosened his limbs. He took off his cloak, hung it over two crosses, and dug deeper and deeper, thrusting and flinging out the earth like a sower strewing seed for the coming harvest. The two Landsturm men talked about their next leave, and of the prospects of peace that seemed to be growing fainter on every side. The two Hamburgers, who had also provided themselves with shovels, got quite friendly with him. There was not room enough for more than four men to work together: at last Grischa was up to his knees in earth and he went on digging with a sullen determination which his guards took for anger, bitterness or hatred. But, in fact, he felt none of these emotions. He had quite lost himself in this work that progressed beneath his hands: it was the enthusiasm of a digger whose task it is to dig well. Sunshine in the air, his breath rising up in steam, above his head a sky growing ever more blue, gold and bluish shadows over the myriad low mounds in that stretch of land, and the deep covering of snow from which the melancholy crosses came forth. This great four-sided enclosure, divided into three sections, seemed to him no longer cut up in squares in the Prussian manner. Like the three battalions of a regiment, faultlessly drawn up, man next to man, with room to move but just near enough to touch, that field of the dead stretched away, a regiment of a vast army, which had for ever abandoned the war that raged over the surface of the earth, and with their rifles at their feet, on a lower story of the edifice of earth that belonged to them alone, waited for the future. Not a bad thing to join that army, thought Grischa, grieved that he could not take with him rifle and ammunition, belt and bayonet, bread-bag and cloak rolled up on top of his haversack, as he had once possessed them. The age-long feeling of the old heathen warriors who did not believe in death on the battlefield but thought they must keep their weapons for future fights, began to stir within him, and lent vigour to the thrusts of his right boot and to his swinging arms. The grave was sinking deeper and was almost too narrow for Grischa to hurl the earth so freely over his left elbow as he had been doing. On the shaft of his spade, which he gripped in his right hand, his left slid up and down with a practised and almost mechanical movement.

"How that Russky of yours does work," said the Hamburgers in astonishment. "He must have greased his joints."

When they understood for whom this Russian had been sent out to dig a grave, they positively gaped, and the elder of the two almost dropped his shovel. From that moment until the stroke of half-past ten they and the two Landsturm-men had plenty to talk about.

Chapter 3

A LAST WILL AND TESTAMENT

THE delegate of the Red Cross, a Knight of the Order of St. John, one Herr von Waggen, happened to be on an official journey to the new Front line. His assistant, a subordinate officer called Mussner, had a round face and childlike eyes which stood out with extraordinary prominence from behind the glasses of his spectacles—he was so far-sighted that he could see practically nothing near at hand, and stared out upon the world in persistent amazement. They both entered the orderly-room in the company of Sergeant-Major Spierauge, to deal with the disposal of Grischa's possessions. A clerk carried in a large sealed paper parcel everything that had been found in Grischa's pockets and rucksack at the time when he had been handed over to the Kommandantur. But the two did not come in alone. With them came the foreign delegate of the Red Cross for Sweden, Professor Ankerström, Count Ankerström in reality, who had arrived the day before to settle with Herr von Waggen and His Excellency von Lychow a number of important questions regarding the care of prisoners. . . . In any case Grischa's effects would be sent to Vologda through Sweden and directed to the Russian Red Cross. Ankerström thought that his unexpected presence at this transaction might give him a real insight into the condition of the war-prisoners in German hands. The long table, clean and dusted, provided enough room for them to spread out everything from the large yellow parcel, and also out of a small box which Corporal Schmielinsky now brought in with a certain diffidence from Grischa's cell, for it was quite certain that a prisoner ought not to have possessed such a receptacle. But no one said a word. Ankerström made a mental note of the fact, that to judge by the presence of the box, this person was humanely conducted. His dark blue eyes, with their golden eyelashes, from behind their rimless glasses scrutinized the cages in which the soldiers slept, the almost mathematical arrangement of all the soldiers' little possessions, and he opened his small sensitive mouth in a gentle sigh at the pitiful state of the world when so many million grown-up men have no more room to live and stretch themselves than the surface of a straw mattress, and four feet of cubic space above their heads. Sergeant-Major Spierauge looked at his watch . . . it was only two minutes past eleven, but a knock was heard upon the door and through it came the man who was to declare his last wishes. His wrists were free, his cheeks were red, though the rest of his face was grey, and from between his eyebrows and his cheek-bones his small eyes peered out upon the company; his body was sound, but his fate had laid upon him the sickness of death. The interpreter informed Grischa what he now had to do.

He nodded, standing at the side of the table, looking curiously at the strange gentleman: he liked the look of his long distinguished face, with its narrow forehead, above the collar of rich black fur. Sergeant-Major Spierauge emphasized the fact that the bag containing his possessions would now be opened in his presence. Grischa took a last look at his watch, his compass, his knife, his several aluminium rings which he had made himself, his flat bronze amulet, pierced for a string and embossed with four holy women in long, bell-like skirts standing round a holy child, a silver watchchain, Bjuscheff's copper identification-disc, with a wire to hang it round his neck, his pigskin purse, a small pair of scissors in a leather case which he had made himself, a razor, three limewood spoons on the handles of which he had carved the figures of two women, one above another, and a soldier's head at the top, a ring on which were strung several contrivances for cleaning pipes, and seven brass buttons slung on a string, which Grischa could have used to make rings. His undergarments—strips of linen to bind round his feet, two shirts, two pairs of pants, a pipe, a tobacco-pouch, two kinds of lighters, an iron knife, fork and spoon plated with tin, folding spoons and forks, and a variety of small odds and ends were taken from the box. The rest of his possessions he carried on his person: his sleeved waistcoat of soft grey sheepswool, his body-belt, another small bag of brightly coloured stuff, much stained with sweat, which he took from round his neck. Then he began to divide them up. His eyes wandered restlessly over this worldly wealth of his, the implements of his daily life for which he was to have no further use. He opened the leather purse: there was still some money in it—sixty-three roubles, partly in Ober-Ost currency, and sixteen German marks in paper. And from the small cloth bag, the contents of which he had often put for safety between the inner sole and the last of his boots, he hesitatingly took a large and a small piece of gold which he had hidden in various places next his skin since the War. He began by saying that this gold belonged to Marfa Ivanovna, and also half the paper, and the silver watchchain and the watch which he had inherited from his father. It was wound with a key, and on the back of it was engraved a stork wading in a pond with reeds; on the bank was a logwood house, and near it a tiny string of washing hung out to dry.

Corporal Langermann was acting as clerk and his pen could be heard gently scratching across the paper.

"Tell her," said Grischa quietly, "that I thought of her to the end, and that I send my blessing to her and my little child, and say good-bye to her in all love and affection. I hope she will think of me, and have no masses said for me, nor give the priest any of my money or hers, because I've very few 'sin-lice' on my hide, no more than any other soldier. And if she marries again, she's to take a man who won't beat my little girl, or I'll have no peace beneath the earth, and I'll come to help the child and stand by the stove in the twilight as I used to do. I'm going to take off my woollen waistcoat afterwards; she's to have that too. She must try and look after the house properly. She must not sell it, and if she wants advice she's to pay no attention to her father, who's always after the money, but ask my mother what she thinks. For the rest she's to do the best for herself and for little Jelisavjeta. She can give those buttons to the child to play with and tell her they came from her little father who loves her and sends her his blessing. This holy brass amulet was given me by a woman, and it must be given back to her. The soldiers know her, her name is Babka. It has not protected me very well, but don't tell her that; there's no medicine against death. At first she had better hang it over the baby's basket or whatever it sleeps in and later the baby can do what it likes with it." Then a sterner look came into his eyes as his hands moved over what lay upon the table. "This paper-money here," he continued, "thirty-three roubles and eight marks, is also to be given to Babka, who is ill in the hospital and just going to have this child. It's my child. That's the sort of thing that happens now. Give her this money and the two shirts to make clothes for the baby. If it's a boy I want him to be named after me, as I would have named my son, Ilja Grigorjevitsch; besides the amulet I send him this ring as a birthday-present. It's made of silver and must not be mixed up with these two rings"—and he held them out on the palm of his hand—"they're only aluminium. I wish her good days. She must not let herself think about Bjuscheff and such things. It was fated that I should not get home; whatever happened I should have come to the same end to-day. I hope she won't mind wearing this aluminium ring with the German cross on it in memory of me. I made it myself in the timber-camp. Besides the money, which I want her to spend on herself and the child, I hope she'll keep this knife, as a souvenir, and the brass disc that belonged to the dead Bjuscheff which she gave to me; but only if it does not trouble her to look at it; I don't want her to reproach herself. Ah," he said, suddenly remembering, "here is a cigarette-box I should like her to use from this day forth. I carved it myself of maplewood, and I give it her in peace and friendship."

Suddenly he glanced up from the homely objects he had been handling, which represented the whole of a man's worldly goods. Someone had entered the room, and although Grischa was deeply absorbed in giving these last instructions, he became aware of the presence of Lieutenant Winfried, who, respecting the general silence, had advanced noiselessly to the end of the table, and was just visible to Grischa as he slightly raised his eyes. As all the men seated at this table, wearing the same uniform, were convinced of the practical good sense and drab reality of the whole proceedings, they were but dimly conscious of the true reason of this solemn stillness. This was no place, they thought, for fuss and chatter. Here was a man disposing of his goods; that was reason enough for them to hold their breath, for goods were ropes that bound us to the solid earth.

A man that untied these ropes would soon thrust out from land and steer his boat into the mists beyond.

Grischa smiled at Winfried. His appearance had relieved him of a great anxiety: he had been wondering how he could safely convey his legacy to Babka, especially the paper-money, without causing offence.

"I'm very glad you've come, sir," he said. "I'd like to ask you to hand over to Babka what belongs to her, thirty-three roubles and the other little things. If a guardian's wanted for the child later on, Babka can choose one herself. She's a good judge of men. But if she dies now in childbirth, or soon afterwards"——

"She's getting on all right," said Winfried, interrupting him, but Grischa only thanked him with a nod, and went on with his instructions:

"In childbirth, or later on," and here he stopped short. He did not know what would be best for his child. His feelings prompted him to say: "Then let the child die; it's a miserable thing to be born into this world," but his good sense told him that a new-born infant hungers for life and growth, and delights in this strange impulse. The only question was to whom he should entrust the child. He would have liked to give it to Täwje, the Jew, for it was well known that the Jews were kind to their children, and not nearly so rough with them as the peasants. Then an idea flashed upon him, clearing all his doubts, and looking calmly at the Lieutenant, he went on:

"Then I should like to ask the Sister with the dark eyes and the little moustache, who was always kind to me, and who danced that day with you, Sir, in the garden at the party——"

"Sister Bärbe Osann," said Winfried quietly to Corporal Langermann.

"Right," said Grischa. "I should like her, as long as she's here, to see after the baby and find some trustworthy woman to nurse it. This compass here is for my friend Aljoscha Pavlovitsch Granki in the saw-mills at the timber-camp, where I escaped from. He's to keep it in memory of me, and I leave him my pipe too. Give one of these carved spoons to Sister Bärbe, one to the other Sister and one to the Lieutenant here, and if Corporal Sacht, who went sick this morning, would like my tobacco-pouch, he's welcome to it. But if he'd rather have my wooden box, he can take it, and Täwje, the carpenter, can have the pouch. Yes, that's better," he added, "Täwje can make a wooden box himself, if he wants one, and every soldier has a tobacco-pouch. That's all."

Count Ankerström, Professor of the Finnish and Ugric languages in the University of Upsala, examined the will to see that it faithfully embodied Grischa's wishes. These simple people, he thought, are everywhere the same. At home in Sweden or over in Germany or here in Russia, everywhere the same enduring stuff of which mankind is made. If only we could—and he corrected himself inwardly: if only society would let these fellows come to the surface, what mighty figures would arise upon the earth!

In the meantime Grischa had picked up the pen, Ankerström handed him the paper, and after the will had been read over to him he made his mark in the form of three crosses at the bottom of it.

"Quite correct," he said.

His pen scratched over the paper, as he made the perpendicular and horizontal strokes that, against the white surface, looked like a symbol of a cemetery in winter, three black crosses on a white background. The witnesses signed, and Winfried with them. A terrible oppression weighed upon them all, as Grischa's belongings, divided into separate portions, were collected and put aside by Winfried and Spierauge, and by Sergeant Mussner for Ankerström. Nobody knew how to put an end to the scene. . . . Herr Langermann folded the papers noisily together, Spierauge cleared his throat, and said:

"What about 'spiritual consolation'? We haven't dealt with that yet. The Russian priest hasn't come yet, though he's been sent for."

Grischa looked up with a frown.

He wanted no priest, he said.

Spierauge was visibly relieved. He would find out at once, he said, whether the Divisional Chaplain had time to come.

Grischa made a grimace, and said:

"Thank you very much. I don't want the Chaplain either. I don't mind dying without a parson. Hell, if there is one, can't be any worse than three years' war and prison. If I've done wrong, I'm man enough to answer for it myself; I'm afraid to die, like everybody else, but people with prayer-books won't make me any less afraid. I've lived like a man, and I'll die like a man, like a common man, who had little time for God, and for whom God had little time too, and if God thinks this insulting, surely death is hard enough, and God, if there is a God, will not be harder to me than I should be to a little child who was rude to me. For," he said with a smile, "if there is a God, and He really did make the world, then He won't simply be as kind as I am to a little child, but a million times more kind, and if He hasn't as much patience with me as I have with a child, then praying isn't much use."

Sergeant-Major Spierauge replied that the regulations required that a clergyman must be present at the execution, and he proposed that the Catholic Divisional Chaplain, Father Jokundus, should be asked.

"Yes," answered Grischa, "I should like to have a cross near me when I die, for I am a Christian, and it's all one to me who carries it; but the parson of yours with the yellow beard once behaved very badly to me, so I'd rather have the other one."

Sergeant-Major Spierauge made a note of this, stuck his note-book between two buttons of his tunic, put his cap on, formally saluted Lieutenant Winfried and the Swedish Count, and took his departure. He was dimly conscious of the embarrassing prospect of having to take leave of the prisoner, but reminding himself that he had plenty of time, he dismissed it from his thoughts. Langermann glanced at Grischa, with a look of fear and horror in his eyes, and followed his chief. The interpreter, with an extinguished cigarette in the corner of his mouth, and an expression of infinite indifference on his sallow face, nodded to Grischa, saluted vaguely towards the ceiling, and slouched towards the door. Corporal Schmielinsky turned pale and his forehead grew damp with nervous sweat at the thought that from now onwards he would be left alone with the prisoner. Fortunately, he could call in the other soldiers again, who, while Grischa was making his will, had been stamping and racketing about outside in the entrance-hall. Count Ankerström buttoned up his fur coat, slowly drew on his left glove, and suddenly, looking Grischa straight in the eyes, he said in Russian:

"Yes, I speak Russian, and I give you my promise in Russian, that your wishes shall be carried out. I will make it my business to see that your wife gets the pension of a sergeant who has fallen in action."

Grischa's face lit up and he thanked the Count.

"I haven't a photograph of myself," he said in a troubled voice. "I'm sure my wife doesn't remember what I look like, and my child won't have any idea of me, when she says 'little father.' Still, I suppose worse things than that have happened in the War."

Ankerström wondered whether a photographer could be found in an hour or so.

"But before you went to the War," he reminded Grischa quietly, "your wife must have had a photograph of you."

"True. That's as it should be. I should like her to remember me as I was then," said Grischa with a nod, divining the Count's intention. "She wouldn't have much use for such a scabby bag of bones as I am now."

The Swede nodded, smiled cheerfully, and said, "You're right, my friend; so God be with you." And he stretched out his hand to him across the table, a small-boned, sinewy hand, and in that pressure there was a human sympathy that warmed Grischa's heart, like a good glass of schnapps.

Ankerström turned to the A.D.C. and asked whether he was coming too.

Winfried pushed his cap back from his forehead, looked at Grischa sadly, and said:

"So the time has come for us to part, Russky. You don't know how I've worried over you. If you'd come with me at once yesterday, perhaps we'd all feel happier now."

Grischa did not speak; he merely glanced at the Count to ask him to translate the Lieutenant's speech almost as if to emphasize his isolation from the rest. Then he answered:

"It had to be, the evil thing could not be avoided, as everyone must see. But I'm grateful to you, Sir; you have always been good to me and taken trouble about me to the end. So we part as good friends."

"Yes, Grischa," said Lieutenant Winfried, "we must part. I

shan't go with you on your last walk, but I shall never forget you, you obstinate old ruffian."

So saying, in the generous sympathy of youth, he swept aside all military forms, and in the presence of a Swedish professor, who was also a Count and an officer, a Prussian lieutenant shook hands vigorously with the humble Russian, raised his right hand to his helmet, saluted once more, and turned to go, standing aside at the doorway to let the guest go through before him.

Grischa watched them both go, and grow smaller in the distance. He felt a little weak at the knees, sank back on his seat, and repeated three times, while his face grew greyer and greyer:

"Alone, alone, alone."

But for Winfried, this handshake with a Russian prisoner, a lousy fellow condemned to death, had, like many another casual gesture, unlooked-for consequences. Corporal Schmielinsky, with glassy eyes, marked the incredible thing. It was only human that he should tell his comrades about it. The men pretended to find fault with it; but secretly they thought very differently, for in those days when the Supreme Command let the puppet-threads of the army fall from its hands, and sword-knots and shoulder-straps got many of their wearers into trouble, someone in the Soldiers' Council would say: "That's the officer who shook hands with the Russky," and these words covered Lieutenant Winfried with a protective aura, which frightened the roughest recruits in the training-camps into an attitude of respect once more. But this is a later and another story.

Chapter 4

LAURENZ PONT

THREE men, of different ages, stood in the entrance to the Tamshin-ski park, just where the black iron scroll-work of the gate rose with its elegant lines and arabesques above the dripping wall into the pale gold sky of winter.

"As for me," said Kriegsgerichtsrat Posnanski, walking up and down, and sucking hard with his bulbous lips at a cigar, "I shan't go; I'm too much of a coward. To see our Russian laid out is not on my programme."

Sergeant-Major Pont laughed, and said: "It isn't on anybody's programme, Herr Rechtsanwalt."

He drew a deep breath of the bright fresh sunny air, glad to be outside his office, and thankfully contemplating the small birds that kept up a silvery twitter in the old ivy of the wall.

"Then no one will be there," said Bertin, conclusively.

He, private soldier as he was, had adopted towards his superior officer a man-to-man attitude, which would have been in no way re-markable between Bertin, the writer, and Posnanski, the lawyer, especially as the two were friends, but when they were in uniform looked rather odd; and Sergeant-Major Pont was not a little amused.

Lieutenant Winfried had made it perfectly clear that, in the first place, the prestige of the Division prevented any officer being present at this melancholy scene; but, on the other hand, that the proper administration of justice required that a witness should be present at the execution. Who this witness was to be, he had, in his charac-teristically insinuating manner, left it to the Herr Kriegsgerichtsrat to decide, and had ridden off on his bicycle, to go for a walk alone, or with Sister Bärbe, in the sunshine on the dazzling white snowfields or through streets of the city. He would probably be passing the hospital, where, strange to relate, he would enquire after the health of a Russian peasant-woman, who had lately been confined. The snow was now neither hard nor melting, but in that condition produced by frost at night and strong sun in the daytime. Bertin bent down, made a snowball, a smooth, soft globe of snow; he aimed at the Tamshinski coat of arms in the middle of the delicate filigree of the iron gate, and hurled the ball, which stuck and scattered; then he said emphatically to his superior officer:

"I shan't go, anyhow. I haven't the nerves for this successful conspiracy to murder. There's one advantage, at least, in being a private soldier. And I shall use it. Now you've no choice, Herr Posnanski."

Sergeant-Major Pont, Pont the master-builder, looked across the smoke from his pipe from one Jew to the other. He understood them. They've got beyond playing at soldiers, he thought. He was a Frank from the lower Rhine, a man of education. When, under Claudius Civilis, his Batavian ancestors had attacked the Romans and had some little success, there came one of the Generals of Vespasian who had lately been made Emperor, and made a bloody ending of that raid by the little tribe of woollen-coated, flaxen-haired Germans. The Emperor, who had formerly been only a General, was at the head of an expeditionary force, for all the world like the English General of to-day, in the eastern part of his Empire, or, rather, of the world: he was fighting with the Jewish people, and later was to hand over the City of Jerusalem to his son and A.D.C., Titus. Sergeant-Major Pont saw as a palpable image before his eyes the difference in their several lines of descent, a short line of Batavians dwelling on the Rhine banks culminating in himself, Pont, contrasted with a long line of nomadic Hebrews down to Posnanski and Bertin. For it was then, under Vespasian, a fat, bull-necked peasant with a small slit-like mouth and fleshy cheeks rounded off by a protruding nose and jowl, that the two lines parted: at that time the Hebrews had a many-sided urban civilization, and eight hundred or a thousand years of history behind them, while the Batavians were still a handful of primitive clans. In those days, thought Pont, as he raised his cap and ran his fingers through his thick grizzled bristly hair, in those days, and once again later, it took the entire resources of the Empire to conquer them, and now they are here and have a right to their nerves. They have been writers and lawyers from the days of Titus to those of William II, and so they'll go on for many a year being good writers and good lawyers. And now they are disputing over which of them can avoid the spectacle afforded to ordinary people by the solemn execution of a fellow-creature. As he pondered all this, he drew with the point of his stick in the snow the two bisecting lines in which he had imaged the course of history, and looked at them in bewilderment. His cloak hung open from his shoulders, and showed how the ribbons in his buttonhole were tied on the inner side. Then, with a look of mild resignation on his face, he turned once more to the present, for he knew already who would ride to the place of execution—himself who in the short cuirass of the legionary, and probably holding something like the rank of sergeant-major, his round shield on his back, his lance across his shoulder, had led the companies of his cohort to similar executions at many places on the globe—the German legionary, the man from the lower Rhine, who had given up his native gods in favour of Serapis or Mithras, and who later on was to worship the new Christ-God that came from the Hebrews. Posnanski, he noticed, had an arm on Bertin's shoulder and was speaking to him with an imploring expression on his face.

"Bertin," he said, "you are a writer. For you, such a business as this may be a decisive influence on your whole life. Go and see it, man, go and see how human justice deals with innocent men. Have you ever seen an execution? Well, then: you have fifty years before you in which to work out your impressions. I cannot do it. I have enjoyed this instructive experience eight times already—nine, I think, if I remember rightly. I ask you as a comrade and a man. What can the whole performance mean to you? No more than a fleck of colour on the painting that is the world. You are a literary man: your enthusiasm is for words and form, and I envy you. But take me; what have I left in the world when law and justice come to blows, and the impotence of justice is made manifest like a picture in a school-book. I am finished with. If I were a logical person and not a man, if I had been invented by one of your colleagues and not a character in God's great Poem, I should go away and take a rope or pistol and destroy my body even as my spiritual entity has been destroyed. Wherefore I beg you to represent me."

But Bertin set his lips and shook his head in refusal. His eyes looked large and black against the snow: he saw the dead man before him already. He saw the blood flowing from his wounds: streams of red flooding the white ground, the dislocated body, the smoke from the rifles. He did not need the experience which so grievously distressed the other. Before every experience, an image lay behind his forehead ready to leap forth into savage and forceful actuality when the hour was at hand. And already in his heart, here by the great gate of the Tamshinskis, he knew all the horror of that agony, the death-struggle, the shattering consciousness of the last moments, and the choking shriek of the murdered man. If—and his horror was such that he grew positively pale—at this moment he explained this to Posnanski, the lawyer would have enough insight to understand him. But Bertin could not speak of it. All these things sank to a level of consciousness not to be expressed in words and plunged into the deep well-springs of his poetic entity and waited for their transfiguration. One day, he clearly realized, he would try to embody in the story of this humble Russian Paprotkin, his conception of the cleavage between this age and the last, and write a play called *"Alarm Überhört,"* * in which he would lay bare the whole process from its earliest origin to its final realization like seed unfolding in an ear of corn.

Laurenz Pont looked from one to the other. He wanted to stand between them, and put his arms, the powerful arms of a mason and a master-builder, on their shoulders. But they might be observed from the window, and the scene would be not quite suitable for the eyes of the clerks and staff-officers; and as he emptied his pipe out by knocking it against the iron-scrolled work its hollow metallic ring made the two disputants start back a little.

"Gentleman," he said with a smile, "since the two asses cannot agree, the bundle of hay—in other words, I myself—must go: am I a satisfactory representative?"

Two pairs of eyes looked with relief and thankfulness into the large, steady, grey eyes of Pont, the master-builder. Posnanski stretched out his hand, laid it on Pont's forearm, and said:

---

* "Warning Unheeded."

"Thanking you very much, yours sincerely, Posnanski."

Bertin spluttered out his relief in some sort of words. But in order to punish himself for the element of cowardice in his attitude, he secretly resolved to watch the procession from a distance or overtake it for a moment, at the point where the circular road round Mervinsk meets the Market Street along which it would have to pass on its way out of the town. Sergeant-Major Pont politely waved aside his companions' thanks: he said he must go off at once to see that his horse, his brown gelding Seidlitz, was properly groomed so as worthily to represent the Staff of von Lychow's Division, which had lost the battle.

So they took leave of one another, Bertin walking on Posnanski's left: and Pont noticed with astonishment that Posnanski limped.

Chapter 5

THE BLACK BEAST

In the corner, behind him in the corner, waits the fear of death, the black beast, and watches him. Soon it will leap upon his neck.

Grischa sat at table eating: he was eating a beefsteak and roast potatoes, and on the table was a tin of preserved fruit. He was drinking half a bottle of red wine. Sergeant-Major Spierauge had sent him three cigars, two of which he had given away, one to Corporal Schmielinsky and the other to Corporal Sacht, to smoke as soon as he was allowed tobacco. Grischa had the third in his mouth. He was going to cut the end off and light it, ready at any moment for the black beast, the fear of death, to leap upon him from the corner. He must keep it off. A soldier was going to his death, by God, a Russian Sergeant, Grischa Iljitch Paprotkin, Knight of the Cross of St. George, alone among a horde of enemies, exposed to the eyes of everyone; and he must go like a man. In spite of all he had eaten there still remained between his palate and his tongue a bitter taste he could not get rid of. The cigar was a good one: it drew and tasted well; but he had to smoke it with set jaws, as his heart was pounding so slowly and so heavily. The door of the cell was open. He would be alone long enough; he would get plenty of sleep, too, if sleep it could be called. Now he must see and hear and breathe; his fingers which he kept lying on the table or stuck in his pockets were continually in motion. They felt the lining of his pockets, and the ribbed surface of the deal table, so rough and pleasant to his touch. His eyes could see the golden light of noon pouring through the window, indeed it was past noon. He saw the spiders' webs on the ceiling, and the winter-flies of Russia—several were buzzing and flying sluggishly along the window-pane, and they reminded him of overfed crows. They were safe enough.

Grischa remembered that he was still wearing his woolen waist-coat which he did not want spoilt. He took it off, drawing it over his head, and then put on his tunic again. Grischa's back felt cold, and he quickly buttoned up his tunic. His head felt hot, so he took off his cap. He felt impelled to walk up and down. From the chair under the window to the cell door by the passage was exactly seven paces, and with bent head, as if he were quite alone, he paced them up and down. He still felt cold. He drew on his overcoat, the good warm Russian cloak. Then the desire to empty his bowels came over him, so he went to the corporal who sent a man with him. He liked the sound of his footsteps echoing upwards from the stone flags. The snow in the yard crunched deliciously under his hob-nailed boots, and the keen blue air felt refreshing against his temples and his nostrils. It is pleasant to sit on a latrine and empty oneself out. All that makes the living man is good, he thought, as he clenched his teeth and wiped away the sweat that burst out on his forehead though it was winter and very cold. It would not last much longer. Then he went back accompanied by the Landwehr man with his rifle. That heavy weight upon his knees had gone. He walked back to his cell much comforted: he felt better now. Next he wanted to wash his face: he was determined to be clean. Hot water takes away the dirt from a man's hands and the skin of his face. The coarse soap, which looks like a soft brown stone, did not lather but it rubbed the dirt off. Anyhow, it would clean him, he thought. Then he asked for the barber—he wanted to be shaved. Erwin Scharski, the company barber, a soldier like the rest, could report in three minutes from the quarters of the first platoon. Grischa was sitting among the South German Landwehr men. They were smoking and reading: two games of nap and a game of chess were going on. It was very silent compared with the usual clatter at that hour. The long tunnel-like room was full of a murmurous hum of talk. With a towel round his neck, pleasantly sprinkled with hot water, lathered with almond soap, Grischa sat with closed eyes—his twilight was upon him. Now that he was being shaved no one could come to fetch him. As long as this business lasted his life was safe. At the moment he had a craving for sleep: but he must be shaved first, and he listened to the barber's gossip while he was stropping the razor.

"I'll put on my St. George's Cross," thought Grischa. "I'll take it out of the pocket of my tunic and hang it on my overcoat: afterwards they can send it back to the Tsar. I hope it may be a reproach to him all his days that he did not keep the peace or come to his senses earlier."

The barber was telling him about the huge rats which they had had in their lines in Champagne, how they were as big as squirrels, nearly as big as cats. But when he came to the point of the story, when the rats with the poison in their bellies lay on their backs with their four paws drawn up, forty-one of them in a single trench, he stopped short. He suddenly hated the idea of these rats lying there so stiff and he grew dizzy at the thought. He was telling the story for the seventeenth or perhaps the seventy-seventh time, but this was the first time he told it with a happy ending. This time the rats smelt the poison and generously left it alone. Grischa smiled, and then let himself be shaved. His skin was now smooth, his hair brushed and parted neatly in the way that soldiers like to have it. The cost of the performance would go down to the office account. The barber would not take Grischa's money. And the soldier, the man of the Landwehr into whom, when his work was done, he so obviously changed back again, shook his customer by the hand and disappeared. As he crossed the yard he heard an unknown clear voice outside:

"Section, halt! Order arms! At ease!"

Something struck at his heart, and he ran into his quarters. A clerk brought in an order to Corporal Schmielinsky; the corporal went as white as a sheet, and his lips trembled in his agitation; then he went in to Grischa, who had just lain down for a moment, though a moment before he had got up because he was tired of lying down.

"Comrade," said Schmielinsky, "it has come. Try and keep calm, old boy."

Grischa felt the sensation of a blow that made his heart leap. And he too went pale. The two men stared at each other. Then Grischa made the movements of buckling up his belt: he would not go forth in slovenly and unsoldierly guise, and he mechanically felt for the broad, once black, infantry belt which had been returned to him with the rest of his possessions, and which he had not yet given away, and buckled it round him. Then he adjusted his cloak in the correct folds over his back, smoothed it down in front, put on his cap, his broad peaked Russian summer cap made of thin linen, straightened himself with a jerk, saluted in the Russian manner (not permitted to German soldiers), and said good-bye to the corporal:

"If it's time, then I must go. Thank you, comrade."

The corporal on duty blew his nose, his arms shook, and for an instant his handkerchief covered his eyes.

A breathless stillness fell upon the room. The guards, who had come in from outside, stood at attention. Grischa, standing on the threshold, looked once more around him: the windows above the long table, the stools on which the chess-players sat motionless and stared across at him, the two groups of nap-players, who let their cards fall, men washing, who ceased to wash, and two men sewing, who let their needles and their garments drop, the bunks with their straw mattresses and haversacks.

"All correct," he thought. "Section, march!"

"I wish you good luck, comrades!"

The Germans made no sound, except for a young soldier, pale, and with eyes starting from his head, who answered him hoarsely: "Keep your heart up, comrade, and good-bye," and another, near him, whispered unintelligible words of horror from where he lay upon his bunk.

"Hurry up," came a voice from without.

Grischa felt slightly dizzy: but with chin well out, he marched with the corporal on duty and two Landwehr men past the sentry at the gate. There waited two sergeant-majors on horseback: Spierauge on a fat lethargic mare, and Berglechner, spruce as an officer, on a dark brown gelding. Four files of four men each, all in the same green uniforms, wearing puttees and steel helmets, carbines on their shoulders—there they stood, Jägers of this machine-gun company, ready for the march.

"But the fellow's arms are free," Berglechner called out to his friend from the office.

Spierauge shrugged his shoulders. It was not really necessary to bind Grischa's hands, he said. But Berglechner was punctilious, and without saying a word, Grischa put his hands behind his back and allowed Corporal Schmielinsky, whose hands were still trembling, to tie a narrow strip of leather round his wrists.

"That'll make me stand up," he thought. "I must stick my chest out with my arms behind my back." And with hard, steady eyes he looked at the horseman, whose voice and manner was quite different from that of the Germans whom he had known hitherto—middle-aged men with their experiences behind them. Then he looked the young Jägers up and down: cool, keen-eyed fellows, he thought. Two files in front of him and two behind, and Grischa in the middle, —and the little procession moved off. The two sergeant-majors started their horses. Berglechner took the lead, and Spierauge was to have ridden behind: but Berglechner would not allow it, he wanted company and conversation, so the leisurely old Liese had to move up to the front. Berglechner, who had already reported to Ritt-meister von Brettschneider, took command: "Section, march!" and the detachment began to tramp rhythmically through the squelch-ing slush of the main street. They went round the Tverskaia, and through outlying quarters of the city.

Grischa gazed straight ahead. The lower edges of the line of helmets in front of him gave the impression of a long grey shield swaying slightly as it moved forward. The men's leather straps and belts, gleaming with fresh buff polish, their puttees, their worn green trousers, their laced boots, so carefully greased, and on an exact level above the helmets the four muzzles of the rifles, and beyond them another four, now visible and now hidden as the heads of the marching men behind them rose and fell. The place for executions at Mervinsk was well known. It lay outside the town, in an easterly direction, on the way to that fortified outlook known as "Lychow's bunion." Years ago it had been a gravel quarry, scooped out of the hillside, and its steep wall offered an excellent background for shooting, and there was a fairly level stretch of ground on which the men could be drawn up. Veressejeff had a sleigh waiting in front of his house so that if the priest, unhappy man, should still come, he could drive to the place at once. Spierauge,

who also had the subject in mind, thought that the clergyman, whoever he might be, would not join them till they were outside the town:
but at that moment Sergeant-Major Pont appeared, helmeted and
gloved, wearing an artillery cloak with three ribbons; he rode up
casually and saluted. He introduced himself briefly and the two
others raised their gloved hands to the rims of their helmets. At a
slow trot they overtook the little party, which of course had not
halted; Pont took up the rear and the two others rode ahead. Some
civilians were sauntering up and down the pavements enjoying the
afternoon sun, and they were splashed with the flying slush as the
men tramped marching with extreme smartness and precision. The
two sergeant-majors felt like officers; they stared straight before
them over their horses' ears, seeing no one. Murmurs and whispered talk followed them along the Magazinstrasse. Women crossed
themselves at the roadside and all the passers-by stared aghast
at the solitary Russian with his hands bound behind him, and the
St. George's Cross on his chest. As yet nobody knew much about
him; but his journey along that humble street of warehouses was to
make him known and famous before evening in Mervinsk, and many
families—Jews, Catholics, and Orthodox Russians—would learn
every detail of his fate. Newspapers were unknown there, but news
was passed all the more eagerly from mouth to mouth.

Grischa went forward, took his eyes off the unbearable steel-grey
line in front of him and the tiny black mouths of the gun-barrels,
and let his gaze wander to the houses on the right and left, where
lived his friends, who could not help him. He filled his lungs with
deep draughts of air. In some·marvellous manner, he no longer felt
the presence of that fear that had so lately threatened to destroy him.
He looked about him and saw all that stood upon the earth.

The shop-signs, on which men announced what wares lay stored
for sale in the caverns behind them. The openings to these
same caverns, four-square windows with wooden frames and
cross-pieces and little double sashes, moss-grown at the joints. The
doorsteps, wooden balks or slabs of stone, smooth and worn with
many steps. He saw the smoke rising like pale pennons from the
chimneys, melting snow pouring in little torrents from every roof,
or falling from the eaves in golden drops; he saw how the wind blew

when they had left the last houses behind them. Every step seemed
to jerk him violently onward; over that white road, monotonously
clanked and tramped a moving body, composed of several members,
each of which was itself a man. Embedded in this complex creature,
his hands behind his back, his legs mechanically moving, marched
in a long buff cloak, the solitary soldier. At last he saw the snowfields, white or pale gold, flecked with bluish shadows. Perhaps
the business of this day was a mad business, but if so it was being
done with such solemnity and so much as a matter of course, that
Grischa alone perceived a little of its madness. His wild eyes
wandered to the right and left of him; there was nothing new to see,
nothing but crows, snowdrifts, and the dazzling shimmer of the
sun's bright golden pathway, before the haze dispersed and gathered
into the blue canopy above their heads.

"O God," he thought, "O God." The only thing that comforted
him was the feel of his broad leather belt round his middle which
kept him stiff and erect. Pride, sad splendid liar, that forced him
to preserve his honour in the face of his enemies by a brave death
in a far country, was like that belt of his: it too held him together.
He kept on swallowing saliva that he noticed had a bitter taste,
and while his gaze wandered from left to right, marking all the
details of that scene, just below his heart he felt a steady pressure
thrusting the overstrained muscle against the vaulting of his ribs.
The horses' harness clinked and there was much rattling of chains
against leather; the soldiers' heavy laced boots, sixteen pairs of
them, crunched in unison into the snow that now began to grow
harder, their bayonets beat rhythmically against their thighs and
on their shoulders the rifles creaked on the leather straps, sometimes
knocking sharply against the steel helmets. This marching body
made its own peculiar noises, and had a heart that was full of fear;
that heart was Grischa.

The young soldiers strode forward, some with serious, others
with different expressions; they were talking in low tones. The
little column was the only eminence in that flat, rolling plain; upon
it the road stretched away into the distance and cut into its surface
like a shallow ravine. Against that glittering scene the soldiers'
cloaks looked olive-green, and their faces a deep red, much darker

than they really were. They were marching out to execute a spy: that was what they had been told. And this was one of the most solemn duties of a soldier. Not till they were coming back, would they light their pipes or cigarettes, talk and laugh, and wave to the women, carrying five bullets less. At the moment they were the very incarnation of discipline as they marched forward with a steady, swinging step. The two horses in front sent up a faint steam of sweat. Liese tactlessly raised her tail before Spierauge noticed it. The soldiers behind her made indignant grimaces and turned their heads aside. Sergeant-Major Berglechner called his colleague's attention to it, and Spierauge drove his heels into the flanks of the fat old creature, and pulled her in to the side of the road.

The little party moved forward: the form of it was oddly symmetrical—narrow at the head, then broadening and narrowing alternately—four files of four men each, a solitary figure in the centre, two horsemen in front and one in the rear. This last horseman, Sergeant-Major Pont, sat meditatively in the saddle. As with all the others the chin-strap of his helmet was drawn tight across his cheeks. But he was the only one of them who realized the martial value of the chin-strap and what many feelings it helped to inspire. All that was distinctive and noteworthy in this game of soldiering he saw before his eyes, and even embodied in himself: war and make-believe, the moving body in front of him, the group soul, if so it can be called, adventure, courage, the solemnity of an official act that was costing a man his life. From his point of vantage he could look over the two files in front of him and their rifles and see Grischa marching with his shoulders drawn back: (but Grischa alone knew how blue with cold his hands were, and cramped and twisted in their leather strap). An infinite pity for that poor, brave, lonely figure, that ragged Russian, brought back from the depths of his unconscious memory a feeling that a tribune was riding here, and that tribune was himself, Laurentius Pontus, riding behind his cohort, on service somewhere in the mighty Empire, German mercenaries marching to his death some rebel against the Imperial law, symbolized perhaps by Hadrian's or Trajan's bust, some hairy Sarmatian, scowling Scythian, laughing Samogetian, or dark, fanatical Jew. That low, white, rolling plain might just as well be white sand or white snow, or again the white lime dust of Galilee or Gaul: and the unchanging nature of man—at least over such short periods as two thousand years—made his heart heavy.

Suddenly they turned off from the main road. Grischa, like a beast lashed by an invisible whip, tossed his head helplessly from right to left, for this parting of the ways made it too horribly clear that the irrevocable place was near at hand. His breath came heavily as though, within his breast, water was contracting into ice. They had reached the rising ground, and after passing a clump of elder, a black and tangled mass of stems and leaves, they came upon a bend in the road, and followed some wheel-ruts into a sunken track, where a grey cart with two half-starved grey horses, and a lumpish Posener peasant lad in uniform, had drawn to the side; near by at the entrance to the gravel quarry, a man on a horse in a grey and purple cloak, with a felt hat turned up on the left side, and the brim hanging down on the right like an African rough-rider, a great silver cross hung round his neck, and a puffy, red-cheeked impatient countenance, the man of God sat waiting. Events now moved forward with incredible rapidity, like a torrent rushing down a mountainside. Grischa, confronted by this lofty yellow-grey wall, spattered with snow, and by the young medical officer, Dr. Lubbersch, who was stamping up and down smoking a cigarette; and in the presence of the long narrow box covered with two tarpaulins, this last grim preparation for the end, Grischa realized that until now he had never quite believed that his last moment would really come; he had thought of it all as somehow hardly serious, though in his heart he knew it must be so. Fortunately for him, the last few minutes sped in rushes towards the end. He tried to tear at the straps that bound him, and he opened his mouth to cry out, but an inner power, engrafted in his soul these hundreds of years ago, forced his wrenching fingers to relax and rub themselves together as though for warmth, and stifled his shriek into a gasp for air. Only the despairing glitter of his watery-blue, wandering eyes above his high cheek-bones betrayed his agony. Luckily, Sergeant-Major Berglechner thoroughly understood such functions: he had had much experience in Serbia and Ruthenia where he had begun his service in the Archduke Frederick's command.

"Pity to spoil a good cloak," he said to Spierauge, who did not in the least know what were the proper steps, as his office regulations did not cover such performances.

One of the Jägers untied Grischa's hands. Grischa smiled gratefully at him and swung his arms against his chest to warm himself. Meanwhile the man of God had begun to recite the prayers for the dead in Latin, which Grischa did not understand; he said them into Grischa's face, honestly troubled for this poor soul, who was going to damnation, and appealing for the grace of Christ, who died on the Cross for the salvation of even this ignorant Russian, although the apostasy and schisms of His Church seemed likely to put something of a strain on God's goodness. He recited the prayers in a sonorous sing-song. Grischa felt very impatient and would have turned his head away from him, but the silver cross hypnotized him for the seconds it took the soldiers to unhook his belt, unbutton his cloak, and strip it off his shoulders; next they took off his tunic and his arms were free for a moment as he stood there in his patched and threadbare grey flannel shirt. High above him towered the semicircle of the stony crumbling wall of the gravel quarry. The path in front of him was now barred. There stood, drawn up in a line, five men, with their rifles at the ready, terrible to look upon, and waiting for a brief word of command. These were the green cloaks and red faces of his destroyers. Grischa stood helpless and forsaken: a crushing weight lay on his throbbing heart, and he cast a wild, fluttering glance past the elder bushes, and watched the sluggish course of a crow flying upwards into the distance, where the town lay hidden below him, that town so full of living men. Sergeant-Major Pont set his teeth, pulled out his handkerchief, and in a quiet matter-of-fact tone that admitted of no question he ordered one of the Jägers to blindfold the prisoner. The priest went on with his muttered ministrations. Now Grischa stood once more with his hands bound and his arms tightly secured. He was terribly helpless now; he could not struggle, he could only groan. He had already almost lost consciousness. The tremendous crushing weight of this thing that was being done to him, and the thought that it was being done without pause or protest, or the least sign of mercy, clouded Grischa's mind. He wanted to beg that he might not be bound or shot, but he could not find the German words to express his anguish, not the Russian words either: all he could think of were the words "Mother, Mother," that came unconsciously to his lips. Then the world was hidden by a soft clean-smelling piece of linen. And within him, ready to spring, crouched that nameless fear, the awful shuddering terror of the black beast, and he stood up tense and stiff with horror, listening for the dreadful sounds that must soon rend his ears. In that instant, as the last order but one suddenly rang out, and he heard the rattle of the rifles brought up to the men's shoulders, the litany came to an end.

The Cross, he thought, was turned towards him, that ponderous hewn symbol was being raised to his unseeing eyes. Then, in that moment when Sergent-Major Berglechner rapped out the sharp command "Fire!" the certainty of death and the extremity of his terror conquered; his soul burst its bonds, and in the same instant his bowels were loosened. The crack of the shots was like a sudden senseless blow shattering a panorama of hurrying pictures in his mind, beginning with the cross in his mother's kitchen at home. He saw Aljoscha with the wire-cutters, the moonlit expanse of the forest camp as he cut through the wires, he smelt the acrid smell of the car in which he had escaped, of the hay in the car next to him when he left the train, the vast white, icy silence of the winter forest, the shuddering loneliness of the deserted artillery position, and there was the black beast creeping towards him, the lynx with her pointed brush-like ears and devilish face, longing to leap upon him and tear him down, yet fleeing in terror at his laughter, his exulting freedom, and the snowball that he threw at her. Once more, now weak and forlorn, he smiled at the beast as she leapt upon him from the five muzzles of the rifle-barrels—this time he knew that she would tear him down. But his sense of life, which had long been broken and effaced from his experience, was suddenly, in the very instant of death, lit by a flame of certainty that burst from the deepest recesses of his soul, a certainty that parts of his being would be rescued from destruction. The ancient germ within him, the mighty source of life, contented with having transmitted itself in women's bodies to new and ever new manifestations, cast into his brain this faint but faithful reflection, and made him believe, as poor besotted men of flesh do believe, in the continuance of the Ego, the immortality of his individual entity which at that very moment had been extinguished.

Three forms of time moved over his fading consciousness. The calculated time of events and hours, the time in which five rifle bullets hiss through space, crash into a body as into a sack full of water, and, rending and flinging aside the contents of that sack, the living, working, breathing human sap and flesh, burrow down into the centre-point of life as a mole burrows through the earth. Next, the flashing electric time of hurrying ideas and images, of dreams that go on all night long, those dreams that endure for so brief an instant before they disappear, that they deceive the mind, and the whirling panorama takes on some semblance of reality. And last of all, time that is conditioned by the body, and is contained in the muscles and the nerves that obey the suggestions and the orders of the central soul. In that less-than-second, from the instant when those five bullets pierced the torn and stained shirt like rams' horns, so senselessly tearing that poor, quivering body, until the moment when the blood-filled veins, the hammering heart, all the intricate network of the lungs was wrecked for ever, he suffered an agony so deadly, so utterly beyond all human conception—struck, pierced, choked, and broken —that the white heat of that destruction must (one would have thought) have burned away his smile of freedom. But from the moment his body, that was himself, cracked and fell, as though from a new joint in his back, and a gush of crimson blood coloured the snow round where it lay, physical time—the time in which his body had lived and functioned—was freed from its vassalage to pain: his body could be no longer altered by it. There lay Grischa Iljitsch Paprotkin, otherwise called Bjuscheff, in the snow, and smiled. His face and muscles had the impress of a cheerfulness that he had not known for this long while. Only his eyes shrieked under their bandage, forced horribly outwards by the suffocation of his death, as the blood welled up into his lungs from his veins and arteries, his heart, ripped from its sinews, fell into the hollow of his chest, and five small holes were torn between the ribs of his back.

And so this huddled human heap died. . . . Stones rattled

down the sides of the quarry, bringing with them little clouds of powdered snow.

"All correct, I think," said Sergeant-Major Berglechner. "Civilians scream, soldiers behave properly"—and he licked his moustache as if he had drunk something. And he had in fact drunk something— his own blood—for without in the least noticing it, as he gave the order to fire, in the dreadful tension of the last second he had bitten his upper lip.

Dr. Lubbersch, whose expression of polite concern had been very little disturbed by these events—indeed, as a philosopher he felt himself superior and impervious to such everyday events—went up to what had once been Grischa, knelt for a moment by the smiling, side-flung head which, awkwardly for him, was lying on one cheek, undid the bandage, closed the eyes, and said:

"Quite dead; perfectly satisfactory. That's what we call the Hippocrates smile."

At that moment there stirred in that slowly bleeding brain what could be called life, but no one noticed it, for men die more slowly than their fellows like to think.

Laurenz Pont dismounted. The handkerchief with which those poor despairing eyes had been bound lay still knotted in the snow, yellow against the white: not a drop of the blood that was trickling slowly nearer had stained it. He felt it as a symbol of Pontius Pilate or Laurentius Pontus, that he was guiltless of the death of this innocent man.

Meanwhile, the men clicked the safety-catches on their rifles, and showed some anxiety to get out of the cold and back to normal pursuits: they had three bottles of schnapps and a free afternoon to look forward to. The long covered object under the tarpaulin revealed itself as a coffin. But no one could be found who took any official satisfaction in putting that pierced body, while it was still soft and could be handled, into this coffin. The Corporal of Jägers pointed out that Sergeant-Major Spierauge should have detailed some men of the prison guard for this purpose. The driver of his cart stood shivering and silent by his horses.

"It isn't our job," grumbled the Jägers.

The difficulty was solved by Laurenz Pont and Dr. Lubbersch, who was prepared to help Pont to carry out this melancholy but philosophic duty. As the Sergeant-Major got off his horse (at the crack of the rifles Seidlitz had merely twitched an ear, and Pont could not help patting him on the neck for it) and took off his gloves, with the actual intention of lifting the dead spy into his coffin with the help of the elegant Jewish doctor, two of the young Jägers nudged each other, took the dead man by the arms and legs and dragged him over the snow with much care so as not to stain their uniforms (his head was already dangling stiffly and horribly from the collar of his cloak), put him into the coffin and arranged his limbs in an easy attitude and folded his hands.

Suddenly the agitated jingle of a sleigh was heard and out of it jumped a flustered old gentleman with long disordered hair and a straggling beard—the Russian priest. The military police post at Bisasni village had kept him back until they could get confirmation of the fact that he was to be allowed to travel urgently: he flung himself down by the side of the coffin, in his long skirts like those of a woman, and prayed with despairing abandonment for the salvation of a soul that these heretical devils had placed in danger of eternal fire.

Pont, in the saddle once more, saw the group of men sharp and clear before him: he saw the kneeling priest place a brightly coloured holy picture framed in tin between Grischa's folded hands, he saw Sergeant-Major Berglechner lighting a cigarette, as the men, without waiting for orders, fell in once more, and the driver waiting to take charge of the coffin and convey it to the cemetery, somewhat troubled as to who would help him get the heavy case into the sleigh after the soldiers had departed, and a deep wearisome feeling of exhaustion made him yawn. He watched the driver standing by, with drooping shoulders and drooping moustache, too tactful to disturb the foreign priest at his prayers; he arranged that the *izvostchick*, the Jewish sleigh-driver, should give the other a hand with the coffin, and turned Seidlitz towards the town. He would have preferred to ride alone: but Spierauge pulled Liese up beside him, Berglechner sprang on to his gelding, Oberarzt Dr. Lubbersch swung himself easily on to his bay, two sharp orders, rifles clattered to the slope, and the little column turned homewards swaying to the rhythm of their march. Pont rode next the doctor. It was obvious that the soldiers wanted to sing, as is the practice on the way back from funerals when the triumph of continuing life over death is celebrated in the cheerful strains of a military march.

"How smart we must look," thought Pont.

But one thing was noticeable. There were four well-turned-out horsemen and sixteen men—one had been left behind. He was not missed. The men talked away to each other and smoked as they did so. A maniple of the Imperial Army, with minds at ease, was swinging back to their camp barracks, which, whether they are built of wood or canvas, leather or corrugated iron, mean to the soldier what hearth and homes mean to other men. When they turned into the avenue and the ground began to slope downhill, Corporal Leipolt did actually start a song; they sang—those sixteen practised cheerful throats—about the little birds twittering in the woods and how one day they all would meet at home again; a simple ditty set for three voices (more or less), and the men, tall erect fellows with white teeth and good-humoured eyes, made the song ring through the streets of the town. Unfortunately, there was a good deal more slush on the way back and the citizens would have to turn out to-morrow with their great wooden shovels; indeed, the street might well be said to be in a disgusting state, but they must give these Jews and Russians something to listen to. Sergeant-Major Pont thought, as he had done all the afternoon, that men change but little and that it was rather tedious to be a man.

Bertin, who was sitting at a window in the Magazinstrasse with a glass of tea in front of him, grew pale. So they had killed him. . . . Very well, he thought, the time will come when we shall win, and our ideas will rule; then let them look out. The room had three windows, it was a tea-room with a few pale indifferent waiting-maids standing about; hitherto it had merely smelt of stale smoke and was full of the musty odour of a place that is used by too many men every day: but suddenly it reeked of blood. He looked at his watch: he had been sitting here, since the men had passed on their outward journey, less than twenty-five minutes. He stood up, pressed his face against the window-panes, watched the moving lips of the soldiers as they sang, their steel helmets, their swaying bodies, their cloaks with the corners thrown back and hooked into the eyes sewn on for that purpose—covered his face and fell back in his chair. He wanted to say, "it is fulfilled," but the word was for him too full of painful associations; so he thought to himself, "it's all over and Grischa is done with." The machine has won; this apparatus of command has mighty wheels, and if it once gets going it goes on. How long, O Lord? He felt the need of company, and decided to go and see Posnanski, who was ill in bed with a fever. Probably he had taken cold, but perhaps it was only a fever of the mind; though he could only hope so, for those were days in which the soul of a man meant very little.

Meanwhile, on one of the town sleighs, covered with two reddish-brown tarpaulins, a long wooden chest was being conveyed to the cemetery just outside the town. With it had been another sleigh containing a Russian priest, but where a cross-road led towards the town they parted company, and the priest drove off. Not a single person was present at the burial of this poor Russian. The two Hamburg Landsturmers lowered the coffin into the grave dug that morning with cries of "hold hard!" and "let go!": they were old hands at the work and, though not careless, could hardly take much interest in it. The driver with the drooping shoulders and moustaches stood by and looked dully down into the grave before him.

"They say the fellow was innocent," said one of the Hamburgers with the sing-song intonation of his native harbour.

"I dare say he was," said the other, "but what's the good of that —we're all innocent."

"I didn't want the War," said the driver suddenly.

It was the first outbreak of that smothered blunted soul, slave among the countless slaves on those wide plains. The two Hamburgers looked at him contemptuously. They did not need to assure anybody that they had not wanted the War. They exchanged a mocking glance indicative of the fact that they thought the driver was balmy, and that, anyhow, the only men of intelligence were to be found in Hamburg; then with a practised gesture they stuck their shovels into the high neat mound of earth that Grischa's body, and not the hands of men, had so raised up.

In that very quarter of an hour Dr. Jakobstadt, the civil doctor, removed the child with pincers from Babka's unconscious body. It was a girl, weighing more than six pounds, well made and with distinctive features whose likeness no one could decide: as a matter of fact, with her short nose, broad cheek-bones, and bright blue-grey eyes she bore a ludicrous resemblance to Grischa's old mother whom none of them had ever seen. It did not cry, and while Babka was being attended to, it lay still, groping with its tiny fingers, red all over, in a rush basket on a pillow which later on was to serve as its eiderdown. When Babka came out of the anæsthetic, she refused to see it, but when it was held out to her all the same, she smiled the faintest suggestion of a smile and would not let it out of her hands.

Dr. Jakobstadt and the motherly midwife, Frau Nachtschwarz, exchanged a few remarks in Yiddish.

"I think we may congratulate ourselves," said the woman as she dried her hands.

And the doctor, with his sallow, drawn face and grizzled, pointed beard, shook his head sceptically and answered:

"If you think that being born in such times as these is a matter for congratulation, then I suppose we may."

Chapter 6

IN THE WAY OF DUTY

THE manor-house of Hohen-Lychow with its narrow-pillared façade facing westwards, looked down an avenue of famous lime trees which reached up to its outer steps. Leafless now, the two lines of them reached away into the distance like tall, black, dripping skeletons. Otto von Lychow with his hands in the pockets of a shooting-jacket stood at the window that reflected the raspberry hues of sunset; his mouth was set and drawn and at its corners were the lines of a new and bitter experience. Frau Malvina von Lychow, whose hair had been grey since the death of her son, Hans Joachim, sat at the end of the sofa by a round table knitting a shawl with large white ebony needles under the light of a lamp. Exactly behind her head, Prince Friedrich Karl looked down from the wall, an old-fashioned photograph but an excellent likeness, complete with whiskers, riding-whip, and hussar's dolman. From time to time she raised her large, still beautiful, dark, grey eyes and looked fixedly across at the old gentleman who, on this period of leave, had been unable to shake off an exhaustion that revealed itself in his whole attitude and expression. Naturally, he hid it from the people of the house: only when he was with her did his bent shoulders and drawn mouth betray how deeply the insolence of this general of New Prussia had wounded one who belonged to what Prussia once had been. Frau Malvina looked towards the other side of the room where the writing-table stood under some electric candles set in stag's antlers—a sixteen-pointer that the General had shot himself. They were not burning: through the blue failing light there shone dully, like a square patch of snow, the long letter which arrived to-day from Paul Winfried with news of all and sundry. It did not occur to Frau Malvina to hate Schieffen-zahn, though whatever her knight and her husband felt, she felt too.

She came of a race that looked upon such officers as too far beneath them to deserve such feelings. The fact that a staff officer of middle-class origin could reach so high a position was only one of the fantastic anomalies of this war in which the cavalry were no longer mounted, bands and colours were left behind, and the infantry only attacked when it was assumed that no living soldier on the other side would be capable of defending himself. She was the daughter of a dragoon family, whose members had been in all the Prussian cavalry charges from Fehrbellin to Mars-la-Tour, and mechanical warfare disgusted her. In earlier times a soldier liked to meet an enemy properly armed and protected against the thrusts of lance or bayonet—to-day he struck him down from a distance, made him helpless and then slaughtered him. "This sort of war suits people like Schieffenzahn. What a name!" she added contemptuously. "Schieffenzahn!" Lychow, without turning, and still staring down the dripping avenue, said with a shrug of his shoulders:

"Well, my dear. You can't deny that Eisenzahn wasn't a beauty, yet he was Elector of Brandenburg and a Hohenzollern."

The gilt clock under the glass case, the dial of which was set between the paws of a recumbent lion, ticked from the mantelpiece. A fireguard, embroidered with imitation pearls, had been pushed on one side, so that the flickering light shone into the room.

"Of course it would be St. Martin's Day with the Rhinselers coming over, not to mention Ludmilla and Agnes. I shall have to be cheerful: we are always being cheerful these days. But if I had my way I should go and sleep."

Frau Malvina, under her crown of white hair, blinked one eye and shot out a quick look with the other as old Fritz used to do. She could not think so fast as in old days. She stumbled from time to time over a chasm in her inner consciousness, and she would have to catch her breath and stifle a groan over her dead boy. Again and again, on the most unsuitable occasions it came over her—the scream of a shell, then death and silence. Yet she said to herself that it was not good for a man of seventy to go about in such a state of depression in bitter weather like this. She was not in the least surprised that Otto had refused to contend with so insolent a creature (she could not utter his name). One came across such people in the way of duty.

"But hasn't Friderici disappeared into the Military Cabinet?" she asked. "Why don't you write to him?"

Otto von Lychow stopped drumming on the windowpane. At that moment five Russian prisoners, with a tarpaulin over their heads to keep off the rain, crossed the great lime-avenue on their way from the fields to the stables: he did not see them though they were right before him. He closed his eyes and from the depths of long-forgotten memories he drew the beloved name of Lieutenant-Colonel von Friderici whom he had once helped, by the loan of seven hundred thalers, out of the most hopeless gambling debt of his subaltern days. He felt relieved at the idea of writing and telling him how outrageous Schieffenzahn's behaviour had been and how contrary to all the traditions of the service. Friderici would be able to find out whether an official complaint to the Highest Authority was likely to do any good. It was true that an executed Russian who had been sent on the way of all flesh without any sort of publicity was a rather unusual subject for a complaint to His Majesty, and would certainly not be understood without further explanation in such times as these, when American flying-squadrons began to rise menacingly above the horizon, although the recent events in Russia which had enabled them to get the upper hand of the peace-besotted Bolsheviks looked very bright and hopeful for Schieffenzahn's schemes. But in Otto von Lychow's mind there was a little point of fire that would not let him rest. He thought he could see a way out: he would describe Schieffenzahn's behaviour faithfully to Friderici and cable to Posnanski to draw up a formal complaint regarding the Quartermaster-General's interference with the judicial authority of the Division and forward it to His Majesty's Military Cabinet accompanied by all the papers and documents. He blew out his cheeks so that his moustache positively bristled, turned away from the window, drew the dark blue curtain, carefully switched on the three electric candles on the antlers above the writing-table and opened the great green leather blotter, on which lay Winfried's half-folded letter. He put it aside, and tested a nib in a thick cork penholder.

"You are quite right," he said, half-turning round: "as you always are. I'll set up a candle to Friderici. Do you mind if I smoke? I know you prefer the smell of cigars from the next room through a closed door. . . ." He laughed: for he reflected that he would have to write his complaint twice over, realizing that his first draft would be couched in very unparliamentary language. The pen scratched and squeaked on the large ivory-laid note-paper like skates upon new ice. The lines of handwriting, with heavy underscorings here and there, but almost no flourishes, and written in the German character, filled page after page. There was anger in what he wrote, obsequiousness, and wounded pride, but there was also a feeling for what was just and fair, and a real concern for the Kingdom of the old Emperor Frederick.

"Don't tell me, my dear Friderici," he concluded, "that the Bjuscheff affair is not important. Are we in dispute over what is important? Prussia is important, Germany is important, the Hohenzollerns are important—on such general points as these we are agreed, within limits of course. Very well then. But you and I and every man in authority know that from time to time the stupidest intermediary, who has to repeat a message by rote, may be of importance, because other matters of importance may hang upon him. Wherefore I consider every individual incident as of possible importance, and a barometer of events. Our ancient Martin Luther, whose birthday we are going to celebrate to-day with cold goose and a glass of warmed red wine, was once only an insignificant unit in the vast army of monks, and when he was young his contemporaries thought he was just an intermediary: and so he was. He was Heaven's intermediary with North Germany—I say nothing of Holland, England, and Scandinavia, because they are on the wrong side to-day. So I should be very grateful, my dear Friderici, if, at the appropriate time—I don't mean to-day or to-morrow—you would try to find out how His Majesty would be disposed to consider a complaint by General von Lychow against the doubtless highly gifted Herr Schieffenzahn. I am too old to sit on broken glass, but what the Newer Politeness appears to demand of an old man like me, that I will not stand even when I come to lie in my grave—every 31st of October I shall get out of my vault at Hohen-Lychow and haunt the place. And I am sure, my dear Friderici, you won't demand it of

Your old Comrade,

O. v. L.

The writer leaned back in his chair with satisfaction. There was a weight off his heart. He took off his spectacles which gave him an almost professional air seen from the front, gathered up the eight sheets between two fingers, and went over to Malvina to show them to her. The old lady at once realized that in this letter he had begun to unburden his soul, and that she had achieved her purpose: now she must get him to read it out.

"Here you are, old lady," he said. "Have a look at this."

"Ah, Otto," she answered shaking her head. "You know I can't read handwriting very well these days. Read it to me."

Before he began, he looked round him and decided that a room like this was a very pleasant place. "Ring for Milchen to bring the coffee," he said, and then, adjusting his spectacles on his nose, he began to read what he had written, slowly and with emphasis.

"I really think rain in Spa is more beastly than rain in Berlin."

"This confounded Belgium is so flat that the Mark of Brandenburg seems positively Alpine by comparison. Hark at it against the window, Friderici."

The two officers listened: the wind howled and moaned and the rain splashed and hissed and rattled on the windowpanes. The trenches would be under water again.

Von Friderici sighed.

"I wouldn't mind being in the East these days."

"I'm for the Balkans. There's still free swimming in Lake Doiran. How did you find His Majesty to-day?"

"Talking about the Eastern Front. Albert Schieffenzahn's been up to his games again. He'll be getting it in the neck, if he isn't careful, good and proper."

"What's up then?"

"His Majesty's remarks are sometimes not fit for publication."

The naval attaché lit a cigarette.

"That's true enough, God knows. What was it all about?"
Friderici yawned.

"Oh, nothing much really. If it hadn't been Lychow . . ."

"What's the matter with the old stiff?"

"Our little Albert's been messing about with Divisional affairs."

"Well, you can't expect Lychow to stand that."

"So His Majesty thought. And if a gold field-flask with a mono-gram in diamonds hadn't arrived for him to-day, Schieffenzahn might have got it much worse. But it really was a most handsome object, with a blue silk case and a gold-topped cork set with diamonds."

"You don't say," said the man in the dark blue uniform with the gilt dirk. "I could do with a thing like that: sounds just in my style."

"Hardly. The arrival of that present was simply providential for Schieffenzahn. His Majesty pretty well blew up, I can tell you. 'I've had enough Cavell cases,' he shouted, and then followed a few kind words about Albert which I unfortunately forgot at once."

The wind beat furiously against the windows. The naval officer stood listening with a fascinated, troubled, anxious look.

"Christ! What weather! It'll be blowing in the canal. . . . And there are some U-boats due back."

Friderici looked searchingly over his eye-glass at his companion.

"Do you think they'll do the trick?"

The other nodded thoughtfully.

"Certainly, if we've got enough of them."

"But have we?"

"Yes, that's the question. What was Schieffenzahn's business?"

"You mean Lychow's? Nothing of any importance. The shoot-ing of a Russian. The real trouble was the question of jurisdiction."

"Ah, yes," said the naval Commander with a sigh, as he stood up and smoothed out the creases in his trousers: "I know those rows. They get the wires all mixed and then His Majesty has to sort them out."

Friderici sighed regretfully.

"Well, commanding an army is a bit harder than looking after geese. Fortunately His Majesty has his enlightened ancestor's natural courage and keen sense of justice": and they both looked up wonderingly and thoughtfully at the portrait of Old Fritz, a new and brilliant oil-painting, with twinkling blue eyes and round cheeks so pink that they might almost have been rouged. The coat, of dark blue silk, was well painted and looked very handsome in the oval gilt frame, and the red and white three-cornered hat looked truly military and menacing on the royal curls.

Chapter the Last

ENVOI

LIKE many others on the Eastern Front, the railway station at Mervinsk was somewhat oddly situated: the Bahnhofstrasse, an avenue of mighty elms, did not connect the town directly with the station; it met the line some hundred yards or so above it, and a side road branched off across the track into the open country, while the avenue followed the line to the station. A barrier painted blue, white, and red in the Russian colours closed this crossing when a train was expected.

Corporal Hermann Sacht was going on convalescent leave. His steel helmet was on his head, his rifle slung round his neck, a small box in his right hand, and in his left the bundle of papers which are as essential as a pair of legs for going on leave—leave-form, delousing certificate, medical certificate, railway ticket with all the necessary stamps; and the corporal hurried along perspiringly beneath the trees. From the level-crossing it took about two minutes to reach the station, another minute to force his way through the barrier, and into an already crowded compartment. Then, and not till them, so far as he was concerned, the train might move off. He prayed fervently in his heart that he might be in time. If he missed his train as it passed through he would lose a good thirty-six hours of that irreplaceable, irrevocable leave. So he made his way along the icy surface of the broad road, and, cold as it was, his forehead and his eyes were damp with sweat: for of course his pack was stuffed with food and supplies for wife and children so that he might be no worse off on his leave in Berlin-East than he was in Eastern Russia. The swine of a delousing corporal had made him wait eleven minutes longer than he need have done for the counter-signature and stamps, so as to get a tip out of him, because as a matter of fact no delousing had been necessary in his case as he had come straight out of the Kommandantur infirmary and was perfectly clean. But there was an ancient quarrel between the Kommandantur and the delousing-station which was always visited on the weaker parties, and no one is so helpless as a corporal who must positively catch a train when he is at the mercy of another corporal whose leave is behind him. As he hurried along, Hermann Sacht saw his two children waiting at the Silesian Station for the arrival of the train, which should already have left the great dark terminus on its way to the Alexander-Platz, looking up and down the platform for Papa who is sure to be coming. His collar was soaked with sweat. He did not dare to spare enough time to look at his wrist-watch. He ran on without a pause, his pack bumping on his shoulders, his steel helmet wobbling on his temples, his box and parcel creaking in their string fastenings, his rifle banging against his right knee from time to time, and his bayonet against the back of his left leg. Suddenly, when he was about fifty yards from the end of the road, he heard the hooting and shrill whistles of a locomotive getting under way. The leave train seemed very long: the engine had probably just begun to move. . . . He would be three minutes too late: but if he missed the train by half a minute he would still be too late . . . too late. . . . He really could have fallen on his knees or sat on his box and howled. But his hurry had so stirred his whole being that he did not stop. He went on hoping for some wonder from Heaven, some miracle of God, in whom he did not believe . . . on and on, although the smoke from the locomotive was already visible between the branches of the first tree: and at the moment when he reached that level-crossing, with its barrier painted with the Imperial blue, white, and red, the huge express engine, its great pistons moving without a sound, its funnel full of smoke and steam, passed him two-and-a-half yards away. Then his despair broke forth:

"Hi," he yelled. "I'm from Berlin," almost staggering as he waved his leave-warrant in his hand.

The fireman by the tender nudged the engineer, who was standing on the plate just about to put on full steam. There stood Hermann Sacht at the barrier as the first coaches glided past; at one compartment-window three cheery officers' faces could be seen watching this ridiculous lunatic of a Muschko, grasping his box, pouring with sweat, with gaping mouth and staring eyes—left behind. In the next compartment someone waved at him jeeringly. Then the first car, with second and third class compartments, passed, and the next car with third and fourth compartments for the rank and file came into view. "It's all up," thought Hermann Sacht; he had run like that all for nothing, and now he would catch pneumonia or pleurisy, for his shirt was sticking to his back, and there were eight degrees of frost in that November air. The fireman shoved his elbow into the engineer's back and said:

"Look, there's another lad wants to come along . . ."

It was the end of November, 1917. . . . The driver's instructions were to let full steam into the bones of his docile iron beast when he reached that point. Hermann Sacht knew this as well as anyone. Soon the next car would pass and then the next, quicker and quicker. Even if he had nothing in his hands he could not, when the train was going at that pace, swing himself up on to the passing footboard. It was frozen, and smooth, and even if he were used to it . . . Oh, yes, if a captain or an officer had been waiting here, and gave an appealing wave of his hand, he might pull it off—he might persuade the driver to put the brake on and stop, against all instructions. But suddenly a rasping grinding sound of iron against steel came from the wheels of the train. It was not going quicker, it was slowing down, it slipped like a roll over a plate and hung like a roll at the plate's edge. Astonished faces looked out of the officers' compartments, but someone bent down from the driving-plate and shouted to Hermann Sacht:

"Get up, you bloody fool!"

In the fraction of a second he realized that the train had nearly stopped on his account. He crawled under the barrier, and rushed with his parcels towards the nearest compartment. The stoppage had surprised the men inside, the window was pulled down, and a number of heads in field-caps emerged. They understood quicker than he did. The compartment door sprang open. Hands reached out to him, took his parcels, seized his left arm, while with his right he held the iron grip outside—he gave a mighty shove with his shinbone and was hauled into the compartment. The door was banged behind him, and once more, with a mighty rumbling, all that gigantic conglomeration of wheels and pistons rasped savagely along the icy rails towards the west. A few officers in their cushioned seats looked at each other. "That's almost . . ." they decided. What it was, they knew very well, but they did not say.

A young pioneer-lieutenant calmly spread a pack of cards out on his leather suitcase, which he put between his knees to serve as a table, ready for a prolonged sitting at his favourite game of "skat."

"You're a cool hand," said an older man, a fat lieutenant of reserve, by profession a traveller in rubber, who had become a marvellous impersonation of an officer. "I tell you what. A couple of months in the trenches wouldn't do that engine-driver any harm. He ought to stick to his time-table. He's got no damned business with anything else."

A young and cheery lieutenant of infantry in a leather-sleeved waistcoat, unbuttoned to show its fur lining, said with a friendly laugh:

"I hope you can take his place on the foot-plate, then: I fancy an engine-driver to-day is more indispensable than Schieffenzahn."

The traveller in rubber sank into an indignant silence. Nine months ago he would have consigned two scoundrels like these to their proper destination. But since the copper fire-boxes had been ripped off the engines to make fuses, the iron beasts were as difficult to manage as hysterical and wealthy aunts.

"The pack is beginning to be aware of itself," he said: "the skilled workmen—all these fellows who have to do with machines."

"They don't know it yet," thought a senior army surgeon, who was allowed to make the fourth in this officers' carriage: "and when they do know it . . ."

The leave-train had got up speed. Forests—black tree-trunks against a white background, snow-covered boulders flecked with scattered oil and soot, sped past the footboards and the windows.

"Well, my boy: I wonder if we shall get away with it," said the engineer to the fireman, spitting on the floor-plate: and with a sort of grim amusement, blackened with soot and grease, they looked at each other.

The incident cost the State seventy marks in wasted driving-power, and two minutes' delay. (Two hundred marks goes up with every shell.)

And so with rhythmic groanings, shaken by its own strength like a dragon in travail, along the surface of the earth's crust, where the air is thick and darkest, that interminable train rolled westwards into the brightening noontide.

AUTHOR'S NOTE

The novel called "The Case of Sergeant Grischa" is the central piece of a Triptych of which the collective title will be "A Trilogy of the Transition." It will be preceded chronologically and dramatically by the novel called "Education before Verdun" (Bertin); the novel called "The Crowning of a King" (Winfried) will follow it. "The Case of Sergeant Grischa," the plot of which is founded on fact, was conceived in the year 1917, composed and written as a play in 1921, and as a novel in 1926-27.

✡

For a complete list of books available from Penguin in the United States, write to Dept. DG, Penguin Books, 299 Murray Hill Parkway, East Rutherford, New Jersey 07073.